**Two brand-new stories in every volume...
twice a month!**

Duets Vol. #55

Look for
THE MAIL ORDER MEN OF NOWHERE JUNCTION,
two linked tales by Jacqueline Diamond, talented
author of over fifty novels, and multipublished writer
Charlotte Maclay, "who has a flair for fun
and romance," asserts *Romantic Times*.

Duets Vol. #56

Delightful Cara Summers is "a writer of incredible
talent, with a gift for emotional stories laced with
humor and passion," says *Rendezvous*.
Joining Cara and making her Duets debut
is quirky Jacquie D'Alessandro,
whose story, *Naked in New England*,
gives readers a real eye-opener!

Be sure to pick up both Duets volumes today!

More Than the Doctor Ordered

"Kiss me."

Lucas studied her uncertainly. "Here?"

"There's nobody around."

"If anyone sees us, they'll gossip."

"Why should you care?" Mimsy was the one who ought to care. Instead, she ached to hold Lucas. She'd been aching for him all day.

It was safer to kiss him out here. Not in the privacy of her apartment. Not in a place where he could sweep her into bed while her inhibitions fluttered away like cast-off clothing.

She looped her arms around his neck. Lucas smiled and touched her shoulders, her neck, the nape of her hair.

His mouth skimmed over hers. He drew back, but she gripped him harder, and then he was kissing her like a man afire.

At last Lucas lifted his head, his breathing rough. "Mimsy, we shouldn't..."

She ignored the words. Whatever he had to say, it didn't matter. Even if Lucas couldn't stay for long, she wanted this night with him.

"Come upstairs."

For more, turn to page 9

A Hitchin' Time

She remembered her vow not to let the next one get away.

No way. No how.

"Welcome to Nowhere Junction. I'm Lilibeth Anderson."

His gaze slowly skimmed over her.

"I'm glad to meet you," he mumbled.

Wasn't that sweet? This adorable, handsome man was *shy*. Didn't it just make a girl want to wrap her arms around him and hug him to pieces?

"Hi, Lilibeth. I'm Alex. Alex Peabody."

She'd died and gone to heaven. His voice was a deep baritone. Soft, yet commanding. Her muscles had lost all their strength, while her heart had turned into a snare drum.

Lilibeth tilted her head to flip her hair over her shoulder. "Will your wife be joining you in Nowhere?" she asked coyly.

His lips curved. "I'm a bachelor."

Lilibeth wanted to punch her fist in the air in a victory salute, but restrained herself. Alexander Peabody had met his match!

For more, turn to page 197

HARLEQUIN DUETS

ISBN 0-373-44121-5

MORE THAN THE DOCTOR ORDERED
Copyright © 2001 by Jackie Hyman

A HITCHIN' TIME
Copyright © 2001 by Charlotte Lobb

This edition published by arrangement with Harlequin Books S.A.

® and TM are trademarks of the publisher. Trademarks indicated with ® are registered in the United States Patent and Trademark Office, the Canadian Trade Marks Office and in other countries.

Visit us at www.eHarlequin.com

Printed in U.S.A.

More Than the Doctor Ordered

Jacqueline Diamond

HARLEQUIN®

TORONTO • NEW YORK • LONDON
AMSTERDAM • PARIS • SYDNEY • HAMBURG
STOCKHOLM • ATHENS • TOKYO • MILAN • MADRID
PRAGUE • WARSAW • BUDAPEST • AUCKLAND

Dear Reader,

Charlotte Maclay and I had so much fun writing the two books in THE BACHELOR DADS OF NOWHERE JUNCTION that we couldn't wait to do it again. And with the encouragement of wonderful editors Jennifer Tam and Birgit Davis-Todd, we did!

It was delightful to meet again with eccentric townspeople like Mazeppa the former bag lady, Finella the cooking fiend and self-important Horace Popsworthy. I hope those of you who are new to Nowhere Junction will enjoy them as much as readers of the original books.

Please let us know if you'd like to see more Nowhere Junction books! You can write to me at P.O. Box 1315, Brea, CA 92822.

Best wishes,

Jacqueline Diamond

Books by Jacqueline Diamond

HARLEQUIN DUETS
2—KIDNAPPED?
8—THE BRIDE WORE GYM SHOES
37—DESIGNER GENES*
44—EXCUSE ME? WHOSE BABY?

HARLEQUIN LOVE & LAUGHTER
11—PUNCHLINE
32—SANDRA AND THE SCOUNDREL

*The Bachelor Dads of Nowhere Junction

For Joyce Wilson

1

IT WAS A DISGUSTINGLY healthy day in Nowhere Junction, Texas, judging by the emptiness of Dr. Mimsy Miles's waiting room.

Sometimes Mimsy almost hoped for an epidemic, of the nonlethal variety. Not that she wanted to drum up business. She just yearned to save people.

To aid the truly afflicted. To prove she was good at her profession. Perhaps to discover a cure that would help doctors all over the country.

With one elbow resting on an open medical journal, she gazed out her office window. Located on the second floor above the currently unoccupied ten-bed Nowhere Hospital, her suite overlooked the school grounds across the street.

Beyond the circus tents that served as temporary classrooms on this sunny October day, workmen hammered at the old school building, stripping it prior to tearing it down and putting up a new one. Soon, Mimsy supposed, a workman would mash his thumb.

Or one of three rambunctious ten-year-olds known informally as the Mean Brigade would set off a firecracker in the vicinity of Principal Dick Smollens, resulting in first-degree burns. Or a golfer with more gusto than skill would trip in the country club golf course and land on a low-growing cactus.

Mimsy sighed and wound a curl of short, dark hair

around one finger. She didn't mean to disparage the routine ills of her fellow townspeople. She just craved a chance to shine.

She was losing hope that it might ever happen. There seemed to be something about her that made people overlook her. A defective gene, perhaps.

In high school, she'd organized pep rallies and made endless banners, but had never been chosen a cheerleader. In medical school, she'd placed near the top of her class, but her boyfriend, Vince, had said everyone assumed it was a computer error.

He soon became her ex-boyfriend. If she'd known then that she would reach the age of thirty-three unmarried and alone, would she have been so quick to dump him?

A tap at the door roused her. "Doc?" A nest of carrot-red hair poked inside. "Some people just came in. And a couple that aren't exactly human, only I'm not going to say so to Murdock Murchison."

Those would be his dogs, George and Lucas, named after the retired rancher's favorite film director. Nowhere Junction lacked a veterinarian and, rather than send for one from the hated rival town of Groundhog Station, some people brought their animals to Mimsy.

She didn't mind. But humans came first.

"Who's hurt the most?" Mimsy knew better than to use a word like *triage* around her recently hired nurse-receptionist, even if her name was Florence Nightingale.

She used to be called Minnie Finkins. After her husband abandoned her to pursue his longtime dream of catching Bigfoot, she'd changed it to the name of the famous nurse. If her ex-husband could start a new life, so could she, Minnie had declared.

"Lilibeth Anderson, I guess," she said. "She caught her hair in the blender while making one of those smoothies at the Anderson Coffee Shop."

"Good heavens!" Mimsy jumped up in alarm. "Did she hurt her neck?"

"She's mostly worried about her hair," said Flo. "She's afraid it might get infected."

"Her hair?" Mimsy asked in disbelief.

"Then there's little Callie Murchison," the nurse went on, ignoring the question. "She's one year old today, you know. She ate something at her birthday party that made her sick."

"What was it?" Mimsy always tried to track down the source of any infection.

"Her mom thinks it was some prune-and-pickle muffins that Finella Weinbucket made," Flo said. Finella based her recipes on whatever items were on special at Gigi's Grocery Store, and the bizarre combinations had been known to cause digestive problems.

In any case, it was impossible to set medical priorities based on Flo's account. Smoothing down her white coat, Mimsy went out to the waiting room.

Grizzled old Murdock Murchison was pacing the floor. He glanced anxiously between his two rangy hounds, one of which sported a makeshift bandage on its paw, and his one-year-old granddaughter, who squirmed on her mother's lap.

But mostly the room resonated with the presence of Lilibeth Anderson.

Mimsy squelched a pang of envy. Golden, gorgeous Lilibeth. At twenty-seven, she had perfect skin and sumptuous long blond hair, with a figure that made the town's cowboys turn purple and stutter in her presence.

Being six years her senior, Mimsy remembered Lilibeth as an angelic little girl. And, later, the captain of the cheerleaders. She had reigned as prom queen all four years at the regional high school.

Currently she worked at her parents' café and drugstore. Someday, she would inherit both properties.

At the moment, tears welled in those melting blue eyes. She looked so distraught that Mimsy could understand why Flo had placed her injury over a one-year-old's tummy ache.

Nevertheless, little Callie was the more fragile of the pair. Stomach trouble could signal any number of problems, including appendicitis.

"Hi, Buffy," Mimsy said to the child's mother. "Please bring her into my office."

"But my hair!" Lilibeth glanced apologetically at the assorted Murchisons. "I'm sorry and I know it sounds stupid, but look at it!" She held up the tangled mess. "Can't this get infected or fall out or something?"

"No, I don't think you need to worry about that," Mimsy told her. "How's your neck? Any sign of whiplash?"

A wide-eyed Lilibeth shook her head emphatically, almost hysterically. "It's fine. But my hair... I've got to look my best. I know it sounds a little strange, but I've been running an ad on the Internet—there's this matchmaking service—and this rich entrepreneur, Mr. McRifle, is coming to see me. Driving a Cadillac!"

Why on earth would the most beautiful woman in Nowhere Junction need to advertise for a mate? Mimsy supposed Lilibeth didn't consider any of the local males worthy of her. That would be understandable, since the town's only millionaire, Quade Gardiner, had recently taken a wife.

"Split ends are not a health threat," she said. "Why don't you stop by Binny's Beauty Salon and get it trimmed?"

"Well, if you're sure..." Lilibeth hurried out the door with an air of desperation that puzzled Mimsy.

Callie let out a loud belch.

"Honey!" said her mother. "Where are your manners?"

The little girl grinned. And uttered a second belch, for emphasis.

"I guess it's just air in her tummy," Buffy said in relief.

"Thank goodness," said Murdock. "Now if my granddaughter's all right, Mimsy, would you check George's paw?"

"I should examine Callie anyway," Mimsy said.

The little girl climbed off her mother's lap and toddled toward the door. "No!"

"I won't give you any shots, I promise," Mimsy said. "I just want to check your tummy." She glanced around for Flo. "We need to take her temperature."

"No!" repeated the baby.

"She's missing her birthday party," Buffy said apologetically. "I'm sure she's okay."

"As long as you're here, you should let me make sure nothing's wrong." Mimsy knew as she spoke that it was a lost cause. If she had a deep booming voice, people might heed her words, but even Buffy, one of Mimsy's best friends, brushed the suggestion aside.

"I'm sorry we wasted your time," she said. "How much do we owe you?"

"Don't worry about it." Buffy's husband, Carter, had towed Mimsy's car for free the last time it broke down.

A lot of her patients paid in free services, produce, eggs, dressed chickens and cuts of beef. Mimsy didn't mind, since the town underwrote the hospital and clinic expenses and she rented her apartment cheaply from the Andersons.

Soon she was alone with Murdock and the hounds. George was the yellow one, Lucas the black, she recalled.

"What happened to your paw, big fellow?" she asked, kneeling on the waiting room floor. She drew the line at putting a dog on her examining table.

"George Weinbucket stepped on it," grumbled Murdock. George, the town banker, was married to Finella, of the prune-and-pickle muffins. "He says it was an accident but I think he resents the dog having the same name as him."

"Carter used to have a cat named Buffy, but Buffy changed it to Tawny," Mimsy reminded him as she unwrapped the paw.

"Nobody's changing George's name," said the old rancher. "That's all we need. Next thing you know, some fellow named Lucas will come to town and want to change my other dog's name, too."

Mimsy signaled Flo for a bottle of disinfectant. "Don't get carried away, Mr. Murchison. You know we don't get many strangers around here."

"All the same," he muttered, "a man's got a right to name his dogs however he likes. Anybody named Lucas had better just ride on by."

TEXAS SURE WAS FLAT, thought Lucas McRifle as his motorcycle whizzed down the highway between wire fences.

He supposed he looked carefree with his shaggy hair

blowing in the breeze. The truth was, he'd had to choose between buying a helmet and being able to afford enough gas to get him from Atlanta to Nowhere Junction and then on to his home base in Los Angeles.

The bike was slim on storage space, so he'd shipped his suitcases back to L.A. Then, right before he left Atlanta, a thief had invaded his hotel room and made off with his laptop and cell phone.

Lucas hadn't been this flat broke since his teenage years. He only hoped Lilibeth Anderson really was an heiress as stated in her Internet ad.

And as hungry for adventure as she'd sounded in her e-mails. He sympathized with her, being stuck in a place called Nowhere Junction out of loyalty to her parents.

He'd grown up in the backwater of Blink, Colorado, and fled as soon as he turned eighteen. Just the thought of visiting a small town gave him a weird creepy feeling touched with morbid fascination, as if he were about to come face-to-face with a black widow spider.

Her e-mails hadn't talked much about marriage, fortunately, because Lucas wasn't the marrying kind. Mostly Lilibeth sounded bored, frustrated and eager for a new challenge.

Well, he could offer her the excitement of a high-stakes gamble, along with a chance to become immensely wealthy. If she was as restless and independent-minded as Lucas, that would make her happier than walking down some worn-out old aisle.

He just prayed Lilibeth didn't turn out to be a con artist or a spoiled rich girl toying with would-be suitors.

Six weeks ago, Lucas's longtime partner had cleaned out their joint bank account and absconded to Mexico. They'd been on the verge of making a fortune by marketing a rare coconut powder with valuable medicinal properties, so his disappearance made no sense. Then a major deal in Atlanta, into which Lucas had sunk his personal savings, blew up because a businessman misrepresented his company's finances. It had rained the whole time he was in Georgia, too.

After those experiences, he wasn't about to trust anybody.

So he didn't entirely regret that the leasing company had reclaimed his Cadillac. Since Lilibeth didn't expect him to arrive on this beat-up Harley, he might have a chance to poke around undetected and learn the truth about her.

As long as the affluent Ms. Anderson helped him save the project of a lifetime, the last few weeks wouldn't seem so terrible. In the meantime, he might as well lean forward and enjoy the trip.

The land was so flat that Lucas couldn't resist the temptation to aim for a personal best land-speed record. He twisted the handlebar, giving the bike gas, and flew over the pavement.

Let the cows turn to stare. There was no other traffic, and he half hoped a bump in the road would send him airborne for real. It was as close to flying as he could afford in his current state of economic depletion.

In the autumn heat, the land shimmered ahead of him. The road wasn't quite as flat as it looked, Lucas realized as he zoomed forward. The dust and rippling waves of heat disguised the pavement's undulations.

The highway dipped in a couple of places, creating long depressions deep enough to hide an oncoming vehicle. He eased off the gas, but he hated to slow down. Not when he was having so much fun.

Lucas sure hoped there wasn't going to be a...

pickup truck rattling out of the next hollow, hogging the middle of the road.

But there it was. He would have cursed, if the wind hadn't been so sharp against his face. Besides, it took all his concentration to hold the Harley to the far right of the pavement.

There was room for him to pass, just barely. Except that something black and furry jutted through the rear slats on the old truck, sticking into his space.

A dog's head.

Lucas edged over slightly. The motorcycle's front tire caught the edge of the blacktop.

He fought for control as it wobbled and sank into the sandy shoulder. Fought, and lost.

The Harley was still going at least 30 mph when it twisted violently out from under him.

And...

And...

And...

He knew he ought to wake up. His shoulder hurt like a netherworld he didn't want to think about when he was this close to descending into it for real.

On the other hand, if he could feel pain, he couldn't be entirely dead.

Lucas slowly opened his eyes and stared at a charming hallucination. A woman with dark curly hair and doelike brown eyes was bending over him with the sweetest look of concern on her face.

Possibly an angel, he mused dazedly. Women never showed such unguarded tenderness toward a stranger.

He stirred.

"Hold still!" the woman said.

"I can take care of myself," he muttered, and tried

to raise himself on one elbow. Agony knifed through him. "Oh God!"

The angel frowned. "I can see we need a tourniquet applied directly to the throat."

He groaned. "Excuse me?"

"To stop the cursing," said the woman, who was wearing a white coat, not white robes, he realized.

Lucas couldn't believe anyone clung to such a Puritan attitude in the twenty-first century. "All I said was 'Oh God!'"

"You took the Lord's name in vain," the woman replied sternly.

He would have shaken his head except he knew it would hurt. "I must be in the middle of nowhere."

"That's right, this is Nowhere," said the lady in white. "And we have our standards. Now, how many fingers am I holding up?"

"Seventeen."

"Don't be smart."

"Three."

"Good."

From a makeshift ambulance near the side of the road, two men carried over a stretcher. There was a carrot-haired woman behind them, Lucas noted dimly.

"I don't need that," he managed to say.

"Indulge me," said the angel.

Lucas wasn't about to let a bunch of yokels cart him off like roadkill. "I can walk." This time he lifted his shoulders two inches off the ground before lightning jolted through him.

"Lie down!" the woman snapped, which wasn't necessary, since he'd already collapsed. "I'm Dr. Mimsy Miles. This is Sheriff Bob Moriarty." She indicated a thirtyish-year-old man in a cowboy hat with sun-streaked brown hair and skin as tan as a saddle. "And my nurse, Florence Nightingale, and Murdock Murchison. He's the driver that you swerved to avoid."

"Didn't see you coming," said Murdock. "Sorry about that. I'll pay your expenses."

The man was taking responsibility for the accident? True, he *had* caused it, but he hadn't hit Lucas. Murchison could have made excuses and, being a local, gotten away with it.

Amazing.

"I'll need your name," said Sheriff Bob.

Lucas opened his mouth to answer, but his better judgment intervened. Once the name McRifle spread around, he'd lose his chance to scope out Lilibeth Anderson on the sly.

Unwilling, in his precarious circumstances, to risk losing his credit cards and driver's license, as well, he'd stuck his wallet inside his boot before setting off for Nowhere Junction. There it lay flat enough to escape notice.

"I don't remember," he said.

The sheriff turned to the doctor. "Is that possible?"

"Very possible." With cool, deft hands, she applied a protective brace to Lucas's neck. "We don't know yet whether he's suffered brain damage, but he's been badly shaken."

Bob knelt and patted Lucas's pockets. "I'm not finding any ID."

"It's probably lying around somewhere in a cactus patch," said the red-haired nurse.

"You mean he has amnesia?" asked Murdock. "I wonder if he's going to be like your grandmother, Bob. You remember, she used to claim she was the real Anastasia, even though she was born in Texas."

"He's not saying he's somebody else," grumped the sheriff. "He said he doesn't know who he is."

"It should clear up in a few hours, or days at most," Mimsy told Lucas. "I'm sure we can find some way to help you. It must be awful, not knowing who you are."

She sounded so sympathetic that he felt a twinge of guilt. "I—I think my name might be Lucas." He'd signed his e-mails L. McRifle, not giving a first name, so he figured his identity might be safe for a while.

"Lucas?" Murdock glared at him. "Dang, boy, did you try to hit my dog on purpose?"

"What?"

"Murdock, how would he know your dog's name is Lucas?" demanded the nurse named Florence Nightingale. Come to think of it, that name sounded familiar. Maybe all rural nurses were called Florence Nightingale, just as cows were called Bossie and dogs Fido...or Lucas.

"I'm confused," he said.

"Let's get him loaded on the stretcher," said the cute lady doctor. "He needs attention, pronto."

EVEN IN SLEEP, the man kept shifting, groaning and muttering. Giving in to impulse, Mimsy stroked a lock of brown hair off his forehead, and he calmed.

Lucas—if that really was his name—had strong, sharp features. He wasn't heavily tanned, and his hands showed no sign of heavy work. Not a rancher, for sure.

Mimsy had given him enough painkillers to last for hours. X rays showed that he'd escaped with only abrasions and a severely bruised shoulder, but those would hurt like heck when he woke up.

The suffering of any patient upset her. For some reason, this man in particular struck a chord. Mimsy found herself wanting to make sure everything possible was done for his well-being.

She wished she had the equipment to scan for hidden brain damage. She debated calling for a helicopter to take Lucas to Austin, but that seemed like overkill. The best thing she could do for the man was try to find out his identity.

Mentally Mimsy reviewed the items Sheriff Bob had retrieved from the motorcycle. There was a sleeping bag and a large duffel bag, neither bearing a name tag. The duffel contained shoes and clothes and a pouch of brownish powder.

Bob, eager to make his first-ever drug bust, had perked up at the sight of the powder. He'd sounded disappointed a while later when he reported that it wasn't drugs nor any other substance he could identify. But then, Bob had been in a bad mood ever since his twin sister, Bobette, got engaged to a mattress salesman from Groundhog Station.

In view of his lack of ID, the sheriff wondered if Lucas could be an outlaw? Bob had sent his fingerprints in for analysis, but she doubted he'd get any results.

Mimsy didn't believe this man was a criminal. Even in severe pain, he'd joked about how many fingers she was raising. And he'd tried to take care of himself rather than impose on other people.

Okay, maybe she was naive, but to her, he seemed like a nice guy. Not to mention incredibly handsome.

Her heart twisted. It was foolish to moon over a man just passing through town. But before he left, she did hope to find out how he looked when he smiled.

It would be worth remembering, Mimsy felt sure.

2

THE FIRST THING LUCAS noticed when he woke up was that his boots were gone.

He was lying on a hospital bed at dawn, the light punctuated by the glow of medical devices. From nearby came the steady beep of a heart monitor, counterpointed by the snores of someone slouching in a chair.

Lucas's brain was fuzzy, probably from painkillers. They must be wearing off, though, because his body felt as if it had been used as a pincushion for the entire Brooks Brothers tailoring operation.

Vaguely he recalled a sweet-faced doctor with a warm, full mouth. If he hadn't been so woozy, he'd have fantasized about the things she could do with that mouth.

There had been another woman, too. Carrot-top Flo. She'd watched over him for a while, Lucas recalled vaguely, but then she'd said something about needing to get home.

So who was snoring lustily in the chair? With luck, it would be the lovely lady physician.

He hadn't been very nice to her out there by the highway, Lucas recalled. He needed to remedy that negative first impression. If he played his cards right, she might even help him learn more about Ms. Lilibeth Anderson.

Not that he meant to exploit anyone in his quest for financial success. Lucas believed in being generous toward others and, until his recent setback, had underwritten an organization that paid veterinary bills for disabled pets. He did it in memory of the many injured stray animals, some of which had become his pets, that had taken refuge in his father's junkyard when Lucas was growing up.

When he made a killing with Lilibeth's help, he would use his share to resume helping the pets, as well as buy this hospital and its doctor all the equipment her heart desired. He'd also give Murdock a new truck. And build an air-conditioned kennel for the black dog that shared Lucas's name.

The first step, however, was to make amends to the lady physician. He couldn't see her clearly from his prone position, but she was slumped in a way that must be straining her muscles. It would be a kindness to wake her.

"Doctor?" he called.

The snoring peaked in a low whistle, then resumed. "Mimsy?" No response. Maybe a little sweet talk would get her attention. "Hey, honey?" The snoring sped up. Obviously, at some level she could hear him. "Angel face?"

Two snorts and a whistle. Promising.

With a grin at his own audacity, Lucas said, "Yo, babycakes! Anybody ever tell you you're beautiful when you're sleeping? But it's time to wake up. Snap out of it, sweetie pie!"

The snoring stopped and the figure on the chair straightened. A gruff masculine voice said, "Are you-all addressing me?"

Lucas wondered if he could blame his stupidity on

the painkillers. Unfortunately that wouldn't make him feel any less embarrassed, he decided. "Sorry. Mistaken identity."

"Oh, that's okay. Nobody pays me no mind anyway." The man shambled to his feet and gave an enormous stretch.

His beanpole proportions explained the oddly angled position he'd assumed on the chair. Tall and thin, long of hair and crooked of tooth, the man was a figure from a rustic fairy tale.

"I'm Billy Dell Grimes." The beanpole approached with his hand extended, then stopped. "I guess I'm not supposed to touch the patient, am I?"

"Are you the night nurse?" Lucas asked.

"Aw, I'm just a handyman. They asked me to fill in," he said. "Flo had to go home on account of she's a single mom and her son, Hank, he's ten, needs to be watched. He's been getting into trouble at school along with my son, uh…" He paused and scratched his head.

"You forgot your son's name?" Lucas doubted that amnesia was contagious. Particularly fake amnesia.

"Well, I got so many of 'em," Billy explained. "We've got nine kids, my wife, Willie, and me."

"No wonder you forgot his name." Nine kids? Lucas couldn't imagine having even one, although suddenly the idea kind of appealed to him.

Maybe it was because of finding himself in a small town, or it might be due to receiving a jolt to the head. Still, it was odd for a man so perfectly suited to the life of a bachelor. "It must be hard coming up with nine names," he added.

"Joe, that's the one that gets in trouble," said Billy. "He's my ten-year-old. Billy's the eldest, and then there's Dell, followed by Willie. She's named after my wife.''

"I see." Lucas gathered that this naming business had tapped out Billy Dell's imagination rather early. "How about the others?"

"We turned to the Bible." Billy frowned in concentration. "There's, let's see, Joseph—that's Joe—and Mary, and then we had Adam, Eve and Abel. Folks was afraid we was going to name the next one Cain."

Despite an aversion to chitchat, Lucas was drawn into the drama. "And did you?"

"Willie went into labor right in the middle of a school-board meeting," Billy said. "I'm on the board because of having so many young-uns, you see. Anyways, people kept accidentally saying the words 'cane' and 'cain't' and shushing each other. But we fooled them. We named the baby after Mazeppa."

"Who's Mazeppa?" asked Lucas.

"She used to be a bag lady until she married Murdock Murchison, the guy that nearly hit you with his truck," Billy said. "It turned out she was rich. She'd been hiding it all these years. She's the one that gave the money to build a new school."

"That's great." Lucas shifted uncomfortably as the invisible tailors resumed their work sticking pins into him. "Did the good doctor leave me any medicine?"

"Oh, gosh!" Billy clapped one hand to his cheek. "I was supposed to call her when you woke up. I guess I'd better do that."

"Wait!" said Lucas.

"What's wrong?" The handyman wore an expression of puppylike anxiety.

"My boots," he said. "Where are my boots?"

"Under the bed," said Billy. "That's where people in Texas always put their boots."

"Who took them off me?" he asked.

"I did," said Billy. "Dr. Mimsy has me undress the males that can't do it themselves."

Lucas didn't want to call attention to the presence of his supposedly missing wallet, but in his present state he could hardly climb down there to check for himself. "Did you find anything in them?"

"Oh, yes, sirree." Billy knelt and hoisted a boot from under the bed. Reaching inside, he produced the wallet. "It's right here. I didn't touch nothing."

"You didn't look inside?"

"No, sir," said the handyman. "I don't mess with nobody's personal possessions." He appeared completely unaware that the wallet might have any significance other than as a container for Lucas's money.

"I'm sure you don't," he said. "Just put it back in there, would you, Billy?"

"Sure thing." The handyman tucked it inside and put the boot away. "It's nice and safe."

"You didn't mention it to anybody?"

"Why would I do that?" said Billy. "People are mostly honest around here, but I wouldn't tempt anyone by mentioning where you keep your cash. There's a few ten-year-olds who might figure it was a divine signal for them to buy more firecrackers and scare the behooties out of Principal Smollens."

"We wouldn't want him to lose any of his behooties," said Lucas, who had never heard the term before, but rather liked it. "By the way, what happened to my motorcycle?"

"Carter Murchison is working on it," Billy said. "He's the town mechanic."

"Is he related to Murdock?"

"His son," said the handyman. "I'll go call Doc Mimsy about your medicine." He hurried away.

Lucas sank back against the pillow. He was beginning to suspect that everyone in this town was either related to each other or had the same name as a dog.

He wished he could leave right now for the relative sanity of Los Angeles, but that pleasure would have to wait.

IN HIS CONDITION, the man couldn't leave, Mimsy reminded herself after receiving the call from Billy Dell. There was no need to hurry, but she did anyway. It was still dark out on a brisk October morning, and she chose a turquoise turtleneck to wear beneath her white coat. The color flattered her light-olive complexion.

He isn't going anywhere, she repeated silently as she rejected a scuffed pair of loafers in favor of sleek flats. Not until his motorcycle gets fixed and his shoulder heals. And, of course, until he gets his memory back.

Even so, she was in such a rush that she forgot her purse and had to go back into her apartment to retrieve it. Then she trotted down the stairs at a half run.

The Anderson Coffee Shop and Drugstore, above which she lived, hadn't opened yet, but as she walked by she could see Lilibeth making coffee inside. When she spotted Mimsy, the former prom queen waved at her to halt, filled a disposable cup and headed for the front door.

It was a kind gesture, performed so frequently that Mimsy had to force herself not to take it for granted. Remembering the young woman's revelation about her Internet ad, she realized she took a lot of things about Lilibeth for granted.

It must be tough for a beautiful young woman to be stuck here. Lilibeth's parents, JoJo and B.K., depended on their only child to help manage the café and adjoining pharmacy with its post-office station. Whatever dreams their daughter treasured, she'd had to put them aside for their sakes.

"Here you go, Mimsy." Morning light clarified the creamy perfection of Lilibeth's skin as she handed over the coffee. "I hear you've got a new patient. What's he like? Is he cute?"

At that innocent question, Mimsy experienced an entirely new emotion. Jealousy.

She hadn't felt it when she was five and had a crush on Billy Dell, and he chose to share his ice cream with Willie instead of her. She hadn't felt it at fifteen when her amorous daydreams about Carter Murchison foundered on the rock of his infatuation with a fast girl named Amy.

But she felt it now, a dark bitter wrench of envy. Lilibeth Anderson could wrap Lucas around her little finger if she so much as simpered in his direction, Mimsy felt certain.

Sharply she reminded herself that Lilibeth never simpered. She'd simply asked a civil question.

"He's in a lot of pain," Mimsy said, "but he takes it well."

"You didn't tell me whether he's cute!"

"I couldn't say. I never notice that kind of thing about patients." Like fun she didn't!

Lilibeth giggled. "I guess you shouldn't. Not if you have to pull their clothes off."

"Billy Dell takes care of that," Mimsy said stiffly.

"Sheriff Bob said the man has amnesia," Lilibeth

went on. "A real mystery here in Nowhere Junction! Do you have any idea who he is?"

"A drifter, I guess." Mimsy supposed it was true. "What else could he be, with that beat-up motorcycle and so few possessions?"

"Oh, a drifter." With a disappointed shrug, the blonde said goodbye and went inside.

Of course, Lucas might have property or a job somewhere. Mimsy recalled how Mazeppa had floated around town for years without anyone guessing she was a millionaire.

People had taken in the crusty old lady out of kindness, letting her stay for months in their tornado shelters and barns. She'd lived for a while in Billy Dell's laundry room until she drove him crazy with her constant carping.

Cradling the cup of coffee, Mimsy continued down Main Street to the corner and turned right on Cross Street. She could hear the whine of saws as the construction workers took apart the interior of the sprawling old schoolhouse that housed grades K-8.

Quade Gardiner, the mayor and chairman of the school board, had announced that the dilapidated building would be brought down by explosives on Saturday, which was tomorrow. The eager townspeople planned to picnic in City Hall Park to watch the big bang.

Mimsy had patched up too many Fourth of July fireworks injuries in the past to relish the prospect of a blast in the middle of town. Especially since the principal, "Uncle Dick" Smollens, was personally taking charge of the detonation.

He claimed that years of being targeted by students' noisemakers had awakened an interest in the subject. There had been firecrackers in the toilets, stink bombs at PTA meetings, and one inventive device—for which credit was never claimed—that blew Uncle Dick's desk two feet into the air and seared the edges of a stack of report cards.

First in search of countermeasures and then with growing fascination, Dick had begun to read about explosives. The past two summers, he'd apprenticed with a demolition firm in Dallas.

Mimsy was not reassured.

At the two-story, white stucco hospital, she went through the side entrance, which was the only one unlocked. Most of the time, no one staffed the front desk. During flu epidemics, the PTA provided volunteers.

Billy Dell came to greet her. "His shoulder's hurting like fire, but he wants to be released," he said.

"What a stubborn man." Mimsy tried to ignore her disappointment at learning that her patient was anxious to leave.

"He said he figures he probably doesn't have insurance. I told him Murdock was paying and he said he doesn't want to run up the old man's bill." The handyman cleared his throat before continuing. "Even when I hinted that Murdock's wife is rich, he said it don't matter."

I knew Lucas was a good man. "Let me take a look at him," Mimsy said.

She found the patient sitting up in bed, his face taut and his hand trembling slightly as he toyed with the frozen breakfast Billy Dell had microwaved for him. "I hear you'd like to be released."

"There's nothing broken, right?" He gave her a wan smile. Stubble emphasized the strong line of his jaw. "By the way, what shall I call you? Dr. Miles?"

"Hardly anybody does," she admitted, picking up

her stethoscope. "The most formal address I get is Dr. Mimsy, but just my first name is fine."

"I'm sorry I was so grumpy yesterday." The skin around his black eyes crinkled, softening the harshness of his expression.

"It's understandable," Mimsy said. "Besides, I'm used to it with patients. They're hurting, after all."

"You shouldn't let people treat you rudely," Lucas said. "Including me. Now, accept my apology!"

"Is that an order?" she teased.

"Yes, ma'am."

"I'm usually the one giving orders around here," Mimsy said.

"We each have our spheres of influence," he responded. "You can order me to get a shot in the rump. I can order you to let me make amends for my bad manners."

"Okay, I agree that you were grumpy as an old bear, and I accept your apology." She smiled, but quickly resumed an air of professional detachment.

Mimsy hoped he didn't mistake her friendliness for flirting. The man could be endearing when he turned on the charm. That didn't mean she had to succumb.

"Is there a motel around here?" Lucas asked.

"A motel?" Good heavens, he not only believed she was flirting, but he expected her to jump between the sheets with him!

"I'll need somewhere to stay till my bike's fixed."

Mimsy felt like an idiot. She hoped he hadn't guessed what she was thinking. "There's no motel. We hardly ever get strangers here."

"Someone must rent rooms," Lucas said.

"Maybe Murdock will put you up, but he lives way

out of town." Mimsy placed the stethoscope against his back.

"That's not very convenient, I'm afraid, considering the state of my motorcycle."

"Breathe deeply."

He obeyed, and winced.

"Your lungs sound clear," Mimsy said. "How's your vision?"

"Twenty-twenty."

"I mean, is anything blurry?"

He shook his head.

She stuck a thermometer into his mouth. The reading was normal; no sign of infection.

"Billy mentioned the Anderson Coffee Shop." Lucas sank back against the pillow. "He said they have a few apartments upstairs. Maybe I could talk them into loaning me one for a few days. Until my wallet turns up."

There was a small vacant unit next to Mimsy's, but she loathed the prospect of sending Lucas to talk to Lilibeth. She'd seen him first. As long as he stayed in town, he was hers, Mimsy thought with fierce determination and more than a little irrationality.

"You can't stay there," she said.

"Why not?"

A good reason occurred to her, one so obvious she should have thought of it sooner. "I can't release you unless there's someone to keep tabs on your condition. A concussion sometimes shows up unexpectedly." It occurred to Mimsy that she had a second bedroom. No! She couldn't possibly let him stay there. "Any idea why you were heading this way? Maybe someone's expecting you."

"I can't remember a thing," he said.

"Exactly my point. You're not well."

"These, uh, Andersons," Lucas said. "Maybe they wouldn't mind checking on me from time to time if I rented a room. How much do you know about them?"

How ironic, that of all the families in town he should inquire about Lilibeth's! Maybe it would be best to say there was insanity in the family, Mimsy thought wildly. Or that a series of boarders had been mysteriously poisoned by substances stocked in the pharmacy.

"They're very nice," she said. "The truth is, I rent one of their apartments over the café. It's right around the corner."

"I gather this hospital isn't normally staffed at night," Lucas said. "So it's a lot of trouble for you folks to be watching over me if I stay here."

"We're prepared to take care of our patients."

"Let me run another possibility by you." He cleared his throat. "You wouldn't have a spare room in your apartment, would you? If I stayed there, you could monitor my progress. We could designate your place as a hospital auxiliary for a few nights."

Mimsy's heart performed a major cardiac anomaly by somersaulting back and forth across her chest. Did she dare say yes? Surely he'd never guess that she felt anything more than professional concern.

He couldn't know how much she longed to hear his voice reverberate through her apartment. Or that she yearned to find out what kind of person he really was.

"I suppose it could be arranged," Mimsy said.

"I'd be grateful."

"Just until you get your memory back."

"Of course."

She'd handled that beautifully. Very cool, very professional. Mimsy felt proud of herself.

LUCAS WONDERED IF THE LADY doctor had any idea how adorable she was. It had been a long time since he'd met a woman who wore her emotions so openly on her face.

She'd been dying to ask him to stay with her. Probably she wanted him there out of curiosity and to relieve the boredom of small-town life, but, he thought, perhaps she liked him a little bit, too.

He certainly liked her. Enough to vow not to take advantage of her. He didn't want to mar one bit of her trusting innocence.

He'd had such negative feelings about small towns that he'd forgotten there were pluses, such as women who didn't calculate his net worth the moment they met him. Mimsy was willing to take him in even though, as far as she knew, he was a penniless loner.

He was not, Lucas told himself, going to think about the delicate curve of her cheek. Or about the small, firm breasts outlined by the white coat as she detached his assorted tubes and sensors.

The woman seemed remarkably unaware of her natural sensuality. He wondered what was wrong with the men in this town, because he'd have bet dollars to doughnuts that no one had awakened Dr. Mimsy.

It was hard to imagine that such a woman could have reached her early thirties as a virgin, so he supposed she wasn't. But whatever man had made love to her, he'd done a lousy job of it.

She needed someone experienced but gentle, a man who appreciated her unaffected beauty and who would take his time. A lover who knew how to stoke the banked embers until the flames leaped high.

A man like Lucas.

"It's time you got up and walked around," Mimsy said. "We don't want you forming any blood clots."

"Uh, sure." Except that, Lucas discovered, he was so fully aroused by his fantasies that he could hardly sit up. All he wanted was to take her in his arms and...

"Lean on me." She sat beside him and looped his uninjured arm around her shoulders.

"I'm kind of achy." Lucas wished he weren't so agonizingly aware of her hip brushing his. "Maybe we should wait."

"You ought to stay here another night, then," Mimsy said. "If I'm going to administer heavy-duty pain medication, I want you hooked up to these monitors."

"Never mind." Leaning on her more heavily than he intended, Lucas hoisted himself to his feet.

During the previous night, he discovered, someone had transferred this hospital to the planet Jupiter. Gravity had doubled or tripled, at least.

"Rough going, huh?" Mimsy asked as she straightened beneath his arm. Lucas guessed her height at about five foot five inches. At six foot one, he towered over her.

"I'm fine," he said.

"Think you could climb stairs?"

"You mean your apartment stairs? Sure."

After all, Lucas reminded himself, he not only wanted to regain a measure of privacy by getting out of the hospital, but he also needed to meet Lilibeth Anderson. And what better way than by living directly over an establishment that belonged to her family?

The heiress must stop by from time to time. In a town called Nowhere Junction, there couldn't be many places to eat out, no matter how rich she was.

Lucas felt a prick of guilt at the thought of misleading the kindhearted Dr. Mimsy. In all honesty, though, he did need a place to stay while he recuperated.

Besides, he liked her. If he worked hard at it, maybe he would come to think of her as the sister he'd never had.

"You're doing fine," Mimsy said as they crossed the room.

Despite the trembling in his legs, Lucas fought an urge to sink into a chair. He had to keep moving. Wasn't that the story of his life, in a way? "It hardly hurts anymore," he lied.

"That's scary," she said.

"What?"

"The way you said that, I could almost believe you. But I know it isn't true." She eyed him assessingly. "You could fool most people easily, Mr. No-Name. You wouldn't be fibbing about this amnesia business, would you?"

It was on the tip of his tongue to enlighten her. To admit the real reason he'd come to Nowhere Junction and to enlist her aid in learning the truth about Lilibeth.

But the odds were better than fifty-fifty that she'd rat on him. A straight-arrow person like Dr. Mimsy wasn't going to cover for him if the sheriff starting asking questions, was she?

"As a matter of fact, I've got a feeling that I'm a hurry-up sort of guy," Lucas said. "The last thing I'd want is to get stuck somewhere pretending to figure out who I am and where I'm going."

At the word *stuck*, she flinched. Instantly he regretted the implication that he didn't want to be here. That he didn't want to be with her.

But she needed to know that he'd be leaving. He wasn't going to deceive her about that.

"So when can I try my luck on your stairs?" he pressed.

"After lunch." Mimsy returned him to the bed. "I'll send Flo down in a minute to assist you."

"She need any help with that boy of hers?" Lucas wasn't sure why he asked, since he had next to no experience with children. Still, he knew what it was like to be a kid growing up in a small town.

"Don't get involved with Hank," Mimsy said, as she helped him back into bed. "He needs people who are going to stick around. Not like his father." And, her tone implied, not like Lucas, either.

The rebuke was well deserved. He didn't understand why it bothered him, so he decided not to think about it.

Lucas leaned his head against the pillow. Everything ached, but he knew better than to say so. Not at the risk of another dose of medication.

He was going to get out of this place today, with his head—if not his conscience—clear.

3

MIMSY HAD A BAD FEELING about tomorrow. Uncle Dick frequently lost control of the students. What if he lost control of a zillion pounds of explosives?

It was a slow day at the clinic, and she needed to distract herself from thinking about the fact that Lucas would be sleeping in her apartment tonight. So after an early lunch, she began making preparations for a possible disaster.

Flo, who shared her misgivings, went to work with a will making up the empty hospital beds and taking stock of bandages, saline solution and antibiotics. Mimsy called the blood bank in Austin and made sure she could have a supply helicoptered in if necessary.

She had just finished resterilizing her surgical equipment when she heard Lucas moving around in the hospital hallway. Mimsy found him walking stiffly but steadily in his bare feet.

He'd taken a shower, she noticed, and put on his spare jeans and a polo shirt that hugged his well-built chest. Unlike other drifters she had encountered, he exuded a mellow self-confidence that made her feel comfortable with him.

Maybe a little too comfortable.

"Exercising?" she asked.

"It's a good idea, right?" He stopped and regarded

her with his head tilted slightly. "I want to get out of here today, as promised."

"Why are you in such a hurry?" she asked.

His eyes were very black, in dramatic contrast to his brown hair. They gave him an intense air that she'd previously attributed to physical suffering, but now she saw as a sign of natural alertness.

"As I told you, I think that's my personality. Always in a rush even when there's nowhere to go."

Mimsy couldn't resist a joke. "We all have Nowhere to go around here."

A crooked smile lit up the guy's face. "It's an unusual town. The name, for one thing."

"The people are unusual, too," she said. "At least, I think they are."

From down the hall came the noise of vacuuming. "You and Nurse Nightingale seem awfully busy," Lucas said. "Expecting a crowd?"

"I hope not." She drew him to a window that overlooked City Hall Park and the adjacent school grounds. "See that building?"

"The school, right?"

"Former school. It's been falling apart for years," she said. "Tomorrow, it's going to be blown up to make room for a new building."

"You're worried about the explosion?" he said.

"I'm preparing for casualties," Mimsy said. "Just in case."

"Who's handling the demolition?"

"The principal. He claims to have expertise," she said. "I'm not sure how he talked the school board into going along with it."

"So you're in charge of disaster preparations for the

town as well as taking care of your patients?'' Lucas asked.

It hadn't occurred to Mimsy to view her activities in that light. "Everyone in town is my patient, so I have to look after their welfare," she said. "There's no public health staff in a town this size. We don't even have a full-time sheriff—Bob spends half his time on the ranch. We all pitch in."

"That sounds a lot different from the town where…" Lucas stopped in midsentence. Ruefully he shook his head. "Darn. I keep almost remembering things, and then they're gone."

"That's a good sign," Mimsy said. "You probably have some minimal brain swelling, and it's abating."

"I hope so," said Lucas. "By the way, if you're going down to inspect the site, I'll come with you."

It hadn't occurred to Mimsy to do so, but now she decided that she should take a closer look. "What's your interest?"

Lucas shrugged. "You never know what might jar my memory. As I said, I'd like to be on my way."

Not too soon. Mimsy knew she was foolish to want to keep him to herself, even for a few days. He didn't belong here. He might even be married, despite his lack of a wedding ring.

But she had so few opportunities to dream. So few chances to tell herself, even for a day or so, that the strong, tender, wonderful man of her fantasies might be real. Mimsy treasured her daydreams, even when she knew she was lying to herself.

"You're more than welcome to come with me," she said. "Let's go."

THAT HAD BEEN A CLOSE CALL, Lucas reflected as he put on his boots. He'd nearly blurted out that he'd grown up in a small town not unlike this one, and that he'd found it narrow and confining.

That would have killed his amnesia story for sure.

Besides, he didn't want to belittle Mimsy's optimism. She obviously had a high opinion of her fellow Nowhereans.

He hoped she was justified, although he doubted it. People might have cooperated with each other most of the time in Blink, Colorado, but they certainly hadn't gotten along with the McRifles.

Lucas had been the town wild child, the kid whom parents wouldn't let their children play with. His mother had stirred gossip by running away when Lucas was young, and his father was an eccentric who cared little for public opinion.

Norman McRifle still lived in Blink, running a salvage yard named Best Rust in the West. Although he took good care of the stray animals that wandered among the car parts and used appliances, his fellow citizens considered the establishment an eyesore and periodically schemed to tear it down.

Lucas tucked his wallet deep into his boot, ran a comb through his hair and came out of the bathroom. Mimsy, he found, had removed her white coat and was waiting for him in his room.

Her turquoise turtleneck brought out the sparkle of her brown eyes and highlighted the color in her cheeks. With her short curls, she looked too young to be a doctor.

"After we see the school, I can drive you around town, if you like," she said. "Flo will page me if any patients come in."

"Terrific," he said. "Thanks."

Lucas hoped to learn a few things from mingling with the townspeople. For one thing, why hadn't the wealthy Andersons helped Mazeppa Murchison underwrite the new school? Were they tight-fisted or more interested in other causes?

He also hoped to meet the reputedly well-to-do Mazeppa, although, judging by the creaky state of her husband's truck, she must have spent all her money on the school. Besides, older folks were less likely to be risktakers than the young.

There was something else motivating him, Lucas had to admit. Being with Mimsy gave him a pleasant buzz.

Around her, he felt alert, stimulated and mildly aroused. Well, sometimes more than mildly. Still, as long as he was stuck in this town, there was no reason not to enjoy her company.

When the two of them exited, sunlight flooded over Lucas's face and shoulders. He was surprised at the relief he experienced at being outside. Time had moved with agonizing slowness in the hospital.

Thanks to a modest dose of painkillers, the throbbing in his muscles had faded to dull aches. A lot of walking would probably make him sore as blazes later, but he preferred to live full-out and let tomorrow take care of itself.

They ambled across an unlaned street. Although there were a few cars parked nearby, Lucas didn't see or hear any traffic.

Trees shaded the park, which was enlivened by a large striped tent and a couple of smaller ones. From inside them came the sound of teachers lecturing and children chattering.

"Where did you get the tents?" he asked.

"Quade rented them from a circus," Mimsy said. "They're quite sturdy. Waterproof, too."

An all-too-familiar figure in a cowboy hat approached. Sheriff Bob. "Out of the hospital already?" he asked dourly.

"Lucas is feeling better, but hasn't recovered his memory," Mimsy said.

"Seems odd," the man grumbled. Although he seemed to be a few years younger than Lucas, his face was creased from the sun or perhaps from his perpetual scowls.

"I'm not happy about it, either, believe me." Lucas assumed a friendly manner.

The sheriff turned to Mimsy. "You heard anything about Lilibeth giving my sister a wedding shower?"

"No," the doctor said. "That would be kind of her, though."

"It's no favor to encourage a woman to make a fool of herself," Bob said. "Marrying a man from Groundhog Station just isn't right. It's against the natural order." To Lucas, he said, "We stick to our own around here."

That was the kind of small-town attitude Lucas had expected. "I see."

"I don't believe there are any plans for a shower," Mimsy said. "I'm sure I would have been invited."

"Well, those two women were gabbing a mile a minute on the phone this morning," Bob said. "Bobette said something about a shower. Or maybe about swimming. There was water involved, anyhow. I didn't pay too close attention on account of a cow got herself stuck in the cattle guard and was bellowing like to bust."

"I'd forget about it, if I were you. We'll find out soon enough," Mimsy said. "Now tell me, how far back are you going to keep the observers tomorrow?"

"Over yonder." Bob indicated a couple of trees behind the tents. "Think that's far enough?"

Mimsy gauged the distance visually. "Hard to say."

"Uncle Dick swears the whole thing's going to implode. He says there won't be so much as a flying brick," said the sheriff.

"I'll believe that when I see it."

"So will I," the man said, and strode away.

When he was out of earshot, Lucas said, "His sister's name is Bobette?"

"They're twins," Mimsy explained.

"And she lives with him?" The woman must be the same age, roughly thirty. Old enough to have her own place.

"They inherited a ranch together. Where else would she live?"

"Anywhere but with him."

Mimsy laughed. "He's not always so grouchy. He just hates Groundhog Station. It's an old rivalry from way back when both towns vied for the railroad and the Groundhogs won. Then not so long ago they got the highway, too."

A robust clanging interrupted her, coming from the direction of the schoolhouse. It was, Lucas realized, a cowbell.

"Lunch! Come and get it!" bellowed a woman.

From the tents issued children's dismayed cries, along with loud gagging noises. Soon about a hundred or so youngsters spilled from the tents. Many of them waved brown sacks in a defensive manner that reminded Lucas of movie peasants wielding holy water and crosses to keep vampires at bay.

"What's going on?" he asked.

Mimsy pointed to an open-air serving setup where a middle-aged woman, her dark hair pulled back beneath a red bandanna, cheerfully ladled food onto paper plates.

Beneath her apron, she wore a red-and-white checked dress with a stiff, full skirt. It looked suitable for square dancing.

The breeze carried cooking scents of fish, chili peppers and orange rind. Construction workers crowded into line, jockeying to get at the food.

"Finella Weinbucket is catering the construction site, and she offered to serve the kids, too," Mimsy said. "Since we don't have a school kitchen right now, the parents were kind of pleased."

"Kind of?" he asked.

"Finella's notorious for her strange recipes," Mimsy explained as they slowly headed in that direction.

"The construction workers seem to like her cooking," Lucas noted. The bruises on his legs made each step vibrate through his nervous system.

"They're from out of town," Mimsy said. "The novelty hasn't worn off yet. Or maybe they've got cast-iron stomachs."

The fortyish woman in the bandanna waved them over. After another sniff brought the mingled scents of cinnamon and garlic, however, Lucas decided to forgo sampling her cuisine.

He shook hands when they were introduced, and politely answered Finella's questions about his memory. Obviously the story of his accident and amnesia had spread quickly.

Although Finella soon turned her attention to dishing up food, other people gathered around. A lady with three double chins was introduced as Gigi Wernicke, the owner of the local grocery.

"You come by my store when you get hungry," she ordered Lucas. "I'll fix you up with this week's specials. Bruised oranges that fell off the truck, chili peppers and freshwater tripe."

"Tripe isn't a fish," Lucas said. "It's cow innards."

"I guess I mean carp," Gigi said. "You come and get some, anyway."

"There's a new shipment of denim overalls down at my dry goods store if you need any," added a red-faced man whom Mimsy introduced as Horace Popsworthy. "They're discounted because they've got little daisies embroidered on the bib. Don't know what dang fool came up with that idea."

"I have to admit, there's a definite lack of flowered overalls in my wardrobe," Lucas said. He could tell the doctor was struggling not to laugh.

"You'll find we're a right welcoming little town," Horace went on, oblivious to the amused undercurrents. "Anything you want to know, just ask me. I'm almost the mayor around here."

"Horace!" Gigi said. "You know Quade Gardiner's the mayor, not you."

"I was the official candidate," the man harrumphed. "He got himself wrote in. That doesn't hardly count."

"Horace! I've got a bone to pick with you!" A man stalked up wearing a black Greek-style sea captain's hat pulled over his white hair. With his square-cut white beard, he looked as if he'd just sailed in on the briny.

"Lucas, this is Dick Smollens, the school principal," Mimsy said. "Dick, I'd like you to meet..."

"Pleased-to-make-your-acquaintance," the newcomer said so fast the words ran together. "Horace, you have to back off this nonsense about making the kids compete in the Great Groundhog Crate Race. I don't have time to supervise them and the only man in town who knows diddly-squat about go-carts is Carter Murchison and he says there's no way we can win without spending a lot of money."

"It was the whole school board that voted on it,"

Horace said. "We want to teach those Groundhogs a lesson."

"Why do I put up with this?" the principal demanded of no one in particular. "As if I don't have enough responsibilities on my hands! I'm telling you, I'd trade it all in for a few blasting caps and a stick of dynamite."

Lucas was glad when Mimsy led him away. Although he was intrigued by the idea of a go-cart race, he wasn't going to be around to learn the outcome, so why get involved?

"By the way," he said, "I heard the school was funded by Murdock Murchison's wife. I'm surprised the townspeople couldn't raise the money themselves."

"We tried," Mimsy said. "Buffy Murchison had the women sewing clothes and selling them. And Finella held I don't know how many bake sales."

"Aren't there other wealthy people in town who could have donated the money?" Lucas hoped it sounded like an idle question.

"There's a few, but their money's tied up," Mimsy said. "Around here, people may own property but that doesn't mean they've got cash to hand out. Believe me, with all the things we need at the hospital, I've hit my share of brick walls."

This was not promising information, Lucas conceded. Nevertheless, even if the Andersons were stingy about making donations, their daughter might have a trust fund of her own. And making an investment was different from giving money away.

"There's something I want to show you." From the eagerness in Mimsy's voice, Lucas gathered it was personally important to her. "Then we'll stop by the garage and check the progress of your motorcycle. I'm sure you're concerned about it."

"Thank you, I am." Impulsively Lucas linked his

arm with hers. He could use some support, since the pavement was jarring him harder with every step.

He also loved the thrum of energy running through this bright-faced dynamo. It was hard to understand why no man in town had swept her to the altar.

It was a good thing, Lucas thought, that he wasn't the marrying kind. Otherwise, if he stuck around too long, he might marry her and get trapped forever in the middle of Nowhere.

MIMSY HAD NEVER ADMITTED to anyone what she was about to tell this stranger. It was too close to her heart to share with anyone else, even her friend Buffy.

In a way, the fact that Lucas wouldn't be sticking around made it safe to confide in him. There was little chance of her hidden wounds becoming idle gossip.

After easing him into her station wagon and tucking his meager possessions into the back, Mimsy drove along worn, pebble-strewn roads. The vehicle rattled and creaked at the slightest dip, and she hoped the aging suspension wasn't hurting Lucas's shoulder.

"How come you drive a station wagon?" he asked. "I picture you owning a perky little car."

"In a pinch, this doubles as an ambulance," Mimsy said. "The hospital has some portable emergency equipment I can load in back."

"How long have you been the doctor here?" he asked as they clunked between clapboard houses.

"Three years, since Ole Doc Winters died with his boots on. Or his scrubs, anyway," Mimsy said. "I'd just finished my residency and was trying to figure out what to do. Lucky thing I was visiting my mother because he dropped from a heart attack right in the middle of delivering one of Billy Dell's kids."

"What made you decide to be a doctor in the first

place?'' He wasn't watching the town go by. He was studying Mimsy.

People didn't usually pay her this kind of attention. She wasn't beautiful like Lilibeth, that was for sure, and most folks considered her kind of scatterbrained.

That was because Mimsy got distracted by her thoughts. Her mind kept working over articles she'd read in medical journals, trying to solve problems and make connections. As a result, she didn't always make connections with the world around her.

Having a handsome man like Lucas turn his full attention on her was a novel experience. He didn't know her well enough yet to realize how dull she was, Mimsy supposed.

''My dad was a doctor,'' she told him. ''I didn't really know him, though. He died when I was five.''

''You decided to follow in his footsteps.''

''It was either that or be a teacher like my mother, and I don't have the aptitude,'' she admitted.

''Your mom taught at the school here?''

''Eleanor Miles was famous, or infamous, as the strictest teacher in the history of Nowhere Junction,'' she said. ''She taught fifth grade and everybody here has a story of how she marked them down for dotting an *I* with an open circle or coloring a picture outside the lines.''

She slowed the car when they reached the southern part of town. They passed the pecan tree where Mimsy had picked a basketful of nuts on her tenth birthday.

Beyond it, she saw the woodpile where a cat named Whiskers had given birth to kittens years ago. It had nearly broken Mimsy's heart when her mother wouldn't let her keep one.

''Was she as tough at home as in the classroom?'' Lucas asked. The gentleness of his tone startled her.

Mimsy nodded, her throat tight. "She was never satisfied. I know she was trying to be both mother and father to me, and she certainly spurred me on to high achievement."

"It must have been hard on you, though," he said.

"What were your parents like?" She stopped. "I'm sorry. I forgot you can't remember them."

"I doubt they were as disciplined as yours," Lucas said. "What is it you want to show me?"

"This house." Mimsy indicated the gray-and-white three-story Victorian sitting at the crown of a patchy lawn. Despite the fact that the trim needed painting, surely anyone could see that the widow's walk and the wraparound porch made it special. "It's where I grew up."

"It must stir a lot of memories," he said.

"I couldn't believe it when my mother sold it. Overnight, practically." Mimsy swallowed hard. "I was in Dallas at a conference. She didn't even ask if I wanted to buy it myself."

"Why'd she sell it?" Lucas asked.

Sitting beside her, he seemed larger than life, Mimsy thought distractedly. She inhaled his spicy scent, and noted how different it was from the smoky cowboys she occasionally dated.

Did he have a woman somewhere? she wondered. Where did he come from, anyway? He didn't strike her as a Texas type, more West Coast. There were lots of beautiful women out there, she'd heard.

He was waiting for an answer, Mimsy realized. He must consider her as dizzy as everyone else did.

"Mom married a long-distance truck driver about two years ago," she said. "He got lost and broke an axle and was stuck in town for a few days while Carter fixed it, and they fell in love. She said she needed the money from the house to start her new life."

"I hope he didn't take advantage of her," he said.

"Not as far as I know," Mimsy answered. "Anyway, she sold the house to Uncle Dick—he's not really my uncle, everyone calls him that—and now she lives in Mystery Meat, Tennessee."

"Why'd she need the money?" Lucas asked.

"Her husband's a widower with ten grown kids, a few of whom still live at home along with some of the grandchildren. They needed a bigger house," Mimsy explained. "I'm glad Mom's happy. I wish she'd at least asked me before selling our home, though."

"Ever think about buying it from Uncle Dick?"

"It's not for sale. He says he'd been waiting years for something like it to come on the market," Mimsy said.

"It's a beauty," Lucas remarked, studying the house. "And I'm sure it means even more because you associate it with your childhood."

She flexed her fingers. "I itch to bake bread in that kitchen like my mother used to. And to see my kids doing homework with their books spread out on the dining-room table. Mom sold our furniture, too, so the table's still here."

Mimsy halted, taken aback by her boldness. Children? She was thirty-three, with no man in sight. At least, not one who was likely to be a marriage prospect.

"Let's go check on your bike," she said before Lucas could see the moisture in her eyes, and pulled the station wagon away from the curb.

4

LUCAS WAS FEELING THINGS he didn't want to feel, over and beyond the throbbing in his shoulder.

Feelings like nostalgia. Yearning. Tenderness. And they were all bound up with both this oddball town and the sensitive woman beside him.

She was different from anyone else he'd met. Highly intelligent but modest, layered with deep emotions yet straightforward. When her golden-brown eyes misted over, he wanted to gather her close and promise that everything would be all right.

But how could he promise that, when he wouldn't be sticking around?

It was a quirky thing, though. Lucas had imagined that a few hours in a small town would send him screaming for the highway. Instead he felt a reluctance as they headed for the garage where his bike was being repaired. He was in no hurry for it to be ready.

His painful teen years in Blink had obscured more pleasant, earlier memories that were rising to the surface. Christmases when the grocer delivered a basket of donated goodies with a few candy bars slipped inside for Lucas. One autumn when his friend Joey's parents took him for a hayride. A summer weekend waterskiing at the lake with his friend Sam's family.

As a teenager, Lucas had grown apart from his friends. For a long time, he'd believed they'd rejected him because of his poverty. Now he wondered if he'd alienated them by his rebellious attitude.

He'd dropped off the baseball team, cut classes and experimented with smoking, although, thank goodness, he hadn't gotten hooked. Sarcasm and messy grooming had become his hallmark.

Inside him twisted a pang of longing. To experience those days again, with the maturity to avoid the rifts. To get a second chance at making things right.

He dragged his thoughts back to the present as the station wagon halted in a short, wide driveway beneath a sign that read Murchison's Garage. They were directly across the street from the school and only about a block from the hospital.

Through the open lift door, Lucas could see a pickup truck sans rear axle, a sport utility vehicle with a bumper sticker that read Eat My Dust, Groundhogs! and his Harley.

The man working on it wore blue overalls and a plaid shirt. He glanced at them with a friendly, down-home smile that reminded Lucas of his old buddy Sam.

"You must be Lucas." The man extended his hand.

Lucas tried to respond in kind, but pain shot through his arm. "Oh, Je..." He stopped on the brink of a curse. "Gee whiz," he finished.

"I'm sorry. I wasn't thinking." The other man lowered his hand. "I'm Carter Murchison. It was my dad that nearly creamed you, so the repair's at no charge."

"I appreciate it." Nobody in Los Angeles would give a guy a break like that, even if their father had smashed the bike to smithereens and performed a juggling act with it.

From a rear doorway stepped an exquisite blond woman with large blue eyes. In her scarf-hemmed red skirt and high-collared bare-midriff blouse, she formed a stylish contrast to the other women of Nowhere Junction.

Could this be Lilibeth Anderson? But if so, why was she hanging around the town garage? And why did she have a year-old baby on her hip?

"Mr. Lucas, I'd like you to meet my wife, Buffy," said the mechanic.

Lucas smiled. "It's a pleasure."

"Nice to meet you, after hearing so much about you," she said. "Everyone in town likes to gossip about strangers. Don't be offended. I was one myself not long ago."

"I don't mind," he said.

"Buffy runs Buffy's Boutique. It's next to the grocery store," Mimsy said.

Carter's wife studied Lucas. "Haven't I seen you somewhere before? Not around here, but maybe in Los Angeles?"

He hoped not. The last thing he needed was to be recognized. His picture *had* appeared several times in L.A. newspapers and once in a national business weekly.

"I can't be sure, since I've lost my memory," he said. "Maybe you knew someone who looked like me. Besides, you've been gone from L.A. for...how long?"

"Oh, I've only lived in Nowhere Junction for about six months," she chirped. "And I love it here!"

Surprised, Lucas glanced at the baby. "I, uh...six months?"

"Carter and I first met in L.A. Sort of," Buffy said. "I was working at this sperm bank and there was this mixup..."

"He wouldn't want to hear that old story." Coloring

in embarrassment, Carter busied himself with the motorcycle.

"Is this him?" Through the rear door marched an elderly lady with straight, unnaturally black hair and a narrow face. "Mr. Forget-it-all? Are you faking, mister? Because if you're pulling a scam, I'll personally ride you out of town in my shopping cart!"

"Mazeppa!" Buffy said. "There's no reason to insult a man you've never met."

"I've met him now." The thin woman, who seemed taller than she actually was, planted herself in front of Lucas. "I'm not some bag lady living in your tornado shelter anymore, Buffy. I'm your mother-in-law, and for the protection of my granddaughter, I'm keeping an eye on this interloper."

Lucas waited for the usual reaction in his gut, the churning anger and resentment that had greeted the snubs of his adolescence. Instead he found himself amused by Mazeppa's bristling defense of the people she loved.

"I'm not here to harm anyone," he said.

"How can you be sure?" she demanded. "From what Mimsy says, you don't know why you're here. Young man, I faked these people out for years. I know what fools they are."

"And you rewarded their foolishness by paying for a new school," he reminded her.

"Someone's been talking," Mazeppa grumbled, clearly uncomfortable at accepting credit for her good deed.

"It's hardly a secret," Carter said, his aplomb restored now that the topic had veered away from sperm banks.

It occurred to Lucas that standing before him was a

woman with, possibly, the resources to fund his business venture and restore his wealth. He doubted she'd be eager to help, though.

Besides, he wanted a partner who enjoyed the thrill of taking risks. He didn't want to drag someone into a venture she didn't wholeheartedly endorse. Not that anyone was likely to be able to drag Mazeppa anywhere.

"In any case, Dr. Mimsy's no fool, and I doubt the other townspeople are, either," Lucas said.

"Well, it was nice meeting you. I've got to get back to the boutique." Buffy handed the baby to Mazeppa. "Lucas, I'll let you know if I remember anything else that might help establish your identity."

"Thanks." Now that the first, and hopefully last, shock of possible recognition was past, his spirits recovered. He just needed time to gather a little information about Lilibeth and he could "spontaneously" recover his memory on his own.

After he said goodbye to Carter and Mazeppa, Mimsy escorted him back to the station wagon. "If you're not too tired, I'll show you the rest of the town."

"That would be terrific." Lucas was beset by more aches and pains than if he'd aged thirty years. However, he was determined to maximize his chances of running into Lilibeth.

If only he dared come straight out and ask about her. But after spreading his amnesia story all over town, he could hardly come clean with Mimsy now. For better or for worse, he was committed to the course.

The car turned left onto Main Street, a wide street with room for parking on both sides. There were hitching posts in front of a couple of stores, although Lucas didn't see any horses.

Glancing from side to side, he took in the plain-wrap store names: Binny's Beauty Salon, Popsworthy's Dry Goods, Weinbucket Real Estate, the First National Bank of Nowhere. Nothing fancy or pretentious.

The facades were painted discreet shades of gray and tan, except for Buffy's Boutique, which was a bright cream thinly striped with lavender and aqua.

On the corner of Cross Street and Main sat Anderson Drugstore, which was attached on the far side to Anderson Coffee Shop. "It looks like the Andersons own a lot of things around here," Lucas said.

Mimsy sighed. "They sure do. Lilibeth owned the title of prom queen for four years in high school. That was a record."

"She must be very pretty."

Wistfully she glanced toward the building. "She sure is. Even prettier than Buffy, if you can believe that."

Lucas was on the cusp of saying that blondes had never been his style, when he remembered that a: he wasn't supposed to know what his style was and b: he wasn't supposed to know the color of Lilibeth's hair.

This amnesia business was tricky, Lucas thought ruefully. Still, he was in no hurry to be done with it, because doing so would mean parting from Mimsy.

There were so many things about her that he wanted to find out first. For starters, why she had such a low opinion of herself even though she was smart and, in his opinion, more than pretty. And what went on in that mind of hers, which, judging from her expressions, was busily jumping from one idea to another even when she kept silent.

Surprisingly, he also wanted to kiss her. Surely it couldn't hurt, just once, to see the startled look in her chocolate eyes and then feel her melt in his arms.

"I'm going to get you settled in my spare room," Mimsy said as she made a U-turn and parked in front of the café. "You need to rest before dinner. I'll have to go back to work, though."

"That's fine." Lucas had a lot to do, and he needed to do it alone.

Mimsy got Lucas's duffel bag out of the trunk and took his arm. As they passed the large café window, he glanced inside, hoping for the sight of a gorgeous blond heiress lingering at one of the tables, perhaps admonishing the staff about some minor lapse. He saw only ordinary folks drinking coffee and eating lunch.

Oh well, he'd be staying right upstairs. Surely he'd meet the heiress soon.

The steps to which Mimsy guided him were steep and narrow. By the time he reached the top, Lucas was dismayed to find his knees turning to Jell-O. He took one pace forward and staggered against the doctor.

She held his weight steadily, although he must have knocked the wind out of her and she was carrying his duffel bag, to boot. "I'm sorry for dragging you all over town," she said. "I've worn you out."

"I guess I need...a nap."

"You sure do." She didn't make a big deal of his exhaustion, to Lucas's relief. He was glad Mimsy wasn't the fussy type.

Together, they staggered through the door into a pink-and-lavender bower straight from a fairy story. Lacy curtains billowed at the front window and soft fabrics swathed the sofa and a small table. Suspended diagonally across one corner was a child-size hammock filled with stuffed animals.

A white arching étagère displayed glass paperweights filled with flowers. Only a discreet white hutch whose door had been left ajar revealed Mimsy's serious side: rows of medical texts and journals.

One misstep and Lucas was likely to crash through the delicate veneer of the room. He halted in the center, overwhelmed by a sense of empathy for bulls that stumbled into china shops.

"Your room is this way." Mimsy indicated a short hallway. "First door on the left. Do you want me to get you settled? You'll probably need help getting those boots off."

That was the last thing he needed. "That's okay. You've done more than enough." Lucas forced himself to stand upright. "Aren't you due back at the office?"

Mimsy nodded. "Even when no one comes in, people call with questions."

"Go on, then," he said. "I'll be okay."

She handed him a vial of pills. "Take two now and two more in four hours, if I'm not back."

"Yes, ma'am," he teased.

When she smiled, her lively face outshone the rest of the sunny apartment. "Get some sleep."

One kiss. Just to see if she really tasted like chocolate.

Lucas shifted toward her, and he felt those imaginary tailors stick pins into his muscles again. He flinched.

"To bed!" Mimsy ordered.

Going to bed alone wasn't Lucas's first choice, but he doubted Mimsy would enjoy a casual relationship. Frankly she deserved better than anything he could offer.

Besides, he'd heard chocolates could be addictive.

"Yes, ma'am," he said.

MIMSY LEFT THE STATION wagon on Main Street. She needed to clear her head on the short walk to her office.

What was wrong with her today? She shouldn't have shown this stranger her beloved house, let alone started blithering about having children. She certainly shouldn't have invited him to stay at her apartment.

But he was so…wonderful.

Even in pain, Lucas moved with an inner grace that marked him as different from any other man she'd known. And the way he looked at her made her blood sparkle.

There was no medical term for her condition. It would take a poet to describe it, and she was no poet.

The only poem Mimsy had written as an adult had been a Valentine to the man she'd dated in medical school. It went:

> "Hemoglobin is red.
> Deep veins are blue.
> Glucose is sweet
> And so are you."

She'd been so embarrassed by her poor writing that she'd crumpled the poem and thrown it toward a trash can. She must have missed. Vince had stumbled across it later and, failing to recognize the handwriting, had copied it over and presented it to her with a flourish.

"I wrote this for you," he'd said.

The discovery that he'd plagiarized her work, and didn't even recognize how lousy it was, had been one more nail in the coffin of their relationship.

No man since then had appealed to her. Perhaps she had unrealistic standards, Mimsy admitted. She wanted a man with honesty, intelligence, humor and gentleness.

Afraid of asking too much, she'd never allowed herself to note that she also liked muscular arms and thick hair. Or a first-class tight butt and an aura of power.

Whoever he was, she felt certain Lucas must have known many women. He was too handsome to be resisted for long. Too handsome for his own good, and for Mimsy's.

She must never yield to him. How could he help comparing her to those other women, who were surely more sophisticated, more feminine, more lovable than she was?

Mimsy blinked away tears. For so long, she'd yearned for a man like Lucas to come to Nowhere Junction.

Now that he had, she almost wished she'd never met him.

SKIPPING THE PAIN PILLS because he didn't want his mind clouded, Lucas took off his boots and lay down for a few minutes. He awoke hours later from a deep sleep, and at first couldn't figure out where he was.

Great fluffy bolsters loomed next to his head and his pillow was so deep he could barely see over it. Overhead, suspended from a four-poster frame, pastel fabric shrouded the bed.

Despite the impression of softness, however, the mattress held his bruised body firmly in place. It was the kind of bed one would expect from a teenage romantic who had grown up to be a doctor.

Reoriented at last, Lucas hauled himself to his feet.

In the kitchen, he microwaved a cup of leftover coffee and sat down with the telephone. Using a thin list of numbers from his wallet, he made a series of phone calls charged to his long-distance card.

The next-door neighbor watching Lucas's Los Angeles apartment reported that his possessions had arrived safely and been stowed inside. His answering service had only a few messages, none of any importance. There was no word from his missing partner, Ray Ryker.

Another call disclosed that the private detective whom Lucas had hired on retainer had found not a shred of evidence on Ray's whereabouts. His former friend had made a clean disappearance with nearly a million dollars in joint funds.

It was hard to believe that his partner would rip him off this way. Worse, the foundation that provided medical care for handicapped pets was running short of funds and was hoping Lucas could make another donation.

It had expanded under Lucas's sponsorship, and now those animals faced an uncertain future. Some of their owners, unable to afford care, might have to have them put to sleep.

As he had several times before, Lucas considered notifying the police. It went against the grain, though, to report Ray without hearing his side of the story. In spite of all the evidence, a thin thread of trust still bound the two men.

When they first met, they had been students at an evening business course in Pasadena, California. With his short stature, round face and wire-rimmed glasses, Ray must have looked like easy pickings to a couple of thugs who strong-armed him one night as he approached his car after class.

They hadn't noticed Lucas waiting nearby for a bus. He'd plowed into their midst like an avenging angel and knocked one of them into a daze. Ray, who had a black belt in karate, tossed the other one around like a sack of flour.

The attackers staggered away, clutching their injuries. Ray offered Lucas a ride home and, when it turned out they lived near each other, made it a standing invitation.

Six months later, they'd both entered a trainee program for a brokerage firm. In their spare time, they'd scanned news sources for entrepreneurial opportunities, and made the most of the ones they found.

Over the years, there had been ups and downs. Profits and losses. Big opportunities that slipped away and small deals that paid off unexpectedly.

So why, with the biggest deal of all practically in the bag, had Ray taken it on the lam?

The front door of the apartment opened. With a jolt, Lucas realized his wallet was sitting in plain sight.

He stuffed the phone card inside and crammed the wallet into his pocket. There wasn't much of a bulge and, with luck, Mimsy wouldn't notice.

He heard the scuff of her shoes on carpet, and the thud of her purse hitting a chair. "In here," he called.

"You're up! How are you feeling?" She was peeling off her white coat as she came through the door. With her curly hair askew and her lips parted, she looked wonderfully beddable.

From his seat at eye-level with her chest, Lucas took appreciative stock of his hostess. Her figure, like the rest of her, was natural and appealing.

Small, round breasts. Well-toned stomach and legs. There was nothing artificial or self-conscious, and her response to a sensual touch would be the same way, he thought. Stimulating and refreshing.

She set a large paper sack on the table in front of him. "People dropped by the office all afternoon to bring you food. There are prune muffins from Finella. Fish from Gigi. Lucy Gardiner, the mayor's wife, brought a box of macaroni and cheese mix. She's not much of a cook."

"Sounds like a meal," said Lucas, who wasn't particular about what he ate unless he was paying large amounts for it.

"And Bobette Moriarty dropped off some zucchini and a few herbs," Mimsy added. "She said not to pay her brother any mind if he's harassing you. She said if he locks you up, she'll make him sorry."

It took Lucas a minute to remember that Bobette was the twin sister of Sheriff Bob. "How does she plan to make him sorry? Cook zucchini every night?"

Mimsy fetched pots and pans from beneath the counter. "She's marrying Barney Dobbs from Groundhog Station. He's promised to open his own mattress store in Nowhere Junction, but she said if Bob makes her mad enough, she'll move to Groundhog. She doesn't mean it, though."

It occurred to Lucas that he ought to help fix dinner, but he was enjoying watching Mimsy. He would clean up, he vowed silently.

"What's Groundhog like, anyway?" he asked.

"About twice the size of Nowhere." Mimsy got out an assortment of spices. "A little overly commercial, if you ask me. There were at least two chain restaurants there when I went to high school."

"You went to high school in Groundhog?"

"The regional high school," Mimsy said. "It's the only school in the state where, at football games, the parents cheer only for the team players from their own town."

"Why do the people hate each other so much?" Blink didn't have a rival. Maybe, Lucas reflected, that was why people had so much animosity to lavish on their fellow townspeople who strayed from the straight and narrow.

"It goes back about a hundred years to when Groundhog Station was chosen for the train station." Mimsy set the oven to a high temperature and began seasoning the fish. "The people of Nowhere claimed there were bribes involved. Anyway, we got bypassed. Then it happened again a few years ago with the new highway."

"Bribes again?" Lucas asked.

"Who knows?" Mimsy shrugged.

"So is there a taboo on intermarriage?" Lucas couldn't help finding the situation amusing, like a pitched battle between two kittens.

"There is for Bob Moriarty. He takes the rivalry personally," she said.

"For any particular reason?"

"Back in high school, right before the senior prom, a guy from Groundhog stole his steady girlfriend," Mimsy said. "When Bob objected, the guy and his two best friends beat him up."

"He can hardly blame the whole town for that."

"The guy is now Groundhog's mayor," she said.

"I see." Lucas leaned back, and felt the wallet rub his hip. It nagged at him like a guilty conscience.

"Is your back hurting?" Mimsy asked. "I could give you a massage after dinner."

It was the best idea Lucas had heard in a long time. "I'd appreciate that."

"My pleasure."

Her words sent tingles running along his legs and chest. Yes, he would definitely enjoy a massage at the hands of Nowhere Junction's beautiful lady doctor.

The baked fish was delicious, the macaroni and cheese tasty and the prune muffins edible. Even the zucchini, seasoned with garlic salt and Parmesan cheese, proved better than expected.

Over Mimsy's protests, Lucas washed the dishes. Then, with a delirious sense of surrender, he pulled off his shirt and lay down on the couch.

After a moment's hesitation, she sat beside him. Her fingertips grazed his back so lightly they might have been butterflies.

"Your bruises are starting to fade already," Mimsy said. "You must have tremendous healing powers."

"You're the one with the healing powers," he murmured.

"Tell me if this hurts." With a rolling, kneading motion, she stroked between his shoulder blades.

Pain took wings and flew away. Whatever aches Lucas felt were nothing compared to the waves of relaxation breaking over him. Underlying them, equally forceful, rose a tide of desire.

Mimsy was both gentle and thorough, working from side to side and top to bottom. At the same time, the heat of her body fanned across his skin. When her fingers strayed near the waistband of his pants, Lucas grew hard.

He wanted this woman. Her teasing, insistent touch was torment almost beyond bearing.

From the speedup in her breathing, he could tell Mimsy was responding to him, too. He forced himself to lie still, head pillowed on his arms. If he turned over, if he made any move, she would scurry away like a turtle into its shell.

It was as if Lucas could read her thoughts. He felt a strong connection to Mimsy that had been there from the moment they met.

He knew that, when it came to making love, she needed to take her time. Besides, in fairness, they must talk openly before they went any further. Lucas wanted her to give herself freely, with full knowledge of who he was and of the fact that he wasn't going to stick around.

He had plenty of scruples. However, he found it hard to remember what they were as Mimsy lifted herself on the couch and flung one leg over his rear end.

"I can do this better if I sit on you," she said. "Does this hurt?"

Given Lucas's bruised condition, of course it hurt. But the strongest sensation was the fiery recognition of her soft bottom pressed against his. They were so close. They could so easily become one.

"It's fine," Lucas rasped.

He wished Mimsy would remove her sweater and rub her bare breasts across his back. He wondered if there was a way to communicate that idea to her without being crude.

"You have well-defined muscles," she said. "Do you work out at a gym?"

"I don't know."

"Sorry. I forgot."

She probed lower, slipping down the band on his pants. Her warm breath whispered across his back.

Nature shouted that there was more to life than caution. Surely they didn't need to wait to make love until she learned the boring details of his identity. There would be plenty of time to talk afterward.

Lucas eased to one side so that Mimsy's fingers grazed his bare hip. He released an encouraging moan.

She shifted position, then halted. After a frozen moment, she said, "Lucas?"

"Mmm?"

"Is there something in your pocket?"

Oh, blast. She'd run into his wallet.

The heat whooshed out of him like air from a balloon. *Think fast, McRifle.*

"Actually, yes." His brain whirred. "I have a...surprise for you."

"A surprise?" She sounded uncertain.

Whatever it is, it's going to be a surprise for both of us.

5

WITH EVERY IRRATIONAL fiber of her being, Mimsy hoped that Lucas had an acceptable explanation. She didn't want him to turn out to be a liar.

But if it wasn't a wallet in his pocket, what was it?

"Do you have any glycerine?" he asked.

"What?" The question was so unexpected that she wondered if she'd heard right.

"Glycerine. That stuff you mix with things to make lotion."

"Yes, I think so." Mimsy experimented with herbs from Bobette's garden, making folk remedies in the never-ending search for better ways to serve her patients. A few ointments did seem to soothe sore joints, but never as well as prescription drugs.

"I found a pouch of powder in my bag," Lucas said. "That's what's in my pocket. I seem to recall that it's good for hand cream. Are your hands dry?"

Embarrassment rushed over her. "Did they feel dry against your back?"

Since Mimsy scrubbed her hands frequently to keep them sanitary, the skin did tend to dry out. All the while she'd been relishing Lucas's powerful muscles, had he been remarking on the poor condition of her skin?

"That's not why I asked you. I'd like to do you a

favor, after all you've done for me. Would you mind fetching the glycerine?''

There was a note of command in his voice. Self-consciously, she scrambled off him and hurried into the bathroom.

Doubts assailed Mimsy as she searched through the cabinet. When Lucas showed her the pouch, it hadn't looked as firm and flat as a wallet. On the other hand, how could she be sure of what she'd bumped with her thigh?

To make matters worse, she could still feel the width of Lucas's hips between her legs. And when she heard that moan, it had stirred an unsuspected wantonness deep within.

Mimsy had never understood women who took foolish chances. Women who jumped into bed with a man they barely knew, who gave themselves to a stranger and held nothing back. Yet she'd come breathtakingly close to doing exactly that.

She emerged with a bottle of glycerine and a small mortar and pestle in time to see Lucas return from the bedroom. ''I took another look in my bag to see if there were instructions, but I didn't find any,'' he said, and set the pouch of powder on the coffee table.

''Are you getting more memories?'' she asked.

''Bits and pieces.'' He shrugged apologetically. ''I think this powder is good for the skin, but that's all I remember about it.''

Sitting beside him on the couch, Mimsy watched him measure a small heap of small white grains into the palm of his hand. ''That smells like coconut,'' she said.

''It does, doesn't it?'' He frowned. ''Do coconuts have any medicinal value?''

"Not that I know of."

"You've never heard of any native treatments? Read anything about rare coconut species?" Lucas probed as he dumped the powder into the small ceramic bowl and squeezed in a dollop of the gel.

"No," Mimsy said. "And I read widely. Most doctors don't have time to keep up with anything but the main medical journals and the drug company literature, but working in such a small town gives me time to dig deeper."

Lucas ground the two substances together with the small, clublike pestle. "Too bad you haven't read anything about coconuts. It might give us a clue to my identity."

"Coconuts grow in tropical climates," Mimsy said, and immediately felt stupid. It was that sort of obvious remark that had made people give her pitying looks in medical school.

The man beside her didn't scoff, however. "That's true. I do have a light tan as well, but not what you'd expect from someone who lived in the tropics."

"I noticed that," she said, and blushed. Darn it, did foolish statements have to pour from her mouth?

"Okay." Lucas wiped the pestle on the edge of the mortar. "Rub this on your hands."

Mimsy scooped up some white lotion with one finger. She wished he wouldn't observe her so closely. Her short fingernails were a mess from frequent scrubbing and, besides, they had a tendency to crack and split no matter what she put on them.

Beneath the cream, her skin tingled. She hoped it wasn't going to give her a rash.

"What do you think?" Lucas asked.

"It feels good." Mimsy sniffed the back of her hand.

"Smells good, too. Like coconut mixed with rose petals."

"It's a rare... I mean, maybe it's some rare kind of coconut. Or perhaps somebody mixed perfume in it," Lucas said.

Mimsy frowned at her hands. "My skin's kind of tingly."

He grinned. "Want to try some on your face?"

That was all she needed, to risk having a rash break out on her cheeks and forehead! "I'd rather wait to see the long-term effects," Mimsy admitted, scooping the rest of the lotion into a baggie. "Although my nails do look smoother."

"Try plunging them in water," Lucas said. "Let's see if the stuff holds up."

Mimsy had no intention of plunging her hands into water any more often than necessary. The mention of water gave her an idea, though.

The night was warm for October and Lucas needed to keep his muscles moving or he would stiffen up. "You could use some water therapy yourself."

"Water therapy?"

"There's a swimming pool at the country club," Mimsy said. "It's not really a country club, since everybody in town belongs. Anyway, it used to close at six o'clock, but Buffy Murchison talked the board into leaving it open until eight, so we've got time."

She was not, she told herself, interested in seeing Lucas in his swim trunks. She was also not keen on having him see her pink flowered one-piece. But he did need to flex those muscles.

When he said, "You talked me into it," she wasn't sure whether to be politely approving or guiltily pleased.

LUCAS WAS A BIT disappointed, although he wasn't sure what he'd expected. Whatever its fine qualities, the cream couldn't be expected to remake Mimsy's epidermis in thirty seconds.

Still, he'd hoped for a more enthusiastic reception. Not that he minded an invitation to go swimming, but the powder and all its properties meant more than Mimsy could imagine.

The stuff was ground-up shell from a species of coconut that grew only on the South Pacific island of Plumpkin, which was near Fiji. Lucas had learned from reading an obscure anthropological journal while searching for business ideas that the shell cured a fungal skin disease and rejuvenated the skin in the process.

The women of Plumpkin were reputed to be unusually youthful looking. Also fungus-free.

In addition, the powder, when taken orally, was said to short-circuit epileptic seizures. With the current popularity of alternative medicines, the commercial possibilities were tremendous.

Lucas and Ray had signed an exclusive contract with the local growers. While Lucas struggled to rescue the deal in Atlanta, Ray was supposed to fly to Plumpkin to set up a manufacturing plant.

Instead he'd taken their investment capital and headed for Mexico. His last e-mail to Lucas had consisted of three words: "So long, sucker!"

Because of Ray's betrayal, Lucas now found himself in a place called Nowhere Junction, trying to drum up money. Although not at this particular moment.

He was too busy donning his swim trunks, a T-shirt and a pair of running shoes. And quivering with unabated passion for the shy, sensuous doctor.

Mimsy kept revealing unexpected depths of intelligence and warmth. Lucas got the idea that he'd barely begun to scrape the surface.

One thing he knew for sure. She was too smart for him to get away with his lies for long.

When he came out of the bedroom, Mimsy had finished changing and was standing across the small living room, flipping through some mail on a side table. Although blue jeans covered the bottom half of her swimsuit, the top molded itself to her body.

Stretchy fabric clung to the gentle contours of her breasts and highlighted the flush of her skin. In the pink suit, she radiated vulnerability and an innocence that made him long to protect her.

But the only one she needed protection from was Lucas himself.

"Ready?" he asked.

She glanced up and her eyes went wide at the sight of him. Darn. He was getting hard just being near her, and in these tight-fitting trunks, that fact would soon be obvious.

"Let's go," he said more brusquely than he'd intended.

MIMSY QUAILED. She'd offended Lucas, she could tell, by staring at him.

It was hard to resist. The T-shirt strained across his broad chest, and his legs, despite their patchwork of bruises, were straight and powerful.

While changing into her swimsuit, she'd noticed a new sensitivity in her body. She'd never felt such hunger for a man before, not even for Vince during their early dating days.

With a lump in her throat, Mimsy led the way downstairs. She took the steps too fast, considering that Lucas was a convalescent, but she was glad to exit ahead of him and have a chance to compose herself.

Was it so terrible wanting to hold him? But it would be wrong, she scolded herself.

He was her patient. He didn't even know who he was or where he came from.

She had no right to take advantage of him. Worse, judging by his curt reaction, he had no desire to take advantage of her.

Although the coffee shop was brightly lit, she didn't see Lilibeth inside, thank goodness. The last thing Mimsy needed at the moment was to have Lucas spot the most beautiful woman in town.

Behind her, she heard him stride out the door. Without looking back, Mimsy led the way to her station wagon.

There were three boys sitting on it, their backs turned to her. Even so, she recognized them. They were the town's notorious ten-year-olds, known among their detractors as the Mean Brigade.

Hank Finkins, Flo Nightingale's son, had peroxided his hair an unnatural yellow-white. Joe Grimes, thin-shouldered and dirty of neck, sat next to him on the hood, while atop the roof perched Boris Norris, the chunky son of gardener and golf semipro Rueford Norris.

Boris swung his heels so they thudded against a side window. "Yeah, I'm sure I've got enough manure," he said. "I took it from my dad's shed."

"I don't know about the vinegar," Hank said. "It smells bad to me, but some people don't mind it."

"They'll mind it when it gets sprayed up their noses," smirked Joe.

"You boys planning something?" Mimsy demanded. "I think Uncle Dick's getting a little tired of your pranks."

Three heads swiveled, and three bodies plummeted to the ground at the same time. "I didn't see you coming, Dr. Mimsy," said Joe.

"Yeah, well, who cares anyway?" sneered Hank, who had developed a bad attitude since his father left town.

Lucas reached her side. Tautly he regarded the three boys. "These kids giving you a hard time?" he asked.

"No worse than usual." Although the boys deserved to be brought into line, they didn't need to hear disparaging comments. Mimsy made a distinction between discipline and disrespect, even toward snotty ten-year-olds.

"Doesn't this town have any organized activities for kids their age?" Lucas said. "They probably have too much time on their hands."

"No, we don't," Boris said, cheeky even to this intimidating stranger. "And we don't want any."

Mimsy checked her watch. "It's nearly seven. Shouldn't you be doing your homework?"

"You're not my mother." Boris, in point of fact, didn't have a mother. No one knew the story of Rueford's past and he'd never volunteered any information. He'd showed up in town eight years ago and stuck around, finally landing a caretaker job at the country club.

"I gotta go." Joe jammed his hands into his pockets and hurried away.

"If my dad were here, he wouldn't let anyone boss me around. Including you!" huffed Hank, before following his partner in crime. Left without his supporters, Boris, too, vanished into the twilight.

"I shudder to think what they're going to pull." Mimsy sighed.

"I don't imagine Billy Dell's son or Flo's kid would do anything really destructive." Lucas went around to the passenger door.

Mimsy got in and started the car. "I don't think they would, either, but Boris is another story. He's been mad at the world since he was a kid. I've never been able to find any evidence of abuse, though. The problem is emotional neglect."

"Kids like that deserve a break." Lucas was staring out the side window, and she couldn't see his face.

Mimsy wondered if he was thinking of something from his own childhood. But surely he'd tell her if his memory had returned. "Boris Norris—the kid on the roof—is a hard one to like. But people change as they grow. Maybe he'll snap out of it."

"It doesn't help that he's got a name like Boris Norris," Lucas said. "He probably gets teased about it."

"Lots of people have weird names around here," Mimsy said. "Including me."

With a sideways grin that made her heart flip-flop, Lucas said, "Yeah, what kind of name is Mimsy, anyway?"

"It's short for Mimosa." She steered past the beauty shop and, beyond it, a scattering of modest houses made of stucco and cement. "Who wants to be named after a shrub with prickly leaves, even if it does have pretty blossoms?"

"A mimosa is also a cocktail," Lucas said. "Place one ice cube in a large wineglass, add orange juice and chilled champagne."

"Your memory does burp up the strangest snippets," Mimsy said.

"I'm almost afraid to find out what else it holds," he said.

"I'm sure it will be a relief, though," she said.

"No doubt." He didn't sound convinced.

The highway ran through cactus-strewn rangelands for a few miles before she turned right beneath an arched sign that read Country Club.

There'd been a lot of discussion about naming the place. The suggestion of Green Acres had aroused derisive laughter. Amber Meadows might be more accurate, but its pretentiousness rubbed the plain folks of Nowhere Junction the wrong way.

They'd balked at The Nowhere Country Club, which might invoke bad jokes by sportscasters if the town ever produced a championship golfer. This wasn't likely, however, given that its nine-hole golf course was one big sand trap. Also, Rueford Norris was rumored to have learned his coaching techniques from multiple viewings of the movie *Tin Cup.*

The country club consisted of a square stone-faced clubhouse with a shaded porch along one side. The building was big enough to hold square dances and the occasional wedding reception.

From behind it, Mimsy saw the glimmer of the pool lights. The other thing that caught her eye was the sole vehicle in the parking lot, a battered pickup with the town insignia painted on the door.

A sticker on the bumper showed a plus sign with a capital *R* hanging off the crossbar. It was the "More R" brand of the Moriarty Ranch.

"It looks like we won't be swimming alone," she said. "That truck belongs to the sheriff."

"He's a real fun guy, isn't he?" Lucas joked. "I can

picture him living it up with an inflatable seahorse and a shaker of cocktails.''

''I've never seen him go swimming.'' Perhaps he'd brought a date, but Mimsy couldn't imagine who. Sheriff Bob wasn't noted for his social skills. ''Gee, maybe Bobette's here.''

She was tempted to turn the station wagon around and make some excuse for leaving. Not that she disliked Bobette. But Sheriff Bob's twin was best friends with the last woman Mimsy wanted to see anywhere near Lucas.

''She's the one who's marrying the mattress salesman, right?'' Lucas said. ''And she grows medicinal herbs.''

''You know a lot about Bobette.'' Reluctantly Mimsy killed the engine.

''In this town, it's impossible not to know everyone's life story,'' he said, and got out.

She hoped Bobette had come swimming with her brother, or alone, although surely everyone knew that was a poor idea. They ought to, thanks to the water safety lectures Mimsy gave at the school and at City Council meetings each spring.

Reluctantly she grabbed their towels from the back seat and joined Lucas. Around them, the land lay flat and silent except for the croaking of insects and the far-off howl of a coyote.

In the emptiness, the man loomed large, a powerful protector against the forces of darkness. Although Mimsy considered herself a country girl, in reality she lived in a world of brainpower and technology. Except at moments like this.

She was grateful for Lucas's companionship, but how much did she really know about him? Crossing the pavement beside him, she was keenly aware of his feral watchfulness. Was that impressive muscle tone the result of workouts at the gym, or was it a clue to his background?

He wasn't likely to be a criminal, since Bob had drawn a blank on his fingerprints. He might be a con artist who had never been caught, though. Or a thief of hearts.

Mimsy supposed she ought to flee in the opposite direction. Instead she wished he would take her in his arms and make her forget she was so darn civilized.

Soon they'd be gliding through the water side by side. Wearing practically nothing. She could picture him reaching for her...

As they came around the corner of the clubhouse, she spotted Lilibeth Anderson.

Starlight, moonlight and electric light all loved the town's beauty queen. They bounced off her blond hair as she arched from the diving board.

No one else in town, except possibly newcomer Buffy, would dare to wear such a minuscule bikini. No one else could display such slender legs, a perfect nipped-in waist and eye-popping large breasts.

Laughter bubbled from Lilibeth's pouty red lips as she surfaced in the water. Her face was exquisite. If she kept on swimming at night and avoided the sunlight, it would stay that way for years to come.

"Who's that?" Lucas asked.

"Lilibeth Anderson." Mimsy's breath caught in her throat. She waited, hoping for some offhand remark that would indicate that the blonde's lusciousness had somehow escaped his notice.

"Now there's someone I'd like to meet," he said.

She should have known this would happen, but all

the common sense in the world hadn't prepared Mimsy
for the sensation of plummeting out of control.

She was in love with Lucas. Halfway, at least. And
she'd just lost him.

6

LUCAS COULDN'T BELIEVE his luck. He'd run into the very person he'd come to Nowhere Junction to meet, under relaxed circumstances that should provide a maximum opportunity to get to know her.

It was a good thing he hadn't had matrimony in mind, though. The woman was too showy for his taste.

Not that he meant Lilibeth any disrespect. No doubt she was a fine person with many excellent qualities. He just hoped they included a large bank account and a keen interest in enlarging it.

Mimsy didn't seem thrilled about running into the other woman. Perhaps she didn't realize how tempting it was for a man to be alone at night with a sexy lady like her. They were both safer with company.

"You sure do have some ten-dollar bruises!" hooted a large-boned woman who must be Bobette. She stopped swimming the backstroke when they came through the gate. "I guess you'd be the mysterious Mr. Lucas."

"At your service."

Lilibeth raised herself decorously from the pool and posed on the edge. The woman's graceful way of moving was no less than Lucas had expected of the town's princess.

"Hi." Even in the dim light, he could see the shimmering blue of her eyes peeking at him through thick lashes. "I'm Lilibeth."

Mentally he cataloged the fact that she had a naturally flirtatious manner. "I'm Lucas. Pleased to meet you."

The women exchanged greetings with Mimsy. She seemed preoccupied as she peeled off her jeans and, although Lucas would have liked to linger and enjoy the sight of her slender figure in a swimsuit, he had business to take care of.

First impressions counted. So, despite a suspicion that the water might not be as warm as he hoped, he strode to the diving board and performed his most spectacular dive. A bounce, a pike in midair, and clean into the water. Not Olympic quality, but not bad, either.

Water broke over his head and shoulders with a cold slap. He hadn't stopped to consider what the impact might do to his sore shoulder. An immediate throb told him that oversight had been a mistake.

Lucas's arm ached. His neck and back hurt, too. He refused to give any sign of it, though. People didn't like to invest with wimps.

"Honey, you're a wonder!" announced Bobette when he surfaced. "You better watch out some cowgirl like me doesn't lasso you on the way down."

"Thanks for the compliment." Lucas swam to Lilibeth, fighting the urge to wince with every motion. "Are you a cowgirl, too?"

"No, I live in town." She tossed back her long hair in classic movie-star fashion. "Bobette's the one who rides the range."

"I'm impressed." He gave her friend a warm smile before turning back to Lilibeth.

What was he going to say next? He could hardly

broach the subject of investing to a woman he'd just met. Going on a date would give him a chance to know her better, but it would violate Lucas's ethics to pretend a romantic interest he didn't feel.

Of course, he was lying to Mimsy about his amnesia. Still, he hadn't known they were going to strike sparks between them when he began this ruse. His motives had been relatively pure.

And they still were.

"Lilibeth's being modest. She's a local celebrity," Mimsy said in a low voice.

She sounded troubled by his interest in this woman. The fact that she was still willing to be generous with praise touched Lucas.

"I am not!" The blonde giggled. "But it's nice of you to say so."

"If getting chosen prom queen four years in a row isn't something to brag about, I don't know what is," replied Bobette. "Of course, Mimsy's no slouch, either. Town doctor! Sometimes I hardly know what I'm doing in such elevated company."

"What you're doing is being the salt of the earth," Mimsy said.

"Well, good. I like lots of salt on my food." The rancher grinned, and Lucas decided he liked her. How ironic that her twin brother was so dour!

"Uh-oh." Lilibeth blinked rapidly. "I've got something in my eye."

Was this a signal for him to approach really, really close and offer to help? Lucas wondered. If so, it seemed a bit brazen.

His suspicion was allayed, however, when she got to her feet. "Mimsy? Would you mind coming to the ladies' room and taking a look at it? The light's a lot better in there.''

"I'll come, too." Bobette winked at Lucas. "The way my brother's been sniffing around you like a hound dog after a rabbit, the last thing I need is for him to find us swimming together."

"Does he come by the country club?"

"He has a gift for patrolling anywhere he thinks he might find me." The woman marched up the steps of the shallow end, shaking out her frizzy reddish-brown hair. "He swears if he catches Barney, my fiancé, anywhere in town he'll trump up some charge and lock him away till the cows come home."

Lucas wasn't thrilled that he was about to be deserted, but he suspected the mote in Lilibeth's eye was a ruse. Most likely, she wanted a private discussion with Mimsy, with him as the subject.

He was flattered and pleased. Piquing Lilibeth's interest marked an important first step in his plan.

"HE'S SO CUTE!" Lilibeth checked her strap in the ladies' room mirror. There was, as it turned out, nothing wrong with her eye. "It's too bad he's penniless. And footloose, most likely, since he rode in on a motorcycle."

Mimsy agreed with every word, from the part about Lucas being cute to the likelihood that he wouldn't stay long in Nowhere Junction. At the same time, she fought to conceal how hurt she felt.

Only a fool could fail to notice Lucas's fascination with Lilibeth. Mimsy had faded into invisibility.

She wanted to fight her way back to the center of his attention. But how could she compete with this dream girl?

"What happened to that man you were expecting, the one from your Internet ad?" Mimsy asked. A new and terrible fear arose within her. "You don't suppose—he couldn't be—"

"You mean, could Lucas be him? Don't be silly," Lilibeth scoffed. "Mr. McRifle will be driving a Cadillac. He's a businessman, not Easy Rider."

"When's he due?" If the man arrived soon, he might keep Lilibeth occupied.

"I don't know." Studying her reflection, the blond woman frowned at a tiny, almost invisible blemish. "I hope he didn't fall for someone else along the way. It would be just my luck."

"If you ask me, it's a good thing he didn't show," Bobette said. "The Internet is not the best place to meet men. Of course, neither is Groundhog Station, but beggars can't be choosers."

"I suppose it wasn't so smart to mention in the ad that I'm an heiress," Lilibeth said. "It's not as if I'm rich."

"Why bother to mention your inheritance, even if you were?" Mimsy asked. "You're so beautiful, you don't need money to attract a man."

To her surprise, the younger woman threw her arms around her. "That's the nicest thing anybody's said all day! Well, except for you calling me a celebrity. That was nice, too."

Bobette sighed. "You have a gift for saying the right thing, Mimsy. I always manage to stick my foot in my mouth."

"I like your frankness, Bobette." Lilibeth gave her friend a hug, as well.

Guilt twitched through Mimsy, that she'd been jealous of this kindhearted young woman. It wasn't Lilibeth's fault that men found her irresistible.

"As for Lucas," she said, "if you're interested in him, well, he's free. As far as I know."

Instantly she regretted offering the other woman carte blanche. But it was too late to take it back.

"You don't have any designs on him?" the blonde asked. "I mean, I heard you're letting him stay in your spare room."

"That's because there's no hotel in town. Besides, he might need medical attention." Mimsy hoped there wasn't going to be a lot of gossip. She valued her reputation.

"I'm not saying I have designs on him, either," Lilibeth assured her. "I just wanted to know the lay of the land."

Bobette stared at her in dismay. "How can you talk to Mimsy that way!"

"What way?"

"Calling her the lay of the land!"

Lilibeth blushed. "That's not what I meant."

"It's a phrase," Mimsy assured Bobette. "It means 'which way the wind blows.'"

"Oh." The rancher chuckled. "Well, that's a new one on me!"

They returned to the pool, where Lucas was swimming with long strokes. The others probably couldn't tell, but it was obvious to Mimsy that his stunt dive had hurt.

It served him right for showing off.

Lilibeth popped into the pool beside him, and soon the two were engaged in conversation. They made a beautiful couple, Mimsy thought. Heartbreakingly beautiful.

She busied herself swimming laps. As a doctor, she was always promoting the value of exercise to her patients, and she tried to get as much as possible herself.

Especially when she was agitated. Like now.

Each time Mimsy passed Lucas and Lilibeth, she caught a snippet of conversation. At one point, they were chatting about surfing the Web. On successive laps, she caught words and phrases.

"Make the most of opportunities," said Lucas.

"Keep a close eye on the bottom line," Lilibeth replied.

"Get the best possible returns."

Mimsy could hardly contain her curiosity. Or her dismay. What on earth were they discussing?

The two leaned toward each other, tuning out their surroundings. Did this mean they were falling in love?

A while later, she found herself beside Bobette in the deep water. At the shallow end of the pool, Lilibeth was draped over the steps while Lucas dawdled beside her.

"You should have told her the truth," Bobette said. "You know she enjoys flirting."

"What do you mean, the truth?" Mimsy asked.

"You can't take your eyes off the feller."

"He's not my type." It was a safe assertion, since no one in town had any idea what her type was.

"He is now," Bobette said. "I don't even stare at Barney the way you're staring at Lucas. Of course, Barney isn't as good-looking as he is, either."

"It's professional interest," Mimsy lied. "I'm afraid he's overexerted himself tonight."

"The only way he's overexerted himself is in being too friendly to Lilibeth." Bobette regarded the couple through narrowed eyes. "Although there's something missing from his body language. If a person lives around animals long enough and sees their courting rituals, they can tell when a man's holding back.''

"He's hardly going to jump on a woman five minutes after meeting her!'' Inside, though, Mimsy felt a spark of hope. Maybe Lucas wasn't finding Lilibeth as exciting as she'd feared.

"It's more than that,'' Bobette said.

Whatever she might have added was cut short by the rattle of the gate. Behind it stood the stocky frame of Rueford Norris.

"Eight o'clock!'' announced the groundskeeper. "Time for you folks to get home.''

"Keep your pants on, Rueford,'' said Bobette. "We're going.''

As the four of them departed, Mimsy waited for Lucas to say goodbye to Lilibeth and Bobette.

In the car, she and Lucas drove for a while in silence. Unable to bear it any longer, she said, "Lilibeth's nice, isn't she?''

"She seems interested in investing,'' he replied.

The observation startled Mimsy. "She does?''

"She's looking to expand her horizons,'' Lucas said. "She said her parents have always been very conservative and she feels they've held her back.''

"You're sure she meant financially?'' Through the windshield, she noticed a big fat moon hanging overhead. She wondered if it was a hunter's moon or a harvest moon. She'd never been able to keep those terms straight.

"We were discussing her portfolio,'' he said.

Lilibeth must have thought he was referring to the folder where she kept bills and receivables. She'd often complained that, despite the purchase of a computer, her parents were slow to embrace more efficient methods of running the café and pharmacy, so she'd set up a portfolio of her own.

Mimsy saw no point in debating the matter with Lucas. Besides, he still hadn't told her what she wanted to know, so she fished a little further. "You seemed to enjoy her company."

"Whose?" he asked distractedly.

"Lilibeth's!"

For the first time in over an hour, Lucas's attention focused on Mimsy. "She seems pleasant. She isn't half the conversationalist you are, though."

That was a compliment, of sorts. "Thanks, I guess."

He took in a breath as if about to say more. Then a shuttered look came over his face, a subtle tightening, and Mimsy could feel him withdraw.

Not for the first time, she wondered if Lucas was hiding something.

"How are your hands?" he asked.

"Excuse me?"

"How's your skin?"

Surprised, she flexed her fingers against the steering wheel. Usually her skin softened in the water, then became rough and irritated when it dried.

Not tonight. "My hands feel wonderful," Mimsy admitted. "Even my nails are softer. That cream of yours is terrific."

"Let's see how long the effect lasts," he suggested. "Tell me how they're doing tomorrow morning."

"Okay."

He'd done a masterful job of changing the subject, Mimsy thought. Well, thank goodness he wasn't raving about Lilibeth the way men often did.

Maybe she hadn't lost him, after all.

THAT NIGHT, LUCAS CAME TO understand what medieval prisoners had undergone when they were put on a rack and tortured. Lying in bed was agony. So was sitting or standing.

At last he yielded and took the pain pills Mimsy had left for him. So much for swimming as a way to loosen his muscles.

It was his own fault, of course. He'd hoped to impress Lilibeth with the swimming and diving skills he'd mastered after moving to Southern California.

She hadn't acted overwhelmed, but at least she'd talked to him about finances, in general terms. He still didn't know how much money she had, but they'd broken the ice.

As his muscles began to unknot, Lucas stretched out and thought about Mimsy. He hadn't meant to make her jealous. It troubled him to cause her any discomfort.

It was better that she didn't get attached to him, though. He couldn't afford to hang around more than another week, if that long.

He ought to go to Murchison's Garage again to see if his motorcycle was fixed. He also wanted to figure out a way to check his e-mail in case Ray Ryker had turned up.

First, though, Lucas needed to get his strength back. In the meantime, why not enjoy the company of the most charming and unaffected woman he'd ever met?

It was a comforting thought, and one that finally, blissfully put him to sleep.

AT NINE O'CLOCK SATURDAY morning, Mimsy arrived at the school site. The implosion wasn't scheduled until eleven, but she wanted to make sure Sheriff Bob, Flo

Nightingale and Billy Dell were on hand to help in case anyone was injured.

Billy had three stretchers ready, which was the total the town possessed. As she'd arranged yesterday, Bob and Flo had set up a first-aid station. Things were on track.

Mimsy had left Lucas sleeping, no doubt under the influence of medication. She hadn't wanted to disturb him.

In retrospect, she agreed with Bobette that something had been missing from last night's interaction between Lucas and Lilibeth. He hadn't leaned toward her with a teasing light in his eyes. He hadn't touched her arm as he talked. He hadn't raved about her afterward, either.

Still, it wouldn't surprise Mimsy if there were subtleties of romantic interaction that she failed to grasp. Lilibeth must know more about those things than she did.

She glanced at her hands. The absence of itchy flakes was remarkable, and her nails had lost some of their brittleness. But she would trade her smooth skin in a flash for one iota of the other woman's sex appeal.

The sound of men calling from within the old school building drew her attention. For one startled moment, she feared something had gone wrong, until she recognized Uncle Dick's calm voice telling Carter where to string a wire.

At last month's City Council meeting, he'd described what he was going to do. Fiddling with his sea captain's hat, the excited principal had said he was going to blow the two-story building off its base, like yanking the legs from beneath a chair.

Some children in the audience had giggled in recognition of a similar prank played on Uncle Dick the previous spring. Except for a frown, he'd been so eager to describe his work that he'd let the interruption pass.

Nearby buildings, he'd said, would be protected by having their windows covered with cardboard. He'd been as good as his word, Mimsy noted. All the glass was covered at the hospital and at City Hall. Murchison's Garage, directly across from the blast site, had its metal door lowered.

Next, the principal had said, he would drill holes in the building's supports. Early on the morning of the event, he would fill them with tubes of magnesium connected by electrical wires, creating a timed pattern of blasts that should cause the walls to fall inward. The explosives would remain stable until exposed to a spark.

The entire process would be taped by three remote-operated video cameras set around the site. Mimsy could see one of them high atop the hospital, and a second one in front of Murchison's Garage. The other must be out of sight around the back.

Taping the blast was something Uncle Dick had learned to do during his summer internship with the demolition company, so that he could analyze the scene if anything went wrong. It would also give the town a record of a key moment in its history.

For safety's sake, Mimsy wished the council had turned him down. This whole thing wasn't necessary. Dick himself had admitted that an implosion like this was usually reserved for high-rises where the use of a bulldozer would be impractical.

But he'd been so persuasive, and so determined, that the council members had caved in. They were well aware of his unhappiness with his job and didn't want to lose him.

She went up to her office to see if there were any patients or messages. A rancher's wife had called with a question about her pregnancy, and Mimsy spent half an hour on the phone reassuring her that queasiness and increased appetite were normal.

Flo popped in. "I don't suppose you've seen my son, have you?"

Mimsy remembered the conversation she'd overheard the day before. "No, but I heard him talking with Joe and Boris. It sounded like they were up to something."

"I hope they're not planning to pull any tricks today!" said the nurse. "That would really rile Uncle Dick."

"Maybe you should advise Sheriff Bob."

Flo sighed. "It would serve those boys right if they got locked up overnight. Teach them a lesson. I can't seem to get through to Hank ever since his dad left."

Mimsy nodded sympathetically and wished she knew how to help. As a physician, she ought to have some sage counsel to give. As an unmarried woman with no children, she didn't have a clue what to suggest.

Going outside, she found the townspeople gathering behind ropes that Sheriff Bob had strung through City Hall Park. A carnival atmosphere prevailed, with people waving Nowhere And Proud Of It! banners, peering through binoculars and setting up a potluck lunch buffet.

Finella, as usual, was first to arrive with food. Mimsy saw that she'd brought her specialty, Spring Salad, whose main ingredients were lemon gelatin and corned beef.

"I plan to make sure the new school has a proper cafeteria," she told Mimsy. "Nutrition is so important."

"It don't do much good if the kids barf it up." Mazeppa plopped a plate of peanut-butter-filled celery onto the table. "Besides, your term on the board's nearly over and since you don't have kids in school anymore, you ought to find some other area to stick your nose into."

"I've got a four-year-old grandchild," said Finella who, accustomed to Mazeppa's barbs, didn't take offense. "I love being around schools. I should have been a teacher."

Zeppa snorted. "Not me! I'd hate being shut up all day in a classroom, or anywhere else, either." She chomped on a piece of celery. "Darn it! I got strings caught in my dentures."

"Some people enjoy their jobs," said Finella's husband, George. "Take me. I like working at the bank."

"That's because you have a private office." Mazeppa yanked a celery string from her teeth. "Think about the poor people out front, having to hold their flatulence all day."

"People do what's polite," said Finella.

"It's unnatural," Zeppa said. "Now that companies are having Casual Dress Fridays, they oughta have Let 'er Rip Thursdays, too."

"Speaking of letting 'er rip, I think we're ready to go." George indicated the school, from which Uncle Dick emerged carrying a small electrical box attached to long wires.

He was flanked by his assistants for the day, handsome Mayor Quade Gardiner and the ever-affable Carter Murchison. Both were frowning. Mimsy wondered if they shared her doubts about the procedure.

"Everybody keep back." Sheriff Bob shooed a few children toward their parents.

Townspeople edged and squirmed, trying to get a better view. The smaller circus tents had been taken down but the larger one obstructed some sightlines.

The citizens of Nowhere weren't accustomed to being in crowds, Mimsy mused. Personally she'd have been happy to watch from her office. As the town's only medic, however, she had an obligation to stay close to the action.

"You folks keep a tight grip on your young-uns," Bob announced.

Flo appeared beside Mimsy. "I can't find my son."

"Bob!" Mimsy called. "Somebody needs to check the school building for..." Her words got lost in the crowd noise.

"Ten!" cried Uncle Dick, holding up his electrical box.

The nurse clapped her hands to her cheeks. "Did you see something move? Behind the circus tent?"

"Nine!"

Mimsy ducked under the rope. "I'll tell Bob."

"Please hurry!"

"Eight!" shouted the principal.

She hurried toward the sheriff. He had his back turned to her as he watched the school, and eager sightseers closed in behind him, blocking her.

"Seven!"

Mimsy spotted a pair of sneakers and the cuffs of jeans sticking out from behind the tent. Someone was hiding there.

It had to be one of the boys. Not Joe, who had been collared and dragged behind the ropes by his big brother Dell. Not Boris, who was standing on the sidelines with his father.

"Six!"

Although the tent wasn't likely to get hit with debris, it was far closer to the school than Bob had deemed safe for people to stand. If anything went wrong, Hank could be seriously injured.

7

IT WAS A SCENE FROM a nightmare. No matter how loudly Mimsy shouted, nobody heard her. Bob didn't even turn around.

"Five!" yelled the watchers. Uncle Dick merely nodded on cue. He'd explained earlier that he wasn't going to pronounce the number "five" because it sounded too much like *fire*.

"Stop! Stop!" she screamed. Still no reaction amid the general whooping.

Hank Finkins peered from behind the tent, his bleached blond hair unmistakable. He was holding a plastic milk carton with a string attached. It looked like a fuse.

"Four!"

A stink bomb. That's what the boys had been talking about. They were planning to throw a stink bomb at the same time as the school blew up.

It had probably sounded funny. Now it wasn't funny at all.

"Three!"

From a far point, a male figure raced toward Hank. The man ran stiffly but doggedly, cutting across the grass on long, powerful legs.

Lucas. He must have awakened and come to investigate the crowd scene. Now he was in danger, too, and outside the range of everyone's attention as they focused on Uncle Dick.

"Two!"

Hank didn't see the man approaching him from behind. He was grinning and slipping around the tent, keeping his eye on Sheriff Bob.

"One!"

Lucas grabbed the ten-year-old around the waist and took off running. A moment later, Flo brushed past Mimsy ready to run after Hank herself. "He's over there!"

"Wait!" she said. "Lucas has him!"

The nurse halted as the rescuer ran toward them, dragging Hank. Still holding his stink bomb, the boy fumbled with something from his pocket as the pair approached the sheriff.

Noticing them at last, Bob grabbed the boy's arm and helped haul him toward the ropes. In Hank's hands appeared a tiny flame.

"Zero!"

Uncle Dick pressed his plunger. Hank made his best attempt at pitching the carton toward the onlookers but, jostled by the two men, he fumbled and dropped it.

A series of booms sounded from the school, a symphony of explosions. A shock wave fanned the crowd.

The brick walls of the school wavered, rose a few inches into the air and seemed to hang suspended. Then, with a series of crashes, they fell inward one by one like a collapsing house of cards.

Black dust roiled from the base and flashed toward the crowd. Most of it landed near the school, but enough sprayed the crowd to set off spasms of coughing.

Near Hank, however, the air was already full of

clumps and particles of partially composted manure laced with vinegar. It smeared the boy, Bob and Lucas from head to toe and shot over Mimsy, Flo and Uncle Dick, as well.

"What in tarnation?" The principal proceeded to unloose a string of profanity such as had not been heard in Nowhere Junction within living memory.

"Stink bomb!" hooted a voice that Mimsy recognized as belonging to Boris Norris. "Yippee!"

Flo wiped her mouth to remove the stuff that had landed on her face. The first words out were, "I'll tan your hide, Hank Finkins! And after I'm done, I'll get Sheriff Bob to tan it, too!"

The boy's smirk died. He looked so frightened that Mimsy almost felt sorry for him.

The sound of running water announced the approach of Quade Gardiner with a hose. He squirted them off one by one, taking the ladies first and leaving Hank for last. When she'd been thoroughly rinsed, Mimsy asked Billy Dell to check the crowd for injuries.

"By the way, your son Joe was part of this conspiracy," she told him.

"He'll be cleaning out the chicken coop for a month," Billy Dell said. "No video games, either."

He came back a few minutes later to report an absence of injuries, just a lot of coughing. Once she'd been reassured on that score, a dripping wet Mimsy took in the fact that the school had collapsed into a compact pile of cement and brick as planned.

It was the sort of demolition one would expect when Uncle Dick was around. Including the stink bomb.

THE POTLUCK LUNCHEON was held, although not exactly as planned. Because the blasts might have contaminated the food, Mimsy as de facto public health official allowed only tightly covered dishes and those brought by latecomers to be served.

Still, there was plenty to go around. Finella, however, looked heartbroken at the loss of her Spring Salad, and her mood wasn't helped by Mazeppa's chortling about God moving in mysterious ways.

Nothing dampened the spirits of Uncle Dick, not even his doused condition. "A complete success!" he announced to anyone who would listen. "I couldn't have hoped for better!"

Horace Popsworthy clapped him on the back. "This town has the finest principal in Texas. That loser they've got over in Groundhog Station couldn't blow up a rat's nest."

Murdock Murchison, who usually couldn't stand Horace, for once agreed with him. "Dick, at the next town meeting, I'm going to move that we award you a medal of honor." Murdock had been named to the City Council the previous month when Fordyce Huggins put his ranch up for sale and left town to join the Mormon Tabernacle Choir.

"That was quite a show," Lucas told Mimsy as they stood to one side, taking in the scene. His dark hair clung to his head and the clothing plastered against his body revealed muscular bulges.

"You were the best part." She hoped she didn't look too much like a drowned poodle. "I can't tell you how glad I was to see you."

"The boy wouldn't have been hurt, as it turned out," Lucas said. "The rubble imploded properly."

"You couldn't have known that. You risked your life," Mimsy said.

A roar from the crowd turned her attention to the star of the day. "Speech! Speech!"

Grinning, Uncle Dick stood on a chair and waved everyone to silence. Although he was normally soft-spoken, his ability to summon a deep orator's voice was one of the reasons for his having been elevated from shop teacher to principal in the first place.

"Thank you, fellow Nowhereans," he boomed. "I'm as pleased as you are that everything went well. Maybe even more pleased."

Cries of "hear! hear!" arose.

"I'm delighted that we've captured the whole event on videotape," the principal continued. "I trust you won't mind if I make copies for myself."

"Not at all," replied Popsworthy, as if he, rather than Quade, were chairman of the school board.

"This demolition project was my farewell gift to Nowhere Junction," said Uncle Dick. "It was also a final exam for my demolition training. As of today, I'm resigning my job as principal and going to work for the Fast Blast Corporation of Dallas. Thank you, and goodbye."

With a wave to the stunned populace, he hopped down from the chair, adjusted his captain's hat and strode away whistling.

For a long time, nobody moved. Mimsy had never seen her fellow townspeople struck mute this way, and she began to worry that they'd been seized by some form of mass hysteria.

All of a sudden, as if a gong had rung, everyone started talking.

"Can you believe that?"

"Where are we going to find another principal?"

"What about the Great Groundhog Crate Race?"

Quade stepped onto the chair, and people quieted. "Seeing all the school-board members present, I suggest we address this crisis immediately."

There were noises of approval. The other board members—Popsworthy, Carter Murchison, Billy Dell and Finella—came forward. Each expressed shock at the announcement, and Popsworthy pressed for them to increase Uncle Dick's salary and beg him to come back.

"Won't work," Carter said. "Anybody can see he's made up his mind."

"Pow! Wham! Ka-blooey!" said Billy admiringly. "Who'd give that up for stink bombs?"

"Well, who're we going to hire?" asked Finella. "None of the teachers wants to be principal, they've all made that clear in the past. Maybe we should choose someone from the school board."

"We've all got jobs," Popsworthy said.

"I don't," said Finella.

"You don't have a teaching credential, either!" said Mazeppa. "Do you?"

"I wouldn't be teaching, I'd be administrating." Nervously Finella pushed back a wing of dark hair and refastened it with one of her twin barrettes.

"We'd be happy to accept your application," Quade said diplomatically. "Any other suggestions?"

A timid hand arose in the crowd. The chairman frowned as if unable to believe his own eyes but, indeed, it was Lilibeth Anderson. "Yes?"

"I think we should advertise on the Internet," she said.

"She's advertised with a matchmaking service," Mimsy explained quietly to Lucas. "For a husband."

"Did she have any luck?"

"Not yet." She still found it hard to believe that Lilibeth had to advertise.

The board members nodded agreement to the proposal, except for Finella, but she had the good sense not to object aloud. "Done," said Quade. "I'll draw up the notice and find an appropriate place to post it."

Pleased with the decision, the crowd dispersed. Mimsy stayed in case any injuries turned up and to make sure the food was disposed of before it could breed bacteria.

"You take your public health duties seriously, don't you?" Lucas said. "Even though they're not official."

"I care about people," Mimsy said. "That's why I became a doctor. It certainly wasn't for riches or glory."

They began walking toward her office. "Did you ever think of moving anywhere else?" Lucas asked.

"Groundhog already has a doctor."

He smiled. "I meant a large city. You're a sharp lady and a very attractive one, too. I don't think you're fully appreciated around here."

His praise warmed Mimsy. Then it occurred to her that, suffering from amnesia, he had no one to compare her to. "Thanks for the compliment, but I know where I belong."

"Too bad." Quickly he added, "I mean, it's too bad you don't get more credit for the contribution you make to this town. You should be on the school board, for one thing. You'd do a much better job than Finella, I'm sure."

"I don't have children," she said wistfully. They'd reached the hospital, where Carter was removing the padding from the windows. "You should go home and take a nap."

"I don't need one," Lucas said, although from the circles under his eyes and the stiffness of his movements, Mimsy knew he was lying.

"Stuff your pride," she said. "I'm your doctor and I'm telling you to go lie down."

"Yes, ma'am!" He saluted playfully before ambling away.

He'd shown a lot of courage in rescuing Hank today, Mimsy thought as she watched him go. He hadn't expected any credit for it, either.

The more she saw of him, the more she knew Lucas wasn't an aimless drifter. A man like him had real value and someone, somewhere surely was looking for him.

She couldn't hold him here forever. No matter how much she wanted to.

LUCAS WASN'T SURE WHY he'd suggested that Mimsy relocate. He'd been on the point of mentioning Los Angeles when it struck him that he had no business planting such ideas in her head.

The last thing he needed was for her to move there for his sake. He was too restless to settle down with one woman.

In the past, Lucas had always made that plain to the ladies he dated. So far, he hadn't broken any hearts that he knew about.

So why was he playing with fire here, flirting with a woman so innocent and trusting?

He really liked Mimsy. He liked the way she cared about others. He liked her modesty, and her quick mind, and the way she transformed from mild-mannered miss to in-charge official when circumstances warranted.

He also liked her bright brown eyes and ready smile. The way she smelled, too, a mix of disinfectant and rose fragrance.

Someday a man was going to engage her at every level, to awaken her potent sexuality and claim first place in that big heart of hers. Lucas shuddered. Some other man would claim her, and she would forget all about him.

It was surprising how much the prospect bothered him.

He needed to wind up his business in Nowhere Junction as quickly as possible, he decided. To tamp out this blaze before one or both of them got burned.

As Lucas limped past the coffee shop, he glanced inside. A fortyish woman was setting out pastries beneath a glass bell.

On impulse, he ducked in, hoping to have another talk with Lilibeth.

"Excuse me?"

The lady at the counter looked up. "Can I help... Oh! You must be Lucas."

"What makes you think so?"

"That limp, plus we don't get many strangers in here," she said. "Billy Dell told me all about you. I'm Willie, his wife. I work at the café on Saturdays, mostly to get away from the kids."

"Pleased to meet you." They shook hands. "I wondered if Lilibeth had dropped by?" He didn't see her, but she might be in a back office.

"Ah!" Willie gave him a knowing look. Why did everyone assume he must be romantically interested in the blonde? "Well, she's not here."

"Too bad."

"I could give her a message, though," Willie said.

"No, thanks." He didn't want Lilibeth to come looking for him when Mimsy might be around.

"She'll be here Monday morning, if you don't see her before then. Good luck." Willie smiled at him. She still showed traces of prettiness, Lucas noted, although years of hard work had roughened her skin.

He'd brought the plastic pouch of leftover coconut lotion in his pocket, hoping to find a chance to try it on someone else. And to do a favor for someone deserving, like Willie.

"Would you do something for me?" he asked. "Would you try some of this cream on your face and let me know what you think of it?"

Curiosity shining in her eyes, Willie took the baggie. "What is it?"

"An ointment Mimsy and I concocted," he said. "It helped her hands a lot. Not meaning any disrespect, but the weather around here sure is drying."

"You've got that right." After opening the pouch, Willie paused in front of a wall mirror and applied a dab of cream to her face. "That does feel powerful good! Thanks, Lucas."

She handed back the baggie with a bit of ointment left at the bottom. "Let me know if you like it," he said.

"Sure will!" She had a fresh glow about her, he thought, but that might simply mean she enjoyed chatting.

By the time he got upstairs, every muscle in Lucas's body was throbbing. Exhausted, he lay down and didn't wake up until Sunday morning.

SINCE SHE WAS ALWAYS UP early, Mimsy baked vanilla-apple bran muffins. They were healthy but, more than that, she wanted Lucas to wake up to the delicious smell.

He'd questioned whether she might want to live somewhere else. What she'd wanted to ask in turn was whether he might consider living in Nowhere Junction.

She had no right to do that. Besides, how could he plan ahead until he got his memory back? In the meantime, she wanted to make this place feel like home to him.

You're too old and too smart to kid yourself. But not too old or too smart to dream, she thought.

At about eight o'clock, Mimsy heard Lucas taking a shower. He came out dressed in the jeans and shirt she'd laundered the previous night at the coin-op past Gigi's Grocery Store.

"You look well rested," she said. "You must have slept sixteen hours."

"I feel a lot better." He stretched. The man looked impossibly big in her little apartment, Mimsy thought longingly.

"Now you need to eat," she said. "How do you like your eggs?"

"Scrambled," he said. "Got any bacon?"

Mimsy hesitated. As a doctor, she knew it wasn't good for people. As a girl whose favorite treat used to be bacon, lettuce and tomato sandwiches, however, she loved the stuff. "Sure."

They were finishing breakfast when a scurrying tap sounded at the door. Mimsy recognized the knock. What was Lilibeth doing here on a Sunday morning?

When she answered, her landlady drooped in the doorway, hair limp and blue eyes glazed. "Are you all right?"

Lilibeth coughed. "I think I'm coming down with a

cold.'' Seeing Lucas in the kitchen, she tried to smile. ''Lucas, Willie said you wanted to see me.''

''No, I...'' When Mimsy looked at him, it seemed as if he'd hoped to avoid this uncomfortable situation. ''As long as you're here, I was wondering if you had any more questions about what we'd been discussing. You know, investment strategies.''

''Oh!'' Lilibeth brightened a little. ''I do want to know more about that.''

''Coffee?'' Mimsy went to fetch some for her guest, glad for a chance to duck out of the room. She didn't want either of them to see how upset she was by the discovery that Lucas had gone looking for Lilibeth yesterday.

Baking vanilla-apple muffins, caring about others and being intelligent obviously weren't enough. Not when compared to the American male's dream of a golden, buxom beauty, Mimsy thought as she poured the already brewed coffee into two mugs.

Mimsy had become invisible again. It was a sadly familiar sensation.

By the time she returned to the living room, the two were deep in conversation. Mimsy set down the coffee, acknowledged their thanks and went into the bedroom.

She'd planned to skip church to take care of Lucas, but there was no reason to stay home now, so she decided to change into something dressier. She was starting to peel off her slacks when the phone rang.

''Mimsy?'' said Buffy Murchison. ''Carter's real sick with some kind of flu. I know it's Sunday, but could you possibly see him this morning?''

''Of course.'' From the living room, Mimsy heard Lilibeth cough. Was there a connection between the two illnesses? ''How are you and little Callie?''

"We're fine."

"Were you at the blast yesterday?"

"No," Buffy said. "I kept Callie home. The whole situation made me nervous. Do you think whatever he's got might be contagious?"

"I don't know. I'll meet him at my office in fifteen minutes." Mimsy put in a call to Flo Nightingale. If there were an outbreak, she needed her nurse.

Flo promised to come to work. She herself felt fine, she said in answer to Mimsy's question.

So much for a connection to the blast, she thought. She, Flo and Lucas had been present but so far none of them were sick.

On the other hand, they'd all been sprayed with manure, and Quade had hosed them off immediately afterward. Either of those occurrences might have stymied an airborne bug.

In the living room, Lilibeth looked even paler than before. Lucas cupped his hand over her forehead.

"She feels hot," he told Mimsy.

She didn't like to see his hand on the other woman. It was such an intimate gesture...but there were other, more pressing concerns.

"Carter Murchison is sick, too," she said. "Lucas, would you help Lilibeth to my office? I'm hoping it's just the two of them and not the whole town."

"There was a lot of coughing after the blast, but I thought that was just from the smoke." He looked worried. "I hope nobody's seriously ill."

"Let's keep our fingers crossed." As she went out the door, Mimsy remembered that, just a few days ago, she'd been half hoping for an epidemic.

Now she fervently hoped there wasn't one.

BY NOON, HER OFFICE WAS filled with patients complaining of weakness, fever and headaches. She heard later that the coughing had been so loud in the Nowhere Nearer to Thee O Lord Church that Ephraim O'Rourke, the ninety-three-year-old pastor, had cut short his sermon for the first time in years.

The sick included Quade Gardiner, Horace Popsworthy, Finella and George Weinbucket, Boris and Rueford Norris, and all of the Grimes family except the mother, who had been working at the café on Saturday.

"There has to be a link to the blast," Mimsy told Flo as she admitted Murdock and Mazeppa, with temperatures of 102 and 104 degrees respectively, to the hospital. "It's breaking down neatly, who got sick and who didn't."

She refrigerated blood samples to be analyzed later. Although she doubted this was a bacterial infection, as a precaution Mimsy administered antibiotics to the most severe cases, which included Horace Popsworthy.

The strength of the illness appeared to be related to how close the observers had stood to the blast and to their ages and physical conditions. The young and strong, like Quade and Lilibeth, weren't quite as sick as their elders.

"I've never heard of a flu like this," Flo said. "To strike so many people on the same morning!"

"Disease mutations can be unpredictable. We need to prepare for whatever may come." Mimsy had already tried to alert state health authorities, but on a Sunday found the best she could do was to leave messages.

Although she entertained fears that this might be the start of a serious epidemic like the hemorrhagic flu outbreak of 1918, she knew she was letting her imagination run away with her. She had no cause yet to call the federal Centers for Disease Control.

She was able to rule out food poisoning, at least. She, Lucas and Flo had tasted every dish that was served, without ill effect. Besides, there were no intestinal complaints.

In midafternoon, Lucas brought Mimsy and Flo peanut butter and jelly sandwiches. "It's not fancy, but it should be filling," he said.

She nodded gratefully. "I'm starved."

"Me, too." Flo wolfed down her sandwich. "Oh, gosh, I forgot all about Hank. He'll eat candy for lunch if I'm not around."

"He's not sick?" Lucas asked.

"Not a trace of it this morning."

"That figures," Mimsy said. Hank had been sprayed with manure and rinsed off, like the three of them.

"Give me your address and I'll look in on him," Lucas offered.

Gratefully, Flo wrote it down and gave him directions. "You're sure you don't mind?"

"I like to be useful," the man said. "Tonight I'll help you in the hospital. With Billy Dell sick, you'll need someone to take over the handyman chores."

Mimsy wanted to refuse. Lucas was, after all, not fully healed himself. But most of the healthy townspeople had ailing family members to care for, and she and Flo couldn't do everything themselves.

"We'd appreciate it," she said.

Only after Lucas left did Mimsy realize one surprising, hopeful, inexplicable fact. He hadn't asked how Lilibeth was doing.

8

FLO NIGHTINGALE, Lucas discovered, lived in a well-kept stucco house half a mile south of the school. It looked shut up tight, and at first no one answered his knock.

Then the door opened and a pair of defiant young eyes met his. With his peroxided hair, Hank could have passed for a California beach boy.

"Oh, it's you," he said. "I don't need any more rescuing."

"I thought you might want to know that your buddies Joe and Boris are sick," Lucas said. He'd decided not to lecture Hank about yesterday's prank, since such a tactic was likely to antagonize him.

The boy's tough-guy stance wilted. "Are they real bad?"

"They're not feeling too great. Boris has to stay at the hospital because his dad's sick, too, but Joe's home with his mother," he said.

"I oughta be sick like them." Hank kicked at the doorsill.

"Actually I came here to thank you," Lucas said.

"You did?"

"If it weren't for you, we'd both be sick," he said. "It seems getting sprayed with manure protects people against this illness. Or maybe it was getting rinsed off afterward."

"That's why we're not sick?" The boy chewed his lip for a moment as he thought it over. "My mom's okay, then?"

"She's fine. She'll probably have to work tonight, though."

A shadow crossed the boy's face, but quickly vanished. "I don't care."

"Listen," Lucas said. "To show my gratitude, I'm at your disposal this afternoon. Is there anything you'd like to do? Need some lunch?"

"I already ate." The boy had a chocolate smear on one cheek, verifying his mother's prediction. "Do you know how to ride a bike?"

"You bet," Lucas said.

"You could ride my dad's bike," the boy said. "I wanted to go down to the creek and catch fish with my hands, but it's no fun alone."

Something like that definitely wasn't fun alone, Lucas agreed silently. He used to go fishing with his friends Joey and Sam, using branches they'd whittled themselves, with backyard worms for bait. They'd had a great time even though the fish mostly outsmarted them.

"You'll have to teach me how," he said.

"Okay." Hank bounded into the depths of the house. "I'll get my stuff."

The rest of the afternoon brought memories crowding from the back of Lucas's brain. He really had been suffering from a form of amnesia, he reflected as, pants rolled above the knees, he splashed in the creek with Flo's son.

He'd forgotten how the interplay of sunlight and leaf-dapple on water stirred a sense of well-being. How thrilling it was to spot a deer in the woods, and how alarming when something slimy slithered past his hand in the water.

They caught three fish. He showed Hank how to gut them with a pocketknife and, at the house, they fried them with baked beans on the side.

They fixed two extra plates of food, covered them in foil and took them to the hospital. Not once the whole day had Hank sneered or smirked or pulled any tricks.

The boy obviously missed his father. And, Lucas felt certain, he didn't like being left alone while his mother worked, although he would never admit it.

If he had a son, Lucas thought, they would spend plenty of time together. It would be fun finding new and interesting projects to embark on.

He wondered if he would feel the same way when he got back to L.A. Having a child in Nowhere Junction would be fun, challenging and rewarding. In L.A., well, he wasn't so sure.

BY EVENING, MANY OF THE patients were on the mend. However, all ten hospital beds remained full and Mimsy had insisted that Flo go home to her son, so, even with Lucas at her side, she faced a long night.

At eight o'clock, Bobette Moriarty arrived, hale and hearty. She'd missed the blast to help a cow deliver a large calf.

"Bob can handle the ranch tomorrow, so I came to help tonight," she said.

"We don't know yet whether the disease is contagious," Mimsy warned. "You could be putting yourself at risk."

"I looked in on some of the other ranchers, so if it's contagious, I'm already exposed," Bobette said. "I might as well work as long as I'm healthy. Show me to the bedpans.''

Thanking her stars for the rancher's can-do attitude, Mimsy put her to work. Half an hour later, Cissy Leroy, the teller from the First National Bank of Nowhere, dropped in.

"I'm glad I missed the action," she said. "I went into San Antonio yesterday to buy some fabric and notions." Cissy sewed clothes for Buffy's Boutique. "George said he'd give me tomorrow off if I came in and helped tonight, and I'm glad to do it."

Lucas listened with a bemused air. After Cissy got to work organizing the hospital admitting records, he said, "I see what you mean about people pitching in."

"People here take pride in pulling their weight," Mimsy said.

"Okay, Doc." Although his shoulder must be hurting again, Lucas gave no sign of it. "Give me an assignment."

She set him to disinfecting her examining rooms. Although Mimsy felt a little guilty asking him to do it, the job was essential.

By the time she finished her nightly rounds, midnight had come and gone. No new illnesses were reported, and several more townspeople volunteered for the overnight shift.

"You go home and get your sleep," Bobette ordered. "The last thing we need is for our doctor to take sick."

"You've had a long day, too," Mimsy protested.

The rancher gave her a mock glare. "Lucas, you escort this stubborn woman home."

"Yes, ma'am," he said.

They walked in companionable silence along the

block and a half to her apartment. At this hour, there wasn't a car stirring in Nowhere Junction and the only sounds were the chirp of insects and the bark of a distant dog.

Overhead, the stars sparkled like Christmas lights. Inhaling the crisp air, Mimsy felt energy surge through her system.

"We should go back," she said. "I'm not tired."

"I predict that in half an hour, you'll reach meltdown." Lucas kept a tight grip on her arm.

"I'm getting my second wind."

"Nothing more than a passing breeze, if you want to use that metaphor."

She supposed she ought to argue, but it felt wonderful to walk with his arm linked through hers. She could feel the heat of his skin and hear the soft intake of his breath.

The heat from his body drew her close. They might have been walking in a bubble beyond whose edges the town wavered and blurred.

Mimsy stopped in front of Anderson Coffee Shop and knew what she had to do. "Kiss me," she said.

Lucas studied her uncertainly. "Here?"

"There's nobody around."

"If anyone sees us, they'll gossip."

"Why should you care?" Mimsy was the one who ought to care. Instead she ached to hold Lucas. She'd been aching for him all day.

Despite the risk of being observed, it was safer to kiss him out here. Not in the privacy of her apartment. Not in a place where he could sweep her into bed while her inhibitions fluttered away like cast-off clothing.

Gently disentangling his arm, she looped her hands

around his neck. Face-to-face, Lucas smiled and touched her shoulders, her neck, the nape of her hair.

Mimsy treasured this suspended moment. They were eagles on the brink of a cliff, poised to fly. At this moment, the world belonged to them.

As Lucas bent over her, the intensity of his concentration drew her soul upward to meet his. When he kissed her, she merged into him, her heart trembling.

His mouth skimmed over hers. He drew back, but she gripped him harder, and then he was kissing her like a man afire.

Mimsy had never been embraced like this before. She hadn't known that beyond the connection of two pairs of lips lay another dimension in which a kiss ignited two people into one white-hot flame.

At last Lucas lifted his head, his breathing rough and his eyes glazed. "Mimsy, we shouldn't... I need to tell you..."

She ignored the words. Whatever he had to say, even if he'd recovered his memory, it didn't matter. After what she'd experienced a moment ago, she knew everything about him that she needed to know.

Besides, she was now so overstimulated and hovering on the edge of a thousand emotions, she couldn't possibly keep her distance. Even if Lucas couldn't stay for long, she wanted this night with him to treasure all her years.

"Come upstairs," she said. And, taking his hand, she led him there.

LUCAS WATCHED MIMSY FLICK on the lamp in her bedroom. The glow played across the sweetness of her face, the wildness of her hair.

He could trace the shape of her swelling breasts beneath the fabric of her blouse. Her hips were softly rounded, the slacks like a second skin. He thought she might scorch him if he touched her.

Inside him stirred a confused mixture of longing and reluctance. The male in him flamed with desire. There was something else, though, that must ultimately keep them apart.

He felt an overriding need to prove himself, to eclipse forever the outcast kid from Blink, Colorado. Lucas hadn't achieved that yet, and until he did he could never be the kind of man Mimsy deserved.

Yet he was powerless to resist her.

He stood, scarcely daring to breathe, as she unbuttoned her blouse. Golden skin gleamed in the lamplight. The dainty fabric of her brassiere was a mere wisp waiting to be snatched away.

"You're beautiful," he said.

Surprise sharpened her gaze. "Me?"

"You're exquisite." If he left her with nothing else, at least he could give her a sense of her own worth. Stepping closer, Lucas curved his palm over the edge of her breast. "Mimsy, you put everyone else in the shade."

"Even...?" Her voice trailed off.

"Everyone," he repeated firmly.

When he rested one hand on her waist, her skin rippled with pleasure. Fascinated, he slipped down her bra and cupped a small, firm mound with his palm.

Mimsy moaned, sending delicious anticipation tingling through him. Yet he owed her more than to take advantage of her faith in him.

Lucas couldn't bring himself to tell her that he'd lied, not right now. The truth was too harsh. Still, he could warn her away and hope she had the strength to pay heed.

"I don't…" His throat clamped shut and he had to force the words out. "I don't know what sort of man I am, Mimsy, but I may not be the trustworthy sort."

"You don't know that for sure!" she flared. "You're always putting yourself down."

"Me?" He hadn't been aware of doing that. Maybe it was only something Mimsy imagined.

"You can be so much more than you give yourself credit for." She appeared not to notice that she was standing before him partially undressed and wholly enticing.

"Maybe I haven't earned any credit," he said. "We won't know until I get my memory back."

"Maybe you never will," she said. "Would that be so bad? You could be any sort of person you make up your mind to be. And you could stay as long as you like."

Lucas wished it were so. To be free of his turmoil, to be able to live here with her.

A wave of longing swept over him, to become part of her goodness. To be the compassionate, honorable man she believed he was.

She was the only woman with whom he could be that man. The only woman in the world.

He took her in his arms. This time, he didn't even try to hold back.

MIMSY COULDN'T BELIEVE HER own boldness. She'd asked Lucas to kiss her in the street, then led him into her bedroom and removed her clothes.

Yet it felt right. It *was* right.

Her last doubt vanished when he kissed her again.

Oh, the seductiveness of his lips on hers, his chest against her bare breasts and his hardness pressed to her soft core.

She had dreamed of being taken by a mysterious, sexy man. Now the man was real. He was her Lucas.

Before Mimsy knew it, they lay on the bed and he was smoothing away the last of her clothes. Only a moment's shyness restrained her, and then she writhed against him, helping to unwork his buckle and coax his shirt buttons free.

Mimsy trailed kisses across Lucas's bare chest and collar. His breath coming fast, he peeled away his pants.

Naked, he was magnificent. Taut muscles, flat stomach, a few intriguing scars. Power and strength and all of it about to be unleashed. She couldn't wait.

"Do you have protection?" Lucas asked.

Mimsy didn't want to stop even for a moment. Was she crazy? How many times had she lectured her patients about the need for caution?

Still, it took great strength of will to reach into the drawer of her bedside table for the packet she'd put there in the hope that someday she would meet a man like this one.

Thank goodness he knew how to put it on. Despite all the demonstrations she'd given with a plastic model, at the moment Mimsy didn't have a clue.

Then something wonderful happened. He caught her wrists and pinned them lightly to the pillow, stretching them above her head. Capturing her, playfully mastering her.

"You belong to me," Lucas said.

"Yes."

His tongue licked fire across her breasts. Down her abdomen. Down to...

Mimsy cried out with joy. Then, without warning, her man mounted and inserted his hardness deep inside her. They fused together in voluptuous abandon.

Lucas moved in and out of her, and Mimsy joined in a rhythm as ancient and enduring as the earth itself. She wanted to touch him everywhere, with every part of herself.

It delighted her to hear him gasp, to feel his movements accelerate. They rode together toward an unseen, unknown, scarcely suspected horizon and cascaded over it into a floating world of bliss.

Warmth flowed around them and carried them along. Mimsy lay nestled against Lucas in a pool of contentment.

She could ask for nothing more.

SINCE REACHING ADULTHOOD, Lucas had prided himself on going where angels feared to tread. On taking risks, on never looking back.

But he'd never gone here before, to this quiet place filled with quicksilver magic. Love, that's what it was called.

Lucas gazed in wonder at the woman cradled against him, her soft curls tangled across her temple and her lids drooping with sleep. A subtle radiance emanated from her.

Why couldn't he stay here with Mimsy forever? Perhaps he could, after all.

He would have to unravel his lies, and give up his quest for wealth and power and eminence. What would he do then? What kind of work was he suited for, in such a little town?

The fact that he was even entertaining such ideas amazed Lucas. He was glad he didn't have to make a decision yet. He just wanted to lie here and cherish the perfection of this moment.

So he did.

ON MONDAY, WHILE LUCAS was still dozing, an early phone call summoned Mimsy to the hospital to release Murdock Murchison. He was demanding to go feed his dogs.

"I'm sure Buffy would see to them," she scolded the still-pallid man. At least his temperature had dropped to normal and he claimed his headache was gone.

"You have it in for my dog Lucas, don't you?" he grumbled, pulling on his shoes. "You want to get rid of him because he's got the same name as your boyfriend."

It was on the tip of Mimsy's tongue to deny that Lucas was her boyfriend, when she realized it was true. She let the comment pass.

"I harbor no animosity toward either of your dogs, Murdock," she said. "Besides, I should think you'd want to stay here with your wife."

Mazeppa's temperature had dropped also. Far from showing normal signs of convalescent weakness, however, she'd dropped to her knees and begun scrubbing the floor the moment she awakened. Bobette was struggling to get her back into bed.

"She looks fine to me," said Murdock. "Our house could use a good cleaning. You sure you're not trying to get some free work out of her?"

"This sudden obsession with cleanliness may not be normal." Mimsy had to admit that nothing about Mazeppa had ever been normal, but she trusted her instincts. "She may be suffering some unusual complication."

"Poppycock!" said Murdock. "I'm taking her home."

It was useless to object. Mimsy did make him promise to bring his wife back for a checkup the following day.

Almost everyone was feeling better this morning. Rueford and Boris Norris had stayed in bed long enough to wolf down the breakfast one of the helpers cooked, then sprinted out before Cissy Leroy could hand them a bill.

They were still wearing their hospital gowns. Quite a sight loping down Main Street, Mimsy supposed.

"Ask Billy Dell to deliver their clothes later, please," she told Cissy. "If they're that hard up for money, we don't want to hold their pants hostage."

The only other patient who troubled her was Horace Popsworthy. He'd mistaken Quade Gardiner for a spy from Groundhog Station and yelled at him, "We'll win that race! Now get your rodent face out of our town!"

"Groundhogs aren't rodents, they're marmots," Mimsy had corrected quietly, while signaling the mayor to slip out of sight. There was no point in riling the shopkeeper unnecessarily.

"He's had it in for Quade since he won the mayor's race," Sweetie Popsworthy noted when she came to collect her husband. "I don't think it's anything to worry about."

"Let me know if he shows any more signs of paranoia," Mimsy said. "It could be a side effect of the medicine I gave him or a complication from the illness."

"Have you figured out what it is yet?" Sweetie asked.

Mimsy shook her head. "No, but I don't intend to let it ride. Whatever it is, it could happen again, and I'd like to be prepared."

Around town, the bets were on Finella's Spring Salad, Flo reported when she arrived for duty. However, Mimsy knew that the dish had only been sampled by a few people before the blast, after which it had been discarded.

"It isn't fair!" sobbed Finella, still weak from her illness, as she and George paid their bill. She'd overheard Flo's report before Mimsy could intervene. "They're trying to blacken my name so I won't become school principal."

"You'd make a great administrator." Her husband patted her hand. "I'm for you one hundred and fifty percent."

Finella beamed. "What a wonderful man."

Well, maybe, Mimsy thought. She'd noticed that George encouraged his wife to get out of the house at every opportunity.

What he liked to do, Cissy confided after the pair left, was eat frozen dinners. He bought them on the sly from Gigi's and kept them in a refrigerator at the bank. He said they were a delight compared to his wife's cooking.

"They have one of the happiest marriages in town, even if they are a bit eccentric," Mimsy said. "As long as they're not hurting each other or anyone else, where's the harm?"

Flo sighed. "I wish that's the worst my husband had done. Going to search for Bigfoot. I'll bet! Going to

search for big breasts, more likely.'' She stalked down
the hall to begin stripping the vacated beds.

Finally Mimsy found a moment to think about what
had happened last night. To nurture the hope blooming
inside her.

Lucas loved her. He must. A man couldn't make
love to her that tenderly if he didn't.

She certainly loved him. She hadn't meant for it to
happen. For all her inexperience with romance, Mimsy
at thirty-three was no starry-eyed adolescent.

She knew the odds were against them. There might
be dark secrets in Lucas's past. Or he might be too
restless by nature to stay in one place.

Nevertheless, their intimacy had transformed her life.
She would never regret it, no matter what might come.

9

ON TUESDAY, LUCAS FOUGHT a battle with his conscience.

He should have relayed his real story to Mimsy first thing yesterday, but she'd left before he got the chance. When she returned at dinnertime, he'd told himself it would be cruel to disrupt their pure happiness so soon. They deserved at least one more night together.

So last night they'd made wonderful love. Then, this morning, Lucas had let her go off to work still naively believing him in the grips of amnesia.

He was selfish. A coward. And still, he admitted, not quite ready to write off an ambition that might take him away from the woman he loved.

His mind a blur of conflicting intentions, he set off on Tuesday morning to check on the status of his motorcycle. Outside the café, he ran into Lilibeth, who favored him with a smile.

"I'm glad you're feeling better," he said.

"Mimsy's a terrific doctor." She straightened her sweater, showing off her sexy figure to advantage. He didn't think she meant anything personal by it, though.

Although he hated to be blunt, he needed to learn once and for all whether Lilibeth was a prospective investor. "You know," Lucas said, "I realized I can't help you plan an effective investment strategy until I know what kind of assets we're talking about."

"Assets?" Lilibeth asked. "You mean, how much money I have?"

"How much is available to invest," he clarified. "That could include savings bonds, trust funds, any property that's readily convertible to cash, CDs…"

She brightened. "I've got lots of CDs! I love music!"

"I meant certificates of deposit."

A couple of ranchers tipped their hats to Lilibeth as they walked past Lucas into the café. "I've got to go," she said, and followed them inside.

To his surprise, Lucas saw her pour coffee for the men. So the heiress helped out while Willie Grimes was taking care of her sick family. It spoke well for her.

Nevertheless, he hadn't learned a thing about Lilibeth's ability to invest with him. Not a blessed thing.

If only he could write off the coconut business as a lost cause, perhaps Lucas could concentrate on beginning a new life. But he couldn't give up until every hope of success was extinguished. And, even then, he needed to find a way to help the disabled animals foundation. He would never forget one orange cat with a missing leg that he'd loved as a child. If only his family had been able to afford proper veterinary care and a prosthetic, Ginger wouldn't have had to drag herself around so awkwardly.

Sighing, he decided to head over to Murchison's Garage and check on his bike. When Lucas arrived, Carter informed him that his motorcycle was fixed. The mechanic looked a bit pale from his illness, but was as enthusiastic as ever. "You can't tell it was ever smashed, can you?"

"You sure can't." The bodywork and paint job were

impressive, especially since Carter must have finished it while recuperating. "Thanks a million. You're sure the bill is taken care of?"

"Absolutely."

Lucas swung onto the seat and revved the motor. It purred like an aging cat in a loving lap.

Off he shot along the quiet streets of Nowhere Junction. The breeze in his hair whispered of freedom. He could keep going if he wanted, leaving behind the complications he'd created and avoiding the consequences.

Lucas's heart clenched. To his shock, his eyes filled with tears.

He couldn't leave Mimsy. He craved her nearness, and ached at the thought of causing her pain.

The intensity of his feelings scared him. He didn't have to stay here forever, he reminded himself. He wasn't trapped. He simply chose to stay for a while longer.

Returning to the apartment, he parked the bike at the curb and went inside. Lucas picked up the phone and began catching up on his business.

There wasn't much left of it. And his partner remained elusive.

After lunch, Lucas went to Popsworthy's Dry Goods Store, which he'd learned had a computer for sale that was hooked up to the Internet. On the pretext of trying it out, he checked his e-mail, but there was no word from Ray Ryker there, either.

"That thing working okay?" Horace Popsworthy asked, peering over his shoulder.

Lucas logged off. "Seems to be."

"Caught a virus in there the other day." The man menaced the screen with a fly swatter. "Killed it with this. It was sent by one of those Groundhog vandals, trying to drive me out of business."

"Now, dear, that's crazy talk." His wife steered him away. "Come and have some tea."

At the back of the store, she tuned the radio to a country music station. "It helps drown out the noise in his mind," she told Lucas. "I hope he gets over this flu complication in a hurry. There's some fiddler on that station who sets my teeth on edge."

Lucas scarcely heard her. The mention of tea had reminded him of something.

It was reported on Plumpkin that a brew made from the coconut shell relieved epilepsy. Could it cure Popsworthy's paranoia as well?

It was kind of a stretch. He doubted there was any connection between paranoia and epilepsy, which, he'd read, involved brain cells releasing abnormal surges of electricity.

Besides, in order to provide the brew, he would have to reveal how he came by his knowledge about the coconut powder. He wasn't ready to unmask himself unless there was a strong reason to believe it would help Horace and Mazeppa, who was also afflicted with sudden obsessive behavior.

"Good luck," he called to Horace and Sweetie, and went outside.

A blast of water barely missed him. To Lucas's right, Gigi Wernicke caught the spray and stood sopping wet, staring in shock at someone on his left.

It was Mazeppa. In her hand, she held a hose, from which water poured into the gutter.

"You get back in that beauty salon!" she shouted at Gigi. "You're scattering little cut bits of hair all over the sidewalk! I can't stand the mess."

Lucas wondered if he shouldn't rethink his reluctance. Curing Mazeppa would be a public service.

"I just had it coiffed," wailed the grocery store owner, whose locks straggled damply across her shoulders. "You're going to pay for this, Mazeppa."

"Add it to my bill!" snapped the older woman.

Her chin thrust out with resentment, Gigi went back into the salon. Lucas raised his hands in mock fear. "I showered today, I promise."

Mazeppa paid him no attention. Instead she was riveted by a man striding out of City Hall across the street and down half a block. "Quade Gardiner!" she yelled.

The mayor turned and lifted an eyebrow questioningly.

"You better cancel that Halloween parade tomorrow night!" Mazeppa roared. "I'm not tolerating crepe paper littering the street. I'll douse the bunch of you!"

He crossed the street and regarded her with fond sternness. "I already canceled it. With so many people sick, nobody's got time to build a float."

"A good thing, too." The woman turned off the water faucet outside the dry goods store, detached the hose and coiled it in her shopping cart. "I've got to go meet my husband." Her head held high, she rattled away down the sidewalk.

"Whatever's ailing her, I hope Mimsy finds a cure for it soon," Quade said, turning to Lucas. "Good to see you again under more favorable circumstances than last time."

"As I recall, you were the one wielding the hose, but it was more than welcome." Lucas shook hands, noting the man's firm grip. "Are the kids going to be real disappointed about the parade?"

"Maybe a few, but it wouldn't have been much to look at this year," said the mayor.

"Sorry I missed it, though," Lucas said. "Small town parades are more fun than big commercial ones."

"Seems like you might be getting a bit of your memory back," Quade observed.

There was no point in denying it. "A little at a time," he said. "I guess it'll flood back pretty soon. Once I remember everything, I suppose I'll be going on my way."

"No need to leave unless you have to," said the mayor.

Lucas wondered why the man should care. Such a wealthy, distinguished citizen had no reason to take an interest in a stranger. "I don't figure I really fit in."

"Heck, what does it take to fit in with Mazeppa Murchison, Horace Popsworthy and Finella Weinbucket?" Quade grinned at him. "Besides, you strike me as a go-getter. This town could use more men like you."

"That's good to hear," Lucas said. "There're plenty of fellows in your position who'd say this town wasn't big enough for the two of us."

Astonishment flashed across Quade's face, followed by amusement. "Despite what Horace contends, I never had any hankering to be mayor. The people wrote me in out of desperation. If you put down roots around here, I've got a feeling that one of these days I'll be voting for you."

It was now Lucas's turn to look surprised. Him, Blink's rebellious teenager, a mayor?

"Think about it," said Quade before he sauntered away.

The man had to be suffering a complication from his

illness, Lucas decided. No small-town bigwig was that generous.

Yet the man's kindness touched him. This whole town was nothing like Blink had been. Or, perhaps, Lucas was nothing like he himself had been way back then.

These people deserved better than to be lied to. So, especially, did Mimsy. Besides, with her brains, she was going to figure out any minute that he'd been faking.

He would tell her the truth soon. Tomorrow. Just for one more day, though, Lucas wanted to enjoy belonging to something and someone.

IN BETWEEN SEEING patients that afternoon, Mimsy scoured the Internet for clues to her epidemic. There were plenty of illnesses with the same symptoms—coughing, fever and headaches—but none with Horace's and Mazeppa's odd complications.

She searched in vain for cases of people becoming ill after breathing dust from an explosion. Watching the videos of the blast didn't help, either.

Mimsy had sent blood samples and scrapings from the rubble to a friend's lab in Austin for analysis. They'd been carried in a cooler by a local resident, Orrin Steppins, who commuted the long drive daily to his computer programming job.

But with so many possibilities to search for, it might take weeks to isolate a common infectious agent, if one were found at all.

She needed to know what was going on sooner than that. Did danger lurk in the dust of the school grounds? Was a quarantine needed?

Like most of the town, the Grimes family had nearly

recovered by the time they came in for their checkups. Willie had not only avoided illness, but she positively glowed. "It's a cream of Lucas's that I tried on my face," she confided in response to a compliment.

Mimsy glanced at her hands. The skin was still smooth and moist, yet she hadn't used lotion for days. "Amazing, isn't it?"

"He's got more on the ball than he lets on," Willie said. "Mark my words, he's destined for great things."

Not too great, Mimsy hoped. Not so great they didn't include her.

Her train of thought broke off as, following the Grimes' departure, Murdock and Mazeppa arrived for their checkups. He had recovered fully, but Mazeppa's obsession with cleanliness was, if anything, worse.

"I had to scrub the whole house with bleach," she complained while Mimsy took her blood pressure. "You wouldn't believe the marks on the walls. And the dogs' water bowl, why, I just washed it yesterday and already there's little specks of mold."

Mold. The subject rang a bell. Mimsy had read something about mold. Now what was it?

She barely restrained herself from running to her computer right then. Even as she completed the checkups, though, her brain was whirling.

The school had suffered a bad water leak last spring. The walls could have become full of spores.

After the Murchisons left, Mimsy did a search on the Internet. At last she found the article she remembered.

During remodeling of a hospital, the construction crew had neglected to use airtight barriers and filter vacuuming to prevent dust contamination. A common fungus called aspergillus had infected a cluster of patients, killing several.

Nowhere Junction was luckier, Mimsy thought gratefully. Or perhaps the healthy citizens, unlike hospital patients already weakened by other problems, had been better able to fight off the illness.

But what about complications? The article didn't mention any.

She had read earlier that strep throat could cause obsessive-compulsive behavior in vulnerable children. Mazeppa's condition might be similar. Unfortunately there was apparently no cure but time.

As a precaution, Mimsy called her friend's lab and asked him to check for spores in the blood samples. Now if she could figure out what had gone amiss for Horace and Mazeppa...

Flo popped in from the outer office. "Lucas is here."

Mimsy's spirits soared. She couldn't wait to tell him what she'd learned. "Please show him in."

A moment later, he appeared in the doorway. No matter how many times she looked at him, there remained something awe-inspiring about him.

He bristled with an inner tension, a wariness, and yet warmth sparked in his gaze. Mimsy wanted him in a thousand ways, and feared losing him in a thousand more.

"Hi." She knew her emotions trembled in her face. A grown woman ought to be more guarded. With Lucas, she couldn't.

"Am I interrupting?"

"No. I've been wanting to talk to you." She leaned her elbows on her desk, atop the computer printouts. "Lucas, I know what the problem is."

"You do?"

"It's mold!"

"Mold?" He sounded baffled.

"From the blast! It must have been in the school walls," Mimsy explained.

Understanding dawned in his expression. "You're talking about the epidemic. I thought you were referring to a different problem."

"What problem?" she asked.

"Me."

Instantly Mimsy was ashamed. In her excitement, she'd forgotten that she had more than one medical mystery to unravel. "I'm so sorry. Of course I want to figure out how to cure your amnesia."

"No hurry," he said. "I'm enjoying myself, in case you hadn't noticed."

"So am I." It was a bit early to leave for the day, but Mimsy had no more patients and suddenly she couldn't stand to be cooped up here a minute longer.

She wanted to spend as much time as possible with Lucas. Physically he was almost recovered from his accident. His memory should return anytime now.

She wanted to believe that he would stay. That nothing and no one would call him away.

Inside Lucas, she believed, burned a clean blue flame of honor and decency and something more. Did she dare call it love for her? She could have sworn that was what she saw in his eyes.

She hoped it was enough to hold him here.

"You could knock off early." As usual, he seemed to be reading her thoughts.

Guilt, bred inside Mimsy from childhood, wouldn't allow her to abandon her duty, but she'd long ago learned how to trick the guilt. "Sure. I'll bring these reports home and you can help me figure out what's causing the complications.''

''We'll think more clearly at your place,'' Lucas drawled, playing along.

''Without all the distractions,'' she said.

''I'll conduct a thorough probe.'' A dimple flashed in his cheek.

Mimsy felt herself blushing. This sort of teasing was new to her. And she loved it. ''Your touch is just what my work needs.''

She gathered some papers and they went out. In her coolest professional manner, Mimsy asked Flo to page her if there were any problems. ''I need to clear my head for my research.''

''Yes, Doctor.'' Her assistant nodded solemnly and winked.

EVERY TIME THEY WERE together, Mimsy grew less inhibited, to Lucas's delight. This time, they made love in the living room, rolling right off the couch and landing with her on top.

Dinner was merely a short break. Then they adjourned to Lucas's room and initiated his bed.

''I'm getting fond of this apartment,'' he said as they lay together afterward.

''Don't get too fond. One of these days I intend to get my hands on Uncle Dick's house.''

''That's right, he's moving out, isn't he?''

''No For Sale sign yet, but I'm keeping my eyes open.''

Heated by their exertions, Mimsy lay naked beside him, lips parted, eyelids half-closed. From her rosy cheeks to the inviting hollow of her hips, she was the most beautiful woman Lucas had ever seen.

He wondered what it would be like if they owned a house together. And made love in every room.

It was one more reason for him to stick around.

EVEN IF LUCAS HADN'T KNOWN that Wednesday was Halloween, the children, many of whom went to school in costumes, would have clued him in. He saw them from where he stood supervising the construction workers as they loaded debris into pickup trucks.

All the workers, including him, wore face masks at Mimsy's insistence. Their appearances fit right in with the holiday.

The kids were cute, he thought, as they spilled out of school at three o'clock. Little bunnies and princesses, space heroes and cowboys.

Finella, who'd taken tofu-spinach brownies to the classrooms, frowned as she emerged with a tray of her uneaten treats. "I didn't see the Mean Brigade in class today," she announced to Lucas, perhaps because there were no other adults around.

Finella seemed to be trying to assume the role of principal, he thought, and wondered whether she would land the job. It was hard to imagine.

"You think they're up to something?" he asked.

"I wouldn't put it past those little hoodlums," she said. "It's Boris who's the real troublemaker. Joe and Hank come from good families."

Lucas's back stiffened. He knew all about good and bad families, having come from one of the latter. "That doesn't mean he's beyond redemption."

"Of course not," said Finella. "But he sure makes other people's lives difficult."

Lucas couldn't argue the point. Being splattered with

manure hadn't been one of the most pleasant experiences of his life.

Although it was only three o'clock, the workmen knocked off for the day. They'd started early, and Lucas didn't blame them after all that hard labor.

"You're being a good sport to help out this way," Finella told him. "Without Uncle Dick here, the men would have made a mess if you hadn't supervised them."

"They'd have managed," Lucas said, although privately he agreed with her. "If you're chosen principal, you'll have to deal with them for the rest of the construction process, you know."

"A woman can do anything a man can do, and a lot more!" Finella declared. "Don't tell my husband I said that, all right?"

"I wouldn't dream of it."

After putting his mask back on, Lucas inspected the school grounds and removed some nails before anyone could step on them. He wished he had the credentials to apply for the principal's job himself, but he hadn't even finished college.

After tidying up the grounds, he was too coated with grime to collect Mimsy from work, so he dropped by Carter's garage across the street and washed up in the lavatory. When he came out, Sheriff Bob stood frowning beside his pickup truck.

"You wouldn't happen to know anything about a theft from Gigi's Grocery Store, would you?" he demanded.

Dumbfounded, Lucas shook his head, and felt the cool air stir his damp hair. Just because he was the only stranger in town, did that make him an automatic suspect?

"Lucas spent all day over at the school, working for free," Carter said from where he lay on his back beneath a car.

"I'm talking about last night," Bob said. "Someone broke a window and took off with a couple of dozen cans of mackerel."

"Sounds like a crazed cat-lover to me." Lucas could see from the sheriff's stiff expression that Bob Moriarty wasn't amused. "As a matter of fact, I was at Mimsy's place all night."

"You might have sneaked out while she was sleeping," the sheriff grumbled. "Being in separate rooms and all, she wouldn't have noticed."

Lucas couldn't respond without ruining Mimsy's reputation. He was grateful when Carter said, "What would he do with a dozen cans of mackerel? Any sensible thief would steal cigarettes or something else that he could resell."

"I suppose that's true." Without apologizing, Bob got into his pickup and jounced away.

"I sure wish he and his sister would come to terms about her engagement," said Carter from beneath the car. "He's driving us all crazy."

"Who would steal that much mackerel?" Lucas asked.

"It's Halloween tonight, remember?" Carter said.

"Trick or treat?"

"You got it."

Mimsy was of the same opinion a few minutes later when Lucas told her about the scene. She wrinkled her nose. "That's going to be one smelly trick."

They left her office and headed companionably toward Main Street. They had agreed to stop by the grocery store to buy food for dinner.

"Figure out anything more in your medical sleuthing?" Lucas asked.

"I have a theory," Mimsy admitted. "I'll tell you while we shop."

The grocery store was small by big-city standards and crammed with merchandise, none of it arranged with any attempt at aesthetics. Also, although Gigi stocked the basics, many of her other selections were eccentric. This week's specials were marinated tofu and frozen creamed spinach.

So that was why Finella had put them in her brownies. He couldn't even bear to guess what they must taste like.

"It's electricity," Mimsy said.

"What?" Lucas frowned, trying to make the connection between her comment and the steak she was putting in her cart.

"The problem with Horace and Mazeppa." She tossed in a bottle of steak sauce. "I checked my records. They're the only two people in town with extensive dental work. It's expensive and you have to go to Groundhog to the dentist, so most people get as little work done as possible."

"I don't understand," he said. "What does dental work have to do with their illnesses?"

"It's just a theory, okay?" Mimsy said. "I read an article about how saliva is a weak conductor of electricity. It occurred to me that the mold might have changed the conductivity of their saliva so that the body's electrical system sends excessive impulses through the metal bridgework, affecting their brains."

"It sounds far-fetched to me," Lucas said.

"Me, too," she admitted. "And there's no way of proving it short of removing their dental work. It's better to wait and hope the conditions improve by themselves."

Lucas would have agreed, except he knew that there was another option. The coconut tea. If it had helped epileptics, it might help Horace and Mazeppa, too.

Also, the coconut powder was reputed to kill fungus. Mold was a kind of fungus, wasn't it?

He had to try it. With their peculiar behavior, Mazeppa and Horace might injure themselves or a bystander before natural healing occurred.

It was time to make a full confession to Mimsy and take his lumps.

"There's something we ought to try," he said.

"What?" Mimsy stacked her purchases on the front counter. It troubled Lucas to let her pay for the food when he had at least a little money right in his boot. It was one more reason to level with her.

"Remember that coconut powder we used in the hand lotion?" he asked.

"Sure."

"I never explained where it came from or what it could do. Well, I have something to confess."

"What?" Her gaze was open and trusting as she awaited his next comment.

Lucas searched for the right words. He never got a chance to find them because right then, outside the store, somebody screamed.

10

GIGI BEAT THEM TO THE DOOR. Lucas had to get close before he could see over her large frame.

Three smallish figures with paper sacks over their heads were vanishing down Main Street on bicycles. On the sidewalk, Mazeppa shrieked and pointed to the pavement.

Even before he identified the little mounds that trailed along the ground, the odor of fish hit Lucas full-bore. "My mackerel!" Gigi wailed.

A cat darted from an alley. Then another. Soon, from everywhere and nowhere, felines materialized along with a couple of dogs.

The bicyclists wheeled around and made another pass, whooping as they went. They'd cut holes in the bags so they could see and breathe. "Cat parade!" shouted one who sounded like Joe Grimes.

"You can't stop us!" taunted another. Boris Norris, Lucas thought.

The third turned his head and caught sight of Lucas. Inside the bag, two eyes blinked in embarrassment, and the boy pedaled hard, trying to catch up with his companions as they surged out of town.

"Stop, thieves!" Sheriff Bob ran out of Anderson Coffee Shop, slopping coffee on himself. "Gol durn it! Lilibeth, take this cup! Where's my truck keys?"

"Lucas, you could catch them." Mimsy pointed to his motorbike across the street.

"Right." Without a second thought, Lucas sprinted to the bike, jumped on and whirred it to life. While Bob was still climbing into his pickup, the motorcycle shot down the street behind the boys.

He came alongside the third rider, who was panting and pedaling hard. Now what? Lucas wondered. He didn't want to risk injuring the boy by grabbing him in motion.

Besides, there were tears in those eyes. "I'm sorry!" the kid called.

Lucas slowed his Harley to keep pace with the bicycle. "You know, Hank, a lot of people recognized you in spite of the bag."

"They can't be sure," said Flo's son. Ahead of them, the other two escapees plunged off the road and along a narrow dirt trail into the bushes.

"People might identify the bikes, although I guess one beat-up bicycle looks like another." Lucas knew he wasn't going to haul this boy in. Let the sheriff do his own dirty work. "I'll give you a tip. Wash your hands and get rid of the fish smell as soon as you can."

"Thanks!" Hank followed his companions off the road.

Behind him, Lucas heard the pickup approaching. He revved his engine and shot down the street as if in pursuit of something.

Bob followed. Boy, was he going to be mad, Lucas thought as he slowed and swung around. "Guess I lost them!" he called.

"You what?" Angrily Bob signaled him to halt. "How could you lose them?"

"They must have cut off the road somewhere."

"Like you wouldn't notice!" Livid, the sheriff got out and walked toward Lucas. "You've been a thorn in my side ever since you got here, mister."

"Not intentionally." Standing astride his Harley, Lucas refused to allow himself to be intimidated. Neither did he wish to annoy the sheriff any more than necessary, so he kept his face blank.

Bob scanned him disapprovingly. The sheriff was about Lucas's height, a bit stockier, but a fair match in a fight. Lucas doubted they were going to resolve matters that way, though, and the man's next words proved him right.

"You've got no business riding a motorcycle without a driver's license," Bob said. "Let's see some ID."

Lucas couldn't bluff his way out of this one. Reluctantly he reached into his boot and took out his wallet.

The sheriff whistled. "You've been lying to us, boy."

"I'm not a boy," Lucas said. "I'm thirty-five."

Bob examined the document. "California, is it? That doesn't surprise me. I had you pegged for some kind of nutcase."

"Don't I get points for not being from Groundhog Station?" Lucas asked.

"Not in your particular case, no." Patting his pockets, Bob found a pad and copied down the information. "You wanted on charges?"

"No," Lucas said.

"Pulling some kind of con?"

"Not that, either."

"Then what?"

This was humiliating, but he had to answer if he didn't want to get dragged to the town jail, or wherever they took prisoners around here.

"I was answering a matchmaking ad Lilibeth posted on the Internet," Lucas said. "When I had my accident, it occurred to me I should take the chance to learn more about her incognito. Ask her yourself. She was expecting a Mr. L. McRifle."

He decided to leave out the part about wanting her to invest in his business. Bob would figure it was some kind of scam.

"You've been taking advantage of our town doctor," the sheriff said.

"Not really. You see, I changed my mind about..." Before he could finish the sentence, a station wagon pulled alongside.

Mimsy's head poked out. "Is anybody hurt?" she asked.

"Just this fellow's pride." Bob waved the license at her. "You're not going to believe what I found out."

Lucas couldn't move. It was as if he were frozen inside an iceberg, unable to hear or speak or move, while Bob's lips moved and disbelief warred with grief on Mimsy's face.

SHE WANTED TO PROTEST that it wasn't true. Lucas hadn't been using her to get to Lilibeth.

He wasn't some Los Angeles lothario who had targeted a gorgeous small-town girl and, in the process, didn't think twice about exploiting a naive, plain-looking woman.

He hadn't tricked and lied to her for the past week. It couldn't be true. But it was.

This end to their relationship was worse than anything she'd feared. Yet the unarguable truth stared her in the face in the form of his California driver's license.

Lucas McRifle, age thirty-five. Yes, she dimly remembered Lilibeth mentioning a Mr. McRifle.

Lucas had known who he was all along. He hadn't had amnesia, not for a minute.

Her instincts had warned that he might be faking, but Mimsy hadn't trusted them. Hadn't wanted to trust them.

Instead she'd trusted *him*. The man of her dreams. And now, her nightmares.

It horrified her to think of the things she'd done with Lucas in the privacy of her apartment. How far she'd gone. How vulnerable she'd been, while it meant nothing to him.

You can't break down in front of the sheriff. Hanging on to the shreds of her dignity, Mimsy said, "I guess he fooled us all. Are you going to arrest him?"

Bob tilted his hat and scratched his head. "I don't know that there's anything illegal about impersonating a stranger," he said. "Did he steal anything from you?"

Only my heart. "N-not really."

"I guess he owes you rent on your spare room," the sheriff went on. "Other than that, as long as he leaves town right quick, I don't suppose I'll take him in."

Mimsy fought to keep her voice steady. "I don't want his money. As to whether he stays, that's up to Lilibeth, isn't it?"

"I don't reckon she'll be interested in a sneak," Bob said. To Lucas, he snapped, "Go on, get back there and tell her the truth."

"You can clear your things out of my apartment, too." Mimsy's throat ached as she forced out the words.

"Listen, we need to talk." His black eyes were as persuasive as ever. His voice as seductive.

"Go now!" she said.

His lips twitched as if to argue. With Bob scowling at him, though, he couldn't seem to get the words out. The lying, weasely, tantalizing words Mimsy knew he was so good at mustering.

"All right." With a twist of the handlebar, Lucas sent his motorcycle roaring toward town.

"Good riddance," Bob said.

Mimsy couldn't answer. She just nodded and drove off to a secluded place by the creek to have a good cry.

LUCAS FELT LIKE A HEEL. Heck, he *was* a heel. The fact that he'd been on the brink of coming clean with Mimsy was no excuse.

He deserved to be humiliated, but she didn't deserve to be hurt like this. He had to find a way to persuade her of the truth, even if she never forgave him.

The truth was that he loved her. He had a feeling he always would.

But it wasn't likely he could stay in this town. Not after people found out he was a phony. Good will only extended so far.

There was nothing he could do to change that now. But he did owe Lilibeth an apology, and before he cleared out he wanted to help Mazeppa and Horace if he could.

He didn't have to look far to find them. When he reached the center of town, Mazeppa was standing in the street hosing down the fish and the cats.

Popsworthy, who had planted himself on the sidewalk in front of his store, waved his fist in the air.

"Groundhog plot!" he yelled. "Terrorists are befouling our streets!"

"Come inside, honey," begged his wife. "I've got the radio turned up nice and loud."

"Spies everywhere!" he shouted. "The radio is bugged!"

Lucas pulled a U-turn and parked in front of Mimsy's place. At Anderson Coffee Shop, a half-dozen people were filing back inside now that the commotion had died down, but Lilibeth lagged behind.

"Did you catch those boys?" she asked Lucas.

"No," he said. "I got caught myself."

"You had something do with this?" she asked in astonishment.

"Nope." He plucked the wallet from his pocket. "But I've been part of an unforgivable deception." He flashed his driver's license at her.

Her flawless forehead wrinkled in confusion. "You're the L. McRifle I was e-mailing?"

"Yes, and I'm sorry," he said. "I got in this accident and faking amnesia seemed like a good way to get to know you discreetly."

"So if things didn't work out, you could go away quietly and I wouldn't know the difference," she said.

"That's right." He took a deep breath. "The trouble is, I fell for Mimsy instead."

Her mouth formed a small *O* of surprise. After a moment, Lilibeth said, "You mean the first fellow to answer my ad went for somebody else?"

"It's nothing personal, Lilibeth. I promise." Lucas didn't suppose he could salvage anything from this catastrophe, but he might as well try. "I was hoping to do some business with you, though. That is, if you're interested in investments, as we discussed."

She drew herself up proudly. "I can handle my own investments, thank you, Mr. McRifle. You know, the truth is, I go for a more intellectual type of man."

"You do?" He'd always considered himself on the bright side, although not highly educated.

"Someone with at least a college degree. I don't suppose you have one, do you?" she asked.

"No." He felt thoroughly deflated.

"It looks like the joke's on you," Lilibeth said. "You've been wasting your time playing these games. I wouldn't have had you anyway."

"I guess not." Although not entirely convinced she was on the level, he respected the way she'd salvaged her pride. "Good luck finding this genius of yours."

"He'll come along one of these days," said Lilibeth, and marched into the café.

Glumly, Lucas went upstairs and began brewing some coconut tea. When it was ready, he poured it into a thermos and took a couple of disposable cups from a cabinet.

Mazeppa was still carrying on in the middle of the street, so he headed for Horace. The shopkeeper's ranting had faded to a mutter, but he remained on the sidewalk, glaring at passersby.

Beside him, Sweetie Popsworthy tugged his arm in vain. She looked up wearily as Lucas approached.

"He's getting worse," she said. "I don't know what to do."

"I've got something that might help." Lucas poured tea into a cup. The fragrance of coconut helped mask the lingering stench of mackerel from the street. "Mr. Popsworthy, this is Nowhere Junction tea, guaranteed to strengthen you for the battle against the forces of Groundhog darkness."

It was utter nonsense. However, Horace didn't dash the cup to the ground.

He sniffed it suspiciously. "Do you want me to taste it?" Sweetie asked.

"Never say I asked my wife to take a risk in my stead!" he declared, and downed the potion in one gulp. "That's got a nice taste."

"How fast does it work?" Sweetie asked.

"I'm not sure. Maybe he should sit down."

"I'm fine," said Horace, before keeling over backward.

They caught him in midplunge and dragged him into the store, where they draped him over a bench. Lucas's heart pounded. What if he'd killed the man, or caused him serious injury?

"I'm sorry," he told Sweetie. "As far as I know, this brew isn't dangerous."

"What's in it?" she asked.

"Just ground-up coconut," he said. "A rare kind from an island in the Pacific."

"That's interesting." Her round, pink face furrowed in concentration. Despite wearing a trifle too much makeup, Sweetie was a pretty woman, Lucas decided. "I heard something on the radio about an island in the Pacific."

Right now a country-music song was blaring. "Do you recall any specifics?"

"They mentioned amnesia," she said.

Lucas stifled a groan. That was the last subject he wanted to hear about now.

He was considering suggesting that Sweetie page Mimsy when Horace snorted and sat up. "What the hey?" he said.

"Are you all right?" Lucas asked.

"Why shouldn't I be?" countered the shopkeeper. "I'm fine. Was I dreaming, or did three boys dump mackerel in the street?"

"Halloween prank," Sweetie confirmed.

"It's the Mean Brigade," Horace said. "Those boys could use a good whupping. And they ought to clean up the mess."

"You don't suspect—" Lucas picked over his words carefully "—any complicity from Groundhog Station?"

"Groundhog Station?" Popsworthy repeated. "I don't think they'd bother to throw fish around. They're too busy getting ready for the annual school tug-of-war and the go-cart race."

Sweetie's gaze met Lucas's. "You did it!" she said. "He's himself again."

"Who else would I be?" demanded her husband, and he lumbered to his feet. "Why's that radio on so loud?"

"I'll turn it right down," said his wife.

Before she reached the dial, the news came on. "Here's more on that American found suffering from amnesia on the island of Wooster, near Fiji," said the announcer.

Wooster? That was right next to Plumpkin! Anxiously Lucas waved Sweetie back from volume control.

"Authorities say the man was found on shore in the wreck of a small boat several months ago following a hurricane. He suffered broken bones and a head injury, and had no idea who he was," the newscaster continued. "Today, officials say he finally recalled a first name. It's Raymond."

Could this be Ray Ryker? Had he been lying in a

hospital bed all the while Lucas thought he'd absconded?

That still didn't explain the flight to Mexico or the kiss-off e-mail, though. Or the whereabouts of their development money. But it was a start.

"Anyone with information about this man is urged to contact the governor of Wooster. Unfortunately the governor is on a fishing trip and the island's telephone service is out of order," the announcer went on. From what Lucas knew of Plumpkin's easygoing ways, this situation wasn't unusual.

Lucas needed to fly to the South Pacific. He still had no money, though, and his credit cards were maxed out.

"What an interesting story," Sweetie said. She turned and stared at Lucas. "Well, aren't you going to go help Mazeppa?"

Lucas blinked, and remembered that he hadn't yet cured Murdock's wife. "Right. I'm on my way."

"Thanks again," she said.

"For what?" asked Horace. "You know, I've got a funny taste in my mouth. You didn't slip me some coconut, did you, dear? You know I hate that flavor."

"A minute ago, you liked it," said Sweetie.

"I never did!"

"I'll fix you some coffee," she answered, giving up the argument. "That'll blunt your taste buds."

Lucas hurried outside to find Mazeppa. There was no sign of her, but Buffy Murchison was closing up her boutique, so he asked after her mother-in-law.

"Murdock took her back to the ranch," she said. "How's your motorcycle running?"

"Your husband did a great job." He smiled, waved and walked to the bike. Obviously word of his duplicity hadn't reached Buffy yet. He could only imagine how cold her response would be if she knew the truth.

He had one more good deed to accomplish. Then he was going to head for Wooster if he had to swim across the Pacific.

WHEN MIMSY REACHED HOME, Lucas's motorcycle was gone, to her relief. She grabbed the groceries from her station wagon and hurried inside before anyone could see her tear-streaked face.

She hated him. She hated herself for being so gullible. She also hated the discovery that he hadn't yet removed his scanty possessions from her apartment.

Maybe he would come back, she told herself as she washed her face. Maybe, in spite of everything, he could explain his actions in a way that made sense.

Her stomach squeezed as she put away the food. Under the circumstances, she couldn't possibly eat anything, except maybe some chocolate ice cream, which was her secret medical cure for disappointment.

Mimsy dished herself a serving and sat down. Her mind began playing reruns.

She saw Lucas racing to grab Hank behind the circus tent. Lucas at the hospital, cheerfully sterilizing her equipment during the epidemic. Lucas bringing her and Flo peanut butter sandwiches.

Who could explain the inconsistencies in his behavior? In Mimsy's experience, selfish people showed their true nature in small ways as well as big ones. Lucas had been kind and brave almost to a fault.

A wayward man could be redeemed by love. That was the theme of many of her favorite books and movies. But love for her or for Lilibeth?

A familiar scratchy noise at the door, ending in a

tentative tap, told her she had company. Lilibeth was almost the last person she wanted to see, but she couldn't be rude.

When the door opened, the lovely blonde tipped up her chin as if gathering her pride. "Hello, Mimsy."

"Hi. What can I do for you?"

Her landlady shifted from one foot to the other. "I wanted to say that, well, I heard about Lucas. I mean, he told me himself that he'd lied."

"I'm glad he 'fessed up." Mimsy wondered what came next.

"I guess the way we talked at the pool and some other times, people might have thought I was throwing myself at him," Lilibeth went on. "Well, it was the opposite."

"The opposite?" Mimsy repeated.

"I was never interested in him." Avoiding eye contact, she toyed with a strand of golden hair. "I only talked with him to be polite, but he wouldn't leave me alone."

The air vanished from Mimsy's lungs. "Oh."

"Just because he was responding to my ad doesn't mean he's my type," Lilibeth said hurriedly. "In fact, he isn't, and I told him so. I'm sorry if I hurt his feelings, but he never had a chance with me and I needed to be honest about that."

"I see," Mimsy heard herself say, as if from a distance.

"So if anyone got the wrong idea, I wasn't the one doing the chasing."

She managed to make a coherent response. After Lilibeth departed, it took several seconds before she found the strength to close the door.

All the while he'd been romancing Mimsy, Lucas

had been hotly pursuing Lilibeth. He hadn't merely flirted with her, he'd practically thrown himself at the woman.

Mimsy hugged herself and leaned against the wall. What did a person do with all this love when no one wanted it?

She wished she'd never laid eyes on Lucas McRifle. At least then she would still have her dreams. Now she knew they would never come true.

Methodically, Mimsy moved through the apartment, collecting his things. Stuffing them into his duffel bag. Removing him and everything about him from her life.

11

MURDOCK AND MAZEPPA Murchison lived in a ranch house twenty minutes outside town, at the end of a long gravelly driveway that wound between clumps of trees.

Lucas came through a grove and halted in front of the one-story adobe house, a large, rambling structure freshly painted and landscaped with native plants. In the yard sprawled two dogs.

Except for their rhythmic panting, they might have been lawn sculptures. Neither reacted to the roar of the motorcycle.

"Hi, George. Hi, Lucas," he said.

The black dog's tail thumped once against the ground. The yellow dog shot it a baleful glance as if to say, "You're setting a bad example."

The front door opened. Grizzled old Murdock folded his arms and leaned in the opening. "Bob Moriarty called."

"Told you all about me, huh?"

"He said you're a no-good, lying scoundrel," the rancher commented, showing no more emotion than his dogs.

"The lying part is true." Lucas held up the thermos. "Before I leave town, I'd like to help your wife. This tea cured Horace Popsworthy."

"I know," Murdock said. "Sweetie called right after Bob."

This town had a grapevine to die for, Lucas mused. "Will you let me in?"

Mazeppa's thin face poked into sight beneath her husband's outstretched arm. "Is that tea purified? I won't drink anything tainted."

"The coconut is sterilized after it's processed," Lucas said. "It should make you feel better."

"There's nothing wrong with me," she said. "But I'll drink it on one condition."

"What's that?"

"Promise you won't let Finella have any of your coconut for her cooking. Heaven knows what kind of garbage she'd concoct."

Lucas grinned. "You bet."

The Murchisons moved back to let him into the house, although Mazeppa did require him to remove his boots. They came off with a thump that made the yellow dog's eyelids twitch.

"You're lucky," Murdock said. "Yesterday she hosed me off in the yard and made me air-dry before I came in."

"Lucas is a cleaner-looking feller than you," replied his wife. "Besides, he chased those boys that befouled the street. I'm cutting him some slack."

"He didn't catch them, though," said Murdock.

"Effort counts," she answered.

The living room boasted rustic couches and hand-hewn tables. Dark-brown woods were brightened by quilted throw cushions.

Everything was spotlessly clean. The air smelled of bleach.

"What's this stuff you've brought?" asked Mazeppa. "Is it going to keel me over like it did Popsworthy? Wish I'd been there to see it."

Lucas handed her the thermos and a crumpled cup. She went out of the room and returned with her own glass, which she filled herself.

"You make sure you're sitting down when you drink it," Murdock told his wife.

She perched on a stool. "Okay, I'm sitting. No, you're not getting me on that couch." To Lucas, she said, "I can't get all the dust out of those cushions, not without destroying the stupid things, and he won't let me."

Murdock sighed. "Just drink it."

With a shrug, Mazeppa tossed off the tea as if she were downing a shot of whiskey. "I don't feel a thing," she said, and keeled over sideways, chair and all.

Poised for such a possibility, Lucas flung himself beneath her. Down smashed the old lady, right on his injured shoulder, and the chair bonked him in the head.

"You all right?" asked Murdock, who hadn't bothered to get up.

"I'd better be." He spoke breathlessly. "There's only one doctor in town, and it's a safe bet she won't treat me."

"Would you look at that?" said Mazeppa, lying across him. "There's two ants on the floor that keep bumping into each other. Look there, one of them found a crumb and the other one wants it. Who's going to lay bets on the winner?"

"I thought you couldn't stand bugs in the house," said her husband.

"I don't mind 'em if they're entertaining." Mazeppa eased herself off Lucas. "No takers? You boys are dull company."

"Hallelujah! She's back to normal!" said Murdock.

"You call this normal?" Lucas stifled a groan as he sat up.

"You'll join us for dinner, of course," said Mazeppa. "We're having frozen waffles with whipped cream and cherries, in honor of Halloween."

Lucas decided not to ask what waffles had to do with Halloween. Besides, he was hungry enough to eat almost anything. "Sure," he said.

"And while you eat, you can tell us what the devil made you take an interest in Lilibeth," said Mazeppa.

MIMSY WAS GRATEFUL SHE had bought a stock of candy the previous week. Although reaching her apartment required climbing a flight of stairs, a steady succession of costumed children made the trek.

The stream of visitors ended by seven o'clock. According to town tradition, no trick or treating was allowed later than that because some townspeople went to bed early.

Mimsy hated the silence. She wished for a parade, or even another explosion. Anything to take her mind off Lucas.

She had left his possessions outside her door, but that wouldn't necessarily stop him from coming inside. The rogue had her spare key. But if he used it, she would...she would...

She didn't know what she'd do. Slap his face, maybe.

When the phone rang, she jumped. And, to her shame, ran to answer it.

It might be an emergency. It might be Lucas. It might be...

"It's Albert." Albert Bertrand was her friend in Austin who ran the medical lab.

"Did you find something?" she asked.

"You bet!" said Albert. "You were on the right track about the mold. There're spores everywhere, in the blood samples and in the scrapings. As you suggested, it's aspergillus, with a slight mutation that might explain the complications."

"We don't know for sure that that's what caused the disease, though," she cautioned. "It could be a coincidence."

"I doubt it." Albert's voice echoed with excitement. "I fed the scrapings to a group of rats. They came down with the illness a few hours later."

Apparently the course of the disease was accelerated in the rodents. Which meant that, if exposed, Lucas would come down with it in minutes, Mimsy thought acidly.

"Any complications?" she asked.

"Based on your theory about dental work, I implanted small wires in the jaws of two of the rats," he said. "The female has been throwing every stray bit of fur and food out of her cage. Tidying up, you might say."

"Like Mazeppa." Mimsy could scarcely believe the correspondence.

"At first, the male kept throwing himself at the bars, trying to attack the rat in the next cage," Albert said. "When that didn't work, he started squeaking angrily and hasn't stopped. Hurling insults, if you ask me."

"A miniature Horace Popsworthy," she murmured.

"If you come up with a treatment, let me know," Albert said. "This squeaky rat is getting on my nerves."

"I will!" she said. "Thanks, Albert."

"I'll send you a written report," he promised.

LUCAS FELT LIKE A COMPLETE chump, and he had no one to blame but himself.

According to the Murchisons, Lilibeth wasn't wealthy. She stood to inherit the drugstore and coffee shop, true, but she had to help her parents by working there full-time.

Money to invest? He'd been dreaming. No wonder the only kind of CD she knew was the musical kind.

So, he reflected glumly as he sat across the kitchen table from Murdock and Mazeppa, he'd gone through this charade for nothing. He'd antagonized the town and broken the heart of the woman he loved to dangle after nonexistent investment funds.

"Why were you so desperate for capital?" Mazeppa asked. When she discussed money, she sat up straighter and spoke more precisely than usual, as if transformed into a business tycoon.

Which might not be far from the truth, Lucas reflected. She appeared to possess considerable business acumen.

"The tea that cured you," he said, "is made from a rare kind of coconut. My partner and I own the rights."

He went on to describe the powder, its amazing properties and the disappearance and possible reappearance of Ray Ryker. "I need to go to the islands and find out what's happened. If we can put this stuff into production, I think we can make a fortune."

"Sounds to me like you've barely scratched the surface of commercial possibilities," said Mazeppa. "Willie Grimes told me about your cream. I swear, that woman looks ten years younger."

"Don't you go trying it," grumbled Murdock. "I like you the way you are."

His wife smiled. "And I love you, honey, even if I

don't always say so.'' She cleared her throat, as if self-conscious about having said something nice in the presence of a witness. ''In any case, you're not going to cut me out of this one, Lucas McRifle.''

''Cut you out?'' he asked.

''How much would it cost to buy a ten-percent stake in this business?'' she asked.

''Off the top of my head, I don't know,'' Lucas admitted.

She named an amount that would more than cover his travel expenses to Wooster, with plenty left over to jump-start production. ''Does that sound like enough?''

''More than enough,'' he said.

''See? I knew he was an honest man,'' Mazeppa told her husband. ''Here's what we'll do, Lucas. You figure out how much of the money will buy me my ten percent, and consider the rest a personal loan. How's that?''

''Incredibly generous,'' he said. ''I can't believe you'd trust me with so much money.''

''Nothing ventured, nothing gained,'' said Mazeppa.

MIMSY HEARD THE MOTORCYCLE while she was finishing her second dish of ice cream.

A moment later, she listened to Lucas's boots thump on her stairs. Those traitorous boots in which he'd hidden his wallet all week.

Except for the time he'd had it in his pocket. Her cheeks burned as she remembered discovering the lump while she was giving him a massage.

He'd tricked her so smoothly she'd never suspected a thing. Distracted her with that business about coconut face cream. What a rogue!

The footsteps stopped in the hall. She imagined him

spotting the duffel bag and bedroll. Hoped he would pick them up and clomp away, never to be seen again.

But how could he? How could she mean so little that he wouldn't even say goodbye?

A key jiggled in the lock. Mimsy contemplated grabbing a broom and whacking at Lucas when he came through the door, but decided the plan lacked dignity. However, she did rush to the sink and wipe her face with a clean towel to make sure she didn't have a chocolate mustache.

"Mimsy?" His voice sounded tentative. "I know you're mad, and you've got every right, but I need to talk to you."

She strolled out of the kitchen. "Fine. Talk."

Oh, heavens, did he have to look so masculine, standing there in her flowery living room? And so appealing, with a clump of brown hair falling to one eyebrow and his black eyes pleading for understanding?

Or, perhaps, for endless indulgence, she reminded herself.

"I thought you'd want to know that this stuff cured Horace and Mazeppa." He held out a thermos bottle. "It's a tea made from the coconut powder."

"How did it cure them?" she asked, intrigued in spite of herself.

"The powder has mold-fighting properties, and apparently affects electrical currents in the body as well," he said. "I thought you might want to test it."

Mimsy set the bottle on an end table. She would send some to Austin tomorrow. "Is this powder available commercially?"

"It may be soon." Lucas regarded her steadily. "I'll make sure you have as much as you need."

He went on talking. Vaguely she heard him explain

that the powder came from an island in the Pacific, that his partner had disappeared and might have turned up again, and that he'd come to Nowhere Junction in a desperate search for funds.

That was why he'd been pursuing Lilibeth, he said. He'd only learned today that she didn't have money.

"Neither do I," said Mimsy. "So there's no reason for you to be interested in me."

"You don't need money," Lucas said. "You're wonderful the way you are."

As always, his words stole beneath her defenses. For a magical moment, Mimsy didn't feel like clumsy, nearly invisible Dr. Miles. She was sexy and desirable.

Who was she kidding? No man could be taken with her short, practical curls, plain brown eyes and less than spectacular figure when he had Lilibeth to compare her to.

"I don't know what your game is, but I'm not playing," Mimsy said.

"I have to leave town," Lucas said. "Mazeppa's investing in my company, and I need to talk to my partner."

"The one with amnesia?" The implausibility of his story struck Mimsy. "How convenient. I can't believe Mazeppa fell for it."

"It's true," Lucas said. "I know I faked mine, but Ray apparently really did lose his memory."

"And I lost my judgment, where you're concerned," she said. "But I got it back today."

"I love you," Lucas said. "I was hoping…"

Angrily she blinked back her tears. "I was hoping, too. A lot of things! But you killed all that with your lies and the way you panted after Lilibeth."

"I wasn't panting," he said. "There was never anything personal about it."

"That's not the way she tells it!" Mimsy cried. She was losing control of her emotions, and she couldn't do a thing about it. "Or maybe that's the way you always treat women. Cozy up to them, make love to them and then deny it was—how did you put it?— anything personal!"

"I didn't make love to her, I made love to you." In one swift movement, he crossed the space between them and caught her arm. "You're the only woman in this town that I care about. Well, maybe Mazeppa, but you can hardly consider *her* competition."

Mimsy almost smiled. Darn the man, how dare he be so charming when she was utterly furious at him!

"I thought you were leaving," she said icily. At least, she was trying for iciness, but the quaver in her voice spoiled the effect.

He cupped her cheek with one hand. "Only temporarily. I'll come back and believe me, that's no easy promise. I used to hate small towns because I grew up in one where I saw the worst side of people."

"I guess they didn't like con artists. Well, I don't blame them," she snapped. It was the meanest shot Mimsy had ever taken at anyone, and it shocked her even more than it must have shocked Lucas.

Reluctantly he released her. Cool air replaced the warmth of his palm against her cheek. "Mimsy, I don't want to leave with matters so unsettled between us."

"They aren't unsettled," she said. "It's over."

Her heart twisted. She didn't mean it. Yes, she did. She had to mean it. She couldn't let this man go on hurting her.

"I don't know how long I'll be gone," Lucas said. "But it isn't over."

Mimsy couldn't speak anymore. If she did, she would burst into tears.

"I love you," he said.

She turned away so he wouldn't see her cry.

"I'll be back," Lucas said, and she heard his footsteps cross the room. The door closed quietly behind him.

"No, you won't," Mimsy said to the empty room.

She wasn't going to fall apart. She was a strong adult woman. A doctor. A person of achievement.

Speaking of which, it was time she started writing an article from her notes about the epidemic in Nowhere Junction. The complications should be noted in the medical literature, along with their apparent cure.

The work would keep her mind off Lucas. For a few blessed minutes at a time, anyway.

Of course, she couldn't finish the article until she'd examined Horace and Mazeppa and arranged for Albert to test the tea on his rodents. Even then, her results would be anecdotal without large-scale trials, but they might give other doctors something to go on if their patients developed the same symptoms.

Mimsy could help people across the country. It was what she had always dreamed of doing.

She decided to call the complications Miles Syndrome after herself. Scientists did that sort of thing all the time.

The article probably wouldn't be accepted for publication. Nevertheless it would make her feel better to send it to *Small Town Doctor,* her favorite publication.

And right now, Mimsy's spirits needed all the boosting they could get.

LUCAS SPENT THE NIGHT at the Murchison ranch. After Mazeppa electronically transferred funds from her account to his own, he reserved a flight from Austin with connections to Fiji.

"I'll e-mail you when I get there," he told his benefactors the next morning as he mounted his motorcycle.

"You're a good man," Murdock said, and clapped him on the shoulder. Not his injured one, thank goodness, although it was nearly better.

"And you've got darn nice dogs, even if you did give them funny names." Lucas stifled the impulse to hug the elderly couple. He could tell it would embarrass them.

"Don't eat any prune-and-pickle muffins," said Mazeppa.

"Count on it." Giving the bike a blast of gas, he roared away.

It was hard to leave Mimsy. And the rest of them. Would Hank Finkins stay out of trouble? Would Finella get hired as school principal? Would Bob Moriarty ever forgive his sister for marrying a man from Groundhog Station?

Nowhere Junction was like an addictive soap opera, Lucas reflected as the landscape whizzed past. He hoped distance and time would dull its grip on him.

Mimsy was another matter. He knew instinctively that the love he felt would burn as intensely a dozen years from now, or a hundred.

He would come back, of course. He'd made a promise, to himself as much as to Mimsy.

But Lucas had to be realistic. He'd betrayed her trust. She was a beautiful, gifted woman who deserved better treatment. Why should she forgive him?

Until now, he'd considered himself a loner, a risk-taker who didn't fit in with conventional society. For the space of the past week, he'd managed to convince himself that things had changed.

He'd fooled himself even more than the people around him. He actually believed, in some corner of his heart, that he'd found the home he'd secretly wanted.

The realization hit Lucas that he'd gotten the second chance he'd wished for, to do things over and make them come out right, and he'd blown it.

Well, he couldn't change that now, he thought with resignation. A man who might be Ray Ryker was lying in a hospital in need of his help. And Lucas had to save the coconut business, not only for his own sake, but for Mazeppa's and for the disabled animals who needed his support.

Also for an unknown number of people around the country who, at this moment, might be frantically bleaching their sidewalks or yelling colorful accusations at their neighbors.

Lucas zipped past a sign that said, Leaving Nowhere Junction. The graffiti underneath read: Eat Our Dust, Groundhogs!

A swell of longing filled his chest nearly to bursting. He wanted to stay, but he couldn't.

And heaven only knew when he'd return.

12

THE WEEK AFTER LUCAS LEFT, Florence Nightingale's husband turned up.

Mimsy, who had accepted a Friday night invitation to dinner, was there when it happened. Ewell Finkins clumped right into his modest three-bedroom home wearing a faux-leather jacket and toting a huge plaster cast of a hairy footprint.

"Lookit, Minnie!" he declared to his wife. "Lookit what I found up there in Canada! I made this cast myself."

Florence, Hank and Mimsy gathered to inspect the enormous print. It might have belonged to a prehistoric cave bear, Mimsy supposed. She couldn't think of any other animal that could have left such a large memento.

More likely, the print was a fake. There was no sense in pointing that out to Ewell, who wasn't likely to believe it anyway. Worse, he might go charging north to try his luck again.

"Did you really see Bigfoot, Pa?" Hank asked in awe.

"No, but it's practically as good," hooted his father, who had grown shaggy himself during his six-month pursuit. Well, partially shaggy. He was balding in front, with a long fringe around the edges.

"You planning to go look for the rest of this beast?" demanded his wife.

"Naw, enough is enough," said Ewell. "I hear you changed your name to Florence Nightingale."

"It suits my job," said the former Minnie Finkins.

"That's fine with me," said her husband. "I'm downright impressed by my wife, the nurse. You figure Gigi'll give me my old job back?"

Ewell had been the grocery store's truck driver, deliveryman and stockman. Billy Dell Grimes and Rueford Norris had been filling in since he left.

"I expect she will," Mimsy said. "Before you start handling food, though, you need to come in for a checkup."

"He sure does," said Flo. "Well, I guess I'm glad you're back, although I'm not done being mad at you yet."

"I'm glad you're back, too, Pa!" Hank threw his arms around his father.

Mimsy was pleased for his family's sake that Ewell had returned. Sometimes men did keep their word.

But she didn't intend to lie to herself. Lucas was gone and someday, no doubt, her longing for him would vanish, too, instead of tormenting her day and night as it did now.

"You reckon we can hang this over the fireplace?" Ewell looked around. "Dang, I forgot, we don't have a fireplace. Maybe I'll build one."

"Let's hang it in the bedroom," Flo said. "That way it'll keep reminding me of how angry I am."

Ewell's shamefaced expression told Mimsy he'd taken the hint. "I'll put it out in my workshed."

"Can I help you, Pa?" asked Hank.

"Yes, you can." His father ruffled his hair. "Let's get started, young-un."

"I'm not quitting my job," Flo told Mimsy after the two males left the room.

"Good." She had no idea where she'd get another nurse if Flo left. Besides, she enjoyed working with her. "I'll see you on Monday, then."

"Sure thing."

Mimsy went home and worked late into the night finishing her article. Then she e-mailed it to the editor of *Small Town Doctor.*

As with Lucas, she never expected to see or hear from him again.

It was Ray Ryker in the hospital, all right. Lucas's partner had lost some weight during the past seven weeks, but his expression brightened when his partner walked into the room.

"I know you," he said. "You're...my friend."

"And partner." Lucas pulled up a chair. "You've got a lot of explaining to do."

Ray had been transferred to a rehabilitation wing, and the room where they met was a sunny outdoor lounge overlooking a palm tree-shaded beach. A lovely place, but far from home.

"I'm as eager to hear my own story as you are." Ray adjusted his eyeglasses, which were taped together at the nose. "It's coming to me in bits and pieces."

Bits and pieces. Lucas squirmed inwardly. He'd used that line himself on the good people of Nowhere Junction.

Unlike him, Ray wasn't faking. He had nothing to gain by sitting here in a hospital for weeks on end.

Over the next few days, prodded by Lucas, his memory did indeed trickle back. Ray recalled hiring a local subcontractor and renting a boat to scout locations for a processing plant.

While rounding the island, he'd been hit by a hurricane and blown into the water. Because he'd landed on Wooster instead of Plumpkin, the boat's skipper must have assumed he'd drowned.

"The subcontractor's name is Mojo Magua Lana," Ray said one morning while they walked along the beach in front of the hospital. "I gave him a large advance payment. Heaven knows what he's done with it."

"You trusted a guy named Mojo?" Lucas asked.

His partner sighed. "He seemed kind of laid-back, with his flowered shirt and straw hat, but several people recommended him."

Lucas had visions of their front money vanishing in the direction of the nearest distillery, or perhaps aiding a large assortment of needy relatives. Still, he'd been wrong before, and he hoped he was wrong again.

"What about that e-mail you sent me?" he asked. "The one that said 'So long, sucker'?"

"Let me think for a minute." Ray lapsed into silence as he dredged up the memory.

A tropical breeze whispered through Lucas's hair and whipped his white slacks against his legs. He wished Mimsy were here. She'd look spectacular in a bikini like the ones those island women were wearing as they surfed toward shore.

Thinking about Mimsy made his chest clench. He'd considered e-mailing her, but it seemed too shallow and impersonal.

Besides, it would be senseless to invite an easy brush-off. The next time he contacted her, he intended to make it as difficult as possible to say no.

"I remember what it said!" Ray announced. "That wasn't the whole e-mail."

"It was all I got," Lucas said.

His old friend shook his head. "You must have thought I burned you."

"The possibility crossed my mind. I didn't call the police, though. I figured you'd have some kind of explanation."

From the appreciation in his partner's gaze, Lucas was glad he'd extended that amount of grace. A rush to judgment might have opened an irrevocable rift between them.

"The e-mail was supposed to say..." Ray's gaze grew distant. "'So long, sucker! Enjoy the rain in Atlanta while I'm basking on Plumpkin! I'll get back in touch when there's progress to report.' Or words to that effect."

"Why did you fly to Mexico?" Lucas kicked a coconut out of his way. It wasn't the rare sort, which for some reason didn't grow in Wooster's soil.

"I had a lot of frequent flyer miles to use up," Ray said. "And I got a really cheap charter flight to Fiji out of Mexico City."

"You were saving us money?"

"Right."

That made sense, now that Ray explained it.

"I'd better go look for that guy Mojo," Lucas said as they neared the hospital.

"They're releasing me today," said Ray. "I'll come with you."

IN NOWHERE JUNCTION, only one application was received for a school principal. The man sounded well-qualified, although there was an odd disclaimer in his letter saying that, despite rumors to the contrary, he hadn't actually blown up the cafeteria at his old school.

"It wouldn't matter anyway. Explosives people make good principals," Carter Murchison said at the next school-board meeting, which was held in the circus tent.

"Sounds like our kind of guy," agreed Billy Dell.

Horace Popsworthy nodded. "Besides, he's got experience."

"He doesn't know our children." Finella sniffed. "We'll be trusting the next principal with our beautiful new building. And let's not forget that some of the kids can be hard to handle."

Not as hard as they used to be, mused Mimsy. Hank Finkins sat next to his father, beaming with pride. He'd become the envy of every kid in town, most of whom had trooped through his parents' workshed to examine the amazing footprint.

"All the more reason to hire a person with experience as a principal," said Quade Gardiner. "Besides, Finella, we're counting on you to set up the new school cafeteria and hire the staff. That's going to be an important job."

She looked slightly mollified. "I suppose so."

"You going to let her poison those kids?" demanded Mazeppa from the back row.

"I'm sure Finella will want to poll the students as to their favorite menus," Quade said.

Billy Dell seized on the idea. "We could form a committee. Put Gigi and Willie on it, too. And JoJo Anderson. She's an expert on account of running the café."

Lilibeth's mother smiled from her seat in the audience. "I'd be glad to help."

The matter was soon settled, and a letter was sent to the applicant, Alexander Peabody, offering him the position of principal.

"WHEN MR. RYKER DISAPPEARED, I decided to go ahead and site the factory." Mojo Magua Lana was a handsome golden-skinned man whose Hawaiian shirt and baggy shorts gave him the air of a beachcomber.

"You didn't believe he'd drowned?" Lucas asked.

Mojo shrugged. "Around here, people sometimes take off for reasons of their own. You never know when they'll show up again."

Finding the subcontractor drinking a Fluffy Ruffles—rum, vermouth and lime—at a seaside cabana-style bar in midafternoon did nothing to reassure Lucas as to the man's stability. However, at least he hadn't absconded with their money.

"You found a site for the factory?" Ray asked, leaning against the bar. He still tired easily, although he'd begun regaining his strength.

"Got it up and running," Mojo said. "We took over an old pineapple processing plant and renovated it. Got stockpiles of coconut powder ready to go. I've planned an ad campaign, if you'd care to look at it."

"Very enterprising," said Lucas. "It sounds as if you've got a business background."

"MBA from Harvard." Mojo stirred his drink with a swizzle stick.

That was news. Good news. "What are you doing on Plumpkin?" Lucas asked.

"It's my home, man," said Mojo. "If your heart belongs in the middle of nowhere, you just have to follow it."

Nostalgia for Nowhere swept over Lucas. For a dusty little town where children studied in circus tents and everyone pitched in during an epidemic. And for a lovely, bright woman whom he missed so much he ached.

"Is the factory far from here?" Ray asked.

"Nothing's far from here," said Mojo. "Come on. I'll show you."

ALTHOUGH SEVERAL FAMILIES invited her to join them for dinner, Mimsy couldn't bear to spend Christmas in Nowhere Junction without Lucas. Instead she drove to Mystery Meat, Tennessee, and spent the holiday with her mother and stepfather.

Having arranged for the doctor from Groundhog to cover for her, she stayed in Tennessee for New Year's, too, catching up on medical journals she'd put aside during the epidemic. After sitting around watching the Rose Bowl game with an uncounted number of stepsiblings, however, she was more than ready to go home to the privacy of her apartment.

Her lonely, too-frilly, Lucas-less apartment.

Once in the sanctuary of her own home, Mimsy opened the bills and was accessing her e-mail when Buffy dropped by with some news. Bad news, although Buffy didn't know it.

"George Weinbucket says a lawyer from out of town arranged for somebody to buy Uncle Dick's house," said the blonde, who was wearing a smart new bias-cut skirt and top she'd designed herself. "Everyone thinks it must be the new principal."

Mimsy, who was opening an e-mail from the editor of *Small Town Doctor,* turned away from the screen. "His house was for sale? George never posted it!"

Finella's husband, who owned the town's real estate office, as well as being president of the bank, usually posted notices of property for sale. Mimsy had checked them right before she left for the holidays.

"I know. That's what's so intriguing," Buffy said. "Apparently the lawyer approached George before he had a chance to post it."

"Someone bought my house!" Mimsy said in horror as the miserable truth sank in.

"Your house?"

"I grew up there," she said. Buffy, being a newcomer, didn't know that. "I wanted to buy it."

"Oh, dear." Her friend glanced past her at the computer. "Hey, what's that?"

"What?" Checking the screen, Mimsy caught a few key words and phrases from the editor's letter. They were "impressed" and "February issue" and "on our Web site." "Oh, my gosh, they're going to publish my article!"

"You're a celebrity!" Buffy said. "Wow, Mimsy. And it's already posted on their Web site. Let's run off copies so everybody in town knows about it."

"Good idea."

When she accessed the magazine's Web site, Mimsy felt a thrill at seeing that the editor had retained her name of Miles Syndrome. He'd also written a special introduction in which he praised her sleuthing as a shining example of what a doctor with limited resources could accomplish.

A glow stole over her. Recognition. It had stung to be ignored everywhere she turned and now, suddenly, she wasn't invisible anymore. Instinctively she fluffed her hair.

"Look, there's a sidebar about Lucas's coconut tea," Buffy said. "It references another Web site. Let's take a look."

Mimsy didn't want to, but she couldn't refuse without making it obvious she was still hung up on the man. "Sure."

They clicked to the other Web site, and then another, and then another. Letters and notices praised coconut tea and coconut hand and face cream. A few minutes later, she discovered an entire bulletin board devoted to people who had sampled the products and were raving about them. Lucas must have gotten his plant up and running almost immediately. He'd apparently distributed samples through a variety of outlets in order to gain good word-of-mouth.

"He's a big success," she said.

"Looks like he's already selling the stuff from his own Web site," Buffy said. "With testimonials like that, the cosmetics companies will be lining up to negotiate for the rights."

"I always said Lucas wasn't a nobody," Mimsy recalled. *I believed in him when hardly anyone else did. But he doesn't care about that now.*

She straightened her spine. So what if Lucas was basking on some tropical island surrounded by beautiful women?

She, Mimsy Miles, was the author of an article in *Small Town Doctor.* She had an entire syndrome named after her. People all over the world would benefit from her research.

She wasn't a nobody, either.

"Let's print out that article," Mimsy said, and went back to the first Web site. "You can distribute copies at the boutique."

"Better than that, I'll have Carter present them at the school-board meeting. Murdock can do the same at the City Council," said Buffy. "I'm really proud of you."

"Thanks." The praise felt good, and Mimsy knew she'd be hearing more of it when the article was circulated.

Best of all, publication had convinced her deep inside that she was an outstanding doctor.

There was only one thing more that she needed to

find: a cure for a broken heart. Unfortunately even a brilliant physician wasn't likely to stumble across that.

LUCAS HADN'T INTENDED to stay away so long. But once the ball got rolling for his business, he didn't dare interrupt the momentum.

The speed of the Internet made everything happen faster these days. Orders for the raw powder poured in from customers large and small. There were offers from cosmetics and pharmaceuticals corporations to buy various rights, and already Mojo was supervising an expansion of the factory.

Much of the initial revenues had to be plowed back into the company. But there was enough left to pay off Mazeppa's loan and provide an initial return on her investment, to give Mojo a well-deserved bonus and to replenish Lucas's and Ray's bank accounts.

By January, Lucas had convinced his partner that it was time for him to set up a base in the United States. Not in Los Angeles, though. They'd lost their old office and he had no desire to return, except to clear out his apartment.

"I have somewhere else in mind," he said.

"Whatever," said Ray, who liked the tropical ambience so much he planned to stay on Plumpkin. "You can be based almost anywhere these days."

Lucas didn't mention Nowhere Junction specifically. It seemed like bad luck to count his chickens in advance.

He decided not to tell Mimsy he was coming, either. It would be best to catch her off guard.

13

"A COUPLE OF PEOPLE JUST came in," Flo announced.

Mimsy was patching the minister's thumb, which he'd smashed while trying to fix a broken pew by himself. At ninety-three, Ephraim O'Rourke had no tolerance for idleness, in himself or anyone else.

"Anything urgent?" she asked.

"Lucy Gardiner brought the twins. They've both got ear infections," said her nurse. "And Boris Norris skinned his knee pretty bad. Finella thought you should look at him." Finella was filling in until the new principal arrived.

"How did he get hurt?"

"He and Joe were skipping school. When Finella spotted them, they made a run for it and Boris tripped over an armadillo," Flo said.

"Did he hurt the armadillo?" Mimsy didn't have much sympathy to spare for the boy, who continued to make trouble even though he no longer had Hank to help him. Besides, Nowhere Junction was home to an endangered species of armadillo with a distinctive geometric pattern on its bony plates.

"I don't think so," Flo said. "They're pretty tough."

"I wish I could counsel the lad, but the Norrises haven't set foot in church in years," said the pastor.

"I tried dropping by their house, but Rueford was downright snippy."

"I'll bet he won't be paying his doctor bill, either," Flo said.

"The boy gets treated whether he can pay or not. But the twins are so young, I'd better see them first." Mimsy patted the minister on the wrist. "You should take some ibuprofen, Reverend. Would you like me to write you a prescription?"

"The over-the-counter kind is strong enough for me." Pastor O'Rourke hopped down from the examining table. "I'll see you both in church on Sunday."

"You bet," said Mimsy.

Lucy came in next, shepherding her two stepchildren. It was hard to believe she'd been a footloose courier until she delivered the kids to their unsuspecting father, Quade. After some initial conflict, he'd joyfully accepted that the kids really were his.

After a stormy courtship, Lucy had settled in happily at his Rocking R ranch. So happily that she was nearly eight months pregnant.

"You'll never guess who I saw near the Murchison ranch," Lucy bubbled. "Lucas McRifle!"

Mimsy hoped Lucy didn't see how her hand jerked as she examined Donnie's ears. When she could trust herself to speak, she said, "There's definitely an infection. He'll need antibiotics."

"I was afraid of that." Despite her girth, Lucy easily lifted her stepson down and hoisted her stepdaughter onto the table. "I guess Lucas was going to see Mazeppa. She sure was smart to invest in his company, wasn't she?"

Mimsy concentrated on Doreen. "I don't see any

infection here. Her throat looks clear and so do her ears."

"She's been rubbing them and complaining." Lucy patted the toddler's hand. "Probably a case of monkey see, monkey do. Should she take antibiotics, just in case?"

"No," Mimsy said. "The bacteria build up a resistance if the drugs are overused."

"Okay. Well, I don't suppose Lucas will be staying long." Lucy, so distracted by her news that she hardly seemed to hear the advice, lowered her stepdaughter from the table. "I imagine he wants to thank a few people who helped him while he was here. Like you, for instance."

Mimsy didn't trust herself to answer. Instead she wrote the prescription, escorted her visitor to the door and cautioned her that some children develop diaper rash on antibiotics due to a temporary milk allergy. "If that happens, you can give him soy milk. And let me know if you start experiencing labor pains."

"Thanks. Don't worry. I feel fine." Both arms full of children, Lucy smiled a goodbye.

Mimsy nodded, wishing the day were over so she could go hole up by herself. She also wished Lucas hadn't come to town and hoped he wouldn't drop by to thank her.

At least, she tried to convince herself that's what she wanted.

THE VISIT WITH MAZEPPA had gone well. She was so delighted at the returns on her investment that she'd forgotten to make any snappish remarks.

Her ranch house no longer reeked of bleach, Lucas noted. He was glad that the coconut cure appeared permanent. And Murdock had announced that he was re-naming his dog Sir Lucas so people wouldn't get the two of them confused.

They obviously expected him to stay in Nowhere Junction. However, Lucas was having second thoughts as he stopped for gas on the edge of town.

How could he expect other people to forgive his blatant lies? No one he'd known in Blink had ever cut him any slack, and in Nowhere he was not only a proven deceiver but an outsider as well.

When the sheriff's pickup pulled into the gas station, Lucas tensed. He didn't look forward to a confrontation with Bob Moriarty.

As the man climbed down, his badge flashed in the sunlight. In the wash of light, Lucas heard a dry voice say, "Howdy. I hear you've done yourself proud."

"Business is good." The pump clicked off, and Lucas removed the nozzle.

"You selling stock on the exchange?" Bob asked.

"Not yet," Lucas said. "We haven't decided when and if we're going public. If we do, I'll be sure to let you know."

"I'd appreciate it." Bob turned to fill up his tank. That, to Lucas's relief, appeared to be all the man had to say.

While he was paying the attendant, Billy Dell Grimes pulled in behind the wheel of his battered sedan.

"Hey! It *is* you!" he cried. "Lucy Gardiner said she saw you, but I didn't believe her. Man, you missed out on a lot of excitement."

"What's going on?"

"We hired a new principal, only he ain't showed up

yet,'' Billy said. ''Finella's miffed, but she's trying not to let on. Oh, and Flo's husband came back.''

''Hank's father?'' Lucas was glad for the boy's sake.

''Yeah, and he hung this great big hairy footprint on the wall.'' Billy let out a whoop. ''It's fantastic! Willie says we ought to start a town paper on the Internet so we could run a picture of it. You've got to see it.''

''I'll do that,'' Lucas said. ''Thanks, Billy.''

When he got back in his new Mercedes, he discovered that he wasn't nearly as nervous as before. The people of Nowhere Junction seemed to have forgiven his misconduct.

He wondered if Mimsy could do the same.

''STOP IT, DOC!'' Boris Norris's swinging leg narrowly missed kicking Mimsy as she cleaned and bandaged his scraped knee. ''You sure are clumsy.''

Mimsy loved kids, but this one was hard to like. With a sigh, she finished wrapping the bandage and picked up a syringe. ''This will keep you safe from tetanus bacteria. It's going to sting a little.''

''I'm not scared,'' Boris sneered, but uncertainty flickered in his hazel eyes as the syringe came closer.

''Good.'' Mimsy plunged it into his arm.

A string of curse words burst from his mouth. He didn't wiggle or try to kick her again, though. Even a ten-year-old could see that jumping around with a needle in your arm wasn't a good idea.

''You're lucky we have vaccines like this,'' she said briskly. ''Kids used to die of this disease.''

''So what?''

Usually she drew the line at lecturing. But darn it, she resented the boy's snide attitude. Dr. Mimsy Miles, discoverer of Miles Syndrome, deserved better treatment.

"You're lucky people like me will treat you even though you're rude and foul-mouthed." She pulled out the needle and slapped on a bandage strip. "If you ever speak to me that way again..."

She wasn't sure what threat she intended to make. Boris, who winced sharply at the contact, drew his own conclusion.

"You aren't going to give me any more shots, are you?" he asked.

"Only if you need them."

"You mean if I'm rude to you?"

He apparently believed she'd been threatening him with more shots. "Boris, I don't use medical treatments to punish kids."

The words went right past him. "I don't want any more shots. I'm sorry I swore, Dr. Mimsy. Okay?"

"Boris..."

The door opened. "I'm sorry, I couldn't discourage him," said Flo. As Lucas entered, the nurse's smile indicated she hadn't tried very hard.

The boy seized his chance to jump off the examining table. "Watch out for her!" he said. "And don't use no bad words or she'll stick you with a needle."

He ran past Flo and out of the office. The nurse winked at Mimsy and followed, closing the door behind her.

Mimsy couldn't spare another thought for Boris Norris. Or for anything except Lucas.

Despite the designer suit and elegant haircut, wildness shone in his black eyes. There was a challenge in the way he angled his broad shoulders and an allure in the twist of his lips that brought back memories of...

"It's good to see you," said the man who had stomped on her heart and left it in the dust.

"I wish I could say the same." Mimsy cleaned up the remains of Boris's treatment, although that was Flo's job. "I want to congratulate you on the success of your enterprise."

"Thank you. I'm glad I can finally pay my debts." He held out a check.

How could he believe she would accept money from him? "No, thank you. The rent was free and Murdock took care of your treatment."

"It isn't for you. It's for the hospital," he said. "To buy whatever equipment the town needs."

Reluctantly Mimsy accepted the check. She couldn't say no, for the sake of her patients.

She glanced down and had to read the amount twice before it sank in. "That's very generous."

"I know I behaved badly," Lucas said. "I would have acted differently right from the start if I'd had any idea I was going to fall in love with you."

It was exactly what she wanted to hear. But she'd trusted him once and he'd made a fool of her.

Although confrontation wasn't in her nature, Dr. Mimsy Miles no longer shrank from mounting a strong defense, even if it took the form of an offense. "Lying comes easily to you, doesn't it?"

He flinched. "Bob Moriarty seems willing to give me another chance. I was hoping you would, too."

"I'm sure a lot of people are impressed by your accomplishments," she said. "I was more impressed by a guy who risked his life to save a little boy and pitched in to fight an epidemic. Unfortunately he was a fraud."

The eagerness faded from his expression. Mimsy

yearned to touch his sleeve and reassure him. *I don't mean it. I miss you so much. Please tell me you love me again and this time make me believe it.*

She held herself motionless.

Finally Lucas spoke. "I'm sorry you feel that way, since we'll be running into each other a lot. I'm planning to stay in town."

Her spirits leaped, and then plummeted as she remembered that seeing him around would only prolong her agony. "Don't you have a business to run?"

"I can do that anywhere," he said. "As a matter of fact, I've bought a place with plenty of room to live and work at home."

He must mean the Fordyce Huggins ranch, Mimsy thought. Located next to the Murchison spread, it had been for sale for months.

"It does need a health inspection, though," Lucas continued in a maddeningly detached tone. "I plan to remodel and I'm worried that there might be some of that mold in the walls."

"You're asking me to inspect your house?"

A boyish grin lit his face. "I'll give you a free ride in my new Mercedes, Doc. How about it?"

Mimsy was on the point of telling him to have Billy Dell bore into the walls and send the samples to a lab. She yearned for Lucas's company, though, even if she knew she was risking more pain.

She had never loved anyone else. With him living nearby, she didn't see how she ever would. Maybe her best bet was to spend some time with him and hope it dulled the edges of her longing.

"All right, if there aren't any more patients waiting for me," she said.

There weren't.

Riding in the passenger seat of his luxury car, Mimsy tried to adjust to this new Lucas. The man she'd known had been a drifter, or so she'd believed.

The man beside her differed in subtle and not-so-subtle ways. He sat straighter. Drove the most expensive car in town. Smelled of exotic aftershave lotion.

And wore the same heart-stopping smile whenever he looked at her.

They headed south. The Huggins ranch lay to the east. "Where are we going?"

"It's not far."

Her stomach twisted when she spotted the pecan tree and the familiar woodpile. Surely even Lucas McRifle wouldn't do this to her.

The car stopped in front of the three-story Victorian. "How do you like it?" he asked.

For the first time in her life, Mimsy understood the expression "spitting mad." She wished she had long claws instead of short utilitarian nails so she could attack the man and render him permanently striped.

Between gritted teeth, unable to force herself to look at him, she said, "How dare you?"

"When I heard it was for sale, I couldn't resist," Lucas said mildly.

"You didn't hear it was for sale! You sent a lawyer to negotiate before anyone else got a chance to buy it."

"Did I?" he asked.

So furious she thought she'd burst, Mimsy swung toward him. "You knew this was my house! How could you steal it?"

"Steal it?" he repeated. "Wait a minute. I paid a fair price."

"That isn't what I mean!"

"Mimsy…"

"I can understand why you used me to get to Lilibeth. After all, she's gorgeous," she said. "But this is vicious…uncalled for. I never thought you would stoop so low…"

"Hold on!" He caught her by the shoulder. "Let's clear up a few points. I wasn't trying to get to Lilibeth because of her looks. I don't even care for her looks. You're much prettier."

"She told me herself that you—" exactly what had Lilibeth said, anyway? Mimsy hadn't paid attention to the details "—practically proposed to her."

"I did nothing of the kind." He spoke earnestly, all trace of cockiness gone. "Mimsy, I told Lilibeth plainly that I was only trying to negotiate a business deal with her. She never appealed to me in the least."

"And I suppose you didn't swipe my dream house? You snatched it out from under me and you think I ought to be a good sport about it, is that right?"

Lucas reached into his jacket and retrieved a sheaf of papers. "Actually the sale isn't final. It still needs your signature."

"My signature?"

"As joint owner," he said. "With your husband."

She stopped squirming and stared at him.

"I guess I didn't make myself clear." With one hand, Lucas brushed a curl back from her temple. "Actually I'm not thinking too clearly at the moment. I keep wanting to kiss you."

Much as she wanted to kiss him, too, Mimsy wouldn't allow herself to get sidetracked. "What was that business about a husband?"

"Me," he said. "If you'll have me."

"Is that a proposal?"

"Of sorts."

"This may be the middle of Nowhere, but we have our standards." She remembered using that line on him before, months ago.

That had been before she fell in love with him. Before she knew how maddening, and how wonderful, he could be.

"You want me to kneel?"

"It wouldn't hurt." Dr. Mimsy Miles, discoverer of Miles Syndrome, deserved the best.

"Hold on a minute." Lucas got out of the car and came around to escort her onto the porch. It creaked underfoot and one of the front railings was peeling.

The place needed work. Loving work.

Ignoring the threat to his expensive tan slacks, Lucas knelt in full view of the street and took Mimsy's hand in his.

"Dr. Mimsy Miles, will you marry me?" he asked. "I promise to love and cherish you always, forsaking all others, not that there ever were any others."

Mimsy nearly burst into tears. Moments ago, she'd thought everything was lost, and now he was asking her to be his wife.

"You don't look very happy," Lucas said. "Did I leave something out?"

"I just don't want this moment to pass too quickly," Mimsy admitted. "I'm enjoying it so much."

"You're not the one down here with a bone spur forming in your knee."

"Yes," she said. "I'd be delighted to marry you. Now please get up. Bone surgery isn't my specialty."

When he stood, she saw a ring in his hand. Not a conventional gold ring, but one made of brownish wood.

"This is for you to wear until I can buy something more suitable," Lucas said. "It's made of coconut shell for good luck."

Mimsy put it on. Lucas leaned down and brushed a kiss across her lips.

She rose on tiptoe and threw her arms around him. "You're the most amazing man I ever met."

He cradled her against him. "I've got a key," he said. "I hear there's furniture inside. Including a bed."

"I've always wanted to get married at the Nowhere Nearer to Thee O Lord Church. Do you mind?" Mimsy asked.

"Fine with me." After opening the door, Lucas picked her up, bride-style. "Any other requests?"

"Don't bang my head on the door frame."

"You're easy to please." He angled her inside. "Welcome home, Dr. Miles."

It was her old home and her new one, too, Mimsy thought in delight as Lucas swept her up the stairs.

After so much loneliness and self-doubt, at last she had everything she wanted. Love had invaded her heart unsuspected, and now it was carrying her away like a raging fever.

This was one ailment that Mimsy had no intention of curing.

A Hitchin' Time

Charlotte Maclay

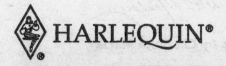

HARLEQUIN®

TORONTO • NEW YORK • LONDON
AMSTERDAM • PARIS • SYDNEY • HAMBURG
STOCKHOLM • ATHENS • TOKYO • MILAN • MADRID
PRAGUE • WARSAW • BUDAPEST • AUCKLAND

Dear Reader,

I met Lilibeth Anderson in my first visit to Nowhere Junction in *Two for One!* She was intended to be only a secondary character, but I had an amazing realization: simply because a woman is beautiful or even a town's perennial prom queen doesn't mean she is happy. So I decided to take pity on poor Lilibeth and give her a beau of her very own.

That wasn't as easy as it might seem. My fellow traveler to Nowhere Junction, Jackie Diamond, kept snatching away prospective heroes for her own heroine.

Finally I invited a stranger to town, Alexander Peabody, the new school principal. He's a perfect match for Lilibeth because he can see past her beauty right into her head and heart, appreciating her for the whole person that she is. That's definitely my kind of man.

Naturally, the course of true love is never easy, and in Nowhere Junction there are bound to be a good many unexpected twists and turns. I hope they will give you a smile or even a laugh or two.

As always, I enjoy hearing from readers. Write to me at P.O. Box 505, Torrance, CA 90508.

Happy reading,

Charlotte Maclay

Books by Charlotte Maclay

HARLEQUIN DUETS
20—NOT EXACTLY PREGNANT
37—TWO FOR ONE!*

*The Bachelor Dads of Nowhere Junction

Once again, my thanks to Jackie Diamond for her sense of humor and to the Lupe Riders, who brighten my days. Finella's Spring Salad lives again!

1

LIVING IN NOWHERE JUNCTION, TEXAS, was about as exciting as eating a mashed-potato sandwich.

With a sigh, Lilibeth Anderson switched on her computer in the tiny back office of the café and drugstore she helped her parents run. Maybe today there would be an e-mail response to her search for a husband via an Internet matchmaking service. So far only one potential mate had shown up, and wouldn't you know! Dark-eyed and handsome, Lucas McRifle had chosen someone else—Mimsy Miles, the town's doctor.

Not that Lilibeth had been interested in Lucas anyway. She hadn't felt an ounce of chemistry between them, but it still galled her to know she'd cast the bait and somebody else had landed the fish.

Clinching her teeth, Lilibeth clicked on her favorite Web site and waited for HitchingPost.com to appear on her screen.

By golly, the *next* time an eligible male showed up in Nowhere, Lilibeth was darn well going to latch onto him herself. She was twenty-seven years old, a former prom queen and didn't have a single prospect in sight. Virtually every man in town was too old, too young, or married, and there had been a terrible contagion of marriages lately, which made Lilibeth feel even more left out.

Tears blurred her vision and the screen went fuzzy.

The thought of living out her life in Nowhere as an old maid was like a life sentence in a convent, including the rules about celibacy. But she couldn't up and leave, as much as she had dreamed about doing just that.

Her parents, JoJo and B. K. Anderson, hadn't made much money running the drugstore for the past thirty years. They'd never wanted to overcharge their friends and neighbors for medicines, or even for milk shakes, not when money was scarce for almost everyone. Except for Quade Gardiner, a millionaire rancher who didn't *walk* Lilibeth down the aisle, despite her best efforts to attract him. Mazeppa was another anomaly. The townspeople all thought she was a bag lady and it turned out she had more money than Quade.

And now, as JoJo and B.K. were facing their retirement, there simply wasn't enough money to support them through their waning years.

Anyway, who in their right mind would want to buy a drugstore in Nowhere that did little more than break even?

Blinking away the film of tears, she stared at the screen and felt her heart sink a little lower. Not one single response to "Fun-loving heiress and former beauty queen seeks matrimony."

Lilibeth prided herself on not resorting to false advertising, no matter how desperate she was to find a husband. Exaggeration maybe, but she would dearly love to have some fun. She'd been the high-school prom queen four years in a row—a real coup since generally only seniors were eligible—and that ought to count for something. And she *would* inherit the drugstore and café eventually, assuming she outlived her parents instead of dying of boredom first.

She'd been as truthful as she thought any woman would be under the circumstances.

Still, she'd only gotten that one nibble from Lucas McRifle, and he'd gotten away. Desperately she wanted a home and family of her own, to be acknowledged as more than that "pretty Anderson girl."

Next time, she vowed...

ALEXANDER PEABODY noticed two things the moment he stepped inside the Anderson Coffee Shop and Drugstore in Nowhere Junction. The bell over the door didn't jingle to announce the arrival of customers, and the woman restocking feminine hygiene products on a shelf looked like an angel.

Instantly his brain began to think of ways he could repair *and* improve the rudimentary carillon system. Another part of his anatomy had a different reaction, focusing instead on the woman's honey-blond hair that fell in gentle waves to her shoulder blades, the finely sculpted arch of her back and the soft, rounded shape of her buttocks.

Rarely did anything distract Alex from ideas that

might lead him to his *grand invention,* the spark of creativity that would place him in a class with Thomas Edison and Guglielmo Marconi, allowing him to achieve his destiny. He'd vowed to bring new pride to the Peabody name and gain the familial approval that had been long denied him.

Simply by kneeling in an aisle between floral-scented douches and deodorized tampons, this woman made him lose all interest in levers and latches, electronic connections and electrical wiring. Confused him. Set up a distressing *physical* reaction that overrode his normally detached demeanor and disrupted his keen analytical mind.

Her presence was a potentially disastrous situation he hadn't anticipated when he signed a contract to be the new principal of Nowhere Junction Elementary School.

When she stood, grace in motion, with a box of contraceptive cream in one hand and a tube of Vaseline in the other, Alex's brain shut down altogether. She smiled, her mouth full and generous, her lips the rosy shade of a desert sunrise, and his throat tightened.

"Hello. I didn't hear you come in." Her voice was what he imagined a nightingale would sound like singing, lovely and lyrical. Her breasts were pressed together in a snug blue-denim dress, the full skirt swaying provocatively at her calves. "Can I help you?"

Oh, yes, he was in desperate need of assistance. In addition to his brain taking a sabbatical, he'd forgotten how to breathe. His fingertips were already beginning to tingle due to the absence of oxygen.

A tiny V formed between her brows, marring her perfect forehead. "What brings you to town?"

Alex struggled to find his voice, to recall just why he was standing in the middle of Nowhere, dumbstruck. "The Internet. I answered an ad on the Internet."

"The Inter-net?" Lilibeth's voice squeaked. This gorgeous hunk of man with gentle brown eyes had come in response to *her* ad? She was so excited, she was afraid she might wet her pants. Barely gathering herself, she remembered her vow not to let the next one get away. No way. No how.

She thrust out her breasts, her very best assets according to the men in town—at least that's what they took the most notice of—and held out her hand. "Welcome to Nowhere. I'm Lilibeth Anderson."

His gaze slowly skimmed over her assets and settled on her hand, but he didn't extend his own.

"Ah, I'm glad to meet you," he mumbled.

Wasn't that sweet? This adorable, handsome man with wavy, saddle-brown hair and broad shoulders was *shy*. Didn't it just make a girl want to wrap her arms around the big guy and hug him to pieces?

She gave him her warmest, most seductive smile and glanced down at her hand...which held a box of contraceptive cream.

Ohmigod! Heat raced to her cheeks.

At that instant in time, Lilibeth would have been

happy if a trap door had opened beneath her feet and she'd have fallen through, never to be seen again.

In a flurry, she jammed the box back onto the cart she'd been using to transport newly arrived merchandise from the stockroom to the store. Her haste caused boxes of Preparation H and bags of cough drops to cascade to the floor. In her effort to snare a tumbling carton of panty liners, her hip collided with the cart. A shampoo bottle with a faulty top tipped over, dribbling its contents down her leg. Tubes of lipstick squirted off the bottom shelf, rolling and spinning down the aisle, circling the stranger's spiffy cowboy boots.

She was one scream short of a hissy fit when he smiled at her, the corners of his eyes crinkling, his teeth beautifully white and straight. All the world suddenly came right again.

"Hi, Lilibeth. That's a really nice name. I'm Alex. Alexander Peabody."

She'd died and gone to heaven. His voice was a deep baritone. Soft yet commanding. "I'm not usually this clumsy," she managed to say. She truly wasn't. Every day she stocked the shelves and she'd never, ever had a disaster like this. Wouldn't you just know she'd make a fool of herself in front of the best-looking man she'd seen in a year full of Sundays.

"Here, let me help you." He knelt to pick up the lipsticks, and she got a good look at all that gloriously thick hair a woman simply needed to run her fingers through. He was wearing a sheepskin jacket against the cool February air and dressy jeans that had never known the feel of a saddle. Not a cowboy. Something much more elegant.

She squatted beside him, picking up a Lovely Lavender lipstick and a box of pads. He had a faint spicy scent, his aftershave, she surmised, instinctively leaning a little closer. His plastic pocket protector, neatly filled with two pens and two pencils, plus a brown faux-leather case for glasses in the opposite pocket, suggested a professional man.

"How did you find me?" Wisely she hadn't listed her address on the Internet. She'd planned to give that out only after she'd exchanged a few messages with a prospective suitor and felt she could trust him.

"Quade Gardiner told me. He's on the school board."

"He's the mayor, too." Although he'd never seemed all that thrilled with either job.

"He told me you and your family were outstanding citizens of Nowhere."

"I'll have to thank him for saying kind things about us." Surreptitiously, she tried to slip a product for promoting regularity out of sight. That wasn't a topic she wanted to discuss at the moment. "I guess you checked out a lot of ads on the Internet before coming here?"

"There weren't all that many, at least not that were looking for someone with my qualifications."

In that case, the women who had placed listings with HitchingPost.com must have some pretty peculiar criteria for a prospective husband. In Lilibeth's book, Alex looked darn near perfect.

"Where are you from?"

"Originally from Cleveland, that's where the family business is. But lately I've moved around quite a bit."

Goodness, things were looking better and better. "What sort of business is your family in?"

"We make Peabody Kazoos." When she didn't immediately respond to that announcement, he continued. "They're the most famous kazoos in the world. Our instruments have been played in concert at Rockefeller Center, the White House, and even at command performances for Queen Elizabeth."

"That's impressive." Far more so than the small-potatoes drugstore her parents owned. "So, you're part of the family's business?"

"Oh, no." He sat back on his haunches, studying a box of Depends Lilibeth had squashed in her scramble to save a tube of Poligrip from falling off the cart. "I can't tell a good kazoo from a bad one."

"You can't?" Who could, she wondered, although her store of knowledge didn't include much about the finer points of kazoo making. Maybe later she'd check out the information on the Internet to broaden her horizons, a habit she'd developed to feed her insatiable curiosity about what lay beyond the borders of Nowhere.

He looked at her, his kind brown eyes so sad she almost cried. "I'm tone deaf."

"Oh, my. I can see that would be a problem." She smiled at him reassuringly. "It does mean we have something in common, though. The girls' glee club teacher at Groundhog High School said a teakettle could carry a tune better than I could.''

They reached for a box of jasmine body powder at the same time, and his hand closed over hers. His fingers were long and tapered, the nails neatly trimmed. Strong, gentle hands.

He met her gaze, his focus entirely on her. "A teacher should never be unkind to a student. Your voice sounds lovely to me.''

"I think he was just jealous because I beat out his daughter for prom queen."

They stood together, although Lilibeth wasn't sure her knees would be able to hold her upright for long. Her muscles had lost all their strength while her heart had turned into a snare drum.

"Is the apartment upstairs?" he asked in his soft baritone.

Oh, dear, he was moving much too fast for her. She wasn't about to go upstairs with him this soon. As a matter of principle, they ought to have at least one date before—

Suddenly a seriously uncomfortable feeling edged down her spine. "Apartment?"

"Yes, the one Quade said you had for rent.''

The one Dr. Mimsy had recently vacated. Lilibeth took a step back and bumped the cart, setting it in motion again. She steadied it.

"You're here to rent the apartment?"

"Quade thought it would work out well for me.''

Even though she knew frowning created wrinkles,

her brows pulled together. "Which Internet ad did you say you answered?"

"The one for school principal here in Nowhere." His sensual lips curled into a self-deprecating smile. "I gather I was the only applicant."

"You're the new principal?" She'd heard one had been hired to replace Uncle Dick Smollens, who wasn't actually anyone's uncle that she knew of. He'd retired to pursue a career in the demolition business, but she hadn't known when his replacement would show up in town. Which meant she had a good reason to feel uneasy. "You didn't answer an ad at HitchingPost.com?"

"Nope. I don't think I know that Web site. Does it have something to do with cowboys?"

Disappointment, so keen it was like a razor blade, sliced through Lilibeth's heart. "Not exactly." She wasn't about to admit it was a matchmaking service. With an effort, she stifled a sigh. "I'll take you upstairs and show you the apartment. It's not very big."

"I'm sure it'll be fine. I wondered, too, if you knew of anyone who might have a garage or old barn nearby they'd like to rent."

"For your car?"

"Not really. I'm an inventor, you see, and I need a place to work on my projects."

"An inventor! How exciting." Another knife of regret slid through her. The most interesting man to come to town in years, and he wasn't here to meet her. "We've got a garage out back my folks might rent to you. It's pretty cluttered, but the only thing we really store there is Aunt Tillie's Cactus Joy Juice.''

"Let's take a look at the apartment first, then maybe I can talk to your parents about the garage.''

She turned to lead him upstairs and nearly fell over the darn cart again. Alex caught her. As he pulled her upright, her breasts collided with his broad chest. She gripped the collar of his sheepskin jacket as she staggered forward, nearly impaling herself on the pens in his pocket.

His eyes narrowed, dark and interested.

"Tell you what, Lilibeth. If your folks rent me the garage, I'll see if I can automate that cart of yours. It's downright dangerous the way it is now.''

A little thrill shot through her. Just because Alex hadn't come to Nowhere in search of her didn't mean they couldn't *find* each other now that the fates had led him here.

She tilted her head to flip her hair—her second-best asset—over her shoulder. "Will your wife be joining you in Nowhere?" she asked coyly.

His lips curved again. "I'm a bachelor.''

Lilibeth wanted to punch her fist in the air in a victory salute, but restrained herself. Alexander Peabody had met his match.

And if any predatory female came within a hundred feet of him, Lilibeth was going to cut her heart out with a spoon.

2

ALEX PULLED HIS PICKUP behind the drugstore and parked it. Everything he needed to work on his inventions was beneath the truck's white camper shell—his tools, a generator, spare parts of all types. He was sure being the principal of a small school in the middle of nowhere would allow him ample time to devote to his real calling.

He was less confident remaining in close proximity to Lilibeth was a wise idea. She was a serious impediment to his ability to concentrate.

Pulling his suitcase from behind the seat, he used the back entrance to the drugstore and went upstairs. The living room of the small apartment overlooked Main Street, an unusually wide thoroughfare where cars were parked randomly dependent upon the driver's whim. A grocery store and a dry goods store were farther down on opposite corners of Cross Street.

Oddly enough, two cows walked single file down the street. A passing pickup drove around them, the driver apparently undisturbed by the wandering animals. Alex carried his suitcase into the larger of the apartment's two bedrooms—the smaller one he'd use as an office.

Idly he wondered if this had once been the Anderson family's home and where they lived now. Especially Lilibeth.

From his bedroom window he could see the south part of town, such as it was. Closest to him was a small medical clinic and beyond that an auto repair garage. On the opposite side of the street a cloud of dust rose, marking the construction site for the new school building. At the moment an adjacent grouping of circus tents housed the students.

The school's situation was chaotic, although no more turbulent than his thoughts had been when Lilibeth had fluffed the pillow on his narrow bed and hugged it to her.

Placing his suitcase on the bed, he unpacked. As soon as he got involved with a project he'd be able to concentrate again. He prided himself on being oblivious to anything that would divert him from his goal.

Not that he hadn't found his own detours. A slight miscalculation in his last project had almost cost the school where he worked a new cafeteria. Only through his quick actions had he been able to release the buildup of pressure in the school's boiler. Unfortunately, the superintendent did not appreciate Alex's heroic efforts.

The timing of Nowhere's need for a principal had been fortuitous.

"YOU COULD HAVE AT LEAST waited until we met him." JoJo Anderson took off her jacket and hung it on a coatrack near the soda fountain where Lilibeth was cleaning up. "I don't like the idea of renting to strangers."

"He's not a stranger, Mama," Lilibeth said. "He's the new school principal. Think of all the status you'll gain by having him here right under your own roof."

"Having a doctor was better, a woman doctor at that. I didn't have to worry about Mimsy having wild parties upstairs."

Lilibeth would venture some hanky-panky had gone on upstairs between Mimsy and Lucas, whether JoJo was willing to admit it or not.

"I don't think Alex is the wild party kind, Mama." Though Lilibeth was counting on a chance for a little hanky-panky herself.

JoJo raised her brows. A former prom queen herself at Groundhog High, she'd fought a valiant battle to keep her looks. Fortunately the arrival of Lucas McRifle and his coconut skin cream had helped her to win her war on wrinkles.

"Just how old is this gentleman?" JoJo asked.

Lilibeth dipped a dirty coffee cup left over from the morning hangers-on into a sink of hot, sudsy water and scrubbed it with a rag. "I don't know, thirty-something I suppose," she answered vaguely.

"You know, Lilibeth, dear, I don't want you setting your cap for some boy who's not a local. Folks who weren't raised here can't appreciate what a fine little community we have. And it would break your daddy's and my heart if you ever moved away from Nowhere."

"Mama, there aren't any *eligible* locals left." At least none who appealed to Lilibeth. "Lucy Gardiner and Buffy Murchison got hitched to the last two a year ago."

"I never thought Carter Murchison was good enough for you anyway, dear. Now Quade's another matter all together." She sniffed. "I had always hoped..."

Lilibeth rolled her eyes. So had she, even if she hadn't exactly been in love with him. He was the best-looking man in the county and so rich he could butter his toast on both sides. But that didn't matter now. She had a *live* one upstairs and she wasn't going to let her mother drive the man away. "Alex would also like to rent the garage out back."

"Oh, no, I don't think that's possible. You know your daddy has—"

"It's all junk, Mama. I'll help Alex clean it out myself."

"But what about Aunt Tilly's Joy Juice? She'd turn over in her grave if she thought—"

"I'll save every drop, I promise." The old family recipe, along with some rip-roaring stories, had been passed down for generations. Drinking the stuff was like a baptism of fire. It was also the only thing that made Finella's Spring Salad palatable. The perpetual PTA president brought the potluck dish to virtually every event in town.

The door to the drugstore opened and Mazeppa wrestled a grocery cart overloaded with junk inside.

"You leave that thing outside, you hear?" JoJo yelled. "I won't have you—"

"Hush, woman. They can hear you screech clear to Tallahassee. Not gonna leave my goods where some fool will come along and snatch them away."

Lilibeth scooted out from behind the soda counter to intervene. She didn't understand why Mazeppa had gone back to pushing around her shopping cart, particularly since she had a perfectly nice home now with her new husband, Murdock Murchison, Carter's father. But perhaps she was still emotionally attached to her former means of hauling her things.

"Here you go, Mazeppa." Lilibeth guided the cart to a spot near the door. "When I rearranged the counters, I took special care to leave a place where you could put your cart while you're shopping."

"Humph!" The old woman relinquished her hold on the cart. "That don't mean I'm gonna name you in my will, you know. I already gave my money away to build that new school what's going up. The whole project's movin' as slow as molasses, if you ask me."

"Yes, well, the new principal is in town now. Maybe he can get construction moving along a little faster." When Mazeppa stepped away from her cart, Lilibeth breathed a little easier. The woman could do a lot of damage to the merchandise with only one run down each aisle. "Can I help you find something today?"

She glanced over at JoJo, then lowered her voice confidentially. "You got any of that medicine what gets a man's juices flowing again?"

"Ah, just exactly what kind of juices did you have in mind?"

She opened her mouth to speak, then closed it again and looked over Lilibeth's shoulder. "I'll take some of whatever that fella's got naturally. Murdock's slowed down some since the honeymoon."

Puzzled, Lilibeth turned to see Alex standing in the doorway that led to the back of the building. Wearing a denim sport shirt with the sleeves rolled up and sun-faded jeans that hugged his muscular thighs, he looked about as virile as any man could. Not even the odd pocket protector he wore in his shirt pocket detracted from his masculinity.

"I don't think they can bottle that," Lilibeth said under her breath. Though if someone could, she and Alex would make a fortune.

A broad smile on his face, Alex strolled into the room. "You must be Lilibeth's mother." He extended his hand to Mazeppa. "I can certainly see where she gets her beauty."

Mazeppa cackled the wicked-witch laugh she'd perfected for Halloween parties.

From the café side of the store, JoJo let out a cry of dismay. "No child of mine would ever look like that old hag."

Alex whirled around. He'd clearly made a tactical error. The woman dressed in layers and layers of clothing wasn't Lilibeth's mother; the far younger and more attractive woman was and she was shooting Texas-size daggers at him from across the room.

In a flurry to smooth things over, Lilibeth hurried to his side, linking her arm through his. "What a wonderful sense of humor you have!" She tittered a high-pitched, nervous laugh. "Here, come meet Mama. She's so excited the school principal is going to be staying with us."

From the woman's dour expression, Alex didn't think that was the case. But then, with Lilibeth's breast pressed firmly against his arm, thinking at all was unusually difficult.

Following the introductions, he managed to apologize to JoJo for his foolish mistake.

"I didn't take no offense," the woman cruising the display of jock itch products yelled from across the room.

"I'll be right with you, Mazeppa," Lilibeth said, not relinquishing her hold on Alex's arm.

Still feeling embarrassed, he expressed his appreciation for the charming apartment upstairs.

JoJo harrumphed. "We don't allow any wild parties or loud music. This is a nice peaceful town, you hear?"

The construction crew down the street chose that moment to drop off a load of steel reinforcement rods. They landed on the ground, the sound like a stick of dynamite going off.

Alex winced. "Yes, ma'am."

"Mama says it's just fine if you want to rent the garage out back. Since we're not using it, she won't even charge you extra rent."

Shifting her expression into a perfect imitation of a

prune, JoJo glared at her daughter. "I didn't say any such thing."

"I'd be happy to pay extra, Mrs. Anderson. It's only fair—"

"I cain't hang around all day wasting my time waitin' for somebody to help me," Mazeppa complained. She grabbed her overfull shopping cart and gave it a yank, nearly knocking over a display of facial creams in the process.

"Mazeppa!" Lilibeth cried.

"I'll get it." In a few quick strides, Alex reached the cart, righting it and steadying the display case. "That's too heavy for you, ma'am. You really ought to have your cart motorized."

Blinking, Mazeppa smiled, revealing a beautiful set of perfectly white false teeth. "Why, thank you, young man. You're the first person in this whole dang town who's shown a whit of compassion for an old woman. Except Murdock, of course, and some days he's about as sympathetic as a fence post."

She shoved her cart toward the door, and Alex held it open for her.

"You have a nice day, ma'am."

"Right now I'm more worried about perking up my nights." She went off down the sidewalk, the front right wheel of her cart wobbling precariously. Alex made a mental note of the diameter of the wheels and the overall weight of the cart.

"Thank you," Lilibeth said.

Alex started, momentarily surprised to find her

standing right beside him. How could he have not felt her bluebonnet eyes on him? Or caught her fresh spring scent? The realization should have been one of relief—he had been restored to his old, undistractable self—except now that he'd noticed those details about Lilibeth, he doubted he'd ever forget them again.

"Would you like to take a look at the garage now?" she asked.

No, he'd rather take her upstairs and—

"Yes, that would be fine. I'm anxious to get back to work on my projects." That surely would be an antidote to his wayward thoughts.

THE OVERSIZE GARAGE smelled of dust and disuse.

One wall was lined with wine racks of liquid-filled green bottles Alex presumed were Aunt Tilly's concoction. Other than that, the space was cluttered with cardboard boxes of various sizes, an old heating-oil drum, which he thought he might be able to use for something, and a long workbench littered with odds and ends that would be perfect for his projects.

"Have you been an inventor long?" Lilibeth asked.

"All my life, I suppose." Dust billowed as he lifted a coil of coaxial cable from the workbench. "When I was about five, my first effort was to invent a robot to hang up my clothes and put away my toys at night. Mother insisted everything be neat and tidy by bedtime."

"Did it work?"

"There were a few glitches," he admitted, peering

into a carton that held Batman comic books. "It kept taking my clean clothes off the hangers and stuffing them in the toy box. Mother wasn't too keen on that."

Lilibeth giggled, and he smiled at her. She was standing in a column of sunlight near the open garage doors, dust motes dancing around her like playful fairies. The impression was magical, as though she'd been transported to that very spot specifically to bring joy to Alex's heart.

"What's the very best thing you've ever invented?" she asked.

"So far?" He considered the question a moment, or rather was unable to give it his full attention because he was focused on the way her waist narrowed above the feminine swell of her hips and how the sun haloed her golden hair. "A few years ago I invented a spoon that measured the fat content of each bite that was about to be taken."

"Oh, that sounds interesting. People are so into dieting these days."

"That's what I thought, too." Although, from his perspective, Lilibeth had no need to worry on that count.

"Did you sell your idea?"

"Not exactly. There were a few drawbacks to my concept." The bowl of the spoon was so large, a person required a mouth the size of Eartha Kitt's in order to get anything to eat. By then, the food had turned into the consistency of mush. "Basically the food industry squelched the concept. They'd just as soon their customers weren't too aware of what they're eating. But I was able to patent the mechanism.''

''Then maybe someday you'll be able to market the idea.''

Alex felt his chest puff out. Most people laughed at his inventions. Lilibeth was different. She actually believed one day he might succeed.

That possibility would never come to fruition if he continued to let his libido be in charge of his thoughts when he should be getting down to work.

''Well,'' he said, picking up a box to carry outside. ''Let's see if we can sort through some of this to make room for my projects.''

Apparently unconcerned she'd get her dress dirty, Lilibeth pitched right in, sorting and repacking boxes, discarding items she felt her parents wouldn't miss. Not every woman would have been so willing, and her presence made it a companionable task.

''Do you and your family live nearby?'' Alex asked as she shook out any possible spiders from a broom that had been worn almost to the nub.

''About a half mile south of Main Street.'' With a toss of her head, she shifted her hair behind her shoulder. There was a smudge on her cheek, which Alex had a desperate urge to wipe away. ''My folks built themselves a new house when I was about ten. Business was much better then, before the main highway was built. Construction skirted around Nowhere and went through Groundhog Station instead, just like they did with the railroad years and years ago. I don't imagine anyone in town has forgiven the folks in Groundhog for either event.''

"Oh, I don't know. If the highway went through here, you'd lose a lot of the town's charm.''

She looked up in surprise. "You *like* Nowhere Junction?''

"From what I've seen of it.'' He smiled at her thinking she was the most charming thing any town could possess. "Of course, I don't know that I'll be staying long. I only signed a contract through the end of the school year.'' With most of his prior jobs, he hadn't lasted that long.

Her expression crumbled. "Maybe you'll find a reason to stay.''

His gaze locked with hers, and he felt a band tighten around his chest. He couldn't make any plans for the future, not until he'd established himself as a Peabody to be reckoned with.

Forcefully setting that thought aside, he glanced around the garage. They'd cleared out a large area, plenty big enough for his workshop.

He eyed the shelves of Joy Juice. "You want to leave those bottles where they are?''

"If they're not in your way.'' Casually she brushed some dirt off her bodice, and he watched her hand skim over her breast, fascinated by the way her rose-tipped fingernails flashed across the smooth cotton fabric. "In fact, how would you like to sample a little of Aunt Tilly's best?''

"Sure. Why not?''

She found a sealed container of wineglasses and removed two, holding them up to the light, then tugged the cork out of one of the green bottles lining the shelves.

"This has quite a kick, so you don't want to overdo," she warned.

The liquid was a rich golden color that reminded Alex of tales of lost mines in Mexico. She poured a finger's width into each glass and offered one to Alex.

"Welcome to Nowhere," she said softly, raising her glass in a toast.

"Thank you." He touched her glass with his, the soft ping like the note of a perfect kazoo, or so he imagined. Continuing to hold her gaze, he felt the liquid slide smoothly down his throat, warming him, until it hit bottom. Then it spread out in rivers of heat that raced down to his toes and up to muddle his brain.

He blinked. "Whew! That stuff is so potent, it must be at least two-hundred proof!"

She laughed and her eyes twinkled with mischief. "The second sip goes down even smoother than the first, which is why we have to warn folks to go easy with it."

"Unless they're planning to use it to launch a rocket."

"I don't think that's what Aunt Tilly had in mind."

Leaning back against the workbench, he swirled the golden liquid in his glass, an almost reckless feeling coming over him.

"There's a special school-board meeting tonight."

"Oh? I don't attend the meetings often. You know, not having any children in school and all, there isn't much point." Although she had been the one to suggest the school board advertise on the Internet for Uncle Dick's replacement. The effort had paid off for the school; she could only hope it would pay off for her, too.

"They're going to confirm my appointment as principal—at least it's on the agenda. It'd be nice to have a friend in the audience. Someone who's glad to have me in town." He reached out to touch her cheek, drawing his finger along the dirt smudge he'd been so eager to erase. "I'd like it if you'd come along...to be that person. *If* you wouldn't mind."

Lilibeth shivered, the heat of Alex's fingertip even warmer than the Joy Juice sprinting through her midsection.

She wouldn't consider missing the school-board meeting. She wouldn't risk a chance encounter between Alex and a single woman in town without being nearby to protect her interests.

She had four months to convince Alexander Peabody to stay in Nowhere. So, until the end of the school year she was going to stick to the man like a burr to a floppy-eared hound dog.

Which wouldn't be a burden at all.

WITH THE SUNSET, the temperature had dropped to the mid-forties and everyone sitting under the circus tent was wearing jackets; a few wore gloves and hats, too.

The entire town—especially the school board—would be happy when the new school was completed along with a decent furnace. It was only due to Quade Gardiner's generosity in renting the big top and several sideshow tents that the students hadn't had to attend their archrival's school at Groundhog Station during construction.

The school board was still debating what to call the new facility, although the name most often mentioned was Mazeppa's Nowhere School since she was the one who had contributed the money to build it.

The school-board members were chatting in the center ring of what used to be a one-and-a-half-ring circus.

"I've got to go shake some hands," Alex said, glancing down at Lilibeth. "I'll see you after the meeting?"

"Sure. Just be careful not to eat too much of Finella's Spring Salad on the potluck table."

He cocked a questioning brow.

"Don't worry. I'll explain later."

He walked off, and Lilibeth tucked her hands in her jacket pockets, admiring the length of his stride, his casual athleticism, and a pair of great buns. A woman could lose her heart to a man like Alex—or get it broken. As her mother had said, it wasn't smart to get involved with an outsider. For the sake of her parents, Lilibeth was stuck in Nowhere. She had to be sure they were cared for in their waning years.

Which meant she might well have to sacrifice her own dreams.

With a sigh, she crossed the tent to say hello to Buffy Murchison and Lucy Gardiner, who had brought their babies to the meeting, as their new husbands were members of the school board.

"Oh, look at these little guys," Lilibeth crooned. "They're growing so fast." She chucked Donnie, one of Lucy's eighteen-month-old twins, under the chin, and gave Doreen a quick peck on the cheek. Actually they weren't Lucy's twins, per se, they *were* Quade's, and he had married Lucy after she'd delivered the babies to him as part of her job as a courier. It was, well, a little complicated to even consider.

Then she eyed Lucy's belly, which was protruding with a pregnancy that was about to pop. "Soon?" she asked.

Lucy groaned. "Believe me, I've got Dr. Mimsy on a short leash. No way is she going out of town again—for a honeymoon or anything else—until this kickboxer inside me decides to make an in-person appearance."

Repressing a sharp tug of envy, Lilibeth laughed and sat down beside Buffy.

"Hey, Lilibeth," Buffy said. Her own daughter, Callie, was playing on her knee with a cell phone. "Who was that hunk you walked in with?"

Lilibeth smiled in a proprietary way. "The new school principal. He's rented Mimsy's old apartment above the drugstore."

The two young mothers eyed each other, then glanced back at Lilibeth.

"You go, girl!" Lucy said.

"Looks like a winner to me," Buffy agreed. "Drop by my shop and we'll see if we can fix you up with a femme fatale outfit that will knock his socks off."

Tempted to deny they'd figured out exactly what was on her mind, Lilibeth started to act embarrassed, but Quade took that moment to gavel the meeting to order.

"Let's get started, folks," he said.

"I move to waive the reading of the minutes," Finella said, not missing a beat with her knitting needles.

From the far end of the table where the board members were seated, Horace Popsworthy, owner of the local dry goods store and defeated candidate for town mayor, popped up. "Does anyone actually take minutes? We haven't heard them since—"

Quade banged his gavel again. "Sit down, Horace. We didn't do anything at the last meeting anyway."

Carter elbowed Quade. "Let's get this meeting over, okay? It's not good for Callie to stay up too late." He glanced in Buffy's direction, a salacious grin on his face. "Isn't that right, hon?"

Buffy sighed. "Isn't he the most commanding man you've ever seen?" she said dreamily.

Lilibeth hadn't ever seen him in quite that light, but there was no doubt the two of them made a perfect couple. As did, to almost everyone's surprise, Lucy and Quade. Lucy had been such a rolling stone, and Quade so wedded to the ranch he'd inherited, few had thought the relationship would last. But together they'd made it work. Lilibeth couldn't help but envy their good fortune in finding each other.

"The minutes are approved as not read," Quade announced. "Now then, the only thing on the agenda tonight is the confirmation of our new school principal, Alexander Peabody. He has furnished us with a résumé—"

"I don't give a fig about his résumé!" Gigi Wernicke, the owner of the Nowhere Grocery Store, raised her bulk from one of the stands previously used by the circus elephants during their shows. "I wanna know if Peabody can figure out a way our kids can beat those varmints from Groundhog Station at *something!*"

Billy Dell Grimes, the only member of the school board with children currently attending the Nowhere school, nodded enthusiastically. "I second that."

"That wasn't a motion, Billy Dell," Quade commented.

"Don't matter. That's how we all feel. There's gotta be *something* our kids can do better than those youngsters over at Groundhog."

As though arising from the sea, Alex stood and walked purposely into the center ring. He turned and faced the audience. They all grew silent. Watchful.

"I know I'm new here, and I haven't had a chance to meet you or the students of this community, but I do understand the need to succeed. I've been striving toward that goal since I was a very young man." The intensity of his gaze swept the tent, energizing everyone there. He straightened his shoulders, flexed his fingers into fists. "If there is any way for the students of

Nowhere Junction to achieve success over your rivals at Groundhog Station, I vow to find it.''

With a cheer loud enough to be heard in Groundhog, everyone leaped to their feet, Lilibeth included. She'd never felt so proud. So confident of any man's capacity to succeed.

Suddenly she was bursting with confidence. Sure, some of his inventions might have been less than successful. But he was determined. That, she knew, was three-quarters of the battle. Without doubt, he'd never give up on his goal.

But then, she wouldn't, either.

She glanced over at Buffy, sharing a conspiratorial smile. ''I'll drop by your boutique tomorrow and see what femme fatale outfits you've got in stock.''

If being sexy was the thing she did best, so be it. For years she'd disguised she had a brain as well as a figure. That's what others expected of her. She'd happily forgo that secret part of her persona to have the home and family she so desperately craved.

3

ALEX PULLED HIS horn-rimmed glasses from his shirt pocket and slid them on. It was the first day of the new semester, his first as the Nowhere principal, and already he could tell the kids were up to some kind of mischief in the play yard.

The glasses were one of his more notable inventions. A small switch on the side of the frame altered the focal length of the lens, much like the zoom function on a camera, changing ordinary glasses into seven-power binoculars. While not a commercial success, the glasses did have their uses.

In this case, for spying on unwary students.

He frowned a little as he focused on the action.

"Bull's-eye!" one youngster shouted.

"Naw. You missed by a mile."

"Did not! It's my turn."

There was some pushing and shoving among the gaggle of preadolescent boys, then a *snap*! "I got him!"

Alex decided to investigate at closer range.

"What's going on, gentlemen?" The gathering of youngsters parted like the Red Sea, leaving one student standing in the middle, a rubber-band gun in his hand—a rather imaginatively designed one as far as Alex could see. "What's your name, young man?"

"Dell Grimes," the boy said petulantly. "You can't do nothin' to me. My dad's on the school board."

"Looks like you've got a multiple-shot, rubber-band gun there. I haven't seen one that clever since I made one in sixth grade."

The boy's eyes widened with respect. "You made one?"

"Of course. I could hit a fly with it from twenty paces, and nail him again if he happened to get away."

"Wow. Rapid fire."

The boys murmured their approval and edged in closer around him.

Alex extended his hand. "Let me see how you made yours."

Cautiously Dell passed the gun over for Alex's inspection. Well made from pine, it had a trigger mechanism that was quite effective. "You'll get a faster release if you put a touch of grease on the front notch."

"Yeah?" Dell and the others crowded in to get a better look. They were all in the twelve- to fourteen-year-old age range, the oldest boys in school and probably the leaders—for good or ill. No doubt they expected him to confiscate the weapon. There wasn't much point, as Alex well knew. The kid would simply go home and make a better version.

"So what's your target?" Alex asked.

"Them armadillos that started showing up since the construction began," a dark-haired boy volunteered.

"They're weird," another youngster said.

"Like they've got a target right on their backs. A big ol' bull's-eye." Dell pointed to a spot about thirty feet away where the strangest-looking armadillo Alex had ever seen was slowly making his way through the dirt and weeds, oblivious that he was a target of the rubber-band militia. Dusty red concentric circles in the form of a bull's-eye looked as if they'd been painted on the armadillo's sides.

Genus bull's-eye armadillo Dasypodidae? He must have missed that biology lesson.

"You guys wouldn't be spoofing me, would you?" he asked. He wouldn't be the first principal to fall for a practical joke.

"Naw. We thought it was a joke, too—like maybe those Groundhog kids were trying to pull one over on us—until we found a whole nest of 'em. Little babies 'n everything."

Alex considered that. If this was a unique subspecies of armadillo, he wouldn't want the local tree-huggers to get wind of it. They'd be sure to slow construction of the new school, which was only about half built. The builders, who were well behind schedule, were only now beginning to dig the foundation trenches for the gym.

It wasn't that Alex didn't favor environmental efforts. He just dreaded the thought of an army of armadillo lovers showing up on the school's doorstep.

"Recess is about over." He handed the gun back to Dell. "Why don't we give the poor armadillo a rest? And keep that gun out of sight, would you?" With the son of a school-board member, he wasn't sure zero tolerance could be enforced without getting himself fired the first day on the job.

Dell shrugged in the disinterested way only an adolescent could. "I guess."

Turning, Alex headed back toward the colorful circus tents, the boys falling into step beside him. He felt like Pied Piper.

"I understand Nowhere would like to beat Groundhog Station at some competition. You boys have any ideas?"

"There's the annual tug-of-war coming up," Dell said. "It's our seventh- and eighth-grade boys against theirs."

"And they've got twice as many guys as we do," a redheaded kid with more cowlicks than freckles pointed out.

A pint-size youngster spoke up. "Besides, they're all lard-butts. It'd take a tank to budge 'em."

"Well, why don't we put our heads together later on, see if we can't find a way for the underdogs to come out on top this time." Alex understood what it was like to be small and outnumbered by a mob of bullies. It wasn't until college that he had begun to put on some weight and muscle. He'd learned early on that the most overdeveloped muscle could be outmaneuvered by a well-developed mind.

That would be a good lesson to teach the kids of Nowhere Junction.

THE STRETCH TOP LILIBETH bought at Buffy's Boutique showed off her endowments to the greatest advantage and left her midriff bare; the miniskirt scarcely reached midthigh, allowing a long, slow look at her legs. The sparkling silver, snakeskin boots added a good three inches to her height. Buffy had assured her no man would be able to resist a woman in this getup.

Lilibeth was ready to strut her stuff.

The moment she saw Alex walking down the street from school, she struck a pose in front of the paperback books display, a copy of *Seductress* in her hand, where he couldn't miss seeing the suggestive cover. Smiling, she practiced a low, sexy growl and batted her eyelashes.

Then she watched him walk right past the store and around toward the back entrance of the building.

Her smile dissolved. The crick she'd gotten in her back from cocking her hip out too far started to ache, and she straightened.

"Well, darn it all!"

Shoving the book back in the rack, she hurried toward the rear of the store. The damn boots weren't worth spit as running shoes.

She reached the storeroom as the back door opened. In an effort to strike another pose, her hand snagged a bin of St. Patrick's Day tie clips left over from last year, spilling them onto the counter and floor.

Fighting to keep her smile in place and act casual, she was appalled she'd once again acted uncharacteristically klutzy in front of him. "Hi, Alex, how was your first day of school?" she said breathily.

He stopped dead in his tracks. His dark eyes flared, and Lilibeth celebrated that she had gained his attention. She threw back her shoulders to add to the effect.

"Shouldn't you wait until after Valentine's Day before you start on St. Patrick's?"

Disappointment ripped through her. He'd failed to notice her or her new outfit, which she was damn well going to return to Buffy for a refund. It had cost her a pretty penny. "I was, uh, just checking to see—"

He swallowed, his Adam's apple bobbing in a fascinating rhythm, and he slowly blinked his eyes.

Before she could finish her thought, he turned and went up the stairs, taking them two at a time. She heard the door to his apartment open and close behind him.

For several seconds, the echo of that closing door reverberated in her head, bouncing around like a ball in a pinball game.

Dadgum it! Alexander Peabody might be a hard nut to crack, but that only meant she had to try harder. Anything worth having took some effort. Until now, Lilibeth hadn't realized how much.

Despite her trembling chin, and the tears that threatened, she vowed she wouldn't give up.

Upstairs, Alex stood in the middle of his small living room with its mismatched furniture and breathed deeply trying to slow his heartbeat. One flight of stairs shouldn't have driven the air from his lungs or left him weak in the knees.

All of his adult life he'd wanted to be met at the door by a woman who asked how his day had gone.

He hadn't expected her to be a blond goddess. Or that he would be so poleaxed he'd make stupid comments about St. Patrick's Day instead of telling her she was the sexiest woman he'd ever seen.

Lilibeth Anderson had him so unsettled he didn't know which way was up. He couldn't allow that to continue, his lack of composure, the sensation that he'd been kicked in the chest every time he unexpectedly caught sight of her, as he had that morning when she greeted him with a cup of coffee at the foot of the stairs when he was leaving for school. It had taken most of the morning for her image to slip from his mind, and then it was only temporary, mere minutes at a time.

He couldn't keep thinking about her full red lips—and what he'd like her to do with them—and hope to get any work done. Either at school or in his workshop.

Changing his clothes, he girded himself for another encounter. If he was prepared, surely his reaction wouldn't be so potent. So out of control.

With measured steps, he went downstairs, only to discover whatever mental preparations he'd made were worse than useless. His heart tripped a beat when he found her sitting on the floor of the storeroom, slowly picking up one gaudy tie clip at a time, dropping them into the basket from which they had spilled. She looked up at him with glistening blue eyes.

Damn! His stupid remark had made her cry.

"Here, let me help." He crouched down beside her, catching a whiff of her sweet scent. Today it was strawberries and her cheeks were the color of rich cream. He had an urge to discover if she tasted as delicious as the combination suggested.

"It's all right." Glancing away, she dropped a tiny leprechaun into the bin with the tie clips.

Frantically Alex searched for a way to make her smile again—and get his thoughts focused on something else. "How about I fix the bell over the front door. I noticed yesterday it's broken. Then I can get started on automating your restocking cart."

"You don't have to—"

"I want to." He covered her hand with his and found her skin warm and soft, her fingers slim, her nails the same red as her lips. She wore no rings. A shudder went through him as he imagined what it would feel like to have her caressing him. Intimately.

She blinked, slowly opening and closing those blue eyes, as if she had experienced the same thought. "If you really want to. Fix the bell, I mean."

He mentally backpedaled. "No problem. I'll just, uh, get my tools from the workshop."

In a cowardly dash, he escaped out the back door. He was definitely going to have to do something about his reaction to Lilibeth Anderson.

He simply couldn't figure out what.

IN THE NEXT HOUR, practically the entire town showed up at the drugstore and café, then stayed while Alex fussed with the bell over the door. Lilibeth was so busy, she barely had time to admire his efforts.

Gigi Wernicke came in from her grocery store across the street to pick up a prescription of her diet medicine, which she'd been taking for years to no effect. Selecting one of the six tables in the café, she lowered her self onto a chair at the ice-cream counter and ordered a banana split.

George Weinbucket, president of the First National Bank of Nowhere, dropped by to read a copy of the *Wall Street Journal* as he did every day, and asked for a cup of coffee. Whenever he was done with the paper, he'd fold it neatly and put it back on the rack. Never in all the years Lilibeth had known him had George actually purchased a newspaper, although he'd been the one to insist Anderson Coffee Shop and Drugstore make them available. Because of delivery problems to Nowhere, the news he so eagerly sought was always two days old. No one Lilibeth knew asked George for investment advice.

Lilibeth made it a point to follow the stock market via the Internet, although she had little money to invest.

Within minutes of pouring George's coffee, Bobette Moriarty, Lilibeth's best friend, slid onto a stool at the counter. "Gimme a cherry cola, will ya, hon." Grinning, she gestured over her shoulder at Alex. "And an order of him to go."

Lilibeth bristled. "He's not for sale. Besides, you're already engaged."

"True." She sighed. A big-boned woman, she had dark blond hair and gray-green eyes that sparkled when she was having fun. At the moment, she looked down.

Scooping some chipped ice into a glass, Lilibeth squirted in some flavoring and filled it with cola from the spigot. "Things are not going well between you and your mattress salesman?"

"They're fine, I suppose. But Bob is really ticked at me for falling for a guy from Groundhog Station."

Bobette's brother, a part-time sheriff, was grumpy most of the time, but he'd been upset for months about his sister's pending marriage. "Doesn't he realize there aren't all that many eligible men around here?" Lilibeth glanced at Alex, who was standing on a stepladder installing a new chime above the door to replace the broken bell. If she were smart, she'd put a fence around the man and not let any woman within a mile of him. Not even her best friend.

"Bob doesn't see any reason to get married at all and can't figure out why I'd want to. Particularly to Barney."

"Men just don't understand, do they? About a woman's need to be loved, to have a family of her own." *And to enjoy a little hanky-panky with a good-looking man.*

Alex climbed down from the ladder, and set it aside. He smiled over at Lilibeth, an adorable grin that creased his cheek and made her think of a little boy who'd just done something wonderful.

"Here we go," he said. With a flair, he opened the door.

The five-note chime started well enough. The first four tones were as clear and pure as the bells on the Nowhere Nearer to Thee O Lord Church steeple. The fifth chime, though, was so off-key, the sour note like fingernails on a blackboard, that Lilibeth covered her ears.

Grimacing, everyone in the store looked up.

George half jumped out of his chair, wadding the newspaper into a wrinkled mess that he'd never be able to refold. "What the devil was that?"

Lilibeth's mother appeared from the back room. "Did somebody let a sick cat in here?"

"Wow! That's enough to wiggle your fillings," Bobette exclaimed, rolling her eyes.

Determined not to have Alex's feelings get hurt because of his tone deafness, Lilibeth darted out from behind the counter. "You've fixed it," she said eagerly. "Now we'll be sure to know if anyone comes in the store."

"Helluva deterrent to thieves," Gigi said. "Ask him if he'll put one of them things on the door at my grocery store. Folks are always walking off with basket loads of my specials."

"How many cans of sardines do you think people want?" JoJo asked.

"My special this week is dried split peas. That's a delicacy, in case you hadn't heard."

"Don't tell Finella or she'll be putting peas in her

yellow Jell-O from now till the end of the school year.''

George visibly paled at the mention of his wife's culinary efforts. ''And I'm the one who has to eat up all the leftovers.''

Lilibeth linked her arm through Alex's and spoke softly. ''Thank you for fixing the door.''

''It's okay, isn't it?'' he asked. ''I mean, did I get the setting right? It might be a little loud.''

''It's perfect. Every time the door opens, I'll think of you.'' Her fillings would no doubt remind her.

She winced as the door opened again.

Stopping in mid-doorway, Lucas McRifle, the newest resident of Nowhere, glanced up at the source of the off-key sound. He shot Lilibeth a questioning look, his dark eyes widening with curiosity. ''Mimsy's out of rubbing alcohol at the clinic. Have you got any?''

''Sure. Second aisle over on the bottom shelf.''

''Thanks.'' Following her directions, his long, jean-clad legs took him to the merchandise and back again with a certain degree of haste. ''Put it on her tab, okay?''

''No problem.''

As soon as the door closed behind Lucas, Alex asked, ''Who was that?''

The one who got away. Not that Lilibeth any longer cared. The Internet had brought her someone even more interesting and more good-looking, or so she thought. ''Lucas McRifle. He married Mimsy Miles, our town doctor, a few weeks ago.''

Alex nodded. "The woman who lived in the apartment before me."

"You and he might enjoy each other's company. He discovered a new skin cream made of coconut oil that takes ten years off a woman's appearance."

Eyeing her, Alex smiled one of his gentle smiles. "You certainly won't be needing any of his cream for a good many years."

A warm sense of pleasure rippled through Lilibeth. Alex Peabody knew how to say the right thing to please a woman.

FOR THE NEXT WEEK, Alex managed to be so busy at school and on his current invention, he avoided any intimate contact with Lilibeth. Not that he wasn't aware of her presence anytime their paths crossed. Which included her appearance in some rather explicit dreams.

Damn! He hadn't had *that* kind of an erotic dream and such a potent reaction since his adolescent years when he was in the throes of true love with Anne Marie Farmer, a whiz at geometry.

At school, Alex had kept himself well occupied teaching special classes on the mathematics of pulleys, weights and levers to the upper-grade boys. Given their motivation to beat Groundhog Station, they took to the elementary principles of physics as though they were the greatest thing since apple butter. In fact, the girls were beginning to complain the boys were getting too serious.

Within another week, he'd have the girls begging to

get into the same class. Unless the boys lost the tug-of-war to Groundhog Station.

But now the moment of truth had come for the automated restocking system he'd designed for Lilibeth. Over the years he'd created a lot of robots. Not all of them had been successful.

He waited until late in the day when the drugstore and coffee shop were closed, and her parents had gone home for the night.

"I call it a Multi-Environment Stock Shelver," he told Lilibeth, who was standing in the test aisle looking terrific in tight-fitting jeans and a crop top. It seemed every day she wore a different outfit, each one more alluring than the one before. "If it works, it could save you hours of work every week."

"I'm sure it will be wonderful. But you might want to think of a different name for your invention."

He frowned. "Why?"

"The acronym. M.E.S.S.? Are you sure that's the message you want to send?"

"Hmm, let's see how it works."

He had a motor attached to the cart's wheels and mechanical arms that could pick up products from the cart, placing them on the shelves in the appropriate places. All the operator needed to do, once the layout of the shelves was loaded into the robot's computer, was place the merchandise on the trays in the preselected slots, then flick on the switch. The robot would do the rest.

"You ready to give it a try?" he asked.

A little smile played at the corners of her sensual lips. "More than ready."

Alex swallowed hard and threw the switch. If this device worked well, he might be able to patent it. Make a name for himself. Become a Peabody of stature.

The cart edged forward on command. A robotic hand on the right took hold of a bottle of shampoo. Without squeezing too hard, the fingers lifted the plastic bottle. The arm swiveled, knocking over six rows of similar products and placed the new shampoo on the shelf with as much delicacy as a mother kissing her baby.

"There might be a few problems to work out," Alex admitted.

"I'm not worried." She smiled at him and he thought he could conquer the world.

The left arm twitched. Its robotic hand squeezed a package of Fantastic Body so hard, bath oil sprayed the air with the scent of sultry magnolias. The excess liquid dribbled down the mechanical arm, shorting the circuits. A tongue of flame spurted out, igniting the oil.

"Oh, damn!" Alex dived for the cutoff switch. Before he got there, the right arm made a swipe at the toothpaste shelf, snared a hapless box and squeezed it until white-and-blue striped goo exploded out of the cardboard.

Overhead, a smoke alarm went off.

"I'll get it." Lilibeth raced for a stepladder, climbed up and disconnected the screeching alarm.

Alex wrestled the cart to a halt, failure once again

heavy in his chest. Of all his projects, he'd wanted this one to succeed. It wouldn't have mattered if he hadn't made a fortune on it. He'd simply wanted to impress Lilibeth.

She rested her hand on his arm. "It's all right. All inventors have tons of failures. That doesn't mean you'll never succeed."

She was so sweet, so caring, her blue eyes so filled with concern and understanding. Her lips so close. Inviting. How could he possibly resist?

Slowly, he dipped his head. Her seductive fragrance easily vanquished the bitter scent of burned wiring, his sense of failure. His lips brushed hers, finding them warm and moist. Intriguing. Offering no resistance. He wanted to delve deeper. Explore the depth of passion he suspected lay beneath her innocent veneer.

But that wouldn't be fair. He had little to offer her.

With a heroic effort, he pulled back. "This is no good," he whispered.

She blinked up at him. "It was fine...as far as it went."

"No, you don't understand. I can't commit to... anything. Not until I've proven myself."

A delicate V formed between her brows. "Proven yourself?"

"I'm the black sheep of the Peabody clan, Lilibeth. Until I've shown them I measure up, I simply can't—" His voice caught. "I'm sorry."

The translucent light left her eyes, the eagerness that

was her hallmark, and Alex cursed himself for disappointing her. But he had to be honest. To be otherwise went against all that he and the Peabody name stood for.

4

LILIBETH COULD STILL FEEL the lingering imprint of
Alex's lips on hers the next morning as she trudged
into Buffy's Boutique, yesterday's bundle of clothes
neatly folded in her arms. She felt like such a failure.
Another eligible man was about to get away.

This was no longer a matter of principle.

She *liked* Alex. A lot. She wanted to think he could
be *the one*. The answer to her dreams of home and
family.

Buffy looked at her aghast. "Don't tell me Alex
didn't notice your bare midriff! You've got a dynamite
figure. How could he possibly not be drooling—"

"He doesn't seem to be the kind of man who
drools." She lay the package on the glass-top counter
that displayed accessories. By offering deep discounts
and going out of her way to know her customers, Buffy
had made a big success of her store. Even women from
Groundhog Station came here to shop.

"You mean he's dead?" Buffy asked.

"Oh, no." Definitely warm and alive, his kiss so
sweet Lilibeth had lain awake half the night reliving
the experience. "He just can't make a commitment."

Buffy made a vague gesture of dismissal in the air. "That doesn't mean anything. No man wants to commit right off. It's the nature of the beast."

"He has a good reason."

"So did Carter, at least he thought so. Quade, too, according to Lucy. But we wore 'em down."

Lilibeth didn't think that was going to work with Alex. The only thing that would solve the problem would be his creating an invention worth megabucks. Then he'd probably go home to Cleveland to his Peabody clan; there'd be no reason for him to stay in Nowhere.

Buffy shook out the designer jeans and lay them on the counter. "Maybe the problem is you scare him."

"Me? Scare Alex? I don't think so." If anything, Alex intimidated her. She'd never known anyone so intelligent and good-looking to boot.

"Guys are funny. You never know what they're thinking." Cocking her head, she studied Lilibeth. "Maybe what we need here is a little reverse psychology."

"If you're talking about breast reduction—"

"No, no. Nothing so drastic."

"No offense, but I don't want to dye my hair, either." Buffy changed hair color almost as often as most women changed underwear, although that particular habit seemed to have slowed since she married Carter. She'd been a strawberry-blonde for weeks now.

"Maybe the problem is we've put too much of you

on display. We haven't left anything to Alex's imagination."

"I haven't exactly been going around naked in front of him." Although, Lilibeth thought, if that would make him consider commitment, she might well give it a try.

"I think I know of something that might just do the trick." Buffy pulled her cell phone from its holster and punched in some numbers. "I'll tell them it's an emergency and talk them out of charging for overnight delivery."

If anyone could persuade a person to do something, Lilibeth was confident Buffy could. She was far less confident of Alex's reaction to whatever costume the boutique owner selected for her.

She was about to leave the shop when Dr. Mimsy arrived. "Hi, Mimsy. I thought you already bought out everything in Buffy's shop for your honeymoon."

A hint of color stained the doctor's cheeks. "I was actually hoping to find a couple of new nightgowns. Something, uh…"

"Sexy?" Buffy provided, after she closed her cell phone.

The color deepened on Mimsy's face. "Lucas does like to see me in pretty things."

Suppressing a chuckle, Lilibeth said, "I've got to get back to the drugstore. You have fun shopping. I'm sure Lucas will appreciate your efforts." Waving goodbye, she left the boutique. She envied Mimsy's newfound happiness and hoped she'd soon be shopping for her own trousseau—including lots of sexy nighties.

WORD GOT AROUND TOWN in a hurry that the new school principal had a scheme for his students to win the tug-of-war between Nowhere and Groundhog. Lilibeth decided the event provided a perfect venue to try out her latest outfit, a loose-fitting Hawaiian muumuu that covered her from her neck to her ankles and disguised her figure. The turquoise floral print went well with her fair complexion, however, and she'd piled her hair on top of her head in studied disarray.

If this didn't work, the next step would be to turn herself into a Mazeppa look-alike and see if *that* attracted Alex's attention.

Filled with anticipation, she drove the forty-five minutes to Groundhog Station.

What she hadn't counted on was the crowd of townspeople from both communities filling the bleachers at the Groundhog High School playing field. Alex might not see her at all, much less notice her among the waving sea of Nowhere And Proud Of It banners.

Oddly enough, each of the Nowhere boys wore scuba-diving weight belts around their waists. Behind the last boy, they'd set up a big wooden frame with pulleys along the top and bales of hay dangling from ropes that were lashed to the far thicker tug-of-war rope. The two teams had lined up on opposite sides of a sand pit that had been turned into a muddy hog wallow.

As the audience quieted, waiting for the event to begin, the heated discussion between Alex and the principal of Groundhog was audible.

"I see nothing in the rules to prevent the use of pulleys and weights," Alex asserted.

"What rules? It's a damn tug-of-war. One team against the other." Clements Vandorphin was livid, his weathered cheeks turning a bright red.

"We both represent institutions of learning. If Nowhere's young men have applied certain principles of—"

"You're cheating, that's what you're doing."

"We're overcoming the handicap of facing superior numbers. It's seems reasonable—"

Someone in the stands shouted, "Come on! Ain't got us all day!"

A "Go Groundhogs!" chant started and began to swell in volume.

The "Go Nowhere!" chant was soon swallowed beneath the cheers of the local crowd.

Vandorphin shook his finger in Alex's face. Alex remained outwardly calm, although Lilibeth could see the tension in his shoulders—the determination to win. She held her breath as the two men stepped aside.

The designated referee, the mayor of Groundhog, Wally Washought, raised a red-and-white striped flag to commence the contest. But before he lowered his hand, the Groundhog boys began tugging on the rope. The Nowhere boys, despite being outnumbered and caught off guard, held their own for a minute, the rope stretching as both sides pulled for all they were worth. The extra weight seemed to be helping. If only—

Then slowly, as the Nowhere team members dug in their heels, their feet began to slip. Like a glacier moving under the heat of the sun, the entire team edged forward toward the muddy pit. Behind them, the wooden frame with its bales of hay began to wobble.

Groundhog supporters came to their feet, shouting, "Go! Go! Go! Hogs!"

Suddenly, one of the critical wooden supports splintered. Hay bales dropped to the ground. Ropes went slack. Encouraged by their success and the cheers of the crowd, the Groundhog team increased their efforts.

In a rush, the Nowhere boys were dragged through the mud. They'd lost again, the twenty-seventh year in a row.

From the stands, Lilibeth saw Alex's shoulders slump, and her heart went out to him. He'd so wanted his students to succeed.

She waited until the crowd dispersed, the dejected Nowhere kids back on the bus, and then walked down onto the field. Alex was picking up the debris of his failed device, tossing the shards of wood into the back of his pickup.

"I'm sorry your boys lost," she said softly.

He looked up, his eyes filled with a deep sadness. He was so distressed even the neat row of pens and pencils in his plastic pocket protector looked out of sorts. "It was foreordained."

"How can you say that? You did everything you could—"

"They greased our side of the mush pit. The boys couldn't get any footing. It's a primitive way to cheat, but I should have noticed."

Lilibeth wasn't surprised Groundhog hadn't played fair. That was the nature of the town's relationship with Nowhere, which wasn't fair, either, since they'd always managed to draw the long straw. "Why didn't you complain?"

"What good would it do?" He picked up a splintered two-by-four and heaved it into the truck. "We're on their turf. But we'll get 'em next time."

"Next time?" A year from now when the tug-of-war contest reconvened? Her hopes flared that Alex was planning to be here—

"The boys tell me the Great Groundhog Crate Race is coming up, and we'll be hosting it this year." He grinned at her, that wonderful smile that creased his cheek and gave him such a rakish look. "This time they'll play by *our* rules."

That wasn't quite the answer she'd been hoping for, she thought, repressing a sigh. "I'll be there rooting for you—and Nowhere school, of course." A breeze caught a wayward strand of her hair, teasing it across her face, and she shoved it back into place.

His gaze followed her gesture, his eyes narrowing slightly. "You've changed your hair."

"I didn't think you'd notice."

"I notice everything about you, Lilibeth." His Adam's apple bobbed as he swallowed. *"Everything."*

A shimmer of pleasure rippled through her. Maybe she wouldn't have to dress ugly after all.

THE FIRST BUSLOAD of protesters arrived at Nowhere Elementary School before seven o'clock the next morning.

Pulling on his jacket, Alex left the sideshow tent that served as the principal's office and went outside to see what was causing all the racket. An early riser, he'd been fine-tuning his recently designed robotic pencil sharpener. Unfortunately the device still reduced every pencil he inserted to precisely one inch, no matter the original length.

Men and women, some with children in strollers, spilled out of the bus, all of them carrying placards.

Save The Armadillos
Armadillos Have Rights Too
Groundhogs Support Armadillos

Alex recognized the leader of the group, who was organizing his followers into a picket line around the school construction site. It was yesterday's referee for the tug-of-war contest, the mayor of Groundhog Station, Wally Washought.

Striding across the asphalt, Alex headed directly for the mayor. "Is there a problem, Mr. Washought?"

"Not at all." The mayor gave him a sly smile that

made him resemble a ferret with thinning hair the color of nutmeg. "Assuming you're willing to stop school construction to protect the habitat of an endangered species."

"Just which species did you have in mind?" As if Alex didn't know.

"You don't have to play coy with me, Peabody. One of your boys let it slip that you've discovered a new species of armadillos here. The Armadillo Survival Society is determined to protect those little critters."

"And block construction of our new school in the process."

"Groundhog Station has the best, most modern school in the county. We have a reputation to maintain."

Another bus pulled up behind the first, as more protesters arrived to the cheers of the original group. The construction crew had begun showing up, too. They lingered on the outskirts of the crowd, apparently unwilling to cross a picket line.

"Your people are on school district property, Washnot. You'll have to ask them—"

"*Washought,*" the mayor corrected.

"Right, *Watchout.*"

Startled, the mayor glanced over his shoulder. "What's wrong?"

Alex smiled. Keeping a bully off balance was something he'd learned at a young age, a coping mechanism he'd developed as the nerdiest nerd in school.

Nowhere's upper division English teacher arrived, a

prissy woman who had once aspired to the stage. With a dramatic flair, Blossom McQuire placed her hand over her heart. "Oh, my gracious. Is there some difficulty, Mr. Peabody?"

"Groundhog Station is trying to shut down our school construction," Alex said.

"We're saving armadillos," Washought insisted.

"Ms. McQuire, would you see if you can reach the sheriff? Tell him he may need to arrest some trespassers."

"Yes, sir. Immediately, sir." With a swirl of her skirt and a wave of her hand, her all-too-obvious wig shifting slightly, Blossom exited stage left.

"Just where do you plan to lock me up?" Washought asked, smirking. "The only jail around is in Groundhog and if you think—"

The sound of a clanging cowbell cut through the chants of the protesters, interrupting the mayor.

"Coffee and doughnuts!" shouted Finella Weinbucket from an open-air serving area near the school's big top. She waved her bell in the air. Immediately the construction workers lined up for their morning dose of caffeine and whatever else Finella was serving.

"What's that all about?" Washought asked.

"It's our catering service. Feel free to buy some to take with you on your way out of town." Alex was confident the good folks of Groundhog hadn't developed the cast-iron stomachs that seemed to be a characteristic of the construction-crew members, who consumed Finella's cooking with a minimum of ill effects.

Washought frowned. "Our school doesn't have a catering service."

"Maybe you can get Finella to expand her services."

He harrumphed. "I'll look into that. But first, I want to make sure that woman's product is up to Groundhog standards. Naturally, if I am to recommend her to our community, I expect she'll let me sample her wares without charge."

"Naturally." The freeloading cheat would think of that.

The mayor headed toward the head of Finella's line while his loyal followers continued to march in a circle around the front of the construction site, waving their signs and chanting, "Free the armadillos!"

Alex didn't know the creatures had been incarcerated.

By now, Nowhere townspeople had begun to show up, drawn by the crowd, and early arriving students were wandering through the Groundhog crowd, heckling them.

Alex slipped on his glasses, adjusted the focus and scanned the crowd. When he spotted Dell Grimes with his multishot rubber-band gun, he knew matters could quickly get out of hand.

The immediate solution to his problem came in the form of an angel—Lilibeth in a flowing skirt and tight-fitting sweater.

"I heard all the ruckus clear over at the coffee

shop," she said. "What in the name of peace is going on?"

"Trouble." Including the problem he had with his libido every time he caught sight of her. "Do me a favor. Go buy some doughnuts from Finella and pass them out to the pickets—as a neighborly gesture." He pulled his wallet from his pocket and handed Lilibeth some money.

She tilted her head, which made a lock of her blond hair slip across her shoulder in a tantalizing way. "Are you sure you want to do that? I haven't tried one of Finella's doughnuts today, but you know how Finella likes to incorporate the week's special at Gigi's Grocery in her recipes. It could be disastrous."

He smiled. "That's what I'm hoping for. You offer the Groundhog folks a new taste treat while I ring the class bell a little early. I think it's best if I keep my students away from our visitors." Even during his short stay in Nowhere, Alex had learned Finella's cooking could have an immediate and potent impact on just about anyone who ate her food.

"We could call Sheriff Bob—"

"Ms. McQuire is doing that. But if it's feeding time for his hogs, it could take him hours to get here."

"Mostly he runs cattle, but you're right," Lilibeth conceded. "His deputy duties sometimes take second fiddle." With a bewitching smile, she hurried off to buy doughnuts for the protesters.

The teachers, as well as the students, grumbled when Alex convened classes early. They trudged inside their

assigned tents just as Lilibeth began delivering doughnuts to the save-the-armadillo crowd.

Within fifteen minutes, the first protester came running toward him. "Where's your rest room?"

He pointed toward the temporary facilities.

"Oh, God..." Groaning, she dropped her sign and
raced toward the outhouses.

Two minutes later the next Groundhog picket ran
across the broken asphalt of the old school yard toward
Alex. He waved the man in the right direction.

Moments later, a call went out for Dr. Mimsy. Alex
greeted the attractive young woman as she hurried
across the school yard, all professional, black bag in
hand. Content he'd staved off construction delays for
the moment, Alex went back to his office to work on
his automatic pencil sharpener. First, however, he'd
have to place an order for more pencils.

Within another half hour, he heard the buses outside
start up. One after the other they rumbled past the circus tents en route home to Groundhog Station.

Yep, as a matter of curiosity he'd have to investigate
just what Finella put in her recipes.

LILIBETH LINGERED NEAR the front of the store waiting
for Alex to come home after school. When she saw
him coming, she stepped outside.

"You were wonderful this morning."

His headed jerked up. "I still don't have it working
right."

"You mean the people from Groundhog came back?"

He looked at her blankly, as if he'd just returned from some other world. Lines of fatigue surrounded his gentle brown eyes and his hair was mussed. Lilibeth had the urge to smooth the thick waves back into place.

"Groundhog? No, I was talking about my latest invention."

"Well, the whole town is atwitter about how you handled the protesters. Even Mama was impressed you'd one-upped Wally Washought this time. Finella's doughnuts made for a perfect counterattack."

Tension eased from his shoulders and he appeared to relax a little. "I don't think Mayor Washought realizes how motivating his stunts are to *our* students. The seventh- and eighth-grade boys are determined to win the go-cart race this year."

"And you'll help them do it, too." She'd already noticed he had quite a knack with the students, far more so than the former principal.

"I do have a plan," he admitted. "The boys started building a wind tunnel this afternoon."

"A wind—" Understanding dawned. "You're going to make the go-cart aerodynamic."

"And jet propelled, assuming I can figure out a reasonable fuel source."

"Land's sakes!" Laughing, she hooked her arm through his. "Come on in and I'll whip up a cherry cola for you. I swear, I don't think there's ever been anybody in Nowhere smarter than you are. Not even Dr. Mimsy.''

He looked at her strangely. ''You're just as smart as I am.''

She took two steps inside the store with him at her side before she stopped abruptly between the displays of fingernail polish and face cream. Alex thought she was smart?

''Everyone in town thinks I'm nothing but a ditzy blonde.'' No one had given her credit for maturing since her high-school prom queen days.

''But that isn't true, is it?'' he said softly, more perceptive than she had realized. ''You virtually run the drugstore and coffee shop on your own.''

''Mama's busy doing her postmistress duties, and Daddy runs the pharmacy.''

''Which is why you're in charge of everything else. I'd say that takes a lot of intelligence.''

Intelligence? She couldn't remember the last time someone used that word in connection with her. Because the townspeople rarely looked past her physical attributes to even care if she had a mind that sought answers to any number of questions, she explored them on the Internet.

Walking Alex to the café counter where he sat on a stool, Lilibeth considered his words acknowledging she was more than a pretty face. Just the thought that he didn't think she was stupid gave her a little shiver of pleasure. Perhaps it took someone new in town to notice the change in her that had taken place over the years.

"When I was little," she said, scooping ice into a glass, "I did well in school, the top reading group and all. I even got a blue ribbon for the school spelling bee in fourth and fifth grades."

"And then you reached puberty and the boys made fun of any girl who was smarter than they were."

Heat crept up her neck and flushed her cheeks. "How did you know?"

"Those same kind of boys made fun of me. I was so nerdy, it was understandable. But I think adolescence is even harder on girls." He smiled at her as she placed the cherry cola on the counter in front of him. "Particularly beautiful girls. Everywhere they look—on TV, in the movies, the cover of every magazine—they're told being pretty is all that counts. Too many of them begin to believe that and give up trying to make good grades."

He was right—she had quit trying. She'd become more interested in being prom queen than figuring out calculus problems. Because that's what had been expected of her by her classmates...and her parents.

"Not only are you intelligent," he continued, "but you also have a kind heart." Sliding a straw into his drink, he took a sip. "Do you really think everyone would make a special place for Mazeppa's grocery cart?"

"Oh, that's self-preservation." She shrugged off his

comment. "I'm the one that has to put the stock that she knocks off with her cart back on the shelves."

"But you did it with such kindness, Lilibeth. That's what I'm talking about."

She was the one who was all atwitter now. Her heart was practically doing jumping jacks. Intelligent *and* kind. A man who saw her as something besides a sex symbol.

"I do subscribe to *Drugstore Management Monthly*," she said. "I learn a lot about customer service from them."

"The way you operate the store so efficiently, you could probably write for the magazine, too."

Without thinking, for she was simply enjoying the sense of being appreciated, she took a straw out of the container on the counter, stuck it into Alex's cola and took a deep, revitalizing sip. The cherry flavor tingled all the way down, right past her palpitating heart.

When she looked up, their lips were only inches apart. Time froze, and her heart all but stopped beating.

Vaguely she was aware of Carter Murchison's tow truck rattling by on Main Street, a firecracker going off in the alley behind the drugstore—probably lit by one of the school's ten-year-old hooligans—and the faint scent of Alex's aftershave. She focused on that and leaned forward.

Suddenly, the door to the store opened, the first four tones of the chime mellow and romantic, the fifth, jarring.

Lilibeth jumped back, nearly tipping over the cherry cola in the process.

"We've got a whole new set of pickets down at the school," Bob Moriarty, the sheriff, announced. "You want I should run 'em off?"

Alex groaned. "Who are they this time?"

"Their signs say something about Save The Sagebrush, Squash Armadillos."

5

HE SIMPLY HAD TO LIMIT the number of hours he spent thinking about Lilibeth. She was becoming an obsession. A serious distraction. A deterrent to his goal.

Even now, as Alex escorted the construction crew through the two lines of pickets to begin their workday, as he had for the past week, he was thinking about Lilibeth. The silky feel of her hair. Her classic cheekbones. The fullness of her lips. Even the protesters shouting "Groundhogs for Armadillos" and "Save the Sagebrush" couldn't distract him from his thoughts of Lilibeth.

At unexpected moments, he found himself imagining how she would feel in his arms. What it would be like to make love to her. Have her beneath him. Be inside of her.

When that happened, he'd lose his train of thought. Hell, he'd forget where he was.

Stopping abruptly, he turned around. He'd walked through the entire construction site and out the other side to the open field, practically falling into a nest of armadillos. Fortunately the workers had stopped at their assigned places. If they'd waited for instructions from Alex, they would have built a new school in the next county.

He sighed. Until now he'd prided himself on his ability to concentrate on any task at hand.

Under other circumstances, if he were not committed to proving himself a successful inventor, he could act on this new obsession of his. But he couldn't take advantage of Lilibeth that way. She was too kind, too vulnerable to be happy with a relationship that couldn't be permanent. Alex was in no position to make that kind of a vow. Not yet.

He squared his shoulders. He needed to redouble his efforts. The world was always in search of a better mousetrap, or its equivalent. He'd invent one. Soon, he told himself. In the meantime, he'd keep his distance from Lilibeth and hope he could keep his focus on his projects.

Fat chance! he realized that evening when she strolled into the garage where he was working on motorizing Mazeppa's grocery cart.

"Hi, how's it going?" she asked.

His focus splintered, arrowing away from the steering mechanism he'd created and zeroing in on Lilibeth's tight-fitting sweater. Cashmere, he thought, a shade that made him think of strawberry ice cream—two scoops with cherries on top. He nearly dropped his screwdriver.

"Fine." His voice came out high-pitched.

"I was about to lock up the coffee shop before going

home. I wondered if I could get you anything. Ice cream?''

Alex began counting backward from a hundred—by sevens. "No, that's all right. Thanks."

He lost count at seventy-nine when she ran her fingers through her honey-blond hair, mesmerizing him.

"Anything I can do to help?" She sauntered toward him, her hips swaying. "I could hold your tools or something."

Hold his— He began to sweat. "I think I've got everything under control," he lied. He knelt down to attach a wire to the motor.

She knelt opposite him. "Four-wheel drive?"

There was only one thing driving him now and its motor was revving. Uncomfortably so. "No, ah, the motor drives the back wheels. The front does the steering."

"I bet Gigi would like some of these at the grocery store."

"You think so?" He hadn't considered that possibility. With this particular design, he'd only been trying to help Mazeppa.

"She likes to try innovative things so people will come into her store and buy her specials."

"I noticed yesterday that she apparently thinks there's a huge, untapped market in Nowhere for pickled beets. She had cans stacked almost to the ceiling right by the cash register."

Lilibeth smiled at him, that perfect smile with perfect teeth and tempting lips. "You watch, the next edition of *Cooking and Sewing with Finella* on cable TV will feature pickled beets in her Spring Salad.''

''Does Gigi give her a kickback for using her specials?''

''I don't think so. Finella would probably think that's unethical, being that she's an important and influential TV personality. Besides, I don't think many people copy down Finella's recipes.''

''For that, we can all be grateful.''

They shared a laugh, and Alex himself was grateful that the width of grocery cart and two rows of wire mesh separated them, because he wanted to kiss her so much he couldn't concentrate on Finella's Spring Salad or Mazeppa's cart. He could only think about Lilibeth's lovely, full mouth and recall its sweet flavor.

''Are you ready to give it a try?'' she asked.

Oh, yes, but he'd vowed to keep his distance and she was way too close as it was. Kissing her, even with the cart between them, would mean actual physical contact. He knew exactly where that would lead.

She stood, forcing him to rise, too, and studied the wires he had connected to the handlebar on the cart. ''How do you turn it on?''

He was already turned on and had been since he arrived in Nowhere. ''It's electric. Just throw that switch. But first you have to—''

The cart shot forward.

''Alex!''

''—shift it into neutral.'' He went running after her. ''Where's the brake?'' Wild-eyed, she sprinted to keep up with the runaway cart, grasping the bar like a novice trapeze artist clinging to a high-wire swing.

"There isn't one yet. That was going to be my next—"

She swerved, barely avoiding a collision with the workbench. Her horrified expression resembled that of an accident victim who had barely escaped with her life and was still in danger of bodily harm.

"—step. On the left of the handle bar, shift the toggle switch straight up. That's neutral."

Fumbling with the mechanism, she forgot to steer. The cart careened toward the bottles of Aunt Tilly's Cactus Joy Juice stored against the wall.

"Watch out!" Alex leaped forward to overtake the runaway cart, stumbled over an uneven board and fell to his knees.

"What in tarnation are you doing with my cart?" Mazeppa bellowed from the doorway.

Lilibeth found neutral, shifted the gear, and the cart coasted to a stop inches from the green Joy Juice bottles. "Oh, my sakes!"

Breathing hard, Alex struggled to his feet, and looped his arm around Lilibeth's waist. Her breath was coming in quick little pants, too, as she smiled up at him, her eyes bright blue with excitement. She'd look like that when they made love, he was sure of it.

"Whew! That was some ride, cowboy," she said.

He wanted to tell her he'd give her an even more exciting ride if he could, such as the one he'd invented using a bungie-cord harness to hold his and his partner's weight while they made love. Unfortunately the young lady who had agreed to participate in the trial run had significantly underestimated her weight, causing a slight miscalculation in both the necessary length and strength of the cord. He hadn't been able to convince her to give it a second try after he made the corrections.

Mazeppa stomped into the garage, yanking the cart away from them. "If you fool youngsters can't behave yourselves in public then you ought'a find someplace private for your carryings-on."

"No, Mazeppa, you don't understand," Lilibeth quickly said, offering reassurance. "Alex has done wonderful things with your cart. I jumped in too fast and didn't ask him how to operate the new motor. You're going to love it, really you are."

Mazeppa didn't look convinced.

"Here, let me show you." Cautiously Alex turned the cart so it had a straight shot out the door, lest anything go wrong. Then he showed Mazeppa how to start the motor, shift into gear and steer. "Careful now, remember there's no brake so you don't want to go too fast."

Her beady eyes raked him. "If I break my neck with this fool thing, you're gonna hear about it, young man."

"Yes, ma'am. Go ahead. Give it a try."

Tentatively Mazeppa grasped the handlebar, then flicked the motor on. She sent Alex a warning look before shifting into gear. A moment later, after a running start, she hopped onto the back of the cart and started doing wheelies around the garage. Only the added weight of the motor on the bottom shelf, which lowered the center of gravity, kept the contraption from tipping over backward.

"Yahoo!" She whizzed past the workbench, spun around and zipped back again, narrowly missing Alex and Lilibeth, who had to scramble for safety.

"She's gone crazy!" Lilibeth said, laughing.

"A little manic," Alex agreed.

"Don't this beat all!" Gray hair flying, Mazeppa's smile was as wide as Texas.

She wheeled a U-turn at the garage entrance, nearly tipping the cart over. "Hold her, boys, she's aheading for the pea patch!"

Alex dived for the cart as it raced by and switched off the motor. When he caught his breath, he said, "I think I need to add a variable speed function."

"Not on your life, youngster." She patted her grocery cart as if it were a bronc she'd saddled and tamed. "I'm gonna have me some fun with her just as she is. Maybe I'll even enter that go-cart race with Groundhog Station. Wouldn't that be a hoot if I won?"

Cackling with laughter, she motored another circle around the garage then came to a halt on her own. "With all the commotion, I forgot what I came to tell you. Lucy had her baby an hour or so ago."

"Oh, that's wonderful," Lilibeth exclaimed. "What did she have?"

"A little boy—Quade, Junior. Dr. Mimsy says Lucy

talked nonstop the whole dang twelve hours she was in labor.''

Lilibeth smiled wistfully, thinking about how exciting it would be to have a child, a tiny baby to love, especially a baby who had Alex's gentle brown eyes. "If anyone could talk that long, it would be Lucy."

"Quade plans to take Lucy and the baby into Austin for a checkup in a week or so."

"Is there something wrong?"

"Not that I know of. I 'spect he trusts Dr. Mimsy well enough, but you know how these new fathers can be. Overprotective 'n all. He wants 'em to see a specialist.'' Mazeppa started to put her "goods," which had been piled near the workbench, back in her cart. "They need somebody to watch out for Donnie and Doreen while they're gone with the baby overnight. I sure ain't gonna volunteer."

Alex helped her shift a bundle of clothes into the cart. "Why not?"

"That little Donnie's a rascal. He always wants me to take out my teeth and then he won't give 'em back."

Lilibeth suppressed a giggle and an idea popped into her head. Maybe if Alex spent a little time around the twins he'd start thinking he'd like to be a daddy himself. He was so good with the children at school, parenthood would be natural for him. And if he spent that time with her, too, well it'd be just as natural for him to think about her being the mama of his babies. She did so much want her own home and family....

"I wouldn't mind watching the twins for a day or

so,'' she said as casually as she could. "Mama could take care of the store. Of course, it would be easier if there were two adults instead of just one."

"That's a fact," Mazeppa agreed.

Pointedly they both looked at Alex.

He shook his head. "I don't know anything about babies."

"You got false teeth?" Mazeppa asked.

"No, but—"

"Then you won't have no problem. You're quick enough to outrun 'em and smart enough to outthink 'em. You and Lilibeth will do just fine. I'll tell 'em to call you." With that, she hopped onto her cart, shifted into gear and rolled out into the alley. "Yahoo! Watch out, Groundhogs, here I come!"

Alex pulled his brows together. "I'm not sure it's a good idea for me to baby-sit—"

"I think it will be wonderful, just the two of us and the twins. And I'm sure I couldn't do it without you," she crooned, batting her eyelashes. Sometimes a woman had to take drastic action to plant an idea in a man's head, particularly a man who was more interested in his mechanical toys than he was in a willing woman.

Although she had to admit he was the only man who had noticed more than just her figure, too. She gave him added points for that. Not that he wasn't already off the scale in terms of sex appeal.

"But if they go to Austin during the week, I'll have to work," he protested.

She waved off his objection. "You can drive out to the ranch after school and spend the night there. That's when I'll need you the most."

"Spend the *night?*" His voice cracked.

Satisfied his resistance would weaken, given the right impetus, she smiled. "I'll even fix you breakfast—the morning after."

"*Morning after?*" he echoed. "Lilibeth, are you sure your parents will—"

"They'll want me to do the neighborly thing, and that's to offer to take care of the twins." She tugged at the hem of her sweater and saw his gaze shift to her breasts. That hadn't been her intention, but if that's what it took, well... "Who knows what we'll think of doing while the babies are sleeping. You might even come up with a new invention for taking care of babies."

"I suppose that is a possibility."

"There, you see? We'll make a terrific team, and I'll be right there to cheer you on every step of the way. I was a pom-pom girl, you know."

He paled slightly, but before he could raise any more objections Lilibeth told him good-night and was out the door.

She drove the half mile home in her aging, bright-red Bronco, her head filled with ways to seduce Alex. Thus far he'd seemed immune to all of her efforts. In desperation, she'd stocked up on every back issue of *Cosmo* she could lay hands on in the past few days and read every article. She was now an expert on Ten Ways

To Arouse a Man, Ten Things a Man Loves You To
Do to Him, His Ten Most Erotic Zones, Ten Ways To
Touch Your Man, and a dozen other lists that were
guaranteed to set your man on fire. She hoped to goodness at least half of them worked.

THE ANDERSON HOUSE was in a neighborhood of Victorian homes, most of them painted white with blue or
green trim, and sporting lots of gingerbread decora-
tions. They all had porches across the front which, on
summer evenings, provided the setting for gossip fests
and informal ice-cream socials.

Now, with the early-spring evening chilly, they were
unoccupied. That didn't mean the neighbors weren't
keeping an eye out for what was going on, however.

"You're late," her mother called from the parlor
when Lilibeth came in the back door. "Was there a
problem at the store?"

"No, Mama. Everything is fine." She tossed her
light jacket over the back of a kitchen chair and went
to find her mother. "Did you hear Lucy had her baby—
a boy?"

"That's nice, dear." JoJo Anderson was sitting in
her favorite wing chair, her feet up on a footstool while
she watched TV. "Of course, in my day a girl waited
to get pregnant until *after* she was married, but I try
not to be judgmental."

"Yes, Mama." Lilibeth sat down in the second chair
and lifted her tired feet onto a matching footstool.

Her parents had been married for ten years before

JoJo got pregnant with Lilibeth and counted themselves lucky to have one child. But the burden of being that only child sometimes rested heavily on Lilibeth's shoulders.

She glanced at her father, who was dozing in the recliner, his mouth slightly open, his hand firmly grasping the remote control. Age spots dotted the back of his hand. Despite applications of Lucas's coconut cream, her mother's hands looked old, too.

Her parents were aging fast, she realized, not for the first time. They needed her to stay here in Nowhere, to run the store and café, to provide care for them as they aged. She couldn't abandon them. Despite how difficult they could sometimes be, she loved them both.

But she wanted a husband and a family of her own. Living in the middle of nowhere, her options had been sorely limited.

Until Alex came along.

She took a deep breath before announcing, "Quade is planning to take Lucy and the baby to Austin for a checkup. I've said I'll baby-sit the twins while they're gone."

"Are you sure you want to do that, dear. You don't know anything about babies."

"Then it's high time I learned."

"Well, it's certainly not right to have those youngsters running around the store all day. They could get into all kinds of trouble. And our house isn't suitable for toddlers."

That was true enough. Her mother had collected all

sorts of knickknacks over the years, which were scattered about on every horizontal surface. The Anderson home was far from baby-proof.

"I'll baby-sit them out at the ranch. That way they'll be around things they're used to."

"I don't know, dear. What about the store—"

"You and Daddy can manage for one day, I'm sure. And Willie Grimes would probably be happy to help out. With all those children she has, she can always use a little extra money." Lilibeth stood, ready to go upstairs to bed. "Alex has been nice enough to volunteer to help baby-sit with me. We'll both be staying out at the ranch overnight."

The recliner's footrest crashed down. "You can't stay overnight with that man," her father said, coming to his feet.

JoJo shook her finger at Lilibeth. "Think about your reputation, child. What will people say if—"

"The twins will chaperon us."

"That's hardly adequate," JoJo insisted.

"Mama, I don't want to die an old maid sitting in a chair with swollen ankles and my feet propped up. And spending a night with a man isn't going to change what people think of me." Most people in town already thought she was on the fast side, a typical blond bombshell, they'd say. But, in fact, the boys in high school had been too shy to ask her out and she'd had few opportunities since then to develop an intimate relationship with any man.

"If that man takes advantage of my little girl," B.K. said, "he'll have to answer to me."

She crossed the room and gave her father a hug. "Trust me, Daddy, if anyone is going to take advantage, it will be me."

THE FOLLOWING DAY AFTER classes let out, Alex went to see Gigi at the grocery store. It was one thing to motorize Mazeppa's grocery cart, but it wasn't patentable; he'd used an ordinary electric motor included in every child's Erector set and juiced it up. What he needed was a more commercial application of the cart plus unique elements he could turn into a franchise-making product.

While he was in the store, he'd ask a favor of Gigi. Using a wooden crate was the single written rule regarding the go-cart competition with Groundhog Station. An avid Nowhere fan, Alex was confident Gigi would contribute to the winning cause.

Then all he'd need was suitable fuel for the rocket he and the eighth-grade boys were designing. A marvelous physics lesson the young men were eating up. Anything to beat their rivals in Groundhog Station.

Gigi Wernicke was a large woman with double chins who reigned behind her cash register like a queen. In some ways, she reminded Alex of his mother, who had been a kazoo-playing protégé at a young age. She eventually met and married his father, the heir apparent to the Peabody Kazoo Company and all the attendant tradition. They'd never expected to give birth to a tone-deaf child like Alex.

He hated that he'd disappointed them.

"Sure hope you've come back to pick up some pickled beets this time," Gigi said. "The special won't last for long, you know."

Alex eyed the stack of cans by the register. At the current rate of reduction, he estimated there would be an adequate supply of pickled beets in Nowhere until the year 2022.

"Maybe there's a way you can move your specials a little faster," he suggested.

Her thin eyebrows rose with interest. "Tell me about it."

Alex described how he wanted to put her shopping carts on tracks that would rove up and down her grocery aisle, selecting merchandise with robotic arms as per the customer's instructions. Ad-libbing, he encouraged her to tie her specials in with other purchases the customer might make, multiplying the chances of selling her high-profit items.

And then he asked for a donation of a grocery crate.

She grinned at him. "You got it, hotshot. Tell me what you need to know and every wooden crate I've got is yours."

Alex left the store pleased with himself. He might have a few details to work out before he declared success, either for the go-cart race or Gigi's Automated

Grocery Access System. A.G.A.S., he'd call it, if he was successful with the invention.

Meanwhile, his far more difficult challenge was to avoid intimate contact with Lilibeth while faced with spending the night in the same house together.

6

AN INTELLIGENT MAN wouldn't be doing this.

He wouldn't be pulling his truck up to a sprawling two-story ranch house well beyond the middle of Nowhere, and a good ten minutes from the main highway, all of it on open rangeland that was part of the Rippling R Ranch property. After spending a full day at school solving problems and arguing with Washought at Groundhog Junction about the Great Crate Race, he should be somewhere else.

A man with only average smarts wouldn't be walking past winter-brown flower beds up onto the wide porch knowing full well there was no one at home except Lilibeth and two toddlers. He didn't know what frightened him the most—the sexy woman waiting inside for him or the thought of being responsible for the care and feeding of two eighteen-month-old babies. God, he hoped Lilibeth knew something about children.

But he'd made a promise. A Peabody was as good as his word.

He had the feeling not everyone treated Lilibeth with the respect she deserved. They took advantage of her good nature. Ignored her needs in favor of their own. Alex couldn't—wouldn't—do that. She deserved his very best efforts at this endeavor *and* the maximum amount of willpower he had so he wouldn't take advantage of her.

Despite the dire warnings screaming in his head, he raised his hand to knock on the door.

Before his knuckles touched wood, it opened so fast, he almost knocked the child perched on Lilibeth's hip right on its head.

"You came!" She threw the door open wide, her smile welcoming but strained. Instead of her usually neatly brushed hair curling below her shoulders, it appeared she'd survived a minitornado, the silken strands crisscrossed like a maze of Pick-up Sticks. Her cheeks were pale, her sensual lips lacked color.

"Are you all right?"

"Fine, now that you're here."

Before he could respond, a knee-high Olympic track star sped past him out onto the porch and headed for the steps.

"Doreen!" Lilibeth cried, juggling Donnie on her hip. "Oh, stop her."

Easier said than done. Alex whirled, reached out for the child, took a header over the welcome mat, snared the youngster's arm, somersaulted ass over teakettle and came up holding the kid high in the air unharmed.

She giggled, a totally infectious laugh Dr. Mimsy would never be able to cure. "Do it adein!"

Despite his best efforts, Alex grinned back at the kid

as he gazed into her sparkling brown eyes. "No way, sweetheart. I don't have chiropractic insurance."

She gave him a full-fledged raspberry that drenched his face.

"Come on in," Lilibeth said from the doorway, her laughter as light and bright as a spring morning. "It's a little easier to corral them inside than out."

Alex imagined that was true. But he also suspected escape wouldn't be easy for him, either, once he was within the close confines of the house with the most exotic, erotic woman he'd ever met. Wearing a simple floral skirt that skimmed her firm calves and a casual sweater that hugged her exquisite breasts, she was a man's fantasy come true. A woman a man instinctively wanted beneath him, hot and eager.

Alex's instincts were honed to perfection. Which, in this case, was a bad thing.

Carrying Doreen inside, Alex tried to distract himself by concentrating on solving the square root of 10,468. That kind of mental exercise had never failed to hold his interest.

Until now.

He caught Lilibeth's faint floral scent mixing with the innocence of baby lotion, a fascinating combination that sang of universal motherhood and elemental creation. Alex was hard-pressed not to consider the man's role in turning a woman into a mother.

An indulgence he had to deny himself until he could prove himself successful.

Lilibeth closed the door behind him, latching it with a double hasp well out of reach of the toddlers.

"I meant to freshen up before you came," she said, "but the twins are pretty active and their naps weren't exactly synchronized. Hard to find a minute to myself."

"You look fine to me." More than fine—*desirable*. A Technicolor dream in the flesh.

A blush tinted her cheeks as she lowered Donnie to the floor and Alex did the same with Doreen.

"Come on, kids, let's show Alex around."

They were standing in a large entryway with gleaming hardwood floors and a plush Aubusson rug. To the right, a picture window brought light into a living room filled with overstuffed chairs, an inviting couch and a classic entertainment center that sat across from a huge natural stone fireplace. In the dining room to the left, a wrought-iron chandelier hung above a table that could easily seat twelve before adding extensions.

Except for the Western flavor and decor, the house reminded Alex of his family's estate in Cleveland, built with the profits of the kazoo enterprise.

"The Rocking R has been in Quade's family since the days of the Alamo," Lilibeth explained. "His roots are sunk deep here."

"I noticed on the drive in that he's sunk a few oil wells, too, plus grazing a fair-size herd of cattle."

"Richest person around, except Mazeppa." Lilibeth smiled at Alex's surprised expression. "She's got millions, but I think she has more fun being a bag lady."

Doreen tugged on his hand. "Play horsey."

Looking down at the knee-high child, he shook his head. "Sorry, I don't ride."

Lilibeth started up the stairs leading to the second floor. "I think she wants to show you her rocking horse."

"Ah, I can probably handle that."

As Alex took the first step toward Doreen, a black-and-gray striped tabby kitten shot between his legs and raced up the stairs, nearly causing him to lose his balance.

"Where did that cat come from?"

"Titty!" Donnie squealed, pointing.

"One of the barn cats had a litter and the twins insisted one of them become a house cat." Lilibeth glanced over her shoulder smiling. "I suspect they wanted the whole litter inside, but Quade drew the line at that." More of a dog lover than cat fancier, Alex could understand Quade's decision.

The twins clambered up the stairs behind Lilibeth, holding on to the mahogany banister for support. They both wore corduroy jumpers—Doreen in pink, Donnie in blue—with matching T-shirts, their little bottoms dirt-stained from a day of play.

"When do Quade and Lucy get home?" Alex asked.

"They said by noon tomorrow."

Alex counted the hours he'd have to resist acting on his baser urges with Lilibeth, grateful for the time the twins would be awake. This was likely to be the most stressful night of his life, requiring every bit of self-control he possessed.

Lilibeth smiled at Alex over her shoulder as she entered the twins' playroom. He looked unsure of himself, keeping his distance from both the children and her. She'd have to do all she could to make him feel at ease. If everything went well, she had big plans for tonight after Donnie and Doreen were tucked into bed—assuming she had enough strength left. Except for an all-too-brief nap, the twins had kept her hopping since she'd arrived that morning.

"Play horsey!" Doreen demanded again. She planted her fists on her hips, looking up at Alex expectantly.

"Right," he said. "Which one is yours?" He took a step toward one of the two spring-mounted horses.

"No, no, no. Horsey! Horsey! Horsey!"

Alex glanced to Lilibeth for guidance and she shrugged. "Maybe she wants *you* to be the horse."

"Me?"

"You know, down on your knees."

He didn't look pleased with the prospect, which made Lilibeth question her strategy. Maybe it was too soon in their relationship to be encouraging thoughts of paternity; she should have stuck with romance. But she did so want to be a mother. Not that she was over the hill, but she wasn't getting any younger, either.

Donnie toddled off in pursuit of the kitten while Alex lowered himself to his knees. "At your service, Miss Doreen." He helped her scramble onto his back.

"Getty up!" She grabbed a fistful of his shirt and whacked his sides with her red tennis shoes.

"*Ouff!*" Wincing, he lurched forward. "Easy, kid! I may need those ribs later."

"Faster! Faster!" Doreen aimed for his ribs again.

Lilibeth repressed a grin as Alex sped up to a fast trot, bouncing Doreen and making her giggle. Alex might not know a lot about being a daddy, but he seemed a natural at the job.

"Faster! Faster!"

"Maybe I can motorize her hobbyhorse and put it on a track," he commented. "It would save a lot of wear and tear on my knees."

"Sounds like a good plan to me." Lilibeth glanced around to check on Donnie. To her dismay, she didn't spot him. He wasn't at his computer or playing blocks. She'd taken her eyes off of him for an instant and he'd vanished.

"Donnie? Where are you, honey?" She hurried to the playroom door. Surely he hadn't gotten out so quickly. "Alex!"

"What's wrong?" He swept Doreen off his back and stood up.

"Horsey! Horsey!" She latched onto his leg.

"I can't find—"

"Titty! Titty!"

At the sound of Donnie's voice, Alex snapped his head up. From the computer desk, the youngster had managed to climb to a high shelf that, more decorative than useful, circled three-quarters of the room. He was crawling along on all fours in pursuit of the kitten, who was scrambling to outrun the child.

"Oh, my gosh," Lilibeth cried. "Be careful, Donnie!"

"I'll get him." Dragging Doreen along because she wouldn't let go of his leg, Alex hobbled across the room. The ceiling was high, leaving the long shelf inches out of his reach. "Over here, tiger. Grab my hand."

"No! No! My titty!" The furry critter scampered ahead of the toddler just fast enough to keep the kid interested.

"Horsey go!" Doreen insisted.

"I need something to stand on," Alex said.

Lilibeth grabbed the desk chair to use as a stool then pried Doreen's arms from around Alex's leg. "Come on, honey. Uncle Alex has to get your brother down so he won't get an owie."

Doreen's wail of protest suggested she didn't much care if Donnie broke his neck or not.

Standing on tiptoe on top of the chair, Alex stretched up to grab the boy, who had now managed to corner the cat. He closed his hand around Donnie's arm just as the kitten tried to escape the child.

A black-and-gray bundle of fur, claws extended, landed on Alex's head, then flew off again to land on the floor.

Alex cried out.

Donnie slipped from his perch, swinging by one arm

as Alex held on for dear life. Doing a quick juggling act, he pulled the boy firmly into his grasp.

"Thank heavens," Lilibeth said.

Alex murmured a silent amen. Raising kids nowadays was more complicated than he'd realized.

It was at that moment he caught the definitive scent of something quite unpleasant.

"Uh, the twins aren't potty trained yet?" he asked.

Lilibeth wrinkled her nose as she got a whiff, too. "Afraid not."

"Is taking care of that part of my job description?"

"I'll do it." She hefted Donnie into her arms.

Bless her. "Maybe I ought to automate a spray-and-wash system for infants and toddlers. I could call it Robotic Action Suds and Hygiene program."

"R.A.S.H." She smiled at him, her lovely lips curving in the most enticing way. "Perfect. Millions of women would be potential customers."

And then he'd be a success, able to do exactly what he wanted—which, for starters, would be to kiss Lilibeth senseless.

DURING THE NEXT HOUR, Alex—unable to concentrate on the potential of his R.A.S.H. invention—prevented Donnie from pouring an entire bottle of white glue down the bathroom sink and rescued Doreen from the giant block fortress Donnie had built around his sister.

For a brief moment, he'd thought Doreen had swallowed his watch, a nifty version that told the time in milliseconds—useful when conducting precision science experiments. Fortunately she'd only choked on a stale Cheerio she'd found under the storage cabinet in the playroom.

A successful Heimlich hug, which expelled the Cheerio, had been the highlight of their hour together as far as Doreen was concerned. She kept asking for "More! More!"

Alex viewed this bonding process as a positive step for that moment when he'd have the pleasure of putting the twins to bed. Finally.

With a twin clinging to each hand, he went downstairs to determine how Lilibeth was progressing with dinner.

"How's it going?" he asked as he entered the kitchen. He noted two high chairs at the circular walnut table and candles ready for lighting. An interesting dichotomy, romance mixed with domesticity.

"Almost there." She bent over to pull a casserole dish from the oven, and he was struck once again with what a truly matchless derriere she had.

Moving gracefully around the kitchen, she placed a Jell-O salad on the table—not one of Finella's recipes, he truly hoped—some steamed vegetables and a plate of homemade muffins. Everything smelled delicious.

"Could you light the candles for me?" she asked sweetly.

Their eyes met, and he knew he could light a whole lot more than her candles if he weren't an honorable man. Never had it been so difficult to maintain his principles. Her cobalt eyes held too much of an invitation; in response, his body developed a serious lack of willpower. He wasn't in a position to offer a permanent relationship; he didn't want to lead her on. She deserved better.

She blinked. "Where are the twins?"

"They're, uh..." He looked down where they'd been standing next to him only moments ago.

Something went clunk in the walk-in pantry off the kitchen. Alex and Lilibeth made a dash toward the open doorway.

"Man, they're quick," he said, bracing himself against the doorjamb. An entire five-pound bag of sugar had been spilled across the floor and the twins appeared to be building modified sand castles with the help of a little maple syrup. "If I could bottle that energy, I'd be famous."

Lilibeth sighed deeply. "It looks like dinner is going to be a little late while we clean up the mess."

"No problem." His appetite had shifted to something far more elemental than mere food.

Minutes later, as Alex was sweeping up the last of the sugar concoction, Lilibeth cried, "Donnie, get down from there!"

Peering out of the pantry doorway, he spotted Donnie on the dining-room table, trying to reach the wrought-iron chandelier. Doreen applauded his efforts and shouted, "Me, too! Me, too!"

Yep, this was really going to be a long night.

"I'M REALLY SORRY I GOT you into this," Lilibeth said as the clock on the mantel struck midnight. Both she and Alex had a baby dozing in their arms, she on the couch and he in the recliner that was Quade's favorite chair. In the fireplace, golden flames danced in an hypnotic rhythm along the length of an age-dried log.

When bedtime had arrived the twins had both thrown a fit, suddenly missing their parents. Lilibeth and Alex had tried reading them books, singing lullabies, giving them each a bottle. Nothing had worked except holding them, and they'd finally drifted off into exhausted sleep only minutes ago.

Not the romantic evening Lilibeth had envisioned.

"You couldn't have known bedtime would be so difficult," he said. He looked a little frayed around the edges; only two pencils remained in his pocket protector.

"I knew I didn't know anything about being a parent. Quade and Lucy would have been better off asking Mazeppa to baby-sit the twins. At least she's raised a couple of children of her own." Her hand curved around Donnie's sweet little head, smoothing his spiky hair. "I guess I simply don't have any mothering instincts."

"How can you say that? Sitting there now you're the picture of Madonna and child."

A ripple of pleasure went through her. "Are you sure you don't mean Whistler's Mother?"

"There, you see? Madonna with a sense of humor. As well as an accomplished businesswoman," he added.

She smiled at him. Alex always managed to say the right thing, to see her in the most positive light, in contrast to the rest of the townspeople who thought of her only as a dumb blonde sex symbol.

Not that she wouldn't want Alex to see her as sexy, too.

"I have been thinking about going to just-in-time deliveries at the drugstore—like they use in assembly lines—so we don't have so much capital tied up in inventory," she said. "No one's used the system in retailing, but I think our suppliers could handle that."

"Sounds like an innovative idea, something worth trying."

Again she felt a sense of pleasure that Alex approved of her plan. But she also wanted to kick herself for mentioning anything so unromantic. How on earth was she going to get him in the mood if she kept talking about inventory control?

Yawning, she shifted Donnie to a more comfortable position in her lap. "Do you think we should risk taking the twins back upstairs and putting them to bed?"

"I'll take Doreen first. She seems to be out like a light." Holding her carefully, he stood. "If she stays asleep, I'll come back to help you with Donnie."

Nodding her approval, Lilibeth sat back to wait for Alex's return—or Doreen's scream from upstairs. Her own fatigue weighted her limbs, making her feel as exhausted as the twins must be.

Closing her eyes for a moment, she imagined Alex taking her in his arms after the babies were safely in bed. They'd smile in relief at finally being alone. Then he'd kiss her. Slowly at first until slow wouldn't be enough. And then...

ALEX CAME DOWNSTAIRS to find Lilibeth sound asleep. He slipped Donnie from her arms. The child muttered in his sleep, but Lilibeth didn't stir. She must be worn-out, he thought as he carried the boy upstairs to his crib.

When he returned, Lilibeth had slipped lower on the couch, curling onto her side, her head resting on a pillow. She looked sweet and vulnerable, a sleeping beauty with golden hair.

This is good, he told himself as he covered her with an afghan that had been folded at her feet. Lilibeth was tired. She needed her rest.

She didn't need him waking her. Exploring the secrets of her lush body. Finding the way his body would fit with hers. Loving her.

Kneeling, he toyed with the ends of her hair, the silken strands spilling over his fingers in a sparkling waterfall. A stream of wanting sped through him with the force of white-water rapids tumbling through the narrows of a powerful river.

Risking further temptation, he placed a soft kiss on her smooth forehead, which was like warm, living ivory. On a deep breath, he drew in her womanly scent.

He couldn't do this. Not until he was worthy of the Peabody name. Lilibeth was too precious; he was unfit to wake her from her slumber when he had so little to offer her.

But the time would come....

Determined, he came to his feet, his hands clenched at his sides. Perhaps the Robotic Action Suds and Hygiene program for infants would be his salvation, the invention with which he would make his mark on the world. His fortune. *Peabody R.A.S.H.* would become a household word. The perfect gift for baby showers. An appliance proudly owned by every family with babies and toddlers. A necessity.

His spirits bolstered, he went out to his truck and rummaged beneath the shell, sorting through the bits and pieces until he came up with an assortment of rubber hoses and valves, a soft-scrub brush, a small motor and makeshift pump.

He silently vowed *Peabody R.A.S.H.* would bring him fame equal to, or exceeding, the notoriety his family had received from Peabody Kazoos. Then, and only then, would he feel free to ask for Lilibeth's dainty hand in marriage.

"What in the world are you doing?"

A crashing sound had awakened Lilibeth and she'd come into the kitchen to investigate. Outside, the sun had edged above the horizon, casting a watery light across the landscape. Inside Alex had all the lights in the kitchen blazing. To her disappointment, she'd slept through the romantic evening she'd anticipated.

Standing at the sink, he turned toward her. His wavy

brown hair in disarray, his shirt and jeans soaked, and a two-inch puddle of water covered the floor.

"My invention. The Peabody R.A.S.H. I've almost got it working." He eyes glowed with the enthusiasm of a zealot.

Lilibeth shook her head to clear her muddled brain. "You've been working on your invention all night?" *When you could have been making love to me?*

"When I'm inspired, I don't dare stop. I might lose my train of thought."

"I see." She eased closer to peer over his shoulder. In the center of the sink, rubber hoses were threaded through a circular plastic pipe about the size of a child's potty, all of which was attached to something that resembled an electric pump from an old well.

"Here's how it will work." He placed one of Doreen's full-size baby dolls on the circular pipe. "Of course, this is just an experimental model. The final version will be much fancier and more colorful."

"Of course."

"When the baby is properly positioned in the center of the device, you throw this switch. The pump begins to operate, providing a gentle spray that will include soapy water, and she's thoroughly scrubbed with a cloth." The baby doll began to rock vigorously on her perch. "Then comes the automatic rinse cycle."

Water began spraying out around the doll and onto the window above the sink. There was clearly too much water pressure for the baby bidet.

"Alex, I'm not sure—"

"That's followed by the dry cycle—a gentle, warm breeze that will soothe the infant and leave her dry and comfortable."

A motor rumbled. A gust of air wheezed up past the doll, quickly turning into a full-fledged gale that would have driven the biggest pipe organ in Texas. The doll rocketed toward the ceiling, bumped her head and tumbled back into the sink. She clipped a valve in the process, causing water to geyser into the air and onto the floor.

Lilibeth jumped back to avoid getting drowned in a combination of suds and icy-cold water.

Alex picked up the doll and set her aside. "I've got a few details to work out, but the theory looks sound. What do you think?"

She thought he was the most adorable man in the world, if a little bit crazy. Life with Alex Peabody would never be dull.

Standing on tiptoe, she kissed him lightly on the lips. "I think you are truly wonderful."

His brows shot up. "You do?"

"Absolutely."

"Are the twins awake yet? Maybe we should try—"

"Why don't we clean up the water first. I don't want Quade and Lucy to come home to this mess."

He looked around as though startled by the pool of water covering the floor. "Maybe you're right."

She patted his arm. "I've never been more right in my life." Now all she had to do was convince Alex they were right for each other.

7

FINELLA SCURRIED INTO THE coffee shop where Lilibeth was serving soft drinks, fries and milk shakes to the after-school crowd.

"Is Mr. Peabody back from school yet?" Finella asked breathlessly.

Lilibeth lined up sodas in front of young Joe Grimes and his ten-year-old cohorts in mischief, keeping a sharp eye out for any surprise firecrackers they might produce. "I don't think so. He usually works late." Which meant Lilibeth had seen little of him during the four days since she'd slept through her *big chance* at Quade's ranch.

"He's working on the wind tunnel with Dell and the guys," Joe volunteered.

"Oh, dear." Glancing around, her dark hair unkempt, Finella appeared unsure of what she should do. "I had a message from him that my Spring Salad has won an award."

All three boys sitting at the counter choked and sprayed their drinks all over the Formica countertop.

"Oh, barfy!" Boris Norris exclaimed.

"An award?" Lilibeth echoed, as surprised as the youngsters. She grabbed a cloth to wipe up the mess.

"Yes, isn't it wonderful? I do hate to bother Mr. Peabody at school but I've never won anything before. Well, except for the time I won third place for a cable TV show featuring local talent." She looked pleased with herself. "Of course, that was in the early days of public access and there were only three programs that qualified."

"I remember." Since then the cable company had only offered two prizes.

"I guess I'll just have to interrupt Mr. Peabody. I can't imagine…" Her hands fluttered around her face and, in a futile effort, she tried to smooth her wind-blown hair. "Perhaps the mayor will want to make a special presentation at the next council meeting."

"I'm sure he will." Although Lilibeth was as curious as Finella about what she might have won. "Why don't I walk over to the school with you? We can both ask Alex about the award."

"That would be nice, dear. I've been in such a state since George told me Peabody had called. It's so thrilling to be recognized for all of my hard work and I can hardly wait to see my prize. I wonder which version of my Spring Salad won. I thought my sardine special was quite tasty—"

Coughing loudly, the boys left the counter and moved themselves and their drinks to the farthest table away from Finella.

"But my layered red beet and garbanzo bean salad

seemed to be the most popular with the construction crew.''

''Just let me tell Mama I'll be gone for a few minutes, and I'll be right with you.'' She slipped off her apron and hung it on a peg, then took a quick peek in the mirror to fix her own hair. The after-school rush had slowed to a trickle so her mother should be able to handle whatever customers came along. Besides, Lilibeth wanted an excuse—any excuse—to see Alex.

He'd been avoiding her, no doubt working on one of his projects. While she admired his determination, she wished he weren't quite so fixated on his inventions. It would be better if they could be *inventive* together, preferably in bed.

She smiled at the thought.

There was a hint of spring in the air as she and Finella walked around the corner and down the street to the school. Trees were beginning to bud and it looked as though Billy Dell Grimes, the town handyman, had been hired to plant some annuals in the flower beds around city hall.

Lilibeth felt spring in her step, too. Surely Alex was the one man who could make her bloom—if only he would take the time to sow a few wild oats with her. In a quiet, subtle way he was the most commanding man she'd ever met. He'd never raised his voice, that she'd heard, yet both adults and young people listened to him. Somehow he brought out the best in people. Her included.

At the far end of the school grounds, the construction

crew was completing the last of the necessary excavations, a deep one for the boiler room, which would be beneath the gymnasium.

Above the colorful circus tents that currently housed the students, pennants fluttered smartly in the afternoon breeze. Lilibeth's long hair mimicked the action, whipping strands across her face that she caught and tucked behind her ear as she entered the big top.

"Yoo-hoo!" Finella waved to Alex, who was crouched on the far side of the tent next to a modified wooden citrus crate, which now included a steering wheel and tires. Against the wall, in front of that contraption was a huge industrial-size fan. Focused intently on what he and the older school boys were doing, Alex didn't look up. Instead he proceeded to attach paper streamers to the go-cart.

With mincing steps, Finella made a beeline for Alex.

Lilibeth followed at a more sedate pace. The pleasure of seeing Alex, his jacket off and his shirtsleeves rolled up, was too great to rush. She suspected, given the chance, she'd always feel that way, wanting to linger near him, eager to admire the breadth of his shoulders, the quick flash of intelligence in his eyes.

He stood. "Okay, boys, let's give it a try." Stepping back from the car, he picked up an electrical cord.

Several teachers were watching the proceedings from various classrooms that had been corded off.

"Mr. Peabody! You called about my award!"

As Finella reached the go-cart, Alex pressed the button that switched on the fan. Slowly the blades began whirling, picking up speed with each revolution until they created a windstorm inside the tent.

Finella threw up her arms as she stumbled backward in the blast. A gray wig Lilibeth recognized as belonging to Blossom McGuire, blew past her like a furry kitten startled into flight.

She screamed, ''My hair!'' Arms waving, she ran after the bounding wig.

From every corner of the tent, papers scattered like so much giant confetti. Teachers scurried to tame the errant missiles and restore some sense of order.

Eyes tearing, Lilibeth had no choice but to hunch her shoulders and turn her back on the wind machine. Her hair parted in the middle, creating two blond ribbons that blew past her face like the pennants on top of the circus tents.

Vaguely she wondered if Alex would ever design a project that worked without creating chaos in the process. Not that she cared. It was his creative nature she esteemed, not his potential for success.

If only he weren't quite so determined to invent something marvelous.

As suddenly as the blizzard had started, the whine of the fan slowed. Blowing papers fluttered to the ground, and Blossom McGuire captured her wig, planting it firmly, if crookedly, on her head. She looked as mad as a cow with a sore teat.

''Alexander Peabody! If you don't get that wind machine out of here, I'm going to take a yardstick to your behind just as I did to my hell-raising boys when they were growing up.''

Alex swiveled his head around and frowned as if he were totally unaware of the havoc he'd created. ''Was there something you wanted, Ms. McGuire?''

The English teacher glared at him. ''You just remember, young man, hell hath no fury like a woman!'' With that, she whirled and stormed out of the tent.

Lilibeth swallowed a giggle at Alex's perplexed look. He truly had no idea what he'd done to upset Blossom.

Looking wild-eyed and ravaged, Finella staggered slightly and resumed her determined trek to Alex's side. ''My award? You said I'd been honored by some organization?''

With obvious effort, he focused on Finella. ''It's in my office. Give me a minute.'' He turned to Dell Grimes, the oldest of the boys working on the go-cart. ''We've got to make the nose of the cart more pointed so it will cut through the air, and the surface has to be smoother. See if you can shape some aluminum cans around the front of the car.''

''You got it, Mr. P.'' The boys eagerly set to work. The same boys Lilibeth knew hadn't done a lick of studying since first grade—until Alex had become the school's principal. He was truly amazing the way he motivated adolescents, and younger children, too.

Not to mention herself.

He walked backward away from the go-cart construction crew. Automatically Lilibeth slipped her arm through his so he wouldn't fall over the uneven surface.

He started, then smiled. "You're here?"

"I came along with Finella."

"Did you see my wind machine? Pretty terrific, huh?"

"Wonderful." If you didn't mind having your head blown off. "You might have Billy Dell Grimes put up some sort of a backstop so the wind doesn't blow the entire school all the way to Oklahoma."

Halting, he turned and gazed at her with his intense brown eyes. His brows tugged together. "Why didn't I think of that?"

"Your job is to concentrate on the important things. What you need is a partner who can worry about the extraneous details so you can do your work." She slid her hand farther up his arm until her fingers curved over his biceps. "I've always been very good at details."

A slow, acknowledging smile curled his lips. "I do believe—"

"Is anyone hurt?" Dr. Mimsy came hurrying into the circus tent, medical bag in hand. "I heard a terrible roar and I was afraid—"

"No harm done except to Blossom McGuire's wig," Lilibeth explained.

The doctor glanced around the tent to assure herself no emergency existed.

"Well, then, I'll just go on back to—"

"Mr. Peabody!" Finella said, ignoring Mimsy. "My award?"

They all jumped.

"Yes, I'm coming," Alex said, but he gave Lilibeth a knowing wink before he strode off toward his office in the sideshow tent.

Her stomach fluttering with pleasure, she hurried after him.

IN HIS OFFICE, ALEX SORTED through the afternoon mail that had arrived and found the eight-by-ten manila envelope he was looking for. Lilibeth was right. He did need a partner. A helpmate who could worry about all the details that escaped his notice because of his tunnel vision. After all, the devil was in the details, wasn't it? With Lilibeth's help, he could achieve success far more quickly. And then the future would be theirs.

Because, in fact, *she* was what he wanted and as more than a business partner. Soon he'd be able to tell her so.

That decision made, he slipped a red-and-gold embossed, calligraphied certificate from the brown envelope and handed it to Finella.

"A P.O.O.P award?" she gasped.

"Third place honorable mention from the Professional Organization of Proctologists. They're headquartered in Rancho Cucamonga, California, coincidentally in the same building that is occupied by a chemical analysis firm I use to test some of my, er, projects."

"Proctologists?"

"Yes, it seems the sample of your salad, which I had intended for the chemists to analyze, was misdelivered." Or perhaps he had omitted the suite number, he couldn't be sure. "Fortuitously the proctology organization was in the midst of a contest to discover cures for constipation. They tested your entry, and well—"

"I won third place honorable mention!" Finella beamed her pleasure.

"Quite an accomplishment, I'm sure."

"Just wait until George sees this." Proudly she held up the certificate. "He's always been pleased I took up cooking for a hobby and now that I'm so successful, he'll be so tickled he'll be able to strut sitting down."

"Absolutely."

Lilibeth said, "Congratulations, Finella. I'm sure the honor is well deserved." The pickets from Groundhog Station had certainly learned to stay well clear of Finella's concoctions.

Finella gazed at her certificate as proudly as if she'd won an Emmy. "I'm going to have this framed, that's what I'll do. And then I'll hang it right over George's desk where he'll see it every single day and he'll just plain forget about those frozen dinners I found out he's got squirreled away at the bank." She looked up at Alex. "Thank you, Mr. Peabody. And if no one else on the school board has mentioned it, I think you're doing a fine job with our young people, and I'm confident *this* year we'll beat the socks off of those Groundhogs in the Great Crate Race.''

He nodded modestly. "We're planning to give it our very best effort, Mrs. Weinbucket."

Beneath his feet, Alex felt a rumbling in the earth. A cattle stampede? he wondered, a dangerous possibility through the middle of town. Surely not an earthquake, not in this part of the country.

Concerned about his students, he started out of the tent just as he heard someone shout, "Thar she blows!" Dark, black oil rained down outside, and he jumped back just in time to avoid getting covered by the greasy muck.

"My God, the workmen must of hit a pocket of oil," he said.

"Probably not." Lilibeth sighed. "Last year Horace Popsworthy hired some phony dowser to drill holes in the school yard hoping to strike oil and save Nowhere school. All he hit was a refinery pipeline from Groundhog Station. Quade was furious."

Reaching out his hand, Alex caught some of the oil and rubbed it between his fingers. "If I'm not mistaken, this is crude oil directly from under the ground. And assuming Nowhere Elementary School owns the mineral rights to the land, I'd say the school district has just achieved a true bonanza."

He frowned at the black oil coating his fingers. If Nowhere became a wealthy school district able to pay decent salaries, they might think twice before retaining a principal with as few credentials as he had to offer.

Which gave him yet another reason to redouble his efforts to invent a better mousetrap before he ran out of time in Nowhere. Before he could express his true feelings for Lilibeth.

EVERY SEAT UNDER THE BIG top was filled for the emergency school-board session. It had taken nearly a week to cap the oil gusher on the school grounds and assess the barrels that could be pumped per minute from the well. In all likelihood, Nowhere Elementary School would soon be one of the richest institutions in the state, although it appeared the new gymnasium would have a derrick in the middle of the floor.

Lilibeth, who recalled the dismaying condition of the old gymnasium with its rotten wood floors and pathetic lighting, thought the students would be able to handle that. And practicing around the obstacle would give them a leg up over the visiting teams.

Banging his gavel, Quade Gardiner tried to quiet the excited crowd. "This meeting will come to order!"

Horace Popsworthy jumped to his feet. "I move we use the money from the oil well to pave the street in front of my house."

"Sit down, Horace," Quade ordered. "It's not the school board's job to pave your street. That job belongs to the city."

"Well, you're the mayor, aren't you?"

"The city doesn't have any money to pave your street. The school's the only one that's going to benefit from the oil well—assuming it doesn't go dry before we have a chance to spend the money."

"Then I move the school district give back all of the tax dollars they've milked outta me over the past twenty years and I'll pave the damn street myself. The school can afford it now."

Several in the audience shouted their agreement.

"No, that wouldn't be right." To her amazement, Lilibeth found herself on her feet challenging Horace and his supporters. "Whatever money the oil well generates belongs to the children, not us. We need to use it to benefit them. Textbooks. Computers. The best teachers we can hire."

She slid a glance at Alex, who was sitting near the row of school-board members. His approving smile gave her courage at the same time it brought a flush of pleasure to her cheeks.

"We can't squander that money on anything frivolous," she continued, really getting on her soapbox now, "because we can't know what the price of oil will be next year, or the year after. Or as Quade pointed out, how long our well will produce. The children of Nowhere need us to steward their money to protect their future."

There was a rippling of applause around the tent.

From the crowd, Mazeppa shouted, "You fools oughta listen to that girl. She's the only one around here with good sense."

"You wouldn't think a paved street was frivolous if

you didn't have one in front of your house," Horace grumbled.

Finella clicked her knitting needles together. "I think we ought to offer a cooking elective for our young people. I could teach them how to make my award-winning recipes."

The audience groaned.

Quade gaveled for silence.

Carter Murchison spoke up. "I think Lilibeth's right. I want Callie to have the best education she can get. And I want that for our next—" His ruddy cheeks colored a bright red, and every eye in the tent whipped toward his wife Buffy, who glowed with a sly smile on her face. "Well, anyway, I move to impeach Horace and appoint Lilibeth to the school board."

"Me?" Lilibeth gasped. "I don't have any—"

"I second that," Mazeppa shouted.

Quade waved off her motion. "You can't, you're not on the board."

"Wait a minute!" Horace complained. "You can't impeach me. I haven't committed a crime."

"We'll think of somethin'," Mazeppa grumbled.

Billy Dell said, "I'll second Carter's motion. Mr. Peabody has done more good with my kids than anybody ever has. He needs all the help he can get. Lilibeth's got a good head on her shoulders. She's the one who'll look after the kids' interests."

Stunned, Lilibeth looked around at the crowd. No one was arguing with Billy Dell's statement. They weren't even laughing. And Alex was nodding his head vigorously as he consulted with Quade.

The board president raised his hand. "Okay, this might not be quite by the book, but here we go. Since virtually every registered voter in Nowhere is here, I declare a special election for the Nowhere School District. All those in favor of impeaching Horace, say aye."

The ayes boomed around the circus tent.

"Anybody say nay?"

"I do!" Horace protested. "You can't—"

"The ayes have it. Now then, all in favor of Lilibeth Anderson serving out Popsworthy's uncompleted term, say aye."

If anything, the chorus of ayes was even louder than the first round had been, followed by whistles, applause and foot stamping.

"Come on down, Lilibeth," Quade said, waving her forward. "We'll have your swearing-in ceremony right now."

"But I—"

A dozen hands lifted her in the air and carried her like an Egyptian queen to the center ring while the crowd cheered.

The next few minutes were a blur. In the absence of a Bible, Quade had her raise her right hand and place her left on a tattered copy of *Moby Dick*, swearing she'd uphold the honor of Nowhere Elementary School and its new mascots, Armadillos Rex.

Her head was still spinning when the meeting ended

and Alex piled a two-foot-high stack of old school district budgets in her arms. She staggered under the weight of paper.

"I'm supposed to read all of this?" she complained.

"Of course," Alex said. "You'll make more sense of it than most of the other board members. You're the smartest woman in all of Nowhere."

Lilibeth wasn't sure that said much about the town. *Or her.* But she was thrilled with Alex's high opinion. Except for a niggling little voice that suggested, where Alex was concerned, she'd *like* to be a sex object.

SHE SPENT TWO FULL DAYS reading the old budgets and everything else she could find about the school district, finding the material as fascinating as a good historical romance that transported her into another time and place.

But now her eyes were weary, her brain on overload, and she needed a break. Instinctively she headed for Alex's workshop where a light in the window showed he was working. She eased open the side door.

He stood at his workbench, his arms crossed and his legs spread in a commanding stance, while chemicals bubbled through an array of test tubes and glass containers. The sharp scent of cactus and sagebrush permeated the workshop as if he'd brought the open range right inside. Which was apparently true, given the pile of prickly cactus beside the workbench.

"What are you working on?"

He started, then smiled at her. "Fuel for the go-cart.

Petroleum-based products are too volatile for the rocket engine, and I can't seem to get a decent solid propellant that won't blow the driver up, too.''

"So you're distilling cactus juice?"

"I thought if your Aunt Tilly could get two-hundred proof—"

"Why don't you use her still? It's there in the corner." She indicated the old heating-oil drum that was covered with dust. "The rubber hoses have probably rotted by now, but the rest of the pieces are around here somewhere."

His eyes widened. "Of course! I should have thought—"

In a few long strides, he'd crossed the garage and was peering into the oil drum like a child discovering a roomful of toys on Christmas morning. He pulled bits and pieces out—a pressure gauge, coils of rubber tubing.

"I'm going to need a fire," he said, examining his treasure trove.

"We've got firewood at home. I can get you some."

"Great. Bring a water hose, too." He didn't look up, already assembling the still.

Lilibeth drove home, loaded the back of her Bronco with all the firewood it could handle, and dropped the garden hose on top of the pile.

"What are you up to?" her mother asked.

"Going into partnership with Alex." A partnership she hoped would last a lifetime.

"Lilibeth, dear, I don't want you getting your hopes

up about that young man. I don't think he plans to
stay—"

"I know, Mama. This is just something I have to
do." She'd given up on schoolwork because others had
convinced her being pretty was enough. It wasn't. She
was smart *and* pretty, and the first person who had
recognized that was Alex. She intended to prove he
was right on both counts.

"I may be late getting home," she called as she got
into her truck and drove away.

At the workshop, she backed the truck up to a device
that looked like a creature from outer space—Alex's
re-creation of Aunt Tilly's still. He directed her to build
a fire under the oil drum while he cut the hose into
various lengths, attaching them to the pressure gauge.
Together they tossed cactus pieces into the cooking vat,
and he closed the lid tight, securing it in place. Flames
began to lick up the sides of the drum.

"Now we wait and see."

Only then did Alex step back from the still and become fully aware of Lilibeth standing beside him. It
seemed natural she be there. Preordained.

He brushed his fingertips to her cheek, wiping away
a dirt smudge. "Thanks for helping."

"You're welcome." She moved closer until their
bodies were almost touching. "How long will we have
to wait?"

The heat of the fire burned at his back. He couldn't
wait much longer before he claimed what he wanted,

needed. His gaze focused on her lips. "Not long, I hope."

Raising her hand, she straightened the pens in his pocket protector. He felt the gesture so intensely, so intimately, as if there were no barrier between them. As if she were caressing his flesh.

She lifted her face to him, her lips temptingly close. "I find I'm not as patient as I used to be."

"Patience is an overrated virtue."

"I agree." Her body pressed against his, breasts to chest, thigh to thigh.

He stifled a groan. "Beth?" He couldn't even manage to say her whole name.

"Whatever you're asking, the answer is yes."

He was lost, unable to help himself. This was the woman he wanted. Not just for tonight but forever. He vowed to find a way to be worthy of her.

Pulling her closer, he covered her inviting mouth with his. She welcomed him, parted her lips, and he let himself go, plunging his tongue into her sweet warmth. His exploration was like discovering a new invention. Exciting. Exhilarating. The sense of being on the brink of something so incredible it would change the world.

He adjusted the angle of their lips for better access. He heard a soft cry of pleasure and couldn't be sure if he or she had made the sound. He only knew the perfection of her kiss.

The explosion knocked them both to the ground.

He covered her body with his own as bits of rubber hose and aromatic cactus juice rained down on them.

When the hailstorm eased, he raised himself up on his elbows. Regret sliced through him that their interlude had been interrupted, that he had failed again. "It seems I may have made a slight miscalculation, and the go-cart race is only two days away."

Her smiling lips glistened with his kiss. "You're calculations were fine. It's my timing that's off."

8

HE'D GOTTEN IT RIGHT this time, he was sure of it. Lilibeth had checked his figures every step of the way. The fuel tank on the go-cart was full of three-hundred-proof cactus juice, the engine primed and ready. So far, no one from Groundhog had questioned the potent smell of fuel hovering around the cart, a scent resembling an overripe cactus.

Alex helped the eighth-grade boys line up the go-cart on the street outside of school where the PE teacher had chalked two lanes. The eighth-of-a-mile course started on a slight rise then dipped to the finish line in front of Carter's garage.

Sweat pooled in Alex's armpits. This would be his final chance to prove Nowhere kids could top the Groundhogs at *something*.

Rival fans lined opposite sides of the street. Banners touted differing loyalties, Armadillos and Groundhogs. At the starting line, Dell Grimes squeezed himself into the go-cart's driver's seat and pulled on his helmet. One of his fellow students fitted a plastic canopy over his head.

"Hey, what's that?" Washought bellowed.

"It will keep the wind out of his eyes," Alex explained, only slightly edging away from the truth through omission.

"My kid's only got goggles."

"We believe in having the very best equipment here in Nowhere."

Washought scowled at him. "Let's show these hard-shelled lizards," he said to his boys.

"Wait a minute!" Mazeppa came running up the incline pushing her grocery cart. "I'm in this race, too."

Washought sputtered, "You can't—"

"I paid for this school, didn't I? I can do any damn thing I please." Whirling her cart around, she lined up between the two student entries. "I'm ready whenever you are, Cecil."

Her reference to Cecil B. DeMille, world-famous screen director, seemed lost on Washought. Alex was suddenly sorry he hadn't arranged for the race to be videotaped.

Quade, as mayor and official race starter, raised a red flag.

"Mr. P.!" Dell lifted the canopy, his face red from the heat of the enclosure. "I can't breathe!"

Hmm, a slight oversight and one that needed immediate correction.

Alex pulled his favorite ballpoint pen from his pocket protector, grabbed the canopy and, in several swift strokes, drove the point of the pen through the plastic, producing airholes—and destroying his pen in the process. A commendable sacrifice.

"You'll be fine as soon as the race starts," he assured the young man, settling the canopy in place again, pleased with himself that he'd had a suitable tool at hand to avert a crisis.

"Get ready!" Quade announced. "Set! Go!"

He dropped his flag. There was a moment's hesitation as the respective teams removed the blocks from in front of the go-carts.

Mazeppa shouted, "Hi ho, Silver!" and away she went down the incline, her electric-powered cart barely making a whisper of sound.

The Groundhog entry edged forward before building up speed down the hill. Nowhere's cart rocked in place, not even crossing the starting line.

Dammit! He'd miscalculated. The ignition system had failed. The cart was mired in his own personal failure.

A murmur of disappointment rippled through the Nowhere supporters, a few turning away so they wouldn't have to watch yet another defeat of their town and their school. Alex's shoulders slumped. Even with his best effort—

Suddenly a ten-foot-long flame shot out from behind the Nowhere cart. The engine roared. People screamed.

Washought complained, "Hey, wait a—"

The cart leaped off the ground. The wheels didn't touch the pavement as it rocketed down the track on a cushion of air, flying past both the Groundhog entry and Mazeppa's grocery cart.

"Hallelujah!" she whooped, waving her arm and veering off course. "Nowhere, at last!"

The Nowhere entry flew past the finish line, two feet above the yellow tape, before crashing onto the ground, its wheels splaying out to the side like the weak ankles of a novice ice skater. The locals cheered; the visitors from Groundhog booed as their cart belatedly broke the yellow tape.

"We win! We win!" Washought announced.

"No way!" Alex pumped his fist in the air. He'd gotten the calculations right!

"Our cart broke the tape first. Yours didn't even come close."

"Because we sailed over it a half mile in front of your old crate."

Washought took a swing at Alex. He parried the strike with his forearm and landed a left uppercut in the process. Quade stepped between them, shouting "Nowhere wins!" and earned a punch to the jaw for his efforts. Washought's next swing clipped Alex.

Sheriff Bob entered the fray. At some point Alex lost track of the action, aware only that the fans had created a melee of flying fists and ugly jeers. At best, the Great Crate Race had ended in a disputed finish.

But Nowhere sure as hell hadn't lost! His kids, as lacking in confidence as they had been initially, had done the job. Alex was so proud of every one of the team, he was almost bursting with it.

"Come on, darlin'." Lilibeth's voice beside him was a soft, Southern drawl, seductive and tempting. She tucked her arm through his, even as the scuffle continued on the street. "Let's go home and celebrate by finishing what we started the other night."

His head still spun from the blow Washought or one of the fans had landed, but he'd follow Lilibeth anywhere she wanted to go. For today, no matter what the Groundhogs said, Alex was going to be a winner.

They made their way through the excited crowd, past the clinic where Dr. Mimsy had set up a sidewalk first-aid station to treat scrapes and bruises. Next to her, Finella was hawking servings of her award-winning Spring Salad for five dollars a piece. The only takers were strangers from Groundhog.

The drugstore and coffee shop were closed for the race, JoJo and B.K. among the fans outside, the building eerily quiet. Lilibeth threaded her fingers through Alex's and led him upstairs. Fear that something would once again interfere with her plans tangled in her stomach with the excitement that this time there'd be no interruption.

She hesitated when they reached the door to his apartment, breathless with the sudden realization that she *loved* this beautiful, sensitive man. Deeply, in a forever kind of way. Not his inventions nor intelligence, his failures or successes, but the whole of him. Until this moment she'd only been thinking of herself, of *her* dreams. Now she wanted to celebrate Alexander

Peabody, the man she'd grown to love. If marriage wasn't in the cards, so be it.

"I want you to know I'm not looking for promises," she whispered. "I simply want to be with you. In every way possible."

An expression crossed his face she couldn't identify. Relief? Pleasure? Or the soft look of her love reflected in his eyes? She couldn't be sure.

Turning the doorknob, he shoved the door open. In a courtly gesture, he scooped her into his arms and carried her inside. The air in the room carried the scent of his spicy aftershave. Discarded clothes were tossed around, draped over the mismatched furnishings provided by her parents to fill the apartment. On a low coffee table, a dozen writing pads were covered with scribbles and figures, the sign of a busy mind at work that could use some organizational help. That's a talent she had in good measure.

She smiled as he lowered her feet to the floor and a pencil in his shirt pocket poked her in the breast.

"This will have to go." Gently she removed the plastic pocket protector and its contents. "I promise you won't need these for the next little while."

His lips twitched with the threat of a smile. "You don't think I'll need to take notes?"

"Feel free to jot down your inventive ideas for improvements later." Crossing her arms, she grabbed the hem of her sweater and pulled it off over her head, then unhooked her bra, letting it slip to the floor beside her.

"Perfect." He said the word on a sigh. As though he intended to worship her, he cupped her breasts with his hands, then lowered his head to brush a soft kiss across the sensitive flesh.

A delicious shudder rippled through her. "I'd like to see you, too, please."

"I'm not nearly as lovely as you are."

"Let me be the judge." She began working the buttons free on his shirt. Although many thought of her as a femme fatale, she had far less experience than they imagined, and her fingers trembled so badly she was afraid she might never finish the task.

With his chest finally bared, she palmed the well-defined muscular contours and ran her hands over the light covering of chest hair, thrilling as his shudder matched her own. The man had been hiding an incredible body beneath ordinary clothes and shirts with pocket protectors.

"You *are* beautiful," she whispered. "In every way." Intelligent. Devoted to his projects *and* his students. A caring man, one worthy of the highest acclaim.

He growled a low, sexy sound and claimed her mouth in a searing kiss. His hunger thrilled her. She responded with the same eagerness. Soon she lost track of where they were, of what had happened to their clothing, aware only of his hands caressing her, his lips tasting her. Everywhere. His murmured words of pleasure and encouragement.

His narrow bed gave a groan as they fell together on

the mussed sheets, which were cool beneath her back in contrast to the heat that seemed to be devouring her. He was hard and muscular; she was soft and pliant. She fought for air, fought to have him join with her, become a part of her heart.

She gasped as he filled her. "Alex!"

"Beth. My sweet Lilibeth." As though he were a master musician, he orchestrated her body to a fevered pitch. Exciting her with every stroke. The tempo hard and fast, then slow and achingly delicious, lifting her to a crescendo again. He played a love song she heard and understood even if he didn't know the words.

Somehow she'd have to teach him the lyrics.

Her climax came in a burst of song worthy of a diva. Moments later, Alex added his baritone counterpoint, then collapsed onto her. She gloried in his weight.

For an endless time, she seemed to float weightlessly in a fanciful world of make-believe, thinking all things possible. A world created in love and buoyed by optimism. Together they'd find a way—

He lifted his body, turning on his side to hold her. "You are so perfect. An incredible lover."

"You, too," she sighed. "I have a confession to make, Alex."

He pulled her closer, cuddling her. "There's nothing you can say that would detract from this moment we've had together."

She hoped that was true. "You remember when you first came into the drugstore?" He nodded. "I was so excited. I thought you had responded to my ad on HitchingPost.com.''

His brows stitched together in confusion.

With her fingertips, she soothed his forehead. ''It's a matchmaking service. I'd been advertising for a mate, object matrimony.''

If anything, the lines on his forehead burrowed more deeply. ''Lilibeth, I can't—''

''It's all right, Alex. What we have together is so special, I simply want to enjoy the time—''

''Lili-beth! Are you here?'' called her mother from downstairs.

Lilibeth started. Oh my God! Her mother! She had to— ''I've gotta go.''

''If you want me to explain—''

''I think you'd better leave that to me.'' As if any explanation would work, forget Lilibeth was well beyond the age of consent. No mother would be that understanding, certainly not hers.

She scrambled out of the bed. Her clothes were scattered like a bread-crumb trail out to the living room. She snatched them up one at a time, trying to reassemble herself as she went along. There was a pleasurable ache between her legs, a less confident one in her chest. And her cheeks were still flushed with Alex's lovemaking.

They'd made no commitment to each other. She'd made it clear she'd hadn't needed one. Which didn't change the fact that she desperately *wanted* one.

With only a quick look over her shoulder, she was

out the apartment door and down the stairs. Before she stepped into the drugstore, she ran her fingers through her hair and gave it a shake.

"Did you call me, Mother?"

JoJo eyed her, a puzzled expression on her face. "Where were you?"

"Right here," she lied, troubled she couldn't tell her mother the truth. That she loved Alex and would marry him in a nanosecond if he asked, and she was afraid he never would. "What's up?"

"There's a man out front. He asked to see you."

"Me? Who is he?"

"I don't know. But he drives a motor home big enough to take a whole herd of longhorns to market and have room leftover to host a decent barbecue for his friends." She started to turn away, to return to the store, then stopped. "He did say something about wanting to meet you because of the Internet, but I can't imagine what he meant by that."

A seriously uncomfortable feeling edged down Lilibeth's spine. She hadn't checked her e-mail in days, even longer since she'd looked for messages at HitchingPost.com. Surely now, after all these weeks, she hadn't gotten the response she'd been hoping for.

And no longer wanted.

9

_____

MATRIMONY.

With a disheartened groan, Alex sat on the side of the bed and put his head in his hands. He could still taste Lilibeth's sweet flavor on his lips, still catch the hint of her strawberry scent in the air and on the tangled sheets where they had made delicious love only minutes ago.

Despite her words to the contrary before they'd made love, she wanted the one thing he couldn't give her. Not yet. Until he could claim a success worthy of the Peabody name, marriage was out of the question.

A disputed win in the Great Crate Race wasn't enough. Not for him. Or Lilibeth. She deserved better.

But he was going to succeed at something! This was no longer about fame or fortune, or even his family honor. This was far more personal.

This was about Lilibeth.

Slowly he dressed and went downstairs. He had to explain to her that the best he could give her, for now, would be his heart. And he'd vow an everlasting pursuit of a success that would make him worthy of her.

He walked into the silent drugstore and down the

aisle of feminine hygiene products to the paperbacks featuring buxom women and virile men. Beyond the plate-glass window, a recreational vehicle the size of a billboard was parked on Main Street, taking up virtually all of the curb space in front of Anderson Coffee Shop and Drugstore.

He frowned. No one came to Nowhere accidentally. He wondered who had gotten so far off the beaten track. And why.

A group of locals, including JoJo and Lilibeth, had gathered around the RV. They parted as Alex approached, giving him his first look at the man who was the center of their attention—a tall, blond Greek god in a spiffy silk shirt with a cravat tied at his neck, expensive dove-gray slacks and Italian loafers.

Alex developed an immediate dislike for the handsome stranger. Instinctively he reached for his pocket protector to make sure his pens and pencils were in order, but found it wasn't there. He'd left it upstairs where Lilibeth had placed it on the coffee table moments before they'd made love.

Suddenly he felt naked. Vulnerable.

"Alex, I'd like you to meet our visitor." Lilibeth held out her hand to draw him into the circle of on-lookers. "This is Roland Marovich, from Hollywood. Alexander Peabody, our school principal."

"He's a movie producer," JoJo said. "Isn't that exciting?"

"About as exciting as an ingrown toenail," Alex mumbled under his breath as he shook hands with the man. For a moment, they measured each other, their grips firm, their eyes assessing, their smiles fixed.

"Nice to meet you, Alex." Roland increased the pressure of his grip.

Alex did the same. "Likewise, I'm sure." He heard a knuckle crack and couldn't be sure if it was his or Roland's. Neither man flinched.

Gigi shoved her bulk forward. "Mr. Marovich is thinking of shooting a movie here in Nowhere. We might all get to be extras."

"Or stars," JoJo added, beaming.

"I'm quite taken with your little town," Roland said, still not easing his grip. "I discovered your community's Web page on the Internet."

"I created a Nowhere page some years ago when Fordyce Huggins was mayor," Lilibeth explained. "Roland managed to follow the link to Hitching-Post.com."

Alex let go of the man's hand. He swallowed hard. "HitchingPost?" The matchmaking service? *Object matrimony!*

A satisfied smile curled Roland's lips. "I've always had a weakness for fun-loving prom queens."

Alex clenched his fists. Not *his* prom queen. He shot a look at Lilibeth, who appeared pale, the rosy flush from their lovemaking erased from her cheeks by the arrival of the stranger.

JoJo elbowed her way closer to Roland. "I was a prom queen, too, don't you know. I was even in a student play, not the star, you understand, but I did have forty lines.''

''Then you'll certainly have to try out for one of the parts I'll be casting,'' Roland assured her. ''*If* I decide to use Nowhere Junction as a locale.''

''Oh, but you must!'' JoJo crooned. ''Just look how quaint our Main Street is. A perfect location.''

''We got us all the characters right here in town you'd need for any movie you can think of,'' Gigi said.

''Montana might be better,'' Alex suggested. ''They've got more trees.'' And it was about two thousand miles due north of Nowhere—and Lilibeth.

''Come on, dear.'' JoJo pushed her daughter forward. ''Let's take Roland inside. I'm sure he's thirsty after his long ride and would love a cherry cola. And a sandwich?''

''You're very kind, Mrs. Anderson,'' he said smoothly, then glanced appreciatively at Lilibeth. ''Something cool to drink would be refreshing, if it's not too much trouble.''

''Not at all. Please come in.'' Lilibeth gestured toward the café door. She had no choice. A customer was a customer, including one who was movie-star handsome and so smooth he could probably talk the legs off a chair. He'd certainly held Lilibeth's mother enthralled with the first words out of his mouth—*movie producer.*

JoJo shooed Roland to a small, round table and held out a chair for him. ''Now, you sit yourself down right here and Lilibeth will get you a big icy soda. She makes a wonderful banana split, if you'd like—''

"Oh, no thank you." He patted his flat stomach. "Have to watch my waistline."

"Mercy, not you, young man. Why, you don't have an extra ounce of weight on you."

Lilibeth's mother was right about that. Roland Marovich was broad shouldered and lean of hip, a man's man from all appearances, but not the *right* man as far as Lilibeth was concerned.

She glanced up from the soda fountain to see Alex take a stool at the counter. His gaze darted to the stranger at the table, then back to Lilibeth.

Leaning forward, he spoke confidentially. "Has he said what kind of movies he produces?"

"Not that I heard."

"You be careful, Beth, honey. I'm betting at best he's a fraud."

She hadn't considered that possibility. Heavens, she hadn't considered much of anything about Roland except that his arrival had interrupted an incredible moment with Alex.

"I'll check him out on the Internet," she said. She wasn't in the least susceptible to his charms, but her mother was and so would a lot of other people in Nowhere.

Alex nodded grimly. "You do that."

"Lilibeth, dear! Don't you have Roland's drink ready yet?"

"Coming, Mama." Using a small tray, she carried

the drink to his table. Before she could set it down, Blossom McGuire burst in through the front door.

"Where is he?" she asked breathlessly, her face a bright red from exertion. She spotted Roland, gulped a breath of air, then strutted across the room.

"'The raven himself is hoarse/ That croaks the fatal entrance of Duncan/ Under my battlements,'" the English teacher intoned, striking a dramatic pose. "'Come, you spirits/ That tend on mortal thoughts, unsex me here—'"

"Blossom McGuire!" JoJo interrupted. "You can't walk into my establishment and start raving on about sex. This is a *family* business and I won't have you—"

"That was Shakespeare, you idiot! Lady Macbeth, to be precise." Blossom smiled enticingly at Roland. "I wanted this kind gentleman to see the range of talent we have here in—"

"Bah!" JoJo planted her fists on her hips. "You don't have a single ounce of talent. Wasn't I the one who beat you out for the school play?"

"For the part of a *jail warden,*" Blossom retorted. "A *male* warden, I might point out. You only got the part because we didn't have enough boys trying out for the play."

JoJo huffed. "At least I had a part. All you could do was paint the scenery and then you—"

"Mama, please. I don't think Roland is interested in any of this." With an amused expression on his face, he'd been swiveling his head back and forth, watching the exchange like a fan at a tennis match.

He patted her hand in a reassuring way. "It's all right, Lilibeth. When people learn I'm a movie producer, I often experience this sort of thing. I'm quite immune, I assure you."

Suddenly Alex was at her side. "You're not immune to a punch in the jaw, which is exactly what you'll get if you don't unhand Lilibeth this minute."

"Alex!" she cried.

"I don't recognize the play," Roland said dryly, "but your characterization is trite and overdone. Don't bother to call us, we'll call you if something comes up."

"Careful, *Moronovich*," Alex said in a low, threatening tone. "Down here in Texas, when there's a brawl we don't use understudies. It's *mano a mano*."

Lifting his hands in surrender, Roland leaned back. "Hey, take it easy, fella. I'm a lover, not a fighter."

A low growl emanated from Alex's throat, and Lilibeth pulled him away from Roland. Gracious! She'd never imagined Alex would actually *start* a fight with anyone.

Minutes later tension was still shimmering in the air like a heat wave when, into the drugstore, strutted Popsworthy. "'To be or not to be, that is the question/ Whether 'tis nobler in the mind to suffer—'"

Right behind him came Carter Murchison, his undershirt half ripped off. His face was beet-red with embarrassment as Buffy practically pushed him inside. "It's you, honey, I promise," Buffy insisted. "You're *sooo* macho!"

"Stella, Stella, Stella—" Carter mumbled under his breath.

Rolling her eyes, Lilibeth sat down heavily on the stool next to Alex. "I don't believe how fast news spreads in Nowhere."

"In this case, bad news," Alex grumbled.

Lucas McRifle and Dr. Mimsy entered the crowded drugstore through the back entrance, both of them wearing old army uniforms.

"Has a war started and we didn't hear about it?" Lilibeth asked no one in particular.

Smiling brightly, Mimsy said, "We thought Mr. Marovich might want to do a doctor series, something like *M.A.S.H.* Lucas thinks I'd make a terrific Hotlips Hoolihan." She hooked her arm through her husband's. "Of course, I've always thought of myself more like Marcus Welby, M.D. You know, the hometown—"

Interrupting Mimsy's explanation, the front door swung open again, chimes sounding their off-key tune. Ephraim O'Rourke, the ninety-three-year-old pastor of the Nowhere Nearer to Thee O Lord Church appeared in the guise of Rhett Butler. "Frankly, my dear, I don't give a damn!"

As THE HOURS PASSED, Alex watched the shenanigans of the townspeople—and Roland—with increasing dismay. He had the troubling feeling if he didn't do something soon, *very* soon, he was at risk of losing Lilibeth.

The moment had come to focus all of his creative energy to gain the success that so far had eluded him. Then he'd be ready to step up to the metaphorical plate and knock Roland's balls—*the* ball, he corrected—right out of the park.

While Finella was singing a song from *Sound of Music,* which put even his teeth on edge, Alex slipped out the back of the drugstore and went to his workshop.

IT WAS WELL PAST THE USUAL closing time before Anderson Coffee Shop and Drugstore cleared out and Lilibeth was able to lock the doors. Virtually every resident of Nowhere Junction had shown up to recite a poem or bit of dialogue from a movie or play, or sing a song. Even people from Groundhog Station had appeared in search of their fifteen minutes of fame at the impromptu audition.

Roland Marovich was the last to leave.

"I was wondering if you'd do me the honor of dining with me," he asked as she was about to lock the door.

"You're asking me out to dinner?"

His smile revealed perfect teeth, although she kept wondering if they were as false as Mazeppa's. "It's an old custom of mine when I meet a beautiful woman."

In spite of herself, Lilibeth felt a blush climb from her neck to her cheeks. Roland did have quite a way about him.

"The only place in town to eat out is right here," she told him. "And frankly, I don't have the energy to cook even one more grilled cheese sandwich." She suspected when she counted up the day's receipts, it would be a record for the store. As an excuse to drop in and perform, people had stooped to buying almost anything from bandages to dental floss.

"We could go somewhere else."

"Like Groundhog Station?"

"I was thinking more along the lines of Austin. As I recall, they have some rather nice restaurants."

Good grief! Austin was hours away by car. To go there for dinner would mean they wouldn't be home until—

"No, I'm sorry. I can't."

He shrugged at her refusal. "Perhaps another time."

She held open the door for him. "I hope you enjoy your stay in Nowhere."

His piercing blue-eyed gaze swept over her, intimate and thorough. "I intend to, Miss Anderson, and I can be a very determined man."

She was sure that was true. So sure that as soon as he was out the door she raced to her office in the back and booted up her computer. Once online, she connected to a variety of Web sites as she followed Roland Marovich's career via cyberspace.

To her astonishment, he was an award-winning producer of movie shorts and TV documentaries, including a foray into live coverage of a miniwar several years ago when he was fresh out of the University of Southern California film school. By all accounts, he was a man on his way up in the movie industry, expected to break out with a blockbuster any time now.

This man was no fake.

But what on earth had made a man like that come to Nowhere Junction in response to her Hitching-Post.com ad? It boggled the mind.

Puzzled, she shut off the computer. She hadn't heard Alex moving around upstairs in his apartment, and he'd left the chaos of the café hours ago. The only other place—

Out back, she saw a light around the edges of the garage doorway. Gingerly she opened the side door and went inside. Hunched over his workbench, Alex didn't look up.

"I checked out Roland on the Internet," she said.

An electric motor whirred, and an artificial arm reached out. Its hand closed around a plastic bottle, squeezing it so tightly the container popped.

"I think I'm onto something." Alex fiddled with his device, his voice low and strained. "Just a few more adjustments—"

"He's legit. Oscars, Emmys, the whole shebang."

Alex straightened, turning slowly toward her. "Is he, now?"

She frowned, not used to hearing that controlled, angry tone in his voice. "A major Hollywood talent, according to several sources."

A muscle flexed at his jaw. "Well, that's good. If he picks Nowhere for a shooting locale, he'll really put the town on the map."

"I suppose." She desperately wanted Alex to take her in his arms. Kiss her. Tell her the movie mogul meant nothing compared to the love they shared for each other.

"You must be pretty pleased he came to town because of your HitchingPost ad."

"That's probably not the only reason he's here." She couldn't imagine a man like Roland needing to respond to an ad at a matchmaking service. No doubt he had women stumbling over themselves to marry him.

Alex studied her for a moment, and she was sure he'd say the words she longed to hear. But instead, he shrugged.

"Look, I'm close to a breakthrough here. If you don't mind—"

She knew a dismissal when she heard one. Alex's hurt more than most. "Sure. I've got to get home anyway. I'll, ah, see you tomorrow?"

"Right." He turned back to his work.

"Congratulations again on beating Groundhog in the crate race."

He didn't respond. His concentration was so intense on whatever project he was working on, he didn't even lift his hand to wave goodbye.

With tears of regret and longing burning at the backs of her eyes, Lilibeth stumbled out the side door. Had it only been hours ago she'd felt so content, so thrilled, to be in Alex's arms? To have him buried inside her, a part of her? Now, he was cold and unfeeling.

Had he gotten what he wanted—a quick tumble in the hay—and was no longer interested? She couldn't believe that was the case. He wasn't that kind of man. He was noble and kind, more thoughtful than any man she'd ever met—if more distractable, too.

Besides, he'd acted so strangely with Roland, she'd been sure he was *jealous!*

Dear heaven! She hadn't known the meaning of confusion until now. Until she'd lost her heart to Alex.

JoJo met Lilibeth at the door the moment she got home.

"Isn't Roland simply the most ornamental man you've ever seen?" JoJo said. "And I do believe he has his eye on you."

"I'm sure he looks at all the women that way."

JoJo hooked her arm around Lilibeth's shoulders and drew her into the living room. "Now you hear me, child. This is your big chance. A rich movie producer, handsome as sin, and he doesn't even strut his okra, like you'd expect him to."

"He seemed nice enough," she admitted.

"There you go. And I'd venture, if you were nice to him, he'd be sure to make his movie here so the two of you would have time to get better acquainted."

"Maybe I don't want to get to know him better." Her heart already belonged to Alex, although he didn't seem to want it at the moment.

"How can you even say that? Like my mama always told me, it's just as easy to fall in love with a rich man as it is with a poor one, and you're a whole lot better off when the shine is off the honeymoon if you've got some green to grease the rough spots."

Grandma Lily's homilies were a world full of mixed metaphors.

Lilibeth made a move to go to her room.

JoJo stopped her. "I know your daddy and me have always wanted you to stay right here in Nowhere. But this could be your big chance. We wouldn't want to hold you back. Not now. And it just plumb doesn't make sense that you wouldn't even try to get Roland to fall for you."

In truth, a matter of weeks ago Lilibeth might have done just that. She would have flirted and thrust out her "assets" at every opportunity in order to get Roland to notice her. She would have been thrilled that he'd responded to her advertisement—object matrimony.

But no longer. Alex had changed her whole outlook on life...and love.

"There's nothing wrong with staying right here in Nowhere," she said. "My friends are here, my family. I have important responsibilities—running the store, being on the school board, watching out for you and Daddy. I don't need money in order to be happy, and I don't have any particular desire to live in California."

"I know you're taken with Alex, but there's no guarantee the school board will even want him back next year. Then you'll be left with nothing—"

"I'll be fine."

"But—"

"Good night, Mama. I'll see you in the morning."

"Now you listen here, young lady. I *insist* you be nice to that young Roland. There's more at stake than just what *you* want." JoJo lifted her chin in a defiant way. "Why, if I hadn't met your father, I might have gone on to Hollywood and become a star instead of being stuck in the middle of nowhere. You *owe* me, Lilibeth Anderson. I'm your mama and I want that chance."

Shock and surprise left Lilibeth momentarily speechless. She'd had no idea her mother had been so unhappy in Nowhere. Or that she'd be so starstruck at meeting a real Hollywood producer that her mother would become a stranger to her.

"I'll be polite to Roland just like I would be to any stranger in town, but that's all I'll promise. I won't try to influence his decision to make the movie here. And I won't jeopardize my own principles just so you or anyone else in town can live out your dreams on a movie set."

Lilibeth's dreams were different than they had been weeks ago. Alex had changed her. But after his rejection this evening, she felt as adrift as a tumbleweed blowing in the wind.

If only Alex could return her love, she'd feel anchored again.

WITH BARELY AN HOUR'S SLEEP, Alex made his way to school the next morning. As Shakespeare might have said, time was out of joint. Aye, that was the rub.

Within the course of a day, he'd gone from the incredible high of celebrating Nowhere's victory in the go-cart race by making love with Lilibeth to the depths of despair as yet another of his inventions failed to emerge as practical. No one would ever invest in one of his robotic designs. For all his tone deafness, he should have entered the family kazoo business.

Added to that, he now had a serious rival for Lilibeth's affections, one with more fame and fortune than Peabody Kazoos had brought to any member of his family.

What troubled him most was that Lilibeth deserved the very best. So far, Alex had fallen short of the mark.

"Hey, Mr. P." Grinning broadly, Dell Grimes gave Alex a high-five. "Was that race great, or what? Guess we showed the Groundhogs a thing or two."

"You were masterful behind the wheel."

"Man, it was like I was riding a rocket. Way cool! I'm gonna be an engineer for NASA or somebody an' build me a rocket to Jupiter."

"I don't know about—" Alex stopped himself. The last thing he wanted to do was discourage Dell from his ambition, so instead he nodded knowingly. "Of course, it would mean a lot of hard work on your part, but I think you could do it. Work for NASA, I mean, building rockets."

Despite his earlier boast, Dell looked surprised. "You think so?"

"Absolutely. You're certainly smart enough when you apply yourself."

"Wow! Way cool!" Slapping Alex with a low-five, Dell trotted off to see his friends.

Alex smiled after the boy. As discouraged as he might be about his own prospects, he didn't want to steal the boy's dreams. Everyone needed someone who believed in him. He was proud of what "his boys," as he'd begun to think of them, had accomplished.

He wondered if a woman like Lilibeth could be satisfied married to a small-town school principal, or if he had the right to ask. Assuming the school board renewed his contract. Given his history, that was no sure bet.

Shoving his hands into his pockets, he strolled into the sideshow tent that served as his office and discovered Blossom McGuire waiting for him. She'd changed from a gray wig to one in a shocking shade of carrot-red.

"I'm so glad you're here early, Mr. Peabody."

"And why would that be?" he asked cautiously.

"Since meeting Mr. Marovich yesterday I've given some serious thought to my future—and my career as an actor."

"An actor?"

"In the trade, actor implies both the male and female form—"

"Yes, I know. But I wasn't aware you were, er, contemplating a career change." Although an entire generation of eighth-grade English students would probably be delighted with the news. Her teaching methods were rigid and offered few opportunities for creativity.

"It's easy to grow complacent about one's life, particularly here in Nowhere. I've come to realize it's never too late to pursue one's dreams." She drew herself up in a way that changed her from frumpy to poised. "Whether or not Mr. Marovich utilizes me in his movie, I intend to pursue a career in the theater. There are some marvelous character parts for the mature woman. I intend to make a name for myself in that endeavor."

"That's wonderful, Miss—"

"I may even contact Dangling Brothers Circus, the organization which supplied us with these tents. I've grown quite fond of working in this environment. It's the colorful stripes, I suspect. And I understand they have an opening for a sword swallower."

Alex gasped involuntarily and felt his throat constrict.

"Regretfully, that does mean I must submit my resignation," Blossom continued, "effective the end of the school term."

Alex could just imagine the sound of students cheering. "No one, er, *Nowhere* will miss you, Miss McGuire."

"That is no doubt true, and thus I wanted to give you ample warning to find a replacement for me."

"That's very thoughtful of you."

They exchanged a few more pleasantries, then Blossom excused herself to break the news to her first period class. The cheers Alex heard in the main tent a few minutes later were quite real and very robust. Her replacement would receive a warm welcome.

Indeed, Alex decided he should conduct a search for an applicant who could both teach English and act as counselor for students like Dell Grimes, who hadn't yet realized their potential. While not precisely killing two birds with one stone, the dual assignment would benefit all the students in Nowhere.

Alex could only hope the school board would renew his own contract at the end of the year so he could see the changes the new school would make in the attitudes of the children.

Or more importantly, that he could remain near Lilibeth until he could claim some grand success.

AFTER SCHOOL, ALEX searched out Lilibeth at the café. What he wanted to do was take her upstairs again. Make love to her. Tell her Roland could never love her as much as he did. That his handsome, *famous* rival was all smoke and mirrors, nothing more than an illusion created by the silver screen.

But Alex was the fabrication, no better than a robot that couldn't give Lilibeth want she wanted. Matrimony. If he tried to act otherwise, he'd hurt her.

That's the one thing he wouldn't risk.

Behind the counter, she moved with the grace of a ballet dancer, blending milk shakes, pouring them two at a time, draining the last drop with a flourish. She made love with the same agility and style. Effortlessly. Enthusiastically. Draining him of all the pent-up need he'd felt since the first time he'd seen her kneeling in the feminine hygiene aisle.

But his sense of fulfillment had been all too brief. He wanted her again. Now.

Her apron hugged the full swell of her breasts, and his palms itched with the memory of their weight in his hands. Their smooth texture. Their taste as he suckled. Strawberries and cream had never had such an erotic flavor.

Knowing what he did, how could he ever be alone with her again without experiencing the thrill of loving her one more time?

She looked up when she finished placing the milk shakes in front of the boys and looked directly at him. A flash of pleasure appeared in the blue depths of her eyes, then slowly clouded over. The brilliant smile that had briefly curved her lips faltered. He knew he'd already hurt her by his actions last night.

He had to talk to her. He had to be honest with her. He had to explain his need, his biological imperative, to be a success before doing those other things he desperately wanted to do—to love Lilibeth as fully as she deserved to be loved, and devote his entire energy to the family they would create together.

"Hi," she said softly, her eyes following him as he walked to the end of the counter where they could talk more privately.

"Hi, yourself." It would take only a moment to slip the yoke of her apron off over her head, slide his hands beneath her sweater...and he didn't dare go there. Not even in his imagination. "I wonder, when you've got some time, if you'd—"

A shadow crossed the plate-glass window at the front of the store like a predatory bird swooping in for the kill. The movie mogul's RV came to a stop at the curb.

"If I'd what?" Lilibeth asked.

Come upstairs and let me make love to you. "Uh, place an Internet want ad for me. Blossom McGuire gave notice this morning. I'll need to replace her for the next term."

Her expression crumbled from one of expectation to the colorless shade of disappointment. "Sure. Just give me a few minutes to get things organized here." Her gaze flicked to the door as it opened, the chime announcing Roland's entrance.

The producer strode briskly across the room to the soda fountain as though it was a movie set and he was Clint Eastwood. "Good afternoon, Lilibeth."

"Hello, Roland. Can I get you something to eat or drink today?"

"On the contrary. I was very much hoping you'd accept my invitation to dinner. I have all the fixings in the RV—steaks, salad, a special wine I particularly enjoy—and I've found a perfect place where we can park and watch the sunset."

Angry heat flooded Alex's face, his hands clenched into fists. He'd never felt so like throwing a punch in his life, not even as a boy when the kids at school had tried to beat up on him, the whimpy nerd. The kid whose mother had made him wear a pocket protector because he kept staining his shirts with ink.

"I'm sorry, Roland." She glanced at Alex. "I promised Alex I'd do a favor for him."

Alex opened his mouth to propose to Lilibeth. Right there at the soda fountain, in front of Roland or anybody else who might care to overhear.

But despite every instinct screaming inside him to do just that, Alex couldn't. He couldn't put his own interests, his love for her, above the chance she might have for a better future than he could so far provide.

His throat ached as he forced out the words he knew he had to say. "It's all right, Beth. The want ad can wait. You go ahead with Mr. Movie Mogul—er, Marovich."

10

LILIBETH'S HEART SANK to somewhere near the linoleum floor. She'd been so happy to see Alex. So pleased he'd sought her out for any reason, she was eager to do him the smallest favor. And then he'd practically thrust her into Roland's arms.

With a determined effort not to burst into tears, she lifted her chin. Alex Peabody wasn't the only cowboy on the range—even if he was the only one she wanted.

But she was an independent woman, a woman of means. An *heiress,* for heaven's sake. She could dine with any man she pleased.

"In that case..." She gave Roland her best prom queen smile, assuming no one noticed the faint quiver of her chin. "I'd be honored to join you for dinner."

Beside her, Alex made a strangled sound, which she forced herself to ignore.

Roland flashed a smile that revealed his perfect teeth. "It is I who am honored. Whenever you're ready—"

With a clatter and bang, JoJo appeared from behind the locked door of her caged-off post office booth in the corner of the coffee shop. She extended her hand as though expecting Roland to kiss her fingers when she reached him and glided across the room past the tables. Her hair was covered with an old-fashioned dust bonnet, her long skirt nearly touching the floor.

"Roland, dear boy, you haven't mentioned what type of movie you have in mind for Nowhere." When Roland didn't take her hand, she covered the omission by patting her bonnet instead. "I've always seen myself in the role of a strong, determined woman crossing the prairie in a covered wagon, her children huddled around her for protection, single-handedly battling the marauding—"

"I actually had in mind a more contemporary story." Roland shot Lilibeth a panicky look. "Are you ready to go?"

"Of course." She slipped her apron off over her head. "Mama, can you look after the store till closing?"

Blocking Roland's path, JoJo yanked off her bonnet. "Naturally there are contemporary women with the same inherent strength—"

"I'll keep you in mind for any suitable parts, ma'am." He reached around JoJo for Lilibeth's hand.

Alex stepped between them. "Just how late do you expect to keep her out?"

"I, uh—"

"I could play the part of a modern-day sheriff," JoJo said. "You know, like that actress in *Fargo*. I may not be pregnant, but I certainly know how to use—"

Alex interrupted. "Remember, Lilibeth has to be up early to open the store. Maybe you shouldn't go far."

"I'll be fine, Alex," Lilibeth said. She slid past him, both puzzled and pleased by the worried look in his eyes. "I promise I'll be home in plenty of time to get a good night's sleep."

Roland managed to catch her hand and lead her to the door.

Filled with regrets and second thoughts, she glanced over her shoulder before stepping outside. Alex's expression was so bleak, she almost turned back. But Roland swept her along to his RV.

Or he would have if Gigi hadn't planted her bulk in front of the truck's door. She'd rouged her cheeks, curled her hair and was wearing a miniskirt that would only have looked good on a teenager. A young, *slender* teenager.

Lilibeth could only assume Nowhere Junction had been struck by some new and terrible epidemic, one she sincerely hoped Dr. Mimsy would discover the cure for soon.

"Well, fancy meeting you here," Gigi crooned, batting her heavily mascaraed eyelashes at Roland.

"Afternoon, ma'am." In an effort to reach the door handle, Roland was forced to do a little dance around Gigi.

"Just wanted to say howdy, so's you know I'd be interested in any ol' part in your little ol' movie. Any ol' part at all." She tittered a girlish laugh, which set her double chins in motion.

"Gigi," Lilibeth said, "Roland and I were about to leave. We're going to go watch the sun—"

"Well, now, why don't I just come along with you. I could read for whatever part—"

"Maybe another time," Roland said, clearly desperate now. He grabbed for the RV door, yanked it open, whisked Lilibeth inside, followed her in and pulled the door shut behind them. "Quick. Let's get out of here."

Lilibeth had a fleeting impression of the RV—a beautifully turned out interior with walnut paneling, a gourmet kitchen, and a huge bedroom to the rear of the vehicle—before she slid into the passenger seat up front. The whole arrangement looked like a luxury penthouse rather than a camping vehicle, and she felt a twinge of anxiety. No doubt Roland dated far more sophisticated women than she, women who were probably willing to—

Gigi pounded on the driver's side window. "If you want me to read a few lines, I could follow you—"

Shaking his head, he started the engine, shifted into gear, and the truck roared forward, nearly knocking over Hank Finkins and Boris Norris, who were on their bikes carrying signs that said Save Kid Actors—Vaporize Grown-ups.

Swerving to avoid them, Roland asked, "Are they trying to get themselves killed?"

"They're probably only imitating the adults they've seen lately. There's been a lot of picketing going on around the school recently."

As the truck sped past the edge of town, Roland sighed.

Buckling her seat belt, Lilibeth settled back into the

soft leather chair. "I don't know what's gotten into everyone. Usually the folks in Nowhere aren't so—"

"Starstruck. It happens everywhere I go. People find out I'm a movie producer and something goes haywire in their brains. They immediately start picturing their names on every marquee in the country."

"I don't," she said softly.

He glanced at her and smiled. "I know. And the fact is, there's something about you that does have star quality."

Heat edged up her neck and warmed her cheeks. "Now you're pulling my leg. I may be a hick from Nowhere, but I know a line when I hear one."

"You're wrong. I'm quite serious. You exude a beautiful innocence that's very appealing to a man, particularly someone like me who has to deal with a lot of phonies in my business."

"I'm flattered you feel that way." But Roland wasn't the man whom she wished found her appealing. She stifled a sigh as she turned to look out the window.

They were driving along the dirt road that separated Murdock Murchison property from Quade Gardiner's Rocking R Ranch. Cattle grazed in the distance and the rolling landscape was tinged green with the first sprigs of spring grass. In a scattered pattern, oil derricks stood like sentinels guarding the cows in open rangeland.

They were miles from town, but Lilibeth's heart was still there—with Alex. For all the good it did her.

"You're thinking about him, aren't you?"

She turned and shrugged, knowing exactly whom he meant. "I'm sorry."

"In love, like the movies, timing is crucial. Looks like mine's a little off." He pulled the truck to the side of the road at the top of a rise where they had a hundred-and-eighty-degree view of the western horizon.

"Maybe it would be better if you just took me back—"

"Nonsense. I'm a darn good cook, but I hate to eat alone. Watching a sunset alone is even worse. Besides, it'll do him good to worry a little." He swung out of his seat and stood, forced to bend his head slightly by the low overhang. "Give me a few minutes and we'll have steak in a burgundy and mushroom sauce to die for. While you're waiting, I'll start you off with a red wine with a light bouquet I promise you'll love."

She couldn't help but smile at his eagerness and smooth patter as he went about the business of opening and pouring the wine. He handed her a glass and lifted his in a toast.

"To your happiness."

"And yours," she echoed, touching his glass. The liquid slid smoothly down her throat, sweet and slightly fruity. "Maybe when we get back I'll treat you to some of my aunt Tilly's Cactus Joy Juice."

"Cactus?" Setting his glass aside, he rummaged in a low cupboard for a frying pan and set it on the stove. "Sounds intriguing."

"It has a bit more bite than this."

He chuckled, a nice warm sound. "Macro vineyards

and breweries are big these days. You ought to consider brewing your aunt's cactus juice commercially.''

Actually Lilibeth had thought about that over the years. It certainly was a popular concoction in Nowhere, particularly when someone was forced to eat Finella's Spring Salad. But until now she'd focused so hard on catching a husband, she hadn't set her sights on other options. Like having her *own* business. Being an entrepreneur instead of running a drugstore.

She looked up as Roland turned the steaks in the pan. The meat sizzled, the rich aroma wafting around the RV.

"What would you think about a cactus cordial?"

He winked at her. "Sounds like a winner to me."

Basking in the possibilities, she got up to help make the salad and set the table he'd placed outside the RV's door. He'd brought a hurricane lamp, linen napkins on a white tablecloth and real silver place settings. *Très elegant.*

They chatted amiably about a variety of topics, and through it all Lilibeth sensed Roland was searching for a woman who would want him for himself, not because he was a successful movie producer.

Some small greedy part of her wished she could be that woman. But it wasn't in the cards. She'd already lost her heart to an inventor who hadn't yet created the masterpiece that would free him from the servitude of his dream.

They were just finishing their dinner as the sun

dipped below the horizon in a flame of orange and red, when she heard a strange hissing noise.

Roland went rigid. "Snakes?" he gasped.

She frowned. "I don't think so." It sounded more like—

The sound repeated on the opposite side of the truck.

"What the devil?" Roland went into the RV, got a flashlight and returned, gingerly scanning the ground around the truck. He walked like a man confident a rattlesnake was about to reach out and nail him.

Lilibeth remained at the table, sipping her wine and smiling to herself.

"I'll be damned! Both back tires have gone as flat as a pancake."

"Really?" She choked a little and coughed. "That's quite a coincidence."

"It sure as hell is. And I've only got one spare."

While Roland was still circling the RV trying to decide what he should do or whom he should call, Lilibeth spotted headlights coming along the dusty road in their direction. Moments later Alex's familiar pickup pulled in next to the RV.

He leaned out the window. "Say, I just happened to be driving by and saw you parked up here. You folks having some problem?"

"You could say that," Roland replied grumpily.

Alex hopped out of his truck, a bit too eagerly in Lilibeth's view. A short discussion ensued. The result was a decision for Roland to call Carter Murchison to come out with his tow truck and a spare tire, and for

Alex to drive Lilibeth back to town so she wouldn't be up too late.

She fumed at the arrogant way the men made the decision for her, yet she couldn't help but be pleased Alex had apparently feared for her safety.

For spite, she gave Roland a good-night kiss. She felt no spark, no chemistry, but imagined Alex wouldn't know that. "You're a good man, Roland," she whispered. "I'm sure you'll find someone soon."

He brushed a second kiss to her forehead. "I hope Alex knows how lucky he is."

Lilibeth hoped so, too, as she climbed into the cab of his truck for the ride back to Nowhere.

ALEX CLOSED HIS FINGERS around the steering wheel so tightly he thought it might break in half. His jaw ached from gritting his teeth.

"You didn't have to do that," Lilibeth said.

He gave her his most innocent look, the one his students used when they knew they'd been caught red-handed. "Do what?"

"Roland's a perfect gentleman. It wasn't very nice of you to give him *two* flat tires."

"Even a gentleman can get the wrong idea about a beautiful woman," he grumbled.

"You were the one who practically forced me to go out with him."

"Maybe I had second thoughts, okay?"

She slid her hand across his thigh, her fingertips

coming to rest in close proximity to a part of his anatomy that ached even more than his teeth.

"What kind of ideas do I give you?" she asked softly. Seductively.

He lost his concentration. The right front tire bounced in and out of a pothole, rocking the truck and causing her hand to press intimately against him.

"Beth?" His voice came out in a strangled sound.

"Yes, Alexander. Is there something wrong?"

"No." His response was little more than a high-pitched squeak as she moved even closer, her breast now brushing against his arm, her hand exploring the seam on the fly of his jeans. He made a rasping sound in his throat.

"You sound like you're coming down with a cold. Maybe I ought to give you a dose of Aunt Tilly's Joy Juice. It has some wonderful medicinal qualities. I'm sure you'll recover in no time."

She squeezed his thigh in a gesture he thought might be intended to reassure him. That's not the reaction he got. "Beth, could you—" The top snap on his jeans popped open.

"Roland thinks I should bottle the Joy Juice commercially. What do you think?"

He couldn't think at all, couldn't even conjure up the formula for the area of a circle, which he was sure had something to do with pi. But he couldn't remember what flavor pie. Strawberry sounded right. And cream.

"I could probably sell it via the Internet," she said idly as the next snap on his jeans came free.

He was suddenly hungry for a taste of strawberries and cream—Lilibeth's own special flavor.

Recklessly he wheeled off the road. The truck bounced over the uneven terrain. The headlights and a few stars provided the only illumination in a vast expanse of darkness, oil derricks barely visible silhouettes against the night sky. He came to a halt next to one and switched off the engine and lights.

Lilibeth grew still. "What are we doing?"

Turning, he framed her face between his hands. In the starlight her eyes glistened like dark blue sapphires but he couldn't read the message there.

"I know I don't have a fancy RV and I can't offer you a big house in Hollywood, but I want you, Lilibeth. I want you more than I've wanted any woman in my life."

Despite not having a right to claim Lilibeth as his own, he did just that. With his mouth and lips, he extracted a soft moan of assent. With his hands, he took her measurements, recording the details of her body in his tactile memory in caressable centimeters and exquisitely flowing curves. If it were possible, he'd patent every delicious inch of her. Register her in his name. And keep her all to himself.

If it were possible...

Everything Alex did sent waves of pleasure through Lilibeth. She craved the excitement he gave her, the internal fire that went from smoldering to a raging inferno as he deepened his kisses, stroked her with his masterful hands to a fever pitch.

Unable to get close enough in the confines of the truck cab, they moved outside, beneath the stars, where Alex took a blanket from the back of the truck. He spread it across the uneven ground and they lay down together. The cool air chilled her nakedness, and he covered her with his own body. Above them, the stars twinkled in silence as Alex entered her. Around them, the soft lowing of cattle provided a musical backdrop in counterpoint to their heavy breathing, their own soft moans of pleasure and delight.

Vaguely she became aware of Carter's tow truck passing on the road. Then later, the truck and RV returning to Nowhere.

Only at some distant level did she acknowledge Alex had not said that he loved her. *Wanted* her, yes. But he'd made no admission of the one thing she longed to hear.

And as she curled with him beneath the blanket, their passion spent in each other's arms, she refused to acknowledge the dampness on her cheeks were tears of regret.

As the bright light of morning pricked at her eyelids, the rasp of something warm and damp swiped at the salty residue of her tears. She rolled over, opened her eyes—

—and found herself staring up into the red-rimmed eyes and white face of the biggest, baddest longhorn bull she'd ever seen.

11

THEY WERE NEARLY TRAMPLED before they could get to the truck. Alex yanked open the door, shoved her inside and climbed in after her.

"I can't believe we did it on a *red* blanket right in front of the biggest bull in Texas," she said, fighting off a fit of hysterical laughter borne of fear and relief.

"Guess he's the jealous sort."

Outside, the bull bellowed and pawed at the blanket, tossing it and an assortment of their clothes into the air. One horn hooked the blanket; Lilibeth's white lacy panties floated down to settle on the other horn. As though he were a star on the rodeo circuit, he twisted around trying to dislodge the unwanted fashion accessories. He roared his fury, lowered his head and charged the truck.

Scrambling to the far side of the cab, Lilibeth screamed again as the whole vehicle shook.

"Let's get out of here!" Alex twisted the key he'd left in the ignition and started the engine.

"Wait! We can't go anywhere. He's got our clothes!"

"He's welcome to 'em. I'm sure as hell not going

back for them.'' The tires spun in the soft dirt before digging in and spewing a storm of dust into the bull's face.

''I can't go home like this.'' Instinctively Lilibeth crossed her arms across her breasts and scooted lower so her shoulders were beneath the window level. She shoved back wayward strands of hair from her face. No question, not only was she stark naked, but she must look completely ravished. Which she had been, of course, but this was hardly the way she wanted to arrive at home.

''We'll think of something.'' He wheeled the truck across the open ground toward the dirt road, bounding along unmindful of the natural hills and gullies. A family of prairie dogs scattered ahead of them, whistling a warning to their neighbors before diving into their holes.

In the rearview mirror, Lilibeth caught a glimpse of the bull following them, the blanket flapping around him. Her panties remained lodged almost demurely on his horn.

Off to the left, she noted another bull loping in their direction. He trumpeted his rival a greeting before lowering his head and picking up speed.

A clutch of cows, who had been peacefully nibbling on the new grass, lifted their heads. For an instant, they hesitated, then as though of one mind they broke into a gallop ahead of the truck as it raced down the dirt road, all of them trying to outrun the bulls.

''Is it mating season?'' Alex asked.

"I have no idea."

"You don't suppose those bulls are nearsighted and have a thing for pickups, do you?"

She certainly hoped not.

To prevent terminal sagging with each bounce the truck took, she hooked her arm beneath her breasts. This was the only time in her life she'd seriously wished for double-A cups.

The stampeding herd, which had picked up a few more strays, swerved onto the road leading into Nowhere. The truck followed. Behind them, the bulls were gaining and had been joined by a couple of their buddies—all of them with threateningly long horns.

"Alex, we can't go into town like this without a stitch of clothes between us."

"Look in the back. Maybe there's something—"

The truck bucked as one of the bulls nudged the back bumper.

Alex swore. "Either those cows are gonna have to go faster or they'll be decorating my front grill in a minute."

She looked over her shoulder. A small window provided access to the space beneath the camper shell. She shoved it open and peered inside.

There wasn't much there. All of Alex's tools were in the garage at home. But she spotted some squares of foam rubber and something that looked like a rag. Getting to her knees, she squeezed partway through the opening.

Alex didn't dare take his hands off the steering

wheel, but with Lilibeth's cute little derriere—creamy white where her bikini had protected her from the sun—he was sorely tempted. She wiggled it once. Twice. He almost lost control of the truck.

She was the softest, most cuddly woman he'd ever known. He wanted to hold her now, make love to her again. And that would be yet another mistake.

What was it about Lilibeth, he wondered, that made him lose every bit of concentration whenever she was near. Particularly when she was naked.

Downtown Nowhere, such as it was, came into view. Shopkeepers, ready to open their stores for the day, were out on the sidewalk, gawking.

"Beth, honey, you'd better find something for us to put on in a hurry. We're almost there."

She wiggled her butt again. "I'm stuck!" she wailed.

That was not a good thing.

He checked his rearview mirror. The bulls were still coming. Six of them now. Horns lowered. Racing full steam after the bull with the red blanket.

"There's a can of lubricating oil on a shelf to your right. Try that."

"What?"

"The *oil!* Rub some on your body so you'll be slippery."

She muttered something unintelligible. Probably something insulting. Which he thoroughly deserved for putting her in this position. A position he would thoroughly enjoy if it weren't for the public spectacle they were about to make.

Kazoo making didn't have this many hazards. Maybe he could learn to be an accountant in the family business. Or a telemarketer selling kazoos over the phone to likely prospects.

Like a cork in a bottle, she popped out of the window. Twisting around in the seat, she pulled one of his old, gray T-shirts over her head, one he'd used as a grease rag for years. There was a tear on the left side, which neatly flapped open to reveal one perfect breast. She snatched the material back together, covering herself, and flopped a piece of foam rubber about a foot square into his lap.

"That's it?" he asked.

"The best I could do. That isn't exactly Buffy's Boutique back there."

"True," he conceded.

By now he'd spotted Roland's RV parked in front of the drugstore. If he could angle his truck ahead of it, the bulls would race on by—or ram into the back of the RV. Either choice would be fine with him.

Meanwhile, the townspeople were shouting and waving anything they could find, including Save The Armadillos picket signs and Buy Nowhere posters, in front of the stampeding herd in the hope of protecting their property from rampaging hooves. So far they seemed to be succeeding. From the way the townspeople acted, he suspected they'd experienced stampedes before.

He cranked the wheel hard, skidding in front of the mammoth RV, and jerked to an abrupt stop.

Lilibeth nearly sailed out of her seat, only stopped when Alex threw his arm out in front of her.

"Oh, my gosh!" she gasped, collapsing back into the seat.

"You're all right now. Relax. The bulls are long gone." Only a cloud of dust lingered.

He'd spoken the truth. Temporarily.

She was all right until JoJo Anderson appeared at the passenger-side of the truck, wild-eyed and crazy like a mother cow on the rampage, and yanked open the door. Her eyes widened as she looked inside to see her daughter in a T-shirt that barely reached to her thighs and Alex's foam rubber effort at modesty, only a marginal improvement over a fig leaf.

Fortunately, the townspeople were so stunned by the stampede down Main Street, they were still immobile in front of their stores and weren't getting the same view as Lilibeth's mother.

"Lilibeth Jodie-Jolene Anderson," JoJo said, "you have a lot of explaining to do."

"Mrs. Anderson, I assure you all of this is my fault." He leaned forward, then realized how precarious his covering was.

Still blocking the door, JoJo planted her fists on her hips. "Then I assume you'll do the right thing by my little girl."

"The right—"

"Mama, what are you talking about?"

"Not that you'd be my first choice for my daughter, but I don't cotton to having Lilibeth's reputation ruined. Even a blind hog could see you two have been eatin' your victuals before saying grace. You'll either have to marry my baby girl or her daddy's gonna take his shotgun to you."

Marry? Alex swallowed hard. There was nothing he'd like better than—

"No."

Both Alex and JoJo gaped at Lilibeth's adamant refusal.

"I don't need a husband, and I certainly don't want one who's been forced to marry me."

"I'm not being forced—"

"Excuse me." With remarkable dignity—considering she was wearing nothing more than an oversize T-shirt—Lilibeth shoved her way out of the truck and past her mother.

"Wait!" Alex started to follow her but he couldn't. Not with half the people of Nowhere standing around gawking from across the street and his entire wardrobe reduced to a single square of foam rubber.

JoJo glared at him as though he were a scumbag. But that didn't bother him nearly as much as Lilibeth's refusal to marry him. That wounded him more deeply, more painfully, than when he'd learned he was tone deaf and might never live up the standards of success set by the Peabody clan.

BY THE TIME HE DRESSED and made his way to school, everyone in town had heard about his ignominious escape from a herd of stampeding cattle and Lilibeth's refusal to marry him. His steps were heavy as he entered the brightly striped sideshow tent that was his office. Maybe Blossom McGuire was right. They all ought to join the circus.

He came to an abrupt halt when he discovered two men waiting for him. Clean-shaven, they wore dark suits, subdued ties and serious expressions.

With a sinking feeling, Alex decided they were either the local morality police or from the State Board of Education. No doubt the result of their visit would be his dismissal.

"Gentlemen." He nodded, wondering if he'd have time to give Dell Grimes and the other eighth-grade boys one last pep talk about their futures before he was tarred, feathered and run out of town.

"Mr. Peabody, I'm Thaddeus Montraville," the taller one said, "and this is Joe Greene. We're from the Ethanol Producers Association."

His eyebrows shot up. "Ethanol?"

"We understand your school won a crate race recently using a rocket engine. We'd be interested in learning about the fuel you used. We may also be interested in licensing the production rights, assuming we can come to an amicable agreement."

Aunt Tilly's double-distilled Cactus Joy Juice. Alex smiled. "It's an old family recipe," he explained. "If you'd like to come with me, I'll let you take a look at the process. It's in my workshop."

LILIBETH STARED in amazement at the agreement the Ethanol people had left for her and her family to study. Unable to fathom the implications, she lifted her head to look at Alex. Except for the two of them, the café and drugstore were empty, the locals having gotten their fill of ogling her after her disastrous return from her night with Alex.

"I don't understand. You were the one who turned the Joy Juice into fuel for the go-cart. Why aren't you signing this?"

"Because it's your aunt Tilly's process, and therefore the rights belong to your family. All I did was find another application for the distilling method. I didn't *invent* it."

She heard regret in his voice, just as she'd heard the hesitation this morning when her mother had insisted he marry her. Lilibeth had jumped in with her refusal before he could make it any more clear than he already had. He didn't love her. And she had too much pride to accept a proposal that had been coerced at the threat of gunpoint.

"If Thad's estimates are correct," Alex continued, "the licensing fees could result in an annual income of several hundred thousand dollars a year."

"You could have told them it was your process and we would have never known the difference."

He looked at her with those gentle brown eyes. Honest eyes. "I would have known."

A band tightened around her chest. She'd never

loved Alex more than she loved him right now, nor had she ever felt more hopeless.

"You could name it Peabody High-Energy Whoopee. Your family would be pleased with that." And Alex might at last think of himself as a success, the inventor he thought he was meant to be.

"P.H.E.W. Yes, that would have been perfect." His lips lifted with the hint of a smile, but his eyes were so bleak, Lilibeth wanted to cry for him.

She set the contract on the glass-top counter between the lip balm display and body lotion. "Mama will be thrilled. With this much money, I think they'll leave Nowhere. Maybe move to Hollywood."

"What will you do, Lilibeth? Will you move to Hollywood, too?"

She could almost hear the words *with Roland* in his question. "No, I think I'll stay right here in Nowhere." At least as long as Alex was here, too. "I'll keep on running the store and café, and I think I'll bottle some of that Joy Juice, too. Roland thinks a cactus cordial would sell pretty well."

"Yeah, well, he ought to know." He stepped back from the counter, bumping into the cart she'd been using to restock the shelves. The useless robot arms Alex had added waved aimlessly. "I've got to get back to school, okay? You'll show that contract to your folks, get them to sign?"

"It shouldn't be a problem." In fact, both her mother and father would be ecstatic. Lilibeth only wished she could be, too.

Alex backed up a few more steps. "I told Thad and Joe to come back tomorrow."

"Fine."

He reached behind him to open the door. The chime sounded, the off-tune note raising the hackles at the back of her neck and making her heart ache one more time. He tried so hard to succeed at everything he attempted. Then, when he achieved his one big success, he handed it over to her and her family.

"Then, I'll, uh, see you around."

Tears blurred her vision as the door closed behind him. Of all the men in the world who answered Internet ads, why couldn't Alex have been the one interested in matrimony—with her?

IT WAS THE LAST school-board meeting of the year and the first one to be held in the new gymnasium. The oil derrick in the middle of the floor posed a few problems for the seating arrangement, but they'd made adjustments so the audience could see the elected officials from most of the bleachers.

Alex took his seat off to the side. The renewal of his contract was on the agenda. He didn't expect it to go well, nothing had since Lilibeth had refused to marry him, even at the risk of her own reputation.

Even his efforts to invent something wonderful so he could properly propose had gone more dismally than usual the past few weeks. Indeed, only with a good deal of luck had he avoided burning down the entire town of Nowhere when he'd shorted out the electrical power trying to get a particularly rebellious robot to do its thing.

A telemarketing job was looking better and better.

"Let's get going." Sitting at a fancy dais—a portable affair on rollers, funded by windfall oil revenues—Quade gaveled the meeting to order.

"I move to waive the reading of the minutes," Lilibeth said in her sweet, clear voice.

In the audience, Popsworthy popped to his feet. "I've been reading Roberts' Rules of Order and—"

"Sit down, Popsworthy," Quade ordered, then accepted Carter's second of the motion.

"I want to know where we're having graduation this year," Billy Dell Grimes asked. "My boy Dell wants to—"

"It'll be right here," Quade assured him. "We've got a couple of important items on the agenda tonight, so y'all just keep quiet for a while."

"Don't forget the potluck after the meeting." Finella set aside her knitting long enough to look up. "My Spring Salad is particularly delightful this evening. Gigi's special is okra and brussels sprouts this week and I—"

The groans from the audience drowned her out.

"The first thing I want to announce," Quade continued as the room quieted, "are the results of the state-wide math test."

Another groan came from the audience, and Alex didn't know why Quade was grinning so broadly. For the past seventeen years, Nowhere Junction Elementary

School had placed dead last in every standardized test that Texas administered. He hardly expected the school to do much better this year.

"It's my pleasure to announce—" Quade looked toward Lucy and Buffy, who did a fair imitation of a drumroll by slapping their hands against their thighs and stomping their feet on the gym floor "—that the eighth-grade class of Nowhere Junction has placed *first* in the entire state of Texas!"

For a moment, the gymnasium was eerily quiet with only the rhythmic rocking of the pumping oil well to break the silence. No one could believe—

Then Gigi shouted, "Hallelujah!" After that the entire assembly burst into applause with catcalls added for good measure.

Mazeppa gave a shrill whistle with her fingers and beat on the side of her grocery cart with an old hubcap she'd probably found alongside the road. "I told you that Peabody knows what he's doing!"

Another cheer went up.

"Furthermore," Quade continued when he could be heard again, "the fifth-graders placed *second!*"

The news stunned Alex. Of course he knew the eighth-graders had been caught up in planning for the Great Crate Race. They'd done the math for the wind tunnel, had even absorbed the physics for the rocket motor and ignition. But he hadn't imagined—

"I believe we owe our principal, Alex Peabody, a special round of applause!"

The entire crowd rose as one, chanting, "Peabody!

Peabody!'' Suddenly Gigi gave him a bear hug that drove the air from his lungs. A half-dozen pair of hands lifted him into Mazeppa's grocery cart, standing him upright, and she whizzed him around the gymnasium like a conquering gladiator to even more cheers of the crowd.

As he circled the board members, he caught a glimpse of Lilibeth smiling at him, clapping, and he wanted to hop off his mechanical mount to take her in his arms. But the surge of people prevented him from doing anything except hang on to the cart.

By the time Quade had the crowd settled down again the only thing left on the agenda was the renewal of Alex's contract—with a substantial raise. The vote was by acclamation.

The meeting broke up, but everyone lingered to congratulate Alex.

Billy Dell pumped his hand as though he was trying to raise oil from a hundred feet down. ''I swear, you've reinvented my boys. Dell's talking about going to college and Joey's so excited about picketing, he wants to be a professional union organizer.''

He'd *reinvented* a kid? Alex hadn't imagined that was possible. For him, inventions had always been devices, bits of metal and wire stuck together, most of which didn't do the job for which they'd been intended.

Carter Murchison stuck his hand into Alex's. ''If I had a vote, you'd get the Nobel Peace Prize. I haven't heard a firecracker set off in weeks. The kids in this town were nowhere before you showed up.''

"Thank you" was all he could manage before someone else grabbed his hand. Bobbing around, he tried to spot Lilibeth over the heads of the crowd and finally saw her near the potluck table. He edged in that direction. By the time he got there, the crowd had thinned and she was standing alone.

She looked beautiful and serene in a sundress that bared her arms, her hair pulled back into a French braid that revealed the elegant arch of her neck. He knew just the spot where he wanted to kiss her...well, one of the many spots, he conceded.

A smile played at the corners of her lips when she saw him. "Congratulations."

"Thanks."

"Nowhere's lucky to have you. I know being the best school principal in the state isn't what you set out to do, but I think your family would be very proud of you. I certainly am." She touched his face with her fingertips, then withdrew her hand. "As far as I'm concerned, you're a success and always will be."

Lilibeth thought he was a *success*? If that was true, nothing else mattered. Not the opinion of his family. Not that he was tone deaf or that he'd failed to discover the Great Invention which would bring him fame and fortune. If Lilibeth believed in him, he'd achieved the most important thing in his life.

"Lili-beth?" His voice cracked.

She arched her brows. "Yes, Alex?"

"I, uh, I wonder if—" He couldn't get the words past the knot in his throat. He couldn't tell her what was in his heart. He'd suddenly been thrown back to his awkward adolescent years—she was the prom queen and he was the school nerd. Self-consciously, he straightened the pens and pencils in his pocket protector.

"Was there something you wanted to say?" When he continued to remain mute, she slowly shook her head. "Good night, Alex. I'm happy for you."

The best he could do was a strangled cry of frustration as she walked away.

He clenched his fists at his side. What he needed to do now, this very night, was to invent the most important robot in his life.

DESPITE THE BRIGHT, SUNNY day, Lilibeth felt as if she had a dark cloud hovering over her head as she walked to the drugstore to open up for the day. She'd been so sure Alex was going to declare himself last night. To admit he loved her.

But she'd been wrong.

Roland's RV was gone from in front of the store. He'd moved on to Groundhog Station to scout a new locale for his movie, to the dismay of virtually everyone in Nowhere, taking with him Lilibeth's one chance at marriage. He'd invited her to go with him to Hollywood, wanted to introduce her to some directors and agents he knew—no strings attached.

She'd turned him down. California wasn't where she wanted to be.

Barely able to see through the blur of tears, she reached the door and stumbled over a three-foot-tall—

—robot? Dressed in a tuxedo? A pair of red lights blinking like eyes?

She looked up to find Alex grinning at her proudly, despite the dark circles beneath his eyes. "What on earth?"

"It's my Automated Robotic Ring Bearer. I've been working on it all night."

"Automated—"

"I've added a sound track to this one. Go ahead, ARRBY, do your stuff."

He threw a switch. The robot rocked and hummed, then broke into an off-tune rendition of "True Love" in Alex's own voice accompanied by the dreadful wailing of a kazoo.

"Alex, I don't think—"

"Just give it a chance," he urged.

A truncated arm extended from the robot's body, its pincer hand gripping a silver ring that looked suspiciously like a metal washer that had been reworked and polished to a high sheen, perfect to fit over a woman's finger.

"I didn't have time to get to Groundhog where I could buy something better," Alex explained. "So you can kind of, well, think of this as a trial run, if you want."

"Are you—" Torn between elation and an attack of hysterical laughter, she swallowed hard. "Turn it off. Please."

His expression crumbled. "I know you said you didn't want to marry me, but I thought since you said I was a success—"

"Alexander Peabody, you can spend the rest of your life building as many robots as you want to. I'm sure they'll all be wonderful, and I'll never complain. I promise." She found the switch. The robot shuddered to a stop. "But if you are proposing to me, I want to hear *you* say the words. Not ARRBY."

"Me?"

"Do you love me, Alex?"

"Oh, yes, I have since I first saw you with a box of contraceptive cream in your hand."

The relief she felt left her feeling light-headed. "Then could you please tell me in your own words?"

He licked his lips and fiddled with his pocket protector.

Taking his hand, she said, "I love you, Alex. You are the most perfect, the sweetest man I've ever known. I can think of nothing I'd rather do more than spend the rest of my life as your wife."

Fiercely he pulled her into his arms, holding her so tightly she could barely draw a breath, and she cherished the feeling.

"I was so scared, I love you so much, Lilibeth, I was afraid—"

"We don't have to be scared anymore. Neither of us do. Not as long as we have each other."

"I realize now I'm a damn good school principal but I don't want you to be sorry I'm not a famous—"

"You're everything I've ever dreamed about. After all, you're the one who answered the ad I placed on the Internet, weren't you?"

A frown stitched across his forehead. "Not on HitchingPost.com."

"But I was the one who wrote that ad, the one for a new school principal, too. And by golly, I promised myself the *next* time an eligible man showed up in town because of my ad, I wouldn't let him get away." She grinned up at him, her heart so full she thought it might burst with love. "Thank you for fulfilling my promise."

Without releasing her, he took the makeshift ring from the robot's pincers and slipped it onto her finger. "Marry me, Lilibeth. Make me the happiest man in the world."

She murmured yes and kissed him. Deeply. With all the feeling she could muster. As far as she was concerned, Alex had invented *love*, and that was the most wonderful invention in the universe.

Harlequin invites you to walk down the aisle...

To honor our year long celebration of weddings, we are offering an exciting opportunity for you to own the Harlequin Bride Doll. Handcrafted in fine bisque porcelain, the wedding doll is dressed for her wedding day in a cream satin gown accented by lace trim. She carries an exquisite traditional bridal bouquet and wears a cathedral-length dotted Swiss veil. Embroidered flowers cascade down her lace overskirt to the scalloped hemline; underneath all is a multi-layered crinoline.

Join us in our celebration of weddings by sending away for your own Harlequin Bride Doll. This doll regularly retails for $74.95 U.S./approx. $108.68 CDN. One doll per household. Requests must be received no later than December 31, 2001. Offer good while quantities of gifts last. Please allow 6-8 weeks for delivery. Offer good in the U.S. and Canada only. Become part of this exciting offer!

Simply complete the order form and mail to:
"A Walk Down the Aisle"

IN U.S.A
P.O. Box 9057
3010 Walden Ave.
Buffalo, NY 14269-9057

IN CANADA
P.O. Box 622
Fort Erie, Ontario
L2A 5X3

Enclosed are eight (8) proofs of purchase found in the last pages of every specially marked Harlequin series book and $3.75 check or money order (for postage and handling). Please send my Harlequin Bride Doll to:

Name (PLEASE PRINT)

Address   Apt. #

City   State/Prov.   Zip/Postal Code

Account # (if applicable)   **097 KIK DAEW**

◈ **HARLEQUIN®**
Makes any time special ®

Visit us at www.eHarlequin.com

◈ *A Walk Down the Aisle*
Free Bride Doll Offer
One Proof-of-Purchase ◈

PHWDAPOPR2

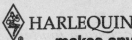

DON'T MISS OUT!

MONTANA MAVERICKS: BIG SKY GROOMS
Three brand-new historical stories about the Kincaids, Montana's most popular family

RETURN TO WHITEHORN, MONTANA—
WHERE LEGENDS ARE BEGUN AND
LOVE LASTS FOREVER BENEATH THE BIG SKY....

Available in August 2001

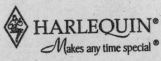